Ken Fry has had a career that has seen him doing everything from grave-digging to working in publishing both in the USA and UK. He has travelled widely and lives alone in deepest Surrey with his beloved Shetland Sheepdog. He has three grown-up children and enjoys long walks, poetry, literature and art. Above all he loves eating and drinking lots...!

DYING DAYS

KEN FRY

Matador
5 Weir Road
Kibworth Beauchamp
Leicester LE8 0lQ, UK
Tel: (+44) 116 279 2299
Email: books@troubador.co.uk
Web: www.troubador.co.uk/matador

ISBN 978-1848763-210

A Cataloguing-in-Publication (CIP) catalogue record for this book
is available from the British Library.

Typeset in 11pt Book Antiqua by Troubador Publishing Ltd, Leicester, UK
Printed in the UK by MPG Biddles, Kings Lynn, Norfolk

Matador is an imprint of Troubador Publishing Ltd

For Sandra

Acknowledgements

Very special thanks to Vernon Holland for allowing me to quote various facts and statistics from his remarkable and definitive work, 'Nobody Unprepared' The History of No. 78 Squadron RAF.

Also special thanks to Linda Tolmie for her constant nagging for me to get this finished.

PART ONE

ONE

January 1975

I shifted around uncomfortably in a creased damp bed. From the bedside clock I can see it's about ten am. Most people are up, moving about or have gone to work. Not me. My pain is unremitting and won't go away. It worsens daily. Doctors told me months back that I didn't have long to live. They're not wrong. Everything's a pain-ridden problem, breathing, walking, washing, cleaning my teeth, eating and pissing. I can't get my fly open and when I do, I piss all down my trousers. You won't want to know what it's like trying to shit. Nothing's easy. Hell, I'm not that old, fifty-nine to be exact. My illness is incurable, fatal.

My name's Anderson, Scott Anderson. Sitting close to the bed is one of my sons, Hugh. He's a healthy twenty-six years of age, bright, intelligent, and with a very well paid job in physics. The pain doesn't prevent me from making observations about people. I've fuck all else to do as I slowly rot away. Hugh's still single, and although he's had his chances with girls nothing ever came of them. I often think the whole of Hugh could do with an iron. His clothes are always creased and his suede shoes look scuffed and battered. He has a well lived-in appearance. The only neat thing about him is the relentless and close crew-cut of his hair. Its shortish height gives him an added air of strength and it's so precise, it could have almost been topped off with the aid of a spirit level. He's always been particular about that. Together we're living in my old house named *Pimlico*, left to my sister and myself when I came of age. My father, Percy, left it to me in an early Will. I shall leave it to my children. It's close to Plymouth, directly overlooking the sea. My sister's name was Elizabeth. She and her partner, Henry lived here before me but he died not long after she did. Then I inherited the house. That was a few years back, so now we have the place to ourselves. Freda my wife lived with me until she died some years back from Parkinson's disease. Originally her father and stepmother opposed my request to marry her but we went ahead and did it in secret. That caused uproar. They didn't speak to us for years until the war was over. An unpleasant pair of arseholes. When we originally moved here we vowed we wouldn't change the house too much as it had its own Edwardian charm we'd always admired. That promise has been kept. Before Freda died she had to have her bed downstairs, as she was unable to get up the stairs. It's ironic; my bed here has now also been moved downstairs where hers used to be. It's close to a toilet. In my state it has to be. Like her, I now also find it too difficult to get up the stairs. I realise how bad I've become, for I caught sight of myself in the bathroom mirror yesterday, thin, bent over and my clothes no longer fit. They hang off my skeletal frame like unwashed laundry thrown into the corner of a room to be washed later. My face is ashen, pinched and bony with faint looking bruises attempting to erupt through my parchment-like skin. Yet in spite of this, *Pimlico* is the only place I want to be. For me, it's full of memories, stuffed with artefacts, antiques and rows and rows of books, which stretch from floor to ceiling. I love the place. I always have. What bothers me is how little time I have left but I guess life can be like that for nothing's truly permanent. The prospect of death gives me a sense of urgency and in particular, that which I'm talking to

4

Hugh about. Over the last year I've realised that there's so much to say about our family and its roots. Who are we? Where did we come from? My sons and daughter have no knowledge of this. Neither do they have too much knowledge of me or what and where I came from or what I did during the war. I know that's all my fault. I want them all to have an idea or understanding of these things. Not to know is like never looking in a mirror and seeing what you look like. It's important to have a sense of roots and culture. Someone has to know this and someone has to hand this information down to other family members or it will all be lost. There's things I daren't talk of but I want them to discover, somehow. Hugh is my choice in this. He's more than qualified and somehow he's going to record all what I've to tell him, and in some way pass it on to his children if and when he has any. My other son and daughter also have to know and hopefully any children they may have and so on. What concerns me is that increasingly of late my brain feels confused when the pain kicks in and it performs memory tricks on me, so I need Hugh to get this all down and put it into some sort of order. I'm getting weaker and more tired by the day and am going to bed more and more frequently. Sooner or later I'll be totally bedridden. I can feel that creeping up on me. So I've asked him to use my old Ferrograph reel-to-reel tape recorder. I brought this from Imhof's shop in Holborn, London, many years back. It was classy then and it still is. Using this he shouldn't have a problem. Hugh looked at it and barely suppressed a giggle.

"Did this belong to Noah?"

"Cheeky bastard! They don't make 'em like that these days."

"That doesn't surprise me!"

I ignored his quips. Before switching it on he got out his

pen and notebook. I started. He doesn't know what he's let himself in for.

I told him that the Andersons descend from a long line of Scots going back as far as I've traced to the early eighteenth century. A common family name with us was James and it has been around for some time in our successive generations. With me, my parents who were a bit different to the set family mould bucked the trend. Percy, my father decided to call me something totally different. He opted for Scott. Whether this was due to our Scottish ancestry or his admiration of Scott of the Antarctic I never did discover. It was different.

Talking hurts my tongue and throat and a racking tiredness is slowly squeezing the life from me. This illness is creasing me in two. I'm determined that I have to force myself on. The morphine helps but frequently puts me out. The doctor is now considering attaching me to a subcutaneous morphine infusion known as a 'syringe driver.' This automatically pumps the stuff in and gives constant relief. It's generally only given to those who have little hope of survival and keeps all pain at bay. I wished they'd hurry up. I need it badly. I have a terminal cancer. Originally my symptoms were symptomatic of Ross River Disease, that I was suspected as having picked up on my recent trip to Australia. The characteristics I had were aching joints in all the limbs, stomach pains plus severe fatigue. So I was sent off to the London School of Hygiene and Tropical Medicine for investigation. The tests proved negative and Ross River Disease was ruled out. A more serious appraisal was called for. After more tests I was diagnosed with Multiple Myeloma. The symptoms are not unlike Ross River Disease. Myeloma, I was told, is invariably fatal and what treatment there is available is usually ineffective, It's a disease of the bone marrow which causes cancerous changes in blood cells, which then spread, growing uncontrollably, producing high levels of calcium known as hypercalcaemia, which in turn causes severe pain, excessive fatigue and bruising. I've got three months at most.

I'm pausing now. The effort of remembering and trying to talk needs concentration and effort and it's not helped by the morphine I take. It makes me woozy. There's much I need to say and I'm worried it will get jumbled up and out of sequence, so pausing is a way I can gather my thoughts slowly and carefully. Even then they're not always accurate. Hugh's always patient and when I'm ready he switches the recorder back on. I told him that I'd traced our family back to 1735 to Charles who was a surgeon barber and there had followed several James in the line with the odd Robert or Charles. None of them were that wealthy and most had died in poor circumstances, so I suppose my father thought a name change might bring me better fortune. I would have hated having a family name, as it can get so confusing. All of them had numerous children, the bulk of whom died in infancy or at an early age. I guess that's why they had so many. The Anderson family had originated in Edinburgh back in early times and Charles the barber had a shop in a side street off The Royal Mile. Later in early Victorian times his descendants moved off to London. For some reason they later started a cheese making business in west London and did well for a while. They got well known and ended up supplying the Life Guards at Buckingham Palace. James, my father's Dad, even became a Freeman of the City of London. My own father, Percy, wanted nothing to do with it and became a teacher. He was also a gifted musician. I never was. I preferred ball games like squash and tennis. I even got into the preliminary rounds of Wimbledon but not much further. My earliest recollection of

Dad was his long forehead and slightly fuzzy but thinning greyish hair. He always wore an unbuttoned brown coloured tweed waistcoat often on top of one of those granddad collarless shirts. That waistcoat was worn even in the hottest weather. Also he was never without a Woodbine cigarette hanging from his mouth. He'd often shout at me that I would never make a living from hitting squash or tennis balls about. What I needed were skills like musicianship or accountancy. I had no idea of what he was going on about and still don't. Since those days I've always striven to distance myself from what he preached about. The chaos that operated in my life, had made it impossible to comprehend what family was all about until some years back before I got ill. It was then I knew I wanted to tell the family story. I'd been documenting material and making plans for some time. I can't do this now by myself. Not enough time and too much pain. Thank God for Hugh. I never really thought much about cancer until I lost both Mum and Dad from it and then never really understood what it meant. After Dad's death I had to go and live with my aunt in Fulham. In those days, cancer was taboo and whispered about in secret. Mum died when I was eleven and Dad died when I was fifteen. She died of breast cancer and he died from throat and mouth cancer. The effort of telling this is beginning to tire me and I'm starting to cough. I told Hugh I needed to rest and to take my medication. He agreed and I asked him to come back in a couple of hours.

He returned as agreed. I felt a little better but told him I was getting things out of sequence and there were a few earlier details I needed to add in.

"Don't worry Dad, take your time. I'll sort it out. You're doing well. Go as slowly as you like. I don't mind at all."

I thanked him and told him I had to try and tell him

everything I knew and also about my own life. I haven't got a lot of time left so it's important, even if what I tell him is out of order. I am just hoping he'll be able to sort it all out. Hugh does have a university first degree in physics so I'm guessing he has an orderly mind. He switched the Ferrograph back on. I proceeded to tell him that our ancestors had fought with Nelson at the battle of Trafalgar. I saw Hugh gasp as he muttered an audible "Phew."

What Hugh hadn't known until I told him was that behind my wardrobe he would find a large antique wooden security chest, which contained all the information and records I'd found over the years and details of what I was telling him. If he got stuck somewhere he might find the answers from my box. It was to be his job to get it all into order then investigate further and present his findings to the family, as I was now in no position to do so. He agreed and I was pleased feeling a burden lift from me. He didn't know he would find some difficult material.

"Hugh," I said, "You and Flora, as you know, are twins." Flora shares a house with Robert my youngest son across in Paignton. "But did you know you were not the first twins in this family?"

"We aren't? There were others?"

"Yep, in 1785 there was James and Helena. They all lived in Edinburgh until the family early in the nineteenth century moved to South Street in Chelsea, which in those days was a poor area. Why they did this is a mystery. James died from diphtheria when he was thirteen and Helena two years later from consumption."

He switched off the recorder. "Dad, why've you never mentioned any of this before? I find it amazing."

"I guess none of us got on too well in the past. I know I've been difficult but aren't most fathers? I didn't think that any of you would be interested. All I want is for you to preserve all that I am telling you and pass it down across our family,

9

children and grandchildren. They should know who they are and where they came from and then they can add to it their own stories and pass them on. In my state I understand the importance of this. Will you do that, please?" I clasped his arm as hard as I was able. I wanted him to understand the strength of my intent.

"Dad, of course I will. It's surprising stuff and I'm fascinated by it. You should have told us this earlier."

I told him there was so much more, like my granddad, James, telling me of yet another James who had started work on the railways up north and lived in communal camps. "Apparently he was handsome and charming and was known as a gambler and 'womaniser.' I never understood what that meant at the time and could only hazard a guess. He was by all accounts a good worker and the bosses were keen to keep him on. One day he lapsed and was caught stealing a loaf of bread. What made him do this we shall never know. Most probably he lost his wages gambling. As an alternative to facing the courts he opted to be confined to camp for fourteen days. How angry and frustrated would he have been? When he'd completed his confinement he quit and started walking from Manchester down to London. He'd lost touch with his father many years back and had little idea where he could find him apart from his old address. He knew his name and had only a faint recollection of what he looked like and where they lived. Were they still there? He had no idea. Eventually after some weeks he ended up in Chelsea. It was a Saturday afternoon and he was in the middle of a street market. It was there he spotted him and all the old memories and pictures flooded into his mind. He went straight up to him and looked him squarely in the face. It was his father. There was no doubt about that. I know all this because I found all their old diaries, which record this from both sides. His father, as if it was only yesterday had said, "Hello son. How are you?"

James was pleased that his father had recognised him but must have been puzzled by the low-key reaction, but had said "Father, I need a place to live for a while."

That was how he became re-instated back into family life. He got a job working in the cheese shop, which in those days was considered a middle class profession, well removed from being a ganger on the railways and that started the beginnings of their own business success. I remember Dad telling me that his father had no idea where some of the family vanished to over a six-year period. The only guess he had was the railway construction programme or the army, as there were no trace or records he could find. Whatever sons achieve is never quite good enough. It's not surprising they up and disappear. Percy wasn't that dissimilar. He would upset me with his constant nagging at whatever I was attempting. Yet I have to admit he did work hard. His solution in dealing with life's upsets was to work even harder, teaching at school or taking on more students for his private musical tutorials.

"I'm stopping for a while, my chest is hurting." I reached for the large grey and black oxygen cylinder standing at the head of the bed. I switched it on, placed the transparent plastic mask over my face, breathing in deeply several times. Relief wasn't long in coming. Hugh paused the recorder. He'd seen me do this many times.

"You had enough Dad?"

I pulled the mask to one side. "No. I'm okay. Just taking a short breather. You'll find all the finer details of what I'm telling you in my box. All you'll need to do is to marry them up to what I'm telling you and more."

"I work hard in the same way if not harder. Dad's focus would drive my Mum, Caroline, mad at times, so much so she would often accuse him of behaving as if she wasn't there. I wasn't that old but do remember how distracted he could become. Even in their deaths they remained distant from each other. He was buried in East London and she was buried in Chiswick, many miles from each other. Caroline was wealthy in her own right and I think this made Dad uncomfortable, less of a man maybe. He was, in a way, living off the money left to her by her mother, Hannah and the sale of her Dad's estate in Devon. This house was part of it.

One thing Dad and I had in common was that we liked to fish. He had all the right stuff, rods, hooks, floats, nets and bait; all that you would expect from a fisherman. When he was in a good mood he would let me try his rods, which were big and manly compared to mine. It was his way of relaxing but it'd get Caroline, very cross, as often we would be away all day. Once he took me in his car to a trout stream he knew of in the country where we fished all day. I actually caught a really massive trout and felt so proud and Dad got irritated because he hadn't caught a thing. I don't think he was too pleased. We got back home late on account of a large herd of deer that had charged across the road. A stag hit the car sideways with its antlers giving the car a large dent in the rear mudguard. Dad stopped the car, got out and walked towards the stag, which was on its back upside down in the middle of the road. Its legs were waving in the air. As he got close to it, it let out a mighty bellow, stood up, shook itself and charged across the road jumping a large fence with ease and disappeared. I shall never forget that. Mum was none too pleased at our late return and our food had gone cold. She fumed away at him. His response was to turn around and wink at me. That made me feel like I belonged in a secret sort of way to his life, a secret society, which few knew about. It was also that year he taught me how to row a boat. That was fun but I think now why he allowed me to do the rowing was that he could sit back with his packet of Woodbines and smoke away to his hearts content."

Telling Hugh this I'm hoping he'll feel connected to the family including Flo and Bobby. It's part of my legacy to them. I refuse now to be a stranger to my family and have been guilty of that so much in the past. I hope it's not too late. I want them to feel that between us all, both the living and the dead there is empathy, connection, identity and a sense of familial unity, a bond that has made us what we are. This is unconditional and includes both the good and bad things discovered. I know I'm coming up to the last hurdle in my life and our history I feel very strongly about. It's become urgent and uppermost in my mind. It's amazing what the knowledge of inevitable death can bring to a man. But now I'm beginning to feel tired again.

"You okay Dad? Do you want to stop?"

"No I'll carry on for a while longer, please."

"When I was just a young boy of eight or nine I had a special girl friend whose name was Emma. What ever happened to her I shall never know. When summer came I would take her out in the rowboat and we giggled and laughed all the time. We squabbled about what to call the boat. I wanted something manly like *Lionheart* or *Jolly Rodger*. She didn't like any of these and insisted we call it a girly name, *Missy* or *Jenny*. Needless to say we couldn't agree and a name never did get painted on the sides. At times she would scare the life out of me as she told stories of the River People who lived on the bottom mud of the river. At night, or when nobody else was near they would surface and eat any children who were about. She was always telling stories to see if she could frighten me. She did that alright. Where she got them from or made them up as she went along I never knew. When she started those stories I remember rowing even harder towards home nearly peeing myself while she laid on gruesome details with a trowel. Invariably she would burst out laughing at my concern and this eventually used to make me laugh. I think I loved her even at that early age." I paused for a while, and Hugh asked if I was ok.

"Yes. I just want to get this part sorted out and done then I need to rest."

"I missed those childhood days when a summer's day seemed to stretch out forever. Sometimes we'd take food with us on our little boat and she used to like hard-boiled eggs. I couldn't stand them. I much preferred corned beef sandwiches with mustard and lettuce. I can still remember her peeling those eggs, the awful smell of sulphur and watching the eggshells she threw over the side go drifting by the boat like an armada before catching up in the willowy weeds by the banks." At this point I looked at Hugh, took a deep breath, closed my eyes and fell asleep.

Next day Hugh returned and told me he had spoken to Flora and Robert and they were coming over to see me at the weekend. What he didn't know is that I'd heard him on the phone saying he didn't think I had long and was wondering whether I'd lost the will to live especially as I was having trouble walking and my constant pain. Well, I guess that's a conversation you can have with relatives and I didn't blame him for it. If anything it reflected his level of concern. I was looking forward to their visit and it would be good to see them all again as normally we only spoke for ten minutes or so over the phone at weekends. This was invariably on Sunday afternoons. Hugh could tell them how my project was shaping up. There were more surprises for him in my box but I thought it might be good for him to find out for himself later when he got around to collating all this. He switched the recorder on, adjusted his black and red notebook, clicked open his Parker pen and asked if I was ready? I told him to never forget, even more so that his roots came from a long line of Scots as we had for a long time lived in England. His true ancestry had been planted in the highlands of Scotland. He said that was something he had never given much thought to but from what I'd begun to tell him he was now finding it important and hadn't realised what all this meant. I smiled for I could see my story was having a positive effect on him.

He sat quietly beside me and I am really beginning to like him being around to take all this in. He's patient and gentle, I feel proud of him. I took five minutes with the oxygen mask and then began speaking.

"After my Mum died I went into myself, became withdrawn, aggressive and my schoolwork deteriorated badly. My enduring memory was of her last days. I could barely recognise her. She would be laying in her bed her skin bruised all over and a large lump protruding from inside her stomach. It was the cancer spreading around inside her. Dad suffered too. He lost interest in everything. Caroline had been a beauty and was his joy. Both myself and Elizabeth who was a year younger than me tried hard to keep the place running but Dad made it more difficult as he had started to drink and smoke heavily. I knew that he'd wake up in the early hours of the morning to drink scotch and have two or three cigarettes and when he finally got up again in the morning he'd start all over again. He wasn't good to have around and how he coped with his teaching and music lessons I'll never know. He got angry very easily and it was like he didn't want us around. He went off his food and all he wanted to do was smoke and drink. Once I found him sobbing out loud in the kitchen holding a picture of Mum. Large tears were streaming down his face. I'd never seen a man cry before. It upset me badly. He put his arms around me and that was something he hadn't done since I could recall. He blurted out between the sobs that he missed her so much and he was finding life and its responsibilities almost impossible. I remember crying with him. Elizabeth kept away; she was always aloof from intimacy. Not long after that Dad started sending us over for long weekends to our Aunt Joan's place in Fulham. I couldn't get on with her and she described me as an unruly boy. Elizabeth was much preferred to me. Dad's drinking and smoking had increased heavily and he never seemed to be without one or the other in his hands. He was also coughing and spitting heavily. This could stop him teaching as he frequently would burst into a coughing fit whilst addressing a class full of pupils. He said that they would find it funny, giggling and snorting as he attempted to gain some control of his spasm. He often had to leave the classroom. We began to worry for him and I recall once he coughed up a mass of blood and phlegm into the kitchen sink. This alarmed him and us and I thought he could have consumption. It didn't stop him smoking. In the meantime my schoolwork had got back on course and regained its momentum. I wasn't pining for Mum so much although a day wouldn't pass by when I didn't think of her. My teacher thought I was bright. I had a skill with mathematics and he said I was a possible candidate for the grammar school. Eventually I passed the scholarship but a year later Elizabeth failed it, not that that made much difference to us the way events were to unfold. Dad was getting worse. He had little idea about anything and couldn't handle money. Even at my young age he'd ask me to try and sort out his bills and bank statements. It was at about this time he told me he could barely afford to keep me at school and my stay there might only be for a short while. I felt disappointed. It was about then he began complaining that his throat was hurting him and his mouth was burning. The doctors told him he had to cut down on his drinking and smoking or this could get worse. Dad's argument was that smoking and drinking reduced his painful symptoms. That was his version of reverse logic. Well it wasn't long after this his condition became far more serious. The family became concerned, as he would frequently go into terrible spasms of pain. His neck and tongue were beginning to swell and blacken. ...."

"Stop there Dad for a moment. I want to ask you a question."

"What's that?"

"Didn't any of those doctors know what was wrong with him?"

"Well medical diagnosis then was not what it is today. Dad found it hard to cut back on his excesses. You see, he never got over the death of Mum. He was diagnosed of having cancer of the throat and mouth. There was little that could be done for him. Not long after he died, painfully and disgustingly, unable to eat or drink. He didn't deserve that. But still, rain falls on both the good and the bad. It's going to happen to all of us sometime, as you can see! Hugh, I was less upset about him dying as I was with Mum. So Elizabeth and I became orphans. The house wasn't left in trust for us so effectively we had nothing until the house was sold. What was revealed to us by the solicitors was that Mum had other properties. This one. It was to be ours when we came of age. Aunt Joan reluctantly took us in. I was withdrawn from school, which devastated me. Any chance of getting on and going to university was lost. I was instructed by her and my Uncle Elgar to get a job and get one quickly. We were expected to pay our way. Meanwhile she helped herself to all Dad's furniture, antiques, jewellery and glassware. We were robbed of everything by that

17

mean and greedy bitch." I paused, "I'll have to stop there. When I think about that it can still upset me. I need a rest please."

"Ok Dad. I'll come back later today."

I thanked him, took a deep breath sank back into my pillow and went through all I'd told him. The events seemed like only yesterday. Sharp pain rode across my back.

After my rest the pain subsided. I felt able to talk again. I decided to speak about the religious side of our family not that there is much to tell but he needs to know how I felt and what I thought of it all.

"All our ancestors, like most in their days were churchgoers and were all buried in churchyards or had Christian gravestones erected to them. I've found plenty of evidence for that."

Hugh doesn't know this but I have a massive family Bible that goes back two hundred years or more. It comes complete with an extensive family tree. This should help him in his collations. I continued, telling him that I had always felt uncomfortable about God.

"I always remember an old American adage that gives my viewpoint some perspective. It always amuses me, 'I'm from Missouri man. Show me!' Not much chance of that I would say. Presumably men from Missouri were great sceptics? That being so I didn't want a Christian funeral as I didn't believe in it and didn't want some priest muttering over me when he hadn't even known me. I used to hate those stiff style vicars giving out those sermons. It embarrassed me and still does. It's as if they had a personal hot line to God's phone."

I knew Hugh would be okay with me telling him as I had already heard his views on this and they were pretty much the same as mine.

"Not going to Sunday school or church on Sundays was frowned upon and my sister and me were dressed up in our best clothes and not allowed out to play. What a bore that was. At least I didn't impose that regime on you, as it seemed important you made your own choices in this respect. When I got to twelve it was decided that I was to be confirmed at his local church, St. Dionis in Fulham. I had no say in the matter. The whole business made me squirm. I rarely ever went to communion. My attitude gave Dad cause to despair. When I got a bit older I got interested in Buddhism as a religion without a God. Dad would have been appalled if he'd been around and been there to see me become so involved. You could say there must have been something missing from my life and maybe this was the path I needed to find it. All my certification and newspaper cuttings about this time are in my box. I can only think that my attraction to it had a lot to with my love of mathematics. Maths are devoid of emotional content. They spoke to me in dignified reverence. They removed me from the stultifying sickly emotions of father's beloved music, frequently blasting the likes of Puccini operas from his crackly old wind up gramophone. I was aware of what maths were about. I could get my head around them. There were always solutions and things fitted into place. For me, God didn't figure in it, that concept was so imprecise. If Einstein had worked out that God $= MC^2$ I might have thought it worth a look at but he didn't. With maths I developed an awareness of cosmic scale, of what time meant and how measurable things could be. At an early age I had little trouble working out simple maths and geometry problems, which surprised my teachers. It all seemed so simple and I couldn't understand why people had such problems with it. Maths had a pure sort of logic with which it ended up with answers. Things became solvable. Six times six was always thirty-six and so on. Basically in understanding the varied rules, which maths is full of, makes for elegant solutions. Numbers didn't lie and there was also a distinct beauty in algebraic formulae, logarithms, roots, sines, co-sines, trigonometry, calculus and so on. This was more so when they were moved and applied into the world of science and physics. I'm sure you know more about this Hugh than I do. I couldn't get any of this with God. Who was he? How long had he been around? Who were his father and mother? Naïve questions from a young boy maybe. Until this day no person or priest has given me a satisfactory answer and probably never will. Maths is not vague in this way. Do you think I deserve to burn in their hell for honest disbelief? It seems so much rubbish."

Hugh chuckled loudly, "Don't worry about it Dad I'm with you all the way. You and I'll fry together!"

A funny sort of shudder passed through me when he said that. That surprised me. It got me thinking as to how much conditioning I must have gone through. Was I now, even in my mature and final days feeling the long arm of religion continuing to stalk me? I quickly dismissed the idea. I carried on talking, "I remember Mum not being too keen on church herself and she would often tell me that the true God was locked away in your heart if only people cared to have a good look. This to me, when I look back, is far more acceptable than a whole army of vicars and bishops quoting things they'd read in a book and have no personal knowledge or experience of. When things got bad for her she would tell me that soon she would be joining her mother in heaven. I recall that that she would walk about the house softly speaking to her mother as if she was still alive. Her grief must have been with her all those years right up to the time of her own death.

When Percy became incapable of looking after himself any longer or us, he was hospitalised. Aunt Joan and Uncle Elgar reluctantly took us in. It wasn't long after Dad died and after he was buried they withdrew me from school and Elizabeth a year later. This bitterly upset me, as I had plans for my education. I was told that there was a suitable vacancy that Elgar knew, with an estate agent and it would help pay my way in living with them. I wasn't consulted, just told. It was the last place I would have wanted to work. Why couldn't I work in photography? This was a subject I was keenly interested in and had plans to save up and buy a decent camera. After a year at the estate agents they put me to work collecting rents. It was awful. There were people who couldn't or wouldn't pay. Others would offer only a fraction of their weekly rent. Where their money went I had no idea. It wasn't my concern. Often my employers would give me a bollocking for not collecting in full. What was I supposed to do? I only hoped they weren't going to turn me into a bailiff! I stuck with it but I had plans to be on my way. Back at home I found Elgar okay in his own way. I discovered he was a survivor of trench warfare in World War One. I could only guess he had seen terrible things and done some also. He wouldn't speak much about it and when I tried to get more information out of him he'd get tearful, hang his head down, shake it or get up and walk away from me. I guessed it best not to ask him any more. Joan who wore the trousers in that place dominated him. She was forever calculating daily and monthly expenditure and at times would increase the contributions I was expected to make for staying there. Elgar was a land surveyor and was often away on a job somewhere. It was then she could really get vicious with us both. I began to think about getting away from there but couldn't quite afford it."

It was at this point I paused and asked Hugh "Would you mind getting me a large scotch. I know I'm not supposed to drink but what bloody point is there of that and as if it mattered in my condition?"

He got up and went out to fetch me the drink. When he did I reached over and gulped an extra dose of my morphine mixture. I didn't want him to see. I wasn't unaware that my condition was upsetting him. When he got back I took the glass from him in shaky and gnarled fingers. It was a large measure, rich with a golden colour and I loved the inviting sound of the ice as it clunked around in the glass and that hint of condensation as it clung to the sides. The aroma was something from heaven. I put the glass to my lips, cautiously sipped at the drink, as I didn't want to splash it about should I get into a coughing spasm. The taste and effect on me as it passed down my throat and sought out my chest and stomach was exquisite. Mixing it with morphine is probably not a good idea and shouldn't be encouraged! Moments like this have become precious to me. My awareness of ordinary things has heightened. The simple act of taking a drink has become full of wonder. The ordinary has become extraordinary and I feel grateful for that, even privileged, which seems a contradiction in terms for someone with Multiple Myeloma.

I continued talking, sipping joyfully on the very large drink he'd poured me. I told him I'd been very fond of girls, much to my Aunt's disgust. I had several girlfriends and she'd attempted to put a curfew on me. She thought that I was like previous male members of our family who apparently had a histories of dalliances and affairs. Well if anyone wants to know I never had full sex until I got married. I didn't want Hugh or anybody jumping to conclusions. I'd received, like Elizabeth, a reasonable sum of money from the sale of Dad's house plus interests in other properties. So on paper I wasn't exactly poor by any degree. However I couldn't touch it until I'd come of age. This gave some impetus for Aunt Joan to tighten her financial straitjacket on us. We were always having to pay extra for something or other. In spite of this I managed to save a good sum of money and brought a camera and tripod. Daringly, I placed an ad in our local paper for taking wedding pictures, christenings, that sort of thing. Even at my young age I started to pick up work to such an extent that I began making enough to think of leaving the estate agents. It was about then I met your Mum. It was an instant attraction for us both and in no time we were discussing marriage. She had a stepmother and neither her nor her Dad seemed to like me and they refused to let her marry me as they thought she was too young. This prompted me to leave Elgar and Joan's and all the items they had decorated their house with from Percy's old house. I rented a small flat; Freda and I married without telling anyone and she moved in. We were husband and wife. Her parents were utterly furious and so was Aunt Joan and Uncle Elgar. So what, it was our life not theirs. She was disinherited, not that they had much to leave her anyway. We were young and in love and that was all that mattered. It was the late thirties and war was just around the corner, which would throw everything into turmoil. I could live at *Pimlico* now but deferred because ….." My voice caught. The scotch, plus the morphine were having their effect. I looked at Hugh. My voice had faded. I took a long deep breath that hurt me. My eyes rolled back and I fell asleep again. I didn't feel him take the glass from my hand.

* * *

It was the end of January. The sky was a swirling mass of an underworld grey and the first late winter snow had begun falling, casting a reflected light on everything on which the flakes landed upon. Scott lay asleep, unaware of the transformation occurring all around him outside. He had always enjoyed snow although he knew there were men who did not. Quietly and gently it continued its descent becoming thicker and increasingly dense, laying a blanket of stillness around the old house, magnifying the silence of his sleep. Scott slept the sleep of the ghosts of his parents, grandparents and all those he and they had loved most. He had known for a long time that one man's coffin is another's cradle. When he awoke he would begin to gather his strength and continue on his inevitable journey.

TWO

Nemo Non Paratus

Today, at this moment I'm pain free. I can only guess my Myeloma is pausing to gather its strength ready to continue its internal devouring mission deep inside. I sensed its spread. On pain free days I experience exceptional clarity and a sense of gratitude. I've lived a full and eventful life although I've had massive regrets. In a muddled way I have to tell Hugh this. He's next to me recorder at the ready and with his pen plus the red and black notebook.

"Hugh, I've travelled around the world, and somehow I have always been attracted to the teachings of The Buddha, which altered my life and thinking in many ways. Yet I was never persuaded to the pacifist aspects of its teachings. People like Hitler and his Nazi's I saw as pure evil. They themselves were a cancer that had to be surgically removed to preserve humanity from monstrous theories and doctrines. This was a time when some people said I was being hypocritical and facing two directions at once. Well maybe I did but I had no qualms. I couldn't stand by in a robe and a shaven head, hands together and making humble bows to those who wanted to wipe out huge sections of decent honest humanity for not being Aryans. I laid down my beliefs, put them away and embraced the frightful prospects of war. For me it felt the right thing to do. I never really again trod totally in the footsteps of Buddhism. Yet many parts of its philosophy have stayed with me and remain priceless. I felt it lacked fundamental compassion for the oppressed and suffering aspects of mankind."

"I've always felt it was very reasonable and logical but at times bloody vague to say the least." Hugh said.

"That may be true, Hugh, but it's not a bad way to live."

"I don't trust beliefs, Dad, until they've been tried tested and found to be true. Not too good for religions, that maxim."

I had no argument with that.

I'm experiencing considerable clarity so it's time to start telling him of the most formulative years of my life and how I ended up in Bomber Command of the RAF and what happened to me.

"War was imminent. I joined the army and became a despatch rider, which I found boring and without challenges. My superiors said I had a very good understanding of map reading and mathematical skills, which they suggested could be put to better use. With this in mind I applied to join the RAF and was surprised that after a few tests that I was accepted and I was immediately transferred. I started off as a cadet in 1939 rising to sergeant within a year and shortly after being promoted to a Pilot Officer. I remember I was supplied with a brand new officer's uniform. It looked conspicuously virginal and almost embarrassing in its stark newness. Mine had a skinny blue Pilot Officer's stripe on the cuff of each arm. My training was intense. Initially I wanted to be a pilot. Who wouldn't? A slight eye defect ruled that out. I was then hopefully to become a navigator."

I asked Hugh if he knew anything about the training and requirements of a navigator?

"No Dad, I don't, but I've a feeling that I'm about to."

We both chuckled and I'm glad I'm having a good day to relate this and so far I'm not feeling too tired.

"Well, I flew in some ancient planes, Ansons, Whitleys, Blenheims and Hampdens before eventually getting into a Halifax. You go through all aspects of complex navigational theory, cross country and sea flights, star observations and map reading. Could I map read and navigate at night? I didn't know, I never tried it but when I did I seemed to do pretty well and my instructor was impressed. They also got you to train in bomb aiming, aerial photography, air gunnery, reconnaissance, meteorology and all other aspects of what a navigator was expected to know. They drummed into us that no details were too small to be overlooked. Our lives depended on meticulous attention to every detail no matter how small or large. Seems silly now but we were always expected to have a stock of sharpened pencils plus a sharpener and a penknife. On top this we had to have Indian rubbers, a 'slipstick' or slide rule, protractors, sets of dividers, a long ruler, time speed scales plus a current *Air Almanac* and appropriate volumes of *Astronomical Navigational Tables*. I remember all this like yesterday, and there were so many other things we had to stock up with as well. Flight plans were essential and without one you wouldn't survive. Every minute spent in preparation on the ground saved nine to ten minutes in the air. It was very much a team effort and no flight should have taken off if anyone had a query or was in doubt about what was intended. I'm not going to bore you with all the mathematical technicalities of navigation but when you get into that box of mine it will all be there if you're interested. It could get tough when flying at altitude trying to work and kitted up in thick furry flying boots, flying jacket plus helmet complete with a microphone and flying gloves. Trying to draw thin elegant plot lines with all that on wasn't easy. On top of this it would be bloody freezing up there and the noise the kite made with its vibration and engines was something else. Added to this you had to use an oxygen mask and then face the anxiety of having to deal with enemy ground and air attacks. I'm out of sequence here, Hugh, forgive me. I'll explain later. I'd been posted to 78th Bomber Squadron. Its motto was *Nemo Non Paratus,* which translated means *Nobody Unprepared.* It was a formidable squadron with a high reputation from 1940 until the end of the war. We belonged to 4 Group and were based in various locations, Dishforth, Middleton-St-George, Linton-on-Ouse and Breighton. In our group we flew the most sorties and we suffered the loss of, if I can recall properly, of 245 aircraft. This was one of the highest loss rates in Bomber Command. From what I can remember also is that we also managed to drop into Germany the largest tonnage of bombs than any other squadron."

"Dad, why have you left all this so late to tell? It's historic and needs to be told, not just to me but also to future generations. Historians are always banging on about Agincourt, Waterloo and Trafalgar but this is equally important."

"I agree and maybe this is part of why I am doing it. It's going to be up to you to tell as many as you can. You'll need to find out more if you can an add it in." As I spoke I was amazed at how clear my mind was. So far, no need for the dull conscious squashing and paralysing infusion of morphine.

"War's an ugly business Dad, but it sadly seems to be part of our lives since time began. I can't begin to imagine what it must have felt like to go out night after night and do what you had to do."

"Let me tell you a little more. You got to know your crew members pretty well but just when you felt a bond developing we would often be allocated to other crews. I guess this was deliberate and avoided the possibility of over attachment to each other and the distress of experiencing the death of someone you had grown to like. I was known throughout as 'Jock' for obvious reasons. Most of us had a funny nickname attached to us. It made you feel you were part of a family. I was never afraid of flying and always enjoyed it and for me there nothing like the feeling of freedom that came when you were up in the sky. You could see forever on some days and it could be so peaceful up there you would have never believed at times that there was a war going on."

It was then I told Hugh I was going to diversify a little and asked him if he minded. He agreed that was fine.

"Well, your Mum had you and Flora to look after. Twins were a shock to both of us especially as there was a war going on. It couldn't have been easy for her especially as I kept getting posted around a lot. As I had to go to Yorkshire she followed up later on the train. When she arrived she had nowhere to stay, so she tramped around the streets of York looking for somewhere or someone where she could stay or be put up. Eventually a lady, a Mrs Pierson, if I recall, took pity on you all and invited you to stay. There you stayed for a year almost. Freda never forgot the kindness of that lady. Isn't it amazing how adversities can often bring out the best in people?"

"Hold on, Dad." Hugh paused the recorder. "I remember all that and in retrospect it's nothing short of a miracle. I remember her husband was some sort of woodworker and he made Mum a beautiful wooden fruit bowl, which we had for years. D'you remember it?"

"Of course I do and it surprises me that you do. If you're going to bring back some memories switch the Ferrograph back on."

He understood and switched it back on. "There's a lot I'm beginning to recall Dad, things like Flora being badly bitten by a dog in the alley behind that house in York. And there was dear old Wren, your Cocker Spaniel dog. D'you remember when we visited you at the airfield and you were standing in your flying kit in front of a huge black bomber with Wren sitting next to you? It seems so clear. I can remember if the air raid sirens went off she would dive for cover and even when the war was over and she heard a programme on the wireless and they played an air raid siren she would still bolt for cover."

I looked up at Hugh because I felt tears coming into my eyes "Hugh, can we stop there for a while. Why don't you come back another time before Flora and Robert arrive and we'll carry on."

Hugh agreed, switched off the recorder and left. Memories are overwhelming me. What happens to them all when I'm dead? "Oh fuck it" I muttered to myself, "If I can't cry now in this state and time of my life then when can I?' So I let it happen. There's lots of it too. I'm feeling overwhelmed with memories. I hadn't expected it would be like this but there's no one to see or hear me. I guess Hugh had a good idea of what state I was in. Crying can be a relief. I can't help wondering where he feels all this is going to lead. To be honest I don't know myself but I'm obsessed that what I have to say becomes part of their family history. There are other things he is going to find out which I can't talk to him about and I hope he or the others don't get too hurt. He might think that what I'm telling him will turn into a book. He's agreed to place all this in order although the way I'm rambling it could get a little tricky. It's about time for my medication as I'm feeling that familiar pain surfacing up and stretching through my bones and body. The dose soon diminishes the advancing pain but I'm left feeling sleepy. I surrender gratefully.

The next morning Hugh arrived early and I'm pleased he has because there's a lot to tell him and I want to do so before I forget. There's so much in my head I keep mixing up my childhood with my adult years and it's getting confusing. It's not a good sign in my state. I think the best idea is to talk about the war years and how I managed in the air and my captivity in Germany, of which I have never spoken before. I know Hugh is in for more shocks.

"You feeling ok this morning Dad?"

"Yeah I'm ok at the moment. So while we have a chance let's get on with it."

Hugh switched on the Ferrograph and we were ready. I ignored the intrusions of childhood memories and focussed on the war.

"I spent endless hours flying about in shaky old training aircraft up and down the length and breadth of this country. It could get very tedious at times. I'd all sorts of pilots flying me around, Canadians, Aussies, Kiwis and Poles mainly. The Polish pilots were mad and very brave and I had a lot of respect for them. I spent about 130 hours day training and about 50 flying at night. My results were good and I was promoted to Flying Officer. My first raid in June 1942 with dear Sergeant Beck as pilot was to attack Bremen. Bremen was my first experience of war and secretly I was terrified. I'm certain I wasn't alone with that feeling. It was pitch black everywhere and then large amounts of heavy flak began exploding all around us. There were bright orange flashes crashing about with odd bits going right through the fuselage and some through the wing tips. I remember thinking quite clearly that I didn't want to die on my first ever op. Fortunately there were no night fighters about and once we had dropped our bombs we circled back towards home. Having made it back to base the feeling in the aircraft was one of high euphoria. Our plane had taken a few hits, which in the morning light the holes looked alarming. Whatever eventually happened to Sgt. Beck I shall never know? When he was posted elsewhere I never saw him again although we'd made many raids together."

"Dad! I can't even begin to imagine what that must have been like. Christ! You were all only just in your early twenty or thereabouts."

"Weren't we all? We'd barely ceased to be boys. The memories are with me and always will be until I die shortly and this is part of the reason why I am telling you. You do understand don't you?"

"I'm beginning to."

"Good. After raids I would be drained but so much adrenalin was pumping about I could hardly sleep. A few pints were normally the order of the day."

"Can you tell me more at the moment?"

"I never wanted to fly over cities and towns dropping bombs and killing God knows who. I would have much preferred to carry on quietly with my photography. I wasn't allowed to do that though, thanks to Adolph. My second op in a great black Halifax was over Dussledorf and was amazingly uneventful for our crew. The bombers created huge fires down below and all across the Ruhr. With over 500 aircraft attacking it must have been as scary down there as it was overhead. There are times when I get to thinking, that I am appalled of what we were both doing to each other, civilians and combatants alike. It still gives me a sense of guilt." My voice broke at this point. I feel overwhelmed. I try shaking my head to stabilise the emotions.

"Take it easy Dad."

"I need to be forgiven. But who will do this?" I continued to shake my head.

"No Dad, you had no choice."

Hugh got up. He knew what was going on with me and

said he would come back a little later. He walked from the room shutting the door quietly behind him. Again I wept.

When he returned I told him that for a while I wanted to talk about his Mum as that might calm me down. He said he had a few memories of his own, which I may not know of. He proceeded to tell me.

"I remember you coming home on leave once and we were only tiny and didn't really know you at all. You were a big man in a uniform who looked scary and you didn't say much. It was all rather difficult as none of us really knew each other. When your leave was over, I can always remember Mum standing at the front gate, waving and crying goodbye to you until you disappeared from the end of the road. I expect she wondered whether she would ever see you again.

"That surprises me you remember that."

"Another thing, I can still see those searchlights over the railway marshalling yards and ordnance factory. The beams were bright white, shining into a black sky bristling and full of the noise of German bombers and our artillery fire. We were all in danger of being hit by bombs and spent most nights in those bloody awful Anderson shelters."

"So you do remember some things then? Work on this, because it will form part of your own story which you must also incorporate and pass on with all that I'm telling you."

"When the sirens went off and we couldn't make the Anderson shelter Mum would throw us into the Morrison shelter in the living room and lay over us covering us with her body for our protection."

"Jesus! I never knew that."

"Well it's true."

"It seems I'm still learning."

"Dad, you've never spoken like this before. God I wish you had done. It's upsetting for both of us."

"Do you want to stop?" It seems odd, me asking him this.

"No. Carry on, I want to know as much as possible."

"Where was I? Oh yes, ops over Germany. I nearly finished a full tour but why don't I tell you later as we go along. You ok with that?"

"Yes, that's fine."

"Should I run out of steam you'll understand won't you?"

"Of course."

I paused and briefly took stock. The pain is under control. I remain lucid and my brain hasn't been attacked, yet. When it is, as it will be, the cancer will eat it. All cognition will go including sight and coordination. Lately I've noticed more bruises and lumps are appearing, erupting from my skin. These are an inky black and purple colour. They're on my legs, groin, testicles, stomach, chest arms and hands. I'd looked in the mirror again earlier and could see my face is now a messy blotch. It's not pretty and it fucking hurts! This disgusting Myeloma is hell bent on my destruction and pursuing its inevitable course. As Dylan sang, "You don't have to be a weatherman to know which way the wind is blowing."

I continued telling Hugh of other raids I'd been on. "I remember a raid over Saarbrucken where we experienced the heaviest flak I'd ever seen. That wasn't surprising, it was an important manufacturing zone for the Nazi war effort. I was busy trying to plot our course leaning over my navigation table and maps and just happened to lean backwards for a moment. I'm glad I did for at that precise moment a large piece of flak burst through the fuselage and went straight through my table where I'd been leaning over. Leaning backwards saved my head being blown off. My startled expression caused some mirth amongst the other crewmembers not wanting a headless Jock navigator to plot them home. Even I managed a laugh. I guess trust and companionship in the face of mutual danger bound us together. These incidences make sweet memories but behind them all always lurked sadness for those who couldn't make it. Do you understand this, Hugh?"

He nodded vigorously and I continued.

That afternoon Flora and Robert arrived. I haven't seen them for such a while that I felt real pleasure that they'd come to see me. So for once, we as a family were all together. I was glad of the break. They drove up in Robert's old MG car. I hope it can get them back in one piece! He's twenty-six years old and works for a large auction house cataloguing and researching the art and antiques due for sale. He has a strong creative personality and a Fine Art degree. Like me he also has a strong interest in photography. He dresses with some flair, complete with billowy colourful silk scarves, outrageous waistcoats and often wears a large black Fedora hat. I've always admired that unconventional side of him. It seems strange to me that brother and sister can live together but these days are so different to when I was their age. When they walked in to see me Robert looked at me and visibly gulped heavily. I guess because I've deteriorated so much physically and so quickly. Having seen me only a few times over the last year and looking at what I've become must come as a shock. Flora looked as lovely ever with her dark auburn hair tumbling around her neck. Her looks are deeply reminiscent of Jane Burden Morris in Rossetti's Pre-Raphaelite painting, *Reverie*. She's wearing a floaty cerise Indian print dress with matching sandals. She's never without an air of control and competence. It's little wonder she works as logistical controller for a major transport concern. She put her arm around Bobby's shoulder and did a good job of pretending everything was normal but I could tell she too was shaken. We all sat around and gradually as the day unfolded we began to relax and to reminisce telling each other stories of what we remembered and did back then. We toasted crumpets and ate them covered in thick butter, washed down with mugs of hot tea and it was just like the good old times. I noticed that Hugh kept the recorder switched on. My, he is taking this seriously, which pleases me. Later we took pictures of each other and like them, I knew that these would probably be the last they would ever want to take of me. When the boys, later in the evening decided to call it a day and go to bed I got Flora to help me with my medication.

"Without morphine Flora, I reckon I would have ended all this some while back."

"Dad don't" I could see her eyes were walled with water. "I know what's happening to you and I know that nothing can stop it."

I held her close but I didn't want to cry and I could tell she was trying not to.

"I won't know much about it, Flora, because I shall just drift off into unconsciousness and that will be that. All over. Doesn't it seem ironic that I survive a bloody and dangerous war but I'm about to be beaten by something I've never seen."

She could see I was tiring and made my bed comfortable, gently kissed me goodnight and slipped out of the bedroom.

* * *

The next morning, when I awoke I got to imagining I was seeing things around me. My eyes were blurred. At the back of my mind I began wondering what dreams were made of and where they came from. I kept seeing most of the pets I'd had throughout my life. My dogs, Wren, Judy, Skippy, my beloved Doris and Charlie the Shetland Sheepdog, not only were they in my head I could now actually see them physically walking around me. Waiting perhaps? It wasn't scary. I wondered if I was going mad? I called out for Flora who I knew had an affinity for such things. She came running in and I apologised for disturbing her and told her what I was seeing.

"That must be so comforting in a way Dad. Can you just accept them being there trying to comfort and look after you as you looked after them?"

"Yes I can. I see what you mean." I smiled up at her. "They're not frightening me, and yeah they're my pals and I still love 'em.

"Good, perhaps you can tell them that?"

"I already have." I've noticed that my hallucinations are slowly on the increase and with this disease it's not a good sign. It's one of a sliding acceleration. A determination gushed through me. I've got to hang on. I must! I must! When everything is said and done I'll surrender and that'll be that. Finito.

Flora and Robert now know what I'm attempting to achieve and said that they would help Hugh where they could. They both had hopes of marrying their boy and girl friends so maybe they would have kids and they in turn could add to this story. I explained to them all how early in my life I had taken an interest in Buddhism and how it impacted on the way I looked at things, the way I brought them up and how that had contributed to us having vegetarian tendencies. It changed so many perspectives but going to war was a contradiction of all it stood for. I noticed again I was lapsing back to childhood memories. So what? It could all be sorted later. Hugh sat beside me and I continued with my story. "I recall that your granddad, Percy, used to tell me not to tell time anything, because it never wanted to hear from us but only sped up past us, faster and faster eventually leaving us stranded. Odd things Percy could come out with. I guess my interest in navigation came from him. I didn't want to be stranded somewhere not knowing where I was or how to get home. I looked forward to when we would spend long nights, wrapped in thick blankets, sitting on the doorstep, looking up at the night sky. He would point out the various formations, individual stars and constellations, The Plough, The Big Dipper, Polaris, Sirius and Vega and talk about where did all this come from? He also liked animals a lot and felt totally comfortable around them. They seemed to be attracted to him. I remember he told me that animals spend a lot of time being still and that included the wild ones and the birds. He said that when we sat still in the woods or wherever, the animals felt safer with us in our stillness. Isn't that strange? But I think that's one thing he got right, and that's the spirit that I've also tried to pass onto you."

They remained quiet and let me ramble on. I then told them about how my mind was now beginning to play tricks on me, what with the vision of the dogs and another I had a short while after. In this vision I saw Mum and Dad quite clearly. They looked terrific, robust full of health and vitality. They spoke to me,

"Scott, we're waiting for you. Don't be afraid to come home."

A bit weird that. All three of my kids looked perplexed and even upset, looking at each other and I guessed I knew what they might be thinking. Maybe it was that I'd lost my marbles. I don't care. I know what I saw and heard. When I think about this, the death of my parents, Buddhism, the war, the universe, time and how much I love these things and them in particular, my children, now adults. It's making it hard for me to say goodbye. I know I don't want to leave them. They'll always be with me. Came early evening and Flora and Robert had to leave.

We'd done a bit of crying, a lot of talking, and laughing, especially when Flora came in wearing an old hat, which belonged to her Mum. She then did a comically passable impression of her getting cross and swearing out loud with the immortal words "Oh shitting bollocks! Shitting bollocks!" We all remembered those stupid words Mum would shout out when things went wrong. They've now become part of our family history and tradition! I'm pleased I can still laugh out loud and it's been some while since I did that. It feels good. Beneath it all, there lurks a sadness. They know that and I know it. We're all having the same difficulty of not knowing what to say and was this to be the last time I would see Bobby and Flora? Bobby spoke. He gave me my answer.

"If it's all right with you Dad, I'll be down next weekend and can I bring Sophie?"

I felt pleased and surprised. I've never met Sophie who is his long-term girlfriend. "Of course, of course. It's about time I met this mysterious lady."

"I'll come down too Dad and can I bring Mark?" said Flora.

"No problem. I haven't met him either and I'd like to meet the man who is courting my daughter. Thank you for that, the pair of you. I'll be all right for a bit; so don't go to any trouble. I still have time left."

That was a remark I shouldn't have made for I saw them flinch. Underneath I couldn't help thinking that it takes a serious problem to reunite a family. Something there to be thankful for in a strange sort of way.

"No trouble Dad. Is there anything you would like us to bring?"

"Some Glenmorangie malt whisky wouldn't go amiss." I smiled at him.

Everyone laughed. "Consider it done."

It's time now for them to go back to Paignton. Flora came close and held me tight kissing my forehead and stroking my face. She whispered, her voice faltering, "Dear Dad." Turning her head away and she gave a stifled sob, stood up, placed her hand over her mouth and walked hurriedly from the room.

Bobby hugged me tight and I can sense his grief. To my surprise he bent forward and kissed my forehead too. "We'll see you next weekend Dad."

"Make sure you do then, and drive back carefully."

"I promise."

Hugh walked out with him and I didn't have to be a mind reader to understand what they must be talking about. I've had a good weekend and it was great for us all to be together again even in these difficult circumstances. Later, Hugh reappeared.

"I think you've had enough for one day, Dad. We can start again in the morning."

I felt a deep sense of weariness flooding through me. "You're right. I'm feeling bloody shagged!"

Hugh laughed, he wasn't used to me speaking like that. I can feel my eyes closing down before lapsing into deep sleep.

* * *

The sea sounded like a tide of voices, meeting me midway in my awakening dream. Covered in a thick mist it moved relentlessly onwards. I could hear, in my head the long tired sounds of fog insulated noises, beshrouded wails of ships, which had travelled many seas and the far strum of fog horns, signals muffled in the mist. Above, a breaking sky, cool and feathery, penetrated my eyelids. as ships sirens and alarms blasted at me through the window, which is going yellow in the wallowing early sunlight. The cries of gulls penetrate my awaking senses. The fog laying on the window begins to vanish. Dreams and perceptions can be a joy and mine of late are intense. When I became fully awake I managed to look out of the window where I could clearly see the sea and the sky above but it wasn't as in my hope filled dream. Dreams can be deceptive.

Eventually Hugh came in with more tapes and asked if when writing this up into some semblance of order he could include the family conversations we had. I agreed. I told him that was exactly what I was looking for and any other stories; facts or memories he or Flora or Bobby could remember should be included. I'm feeling refreshed from the day before. Yesterday's company boosted my spirits. After having breakfast Hugh came back to see me ready to switch on the reel to reel together with his notebook and pen. I'm impressed. I decide to tell him more about what happened to me during the war.

"It was harrowing to go out night after night getting shot at and attacked from all sides all the time. I can understand why they took you off ops after a tour of thirty and remove you from combat duties for something less dangerous and useful at home. I'll tell you the more dramatic events I can remember, others you will also find in my log book in the box. If I get breathless or start coughing bear with me and get the oxygen ready please."

"Okay. I'm not pushing it. Go at your own pace."

I've decided to try and tell this as a story, which should make it easier for him. From this he should be able to understand what we went through.

"It was about 11pm and we were part of a massive raid over the Ruhr yet again. It was a destination we all hated because of the substantial defences it had trying to protect

41

vital components of their war effort. Even now, I can still hear the roar of our Merlin engines straining in the darkness. I don't think I shall ever forget them. I was wondering why the Germans hadn't switched on their searchlights. It was as quiet as the grave and the blackness was highlighted by a bright new moon. This was almost like a ritual, sacred yet terrifying. We were all on edge because we knew what they could throw at us. We were just planes, large planes full of the flesh and blood of men, many who were about to die. I prayed I wouldn't be one of those. People down below us were about to die also. I got to thinking how an aircraft was built. It involved ships carrying metal and iron, the factories which shaped and forged it all, men and women who laboured night and day separated from their loved ones in relentless shift work twenty four hours a day. The workers, the plane and us were connected and joined together. We were as one. What brought on those thoughts I'll never know? The concept of war in planes had dramatically changed and was now far more technical. The men who flew them were ultimately pawns on the military chessboard, gone today and probably forgotten tomorrow. We were there for a purpose and we would carry that out as best we could. We were in the advanced formation of the attack and inside the plane we're all quiet apart from me as I constantly wrestled with maps shuffling papers and charts and plotting courses. Behind and above me the gunners are straining their eyes looking for enemy fighters. Back home in the ops room everything is being plotted out and they no doubt want to hear the words, 'Mission Completed' but there would be other messages, 'Mission Abandoned' 'Bombs Jettisoned' 'Injuries and require medical assistance on landing' 'Fighter attack developing' or worst of all 'We're going down. Preparing to bale out.'

"Stop there, Dad, for a moment. Was this how it was every time?"

"Mostly. You could never predict what would happen. On this raid German night fighters attacked us and you could just make out the painted swastikas and black crosses outlined in white on them. Our rear gunner, Pat Leyton took the brunt of it all and a burst of shells got him. He was cut in half, literally, spreading his insides all over the turret. He'd been a good friend of mine and having to witness him being hosed out of the turret when back at base by the Fire Service was for me a distressing experience. It was traumatic and war seemed so fucking stupid! It was one of the worst nights I ever recall. The night sky was suddenly lit up with orange flashes. They were shooting at us in earnest. Jesus, it was scary. There was an almighty whack and you didn't need to be an engineer to work out we'd been hit, not by a fighter but by large quantities of flak. One by one the engines packed up bar one and the Halifax leant alarmingly to port descending at a rapid rate and now seemed unflyable. I was first designated to jump. I was completely terrified with my legs dangling into the blackness of the night and just waiting for the green light to go on for me to jump down into Germany. My God! I had no thoughts of Freda or you. There was just pure terror of what was going to happen to me leaping into a hostile and unforgiving Germany. Miraculously the green light didn't come on. The pilot had held the Halifax up and the engines refired. God knows how but I clambered back inside. He'd saved us with seconds to spare. We turned around and dropped our bombs and headed full speed for home. I was shaken but jubilant. That had been close. That pilot was awarded a DFC.

"Bloody hell Dad! You've never said a word about this. That's astonishing."

I can tell Hugh is having an eye opening time and I tell him that these things are important and there is more to come later. He is shaking his head, "This is so hard to believe."

"Come back later this afternoon. There's more to tell you."

"I can't wait."

It's getting worse. Pain stabs at every crack, crevice and bone I possess. I try to go easy on the morphine. God knows why, that's what it's there for, to relieve pain. I've plenty of that. There are now wracking and increasing surges, which rush in flowing waves assaulting my arms and back. I can see the bruises and swellings are growing. I'm not a pretty sight. I always thought I'd been an ugly bastard but this is making me more so. Walking is also a real problem as it hurts so much and I'm practically bent double when I have to. It's time to stop trying. I've got to thinking that I haven't achieved too much with my life and don't in any way have much to show for it. Yet my kids are a source of wonderment. Their patient kindness overwhelms me, and it can make me tearful when I lay awake at night in the dark, becoming contemplative about life, trying to make some sense of it all. Who wouldn't if they were like this. Zen mantras are coursing through my mind, 'Namu Shakyamuni Butsu!' was always one that I felt at home with most but never did find out what it meant. It sounds relaxing. So in the privacy of my room I chant it softly, but croakily to myself. It brings me some comfort.

Over the last few days I've prepared instructions on how I want my funeral ceremony to be run. It focused my mind. Planning your own funeral feels strange. It gave me a surreal floating sense of being nowhere but everywhere all at the same time. But it's also proved to be highly satisfying. Funerals are ultimately for the living and not the dead who I'm reckoning can't see or hear them. However I know that the family will want me to indicate how I want it done. At least, if they're uncertain I can point them in the direction they need to go. I've kept all my instructions in a blue folder and will give it to Hugh later. It's for him to organise and that at least for a while will prevent him from getting too upset. That'll come later when it's all done and dusted.

When I see Hugh next I tell him not be too surprised at what I'm about to tell him and to keep all his questions until later when I've finished. He agrees and I begin. " This isn't going to be easy for me or you. I told you I never completed a full tour of ops and this might help you to understand why. I've struggled to get this right in my head but I think it's mostly accurate give or take some minor errors. We'd embarked on a raid on Lorient in Brittany where the Keroman U boat submarine pens were based. It was reckoned the pens were so well built they were virtually indestructible at the time. So the only alternative was to stop them going to sea. Bombing the city was the only way to do this, which would cut off their fuel, ordnance and food supply lines. If they couldn't get these things they couldn't go to sea and attack shipping. Another problem was the whole area was bristling with defences including night fighters. This would be my second run to Lorient so I knew what to expect."

I asked Hugh if he would get me a large scotch with a dash of water, which gave me a chance for a short break. When he handed me the drink I could see that he had noticed my blotchy arm and my shaky hand as he gave me the drink. This was evident more so as I attempted to sip at it without slopping it all down me. That wasn't successful and he mopped me up with a nearby tea towel.

"Want to give it a break, Dad?

"Just for a few minutes." I took a large breath, which sent a rush of pain through my lower back and chest prompting another huge messy slurping gulp of scotch.

"Oxygen Dad?"

"Yes."

Hugh fitted the mask to my face and turned on the cylinder. Several minutes passed as I let the pain calm down, before continuing. I signalled I was okay to carry on.

He picked up his pen, made some notes and switched the Ferrograph back on. "Phew! U boat pens! What can I say!"

"The flight down there was uneventful until we arrived then all hell broke out. Green and orange tracers plus shells burst all around and surrounded us. It was a barrage that never seemed to stop. I remember in spite of the dense cold being soaked in sweat as a searchlight managed to pick us out, which is just what their artillery wanted. It was what we all dreaded. The astrodome was blown out and bright yellow flashes were bursting all around us as they kept up the attack. A night fighter came up from beneath us where he couldn't be spotted, swooped from underneath us and swept onto our tail. Shells began raking through the bottom fuselage and the thin deck of the Halifax. How I wasn't hit I'll never know but yet again our rear gunner had bought it because his turret was missing, shot away. He wasn't there. Whoever that Hun pilot was he knew his business because once he finished his attack he disappeared and our plane was beginning to burn like a torch. I have a mortal fear of being burnt alive and I knew this beloved kite couldn't be saved. We awaited the command to bale out, which seemed an eternity in coming.

Our pilot, Hugh Henty, shouted "This is it lads. Time to bail out! She's had it. See you back home!" With that the green light came on and we knew what we had to do. My parachute was on and I got to the rear door trying to keep upright as she rocked across the sky. This was now the second time I had been in this position but this time there was no alternative. She was going down and there was nothing that could be done. I opened the rear door and I could see the plane was alight with masses of yellow and orange flames. We had to get out before they got to the fuel tanks. I looked down below, and yes, I was petrified as there was nothing to be seen in the ink like darkness. Jesus, I thought France is down there somewhere. Thank God it's not Germany. I saw three shapes drop down to my left and knew three of them had jumped. There was nothing left but to do the same, close my eyes and do it. I did. Cold dark air gushed alarmingly fast past me as I hurtled into a black vacuum. I gave the mandatory count and pulled on the D ring. I felt a sharp jerk as the chute responded and billowed open up above me. I began drifting slowly downwards. I was bloody frightened, cold and pumped up with adrenalin. Hugh, telling you this after all these years still makes me tense and sweaty. I'm pausing for a drink to calm me down." I started to cough badly and grabbed for the tissues. This is taking more from me than I imagined.

"I can't believe that you or Mum never mentioned this to us all those years ago. I'm beginning to feel angry. We've been denied and cheated. Why didn't you tell us?"

"Hugh, please don't get angry. I need to explain and don't have a huge amount of time to tell you. There's more. It's been something I swore your Mum to secrecy about, never to tell any of you. You see, I felt so ashamed. I had failed. I couldn't help plot the plane out of trouble. Its fate was part of my responsibility. I wasn't able to do it." It was then I felt the tears bubbling up in my eyes. I don't need this extra pain in my condition but something is pushing me ever onwards. The tears ran down my face. Hugh embraced me.

"I'm sorry Dad. I didn't mean to upset you. How on earth can you place yourself in that position? Don't be so stupid! You were shot down like so many others at that time. It was not your fault in any way whatsoever."

I took another large gulp on my drink, which swept through me as an anaesthetic. "Thanks Hugh. You just don't know how long I've wanted to tell all this and it's taken so long and at last it's out. I should feel better about it but at the moment I'm not so sure."

He said nothing and was looking incredulous, staring hard at me. He was obviously shaken. Eventually he simply asked.

"What happened then, Dad?"

I knew there must be a thousand questions he would want to ask. As this part of my life has been kept from them all for so long I'm going to have to take it slowly, one piece at a time.

"I knew you'd ask that. It was a nightmare, drifting downwards, not a thing to be seen in that pitch darkness and not knowing where the others were or if they had all got out in time. The Hali' had also disappeared somewhere in a ball of flames. I couldn't see a thing. I didn't hit the ground, I got caught up in a tree. We'd always been told to conceal or dispose of our chutes after baling out. There was nothing I could do. I couldn't budge it. I seemed to be unhurt. I unclipped the harness and somehow managed to climb down the tree, complete in my flying kit. I didn't know what to do with it. I dumped most of it under hedges. I had a small compass and a torch and headed off in a northerly direction not knowing where the hell I was and what I might come across."

At this point in my story I started to cough again and gasp

for breath as another sudden attack of pain hit me. It was time to stop. I reached out for the morphine.

"Take it easy Dad. Let me do it for you." I took two large spoonfuls. The pain is excruciating. It's definitely on the increase. This disease has also disrupted my bowel functions, which are now almost extinct. I've been supplied with an antiseptic, undignified looking white plastic commode. I've only used it once or twice. Mainly all I manage is the odd minor fart or two, one of which has just happened. It's an event that can still make me giggle even in this pain.

"Let's leave it there Dad. Shall I come back later?"

"Yes that's a good idea." This pain is totally distracting me from what I'm saying and I can't get my mind or memory to function properly. I can feel my eyes glazing over as they roll upwards before I partially and mercifully pass out. When I awake I can see from my clock that some hours have passed. The bed is lumpy and wet with sweat. My man-sized nappy is irritating my crotch. It's riding up into the crease of my leg causing me to keep on scratching and pulling at it. It needs changing, as at times I'm unable to control my bladder. This is one of those times. When my eyes complete their focus I can see Hugh come into view. He's holding my arm.

"How you feeling?"

"I'm not sure. That was a bad one. They're getting worse."

"Shall I get the doctor?"

"No. She's due here in an hour. I'll be fine for a while."

"No more story telling today Dad, please. Frankly I'm astonished at what you're saying and I know Flora and Robert will be when I tell them."

"Didn't mean to upset you but let's carry on tomorrow."

He agreed and I can tell that I'm feeling exhausted. Later I heard the doctor arriving and her and Hugh talking in the other room. I don't have to be a mind reader to know what they are talking about. A few minutes later Dr. Adams came in to talk to me. She's in her late thirties and always dresses a generation or so below her years. Today she's got a pair of red-framed glasses, and her black skirt is tantalisingly short and her tightish white silk blouse has a button too far undone. Even in my condition and age, whenever I see her I realise that all has not passed me by. The old urges can still surface. I'm glad to note I'm still able to fantasise! She's incredibly competent and caring and asks me lots of questions. Finally she suggests that a Macmillan nurse be appointed to visit the family and me on a regular basis. Additionally she arranges for a Marie Curie nurse to sit in through the evenings into the early mornings. This would be a help to me, and remove the strain of Hugh and other members of the family watching over me at night. I agree to this. The plan is put into action immediately. She would let us know within a day or so when to expect her. I asked what the nurse would do? She told me they are highly trained with terminally ill patients and can provide me with all sorts of advice and help the family too. Dr Adams doesn't mince her words. She knows roughly what time I have left and tells me. I see Hugh wince. He's not used to such directness and all in all he's had a bad day. He shakes his head and I can tell he's distressed.

"Don't get upset, Hugh. We all know what's happening here."

He turned away from us and walked quickly from the room.

I'm left on my own. I'm beginning to realise I get comfort from understanding that whatever, now or in the future, when I am gone from here, that there can be nothing that can take away from us the knowledge of who and what we are. There will always be people and family. For friends and lovers though, maybe definitions of love will alter and vices diminish as times change but affections will not lapse. It's as the seasons, it's never ending. It has an elegant simplicity almost mathematically beautiful. In doing this I know deep within that I'm attempting to articulate wrongs and redress errors I've made. These are the things I can't tell Hugh or anybody else about. I'm afraid to. They'll discover them later. I've set into motion a hidden agenda, which they will discover. Doing this gives me comfort and comfort is what I want but daren't ask for. I recall drawing comfort when I was younger from sitting, huddled around a small fireplace with my weekly *Beano* comic, where outside I could see trees without leaves. There was a silent happiness from this childish simplicity, which left a scent on my life filling and dancing over and over casting its shadow. That memory will always be entwined inextricably with my life. But I couldn't keep it simple. Later I fucked it up. The light is beginning to fade and flowers are closing up their blooms, a gathering metaphor for the transitory nature of life. I am unafraid of the inevitability of my condition. Making efforts for all to know has given to me a deep feeling of peace that curls around me.

The following morning Hugh reappears and he looks composed once more. He's carrying his notebook and bends to switch on the Ferrograph.

"Sorry about last night Dad but it got to me."

I tell him not to be concerned. It was a perfectly natural reaction.

"Shall we carry on where you left off? I want to know what happened next."

I agree and take my medication, which now includes about ten pills a day, one lot to control the other lot and any brain inflammation and the possibility of having a fit plus the morphine. So far my mind is behaving itself.

"I'll tell you what happened in France."

The recorder reels begin to turn slowly in their subtle hypnotic way as I start to relate what happened next.

"I found a road and walked along it in the dark. Thankfully it was getting lighter but I hadn't a clue where I was. Some navigator eh! As daylight expanded I was able to look at my watch without using the torch and it read five-thirty, which probably wasn't local time. Without warning from around a bend came a man pedalling a bicycle. No, he didn't have onions round his neck but from his overalls and at this time of morning he must have been on his way to work. He braked his bike abruptly and we both stood staring at each other without saying a word. He obviously guessed what I was. With sign language he indicated that I should hide. I speak some French but not a lot but he showed me where to hide beneath a hollowed out mound concealed from the road behind a large canopy of hedges. I was able to stretch in it comfortably without being seen. He indicated that he would be back later with food and drink and I wasn't to move from where I was or reveal myself in any way. I was mightily relieved he wasn't a German but a friendly Frenchman. It didn't escape me that his activities could get him shot. An hour or so later he returned with denim overalls for me to help disguise myself. Also he had bread, cheese, water and wine. My God it tasted like food from the Ritz. The overalls concealed my uniform but I reckoned I had to keep moving as I could still be too close to where the plane had crashed. I shall always be grateful to that unknown and very kind Frenchman. Knowing of the thoroughness of the enemy they would certainly be looking for us. We couldn't be that far from each other. I decided to travel at nights and rest and hide during the day. There were signposts on the road but for small villages I'd never heard of. Sometimes I broke my rule and travelled cautiously in the daylight. I got food from the fields, anything that could be eaten and water from streams and brooks. A short while later I began heading in a north-westerly direction towards the coast avoiding contact with anyone or wishing to be seen. I had no plan as to what I would do when I got there. Disregarding my daylight rule I began travelling along a quiet rural track when three bicycles came up behind me. I instantly dodged into a hedge but I'd been spotted. They all stopped, surrounded me and spoke to me in rapid French most of which I couldn't understand. One spoke to me slowly and clearly after looking me up and down, asking me if I was English. At the same time he bent down and pulled up my trouser leg to reveal a flying boot. That was a give away, wasn't it? With my mediocre French and their schoolboy English plus lots of sign language we made communication. I was told to keep on walking for two kilometres when I would see a slip road on my right sign posted to the Chateau de Locguenole. I was told to wait at the beginning of the footpath, out of sight and they would meet me soon with fresh clothes and real food. This would be welcome change from stolen root vegetables, grapes, apples and the odd peach or two. They were as good as their word and I was led to a farmhouse and told to get to bed as soon as possible and not to go walking until I was told it was safe to do so. The farmer was as you might imagine with his Breton cap and denim overalls. He wasn't tall but he was muscular with enormously strong looking hairy hands. I was sure he would be capable of looking after himself if he had to. I was given a huge bowl of hot onion soup, French bread, cheese, together with a bottle of red wine. Bliss! Whilst I was eating he brought in his married daughter who spoke good English. This was a relief but I think they were checking that I wasn't a German spy. They soon worked out I wasn't. I was holed up there several days not doing much until they brought me several maps and I worked out where I was. The area was full of German military and Gestapo who were anxious to deal with the local resistance, which was highly active in this area. This was a dangerous place to be."

As I was speaking I felt a slippage, a twitch maybe from my mind, for brief seconds my memory went blank with an almost audible click. It made my head jerk. It was distinct and very clear but normality returned quickly. This is not a good sign and is, I'm sure, indicative of things to come. It's a worry I don't need at this stage. The doctors had warned me this could happen but please God not now. I have much to say before I'm finished. Hugh sensed my confusion and must have seen the look on my face.

"You want to call a halt there, Dad?"

I knew the impact this was having on him and told him, no I'd continue, it was just a minor memory lapse. "Let's push on while I'm able." I continued. "I had thought of heading to Spain towards Gibraltar via the coastal route but they told me it was too far and too dangerous. They were so caring I can never forget their courage and fortitude. It was very obvious they were part of the French resistance movement. The Maquis? I could only guess. They were secretive but asked me if I would like to send a message to England. I trusted them and in full trust, wrote one telling my superiors of our crew's predicament, gave it to them and they confirmed later that it had been sent. They also informed me that if I wrote a letter to my wife they would arrange for it to be sent also. God knows how they could do that but I had faith in them. They also told me that if I could get to a certain location in Lorient they could arrange for me to picked up by a British submarine and taken back to England. But wasn't Lorient a German u-boat pen? How could this be done? I was told not to worry as it had been done before. I was amazed at their attitude. We had just bombed the shit out of their city yet they seemed to understand why it was bombed and accepted it. They then told me that the Germans had captured three airmen. That gave me a burst of high anxiety. I knew it had to be my crew and I didn't want to be the next. So reluctantly I agreed to their suggestion but it was obvious that there was tension amongst them and I suppose my presence didn't do them any good either. The Gestapo was particularly active in this region, which I now know to have been a hot bed of resistance fighters. My rescuers were continually monitoring their activities and movements and of people who lived nearby. The Gestapo were now encamped in the nearby town and so I was, as a precaution, moved to another farm"

"Stop Dad! Stop there please. I'm having trouble taking all this in. Frankly I'm astonished. It's like a book or a film. I don't know what to say or think."

"Don't try." My voice was beginning to croak. I needed to rest. "Is there any scotch left?"

"Of course." He got up and poured me a generous measure.

I sipped at the scotch, without spilling it, savouring its warm glow as it moved around inside of me. I silently wondered how long it will be before this would be no longer possible. Although I'm at peace with myself I still feel a deep sadness at the thought of saying goodbye to them and knowing they were in for a few more nasty shocks yet. I'm going to miss many things like never to see snow falling again, or delight in the warmth of a summer sun on my body. Such simple things that are often taken for granted now seem so important. They have enacted around my life and I hardly ever knew, that is, until now, which is a bit late in the day. I look directly at Hugh but don't really see him. My mind is elsewhere.

"How many more shocks are you going to give me Dad,? I've got a feeling there's more to come."

I'm oblivious to what he's saying. My mind is far away remembering myself as a small boy in the Cubs. It's a hot sunny afternoon and I'm on a summer camp running through a ripe sunlit cornfield behind the farmer's harvester and chasing rabbits as they bolt for cover to escape the farmer's gun and dogs. I'm locked into this scene and only when Hugh gently shakes me by the arm do I come out of my reverie. He asks me if I'm okay as I got him worried for a moment. I guess this is symptomatic of someone in my condition. I apologise and begin talking where I left off. Is my mind now under attack? My throat is also giving me a problem and I get Hugh to move closer with the microphone as my voice at times descends into a whisper.

"The farm where I was hiding got searched several times by German patrols but I was never found. Had I been, the farmer would have probably been shot and his family into the bargain. It was made clear the Germans were searching for a parachutist, which I guessed was me. I was moved again to another farm before I was taken back to the Chateau de Locquenole. They kept me on the move as it minimised the possibility of capture. The Gestapo were swarming through the area. They seemed to know I must be somewhere around. The local priest supplied me with forged identity papers. How he could do this I had no idea. I can even to this day see his kindly face and all those brave people to whom I'm eternally grateful."

I paused as a tide of emotions stuck in my throat and my eyes got watery. Hugh paused the recorder and stopped writing. He waited for me to continue.

"Then I was told that the chances of being picked up by a submarine didn't seem too good as it was apparent that there

56

was the possibility of an allied invasion about to take place. At the Chateau there were two other escapees trying to avoid capture. They too had been shot down and had been there for some weeks. Like me, they had been shunted around from hiding place to hiding place, awaiting a suitable time to be on the move again. All this was at great risk to the owner. This place was not going to be safe for much longer. It was decided that we had to leave as luck was looking thin. We were told to head across a nearby river and towards a small village the name of which escapes me. On our way there we were stopped by a group of Frenchmen and it was immediately obvious we were not French even with our forged papers. We were taken to a back street café and we assumed they were members of the Maquis. After some fierce questioning they knew we were not spies and gave us pistols, why I didn't truly know, and then drove us off to another lodge. Here was another escaped parachutist. So we were now four. Here the Maquis, were what we would now call a bunch of cowboys, trigger happy with no idea of order or discipline. What none of us knew, including them, was that the noose was tightening around us. Then it happened. Early next morning a German patrol marched into the courtyard. We bolted into some nearby woods but we'd been seen and were soon captured and I thought we were due to be shot as they disarmed us and we were bundled into the back of a large lorry. I was feeling petrified as they drove us to God knows where. When we came to a stop we were physically thrown off the lorry and the soldiers set about us with their rifle butts and then tied us up with wire. I remember thinking, this must be it as they threw us down on the ground and began stamping on us with their heavy army boots. At first the pain was excruciating but after a while, the nerve centres switched off and there was no more pain to feel. They didn't stop until a German officer arrived and commanded them to stop. I was covered in blood and sweat and so were the others. We were dragged off to the local Municipal Buildings to be interrogated. The Gestapo had set up their HQ there. The mention of that word 'Gestapo' filled most with dread. I wasn't any different. What I told them, I can't remember. I was interrogated for three days but didn't have much to offer. I was in severe pain with a fractured wrist and two or three broken ribs. These were gifts from both the soldiers and the Gestapo. I was put through questioning again but survived the ordeal. As an officer I was eventually despatched to a P O W camp, Stalag Luft 3 Safan. There I remained, virtually until the end of the war. I now also know that my French rescuers paid a heavy price for their bravery. Some were shot and others sent to concentration camps."

At this point I stopped and looked up at Hugh. He looked white. I told him that I was the one who was supposed to look ill not him. I smiled and reached for his hand. He was obviously upset and hung his head down.

He whispered, "God knows how Flora and Robert will react when they hear all this. Why couldn't you have told us all this years back?"

"I've already told you why." I was getting irritated. Maybe with age it's easier to accept some things that the younger can't. "You always want to hear and know all the answers." I try deflecting him. "When are your brother and sister turning up?"

"Tomorrow, Friday night."

He's gone tense and I sense an anger in him. It's a good barometer of his level of concern.

"They bringing Sophie and Mark?"

"Yes, I think so."

"Hugh, I'm sorry that this story has waited over thirty years to come out. I never wanted to hurt your feelings and I hadn't realised how upsetting it would be for you. Will you forgive me my stupidity?"

"Dad, I'm struggling with this and the enormity of it all. I feel devastated. Of course I forgive you."

He embraced me for some time.

"There's more, isn't there, Dad?"

"Yes, there's lots more. You sure you want to hear?"

"Yes. But let me take this in first and I want to speak to Robert and Flora."

I agreed. The trauma of what I have told him has made me weary, underlined by a residue of continuous nagging pain as my bones and marrow are once more under attack. This cancer is relentless.

THREE

Peace and War

It's late Friday morning just before lunchtime. Flora, Robert, Mark and Sophie have just arrived to stay the weekend. I'm hoping I won't get too bad and spoil it for everyone. I don't look too good eating and drinking. That worries me. I'm introduced to Mark and Sophie and immediately like them both. Flora and Bobby have made fine choices for they seem a happy and cheerful bunch. Bobby produced, as promised, a bottle of Glenmorangie single malt whisky. They all declined a tot so Hugh poured me a handsome measure. It never fails to amaze during these final days how the simplest pleasures almost overwhelm me in their intensity. The whisky tastes like nectar and I can never recall it tasting as good as this. It's decided that I might like a trip out to a pub for some lunch later. I think that's a good idea. I'm not going to get many more opportunities to see the outside world again. The wheelchair folds up easily enough and can take up a small space in the boot. So I agree. Outside later, the sun feels warm and I feel excited at being taken out. It's been a while since that's happened. I make sure I've enough medication with me, sufficient for any sudden attacks. I need tissues, plenty of them. They'll mop up slop and any body fluids that make an appearance. Sophie is a sweetie. She has a natural charm about her and seems to be totally comfortable about my situation. Her dress style is her own, which has throwbacks to the twenties and thirties. When she came in she was wearing a largish biscuit coloured cloche hat held down with an extravagantly large glittering bejewelled pin. From beneath this glowed the most liquid warm brown eyes I can ever remember seeing. They came with an enormous smile. Around her neck, unbelievably, hung a feathery silver coloured boa. She wore a light blue-tiered tasselled dress, which gave her an added femininity of movement. On her feet were a pair of gold wedge style sandals. She compliments Bobby's unconventional dress sense beautifully. I just love the way she is fussing around me ensuring I'm comfortable in every way. Mark has an intensity about him but he is a good-looking man with dark black hair, a flashing white grin and a hard jaw. Oddly, he wears black horn rim glasses, which definitely set him apart from others. They remind me of 'Brains' from the TV series *Thunderbirds*. Under his black corduroy jacket is a matching lightweight, jet black, roll neck sweater. His tight faded blue jeans are matched with a pair of safari boots. He tells me he has a doctorate in Medieval History in which he lectures at Exeter University. That part of history always fascinated me in the past. Sadly I can't read about it any longer, as now I don't have the strength to concentrate. From the corner of my eye I notice Flora, Bobby and Hugh in deep conversation and I see Flora's jaw open wide and her hand comes up to cover her mouth. Bobby clearly says "What!" It's obvious what they are talking about. I called Hugh over and quietly asked him not to bring this up while Sophie and Mark are about. He agreed totally. I relax. I'm feeling good being around such pleasant people.

We drove off to the *Armada Arms*, a pub restaurant I haven't been to for some time. It's located overlooking the sea close to where Sir Francis Drake, famously and allegedly played bowls as the Spanish Armada was preparing to attack England. This became one of my favourite areas. It's now a district now full of small businesses, smart shops, delicatessens and a range of cosmopolitan restaurants clustered around in close viewing proximity of the Channel. Once it was run down and seedy and no self-respecting citizen would have dreamt of living or eating out here. Times have changed. The *Armada Arms* has it's own dubious brand of charm and atmosphere. The landlord, remarkably, remains the same as I remember him years ago. He's large and laughs heartily and frequently. His name is Joe. He was and probably still is, known as 'Laughing Joe.' He's a living caricature, pure Dickensian. Who knows, perhaps he's holding off at arm's length with his constant laughing all the nagging problems of his life, which could be threatening to devour him? He should try my life. He's decorated the pub and restaurant as a galleon, which I think looks awful. He recognised me. "Bloody hell! It's been a long time since I've seen you, squire. Where've you been?"

"I haven't been too well of late Joe."

"I can see that. Hope it's nothing serious."

"It won't last forever."

He hasn't a clue and no one lets on. We are shown to a table and as we sat I felt a profound weariness sink through me. The pub's depressing. Talking and being amongst a host of people can be a trying experience. I suppose once I was part of the 'atmosphere' of this place before it got themed up as a jolly fake galleon. Hugh seems to know the place well enough and perhaps he's already part of Joe's synthetic atmosphere. The tables are situated in booths mocked up to look like ship's cabins. The menu has a pirate on the front cover and inside is full of 'Shipmate's Hearty Suggestions' and 'Ahoy There's!' This, if I let it, will depress me further. Everybody seems to know everybody else and there's a lot of laughter and a false air of joviality hanging in the air. This is so typical of pubs.

Maybe I'm over sensitive. It's been such a while since I went out and coming here I can see why! Hugh went off to speak to some people he knew nearby and Robert leant over and quietly asked me that when everybody had gone home would I be continuing my story with Hugh.

"Yes I will but only when everybody's gone home. It also depends on how I feel."

"I know Dad. I'm staggered with what Hugh has told us and so is Flora."

I ask him not to speak about it anymore and he nods his assent. We ordered our food and it's strange to note I used to enjoy eastern, Indian and exotic foods but all I want now is plain English fare, which can be hard to find these days. This illness has buggered up my taste buds, metabolism and appetite. Vegetarianism has gone out of the window. I crave sausage and mash, liver, roast beef dinners. It's as if I'm regressing backwards as there is now no way forward that I can travel to, so retreat is a natural response. Am I making sense? I get to talk to Sophie in more detail and it turns out she's a researcher for a prominent M.P. "My, that sounds impressive. Just what do researchers do?"

She explained that much of it involves social, plus global statistics, current economic intelligence and analysis. Importantly for the M.P. she's working for, it also involves digging up who said what and when, which the M.P. can use to attack his opponents or to defend himself. As she is explaining this I begin to experience a bone-breaking wave of pain, which triggers off a breathless coughing spasm. She stops talking and gives Hugh a concerned look. I'm not being let off the rack, even for the afternoon. They are all aware of what's happening. Hugh is over in a flash and reaches for my medication and administers it. The others look away and Flora's eyes flood with concern as she grasps my hand.

"C'mon, Dad, we'll take you home."

I'm determined not to let this screw up everyone's lunch and splutter my reply. "No, I'll be okay in a moment or two. I want my food anyway."

The attack passed quickly and the only other embarrassing thing I now have to face is my inability to eat properly. I've always hated messy and noisy eaters. I've now become one. I frequently rely on being helped to place food in my mouth. A roast dinner sat in front of me. The others opted for curries or fish. I tried for a third time to cut and spear a slice of roast beef but couldn't get it onto the fork properly. My hands won't function. It's frustrating and embarrassing. Hugh did it for me and then lifted it to my mouth for me to chew and swallow. That's not easy and swallowing hurts my throat. My hands are swollen blue and seemed to have a life of their own. I hate the idea of being spoon-fed. I feel humiliated. Hugh continued lifting my fork and I opened my mouth swallowing the food. Flora sat on the other side of me and frequently wiped the solid half chewed, mushy food or liquid away from my mouth and chin. I put up with it. After frequent chin and mouth wipes my plate was finished. Lifting a small glass with a shaky pair of hands I managed to steer it carefully and slowly to my lips but the drink dribbled down my chin and neck as much as going down my throat. I finished drinking but inwardly I'm wincing with dreadful pain, waiting until the morphine to completely kick in and subdue the attack. I've gone as white as a ghost and I'm covered in a hot and cold sweat. It's as quick as that as I struggle to breathe normally. This could get worse but I'm not letting them know that. Hugh understands what's happening and he gives me a second dose and gradually I feel it overcoming the pain. What would I do without him?

Joe saunters over, "You ok there, Scott? I hope our food's

wasn't that bad." A broad grin crosses his florid face and he let out one of his enormous laughs.

He's not to know and I can't be angry with him and smile. "Yep I'm ok Joe and the food was fine." In spite of the dreadful Kitsch décor the meal *was* excellent. I'm also taken aback he remembered my name. People are surprising. "I've been well looked after thanks." He nodded and walked away and I appreciated his concern.

I worry secretly of the affect I'm having on my family. They're seeing me dying in front of them, slowly, inextricably. This afternoon I am determined not to succumb to anything. I don't want to rot up their afternoon. I'm thinking back to our ancestors who lost handfuls of children before they even reached their teens. What must it have been like for them? This in some ways is a late rerun of what happened to my parents. It's not uncommon, is it? It's said that diseases are often inherent and hereditary in families. To me life and death walk hand in hand. They are one and part of the same thing. My thoughts ramble on. I'm aware of everyone trying to talk as if nothing has happened. I can see that both Sophie and Mark have been well briefed. There's something really nice about them and I like them more. The lunch moves on. My attention is on my scotch. Hugh once again assists me and I'll be ready for another soon. Its warm embrace circulates through my rotting frame but I realise how incredibly tired I'm feeling. I'm spoken to but lack the vigour to get involved. I suspect they know this and know when to stop.

Back home, Hugh and Robert put me to bed and I reach out for their hands and thank them for their understanding and kindness, telling them I would be okay shortly.

"We'll pop in and see you later Dad. If you need us just give a shout."

In the cool quietness of my room I fell asleep. It was still light when I awoke. In the distance, from the living room I could faintly hear muffled voices and occasional laughter. I wasn't paying any attention to that. Laying there alone I found myself slipping into a reflective mood. I thought of and began to question the purpose of life. It slid into an intensity. I lost track of time. It was then, I sensed an odd shift occur in my mind. Was the Myeloma attacking my brain? It didn't seem so for I was totally lucid. My pains were nowhere to be felt and suddenly I was experiencing the pleasure of normality. This is an almost forgotten but wonderful sensation, when all I'd known over the last months was the burning fires and agonies of a bone eating cancer. Instinctively I sat up and for some unknown reason had an overwhelming desire to meditate. Tentatively I inched and gradually hauled my body out of the bed. Miracle of miracles it was without pain! It could move almost freely, albeit, I was cautious. I quickly found a hefty cushion and sat on it 'Burmese' style, my legs descended slowly, effortlessly to allow my knees to touch the floor …. NO PAIN! … legs fine … ankles fine … feet fine …THERE'S NO PAIN! I began to breathe slowly and soon a feeling of delightful lightness enveloped me. My mind began to freewheel. There was nothing I needed or wanted to hang onto. There was a dropping way. At that moment a felt a brush of unbelievable bliss ripple through me up the region of my spine. I became aware of an astounding revelation that bridged the gap across our understanding of the 'now' and chronological time towards a realm of utter timelessness. Life's light and dark shadows dissolved into the breathtaking wonderment of life being one, just one never ending, unassailable complete whole, where we're all as one, deeply connected and not separate It was a release from birth and death. I couldn't explain it. I stood on the edge of an inexplicable and uncreated emptiness. I could only hold my breath and gasp. In a blink of an eyelid it would be just a brief memory and it would be gone. My 'self' had vanished. Life was a continuous whole, there was no living no dying. For a microsecond it all seemed so simple, so understandable like sleeping and waking countless millions of times. What is there to fear? I knew that I was safe and there is nothing to dread. The ripples of birth and death take place and are no different from the action of wind on a lake of mirror like water. Just as quickly as it came the insight faded away.

I sat stunned not knowing whether to laugh or cry. Whatever it was I experienced I thought could not have lasted more than a minute. When I checked my watch I was amazed to see I'd been sitting for forty minutes. Had I been knocking at the door of life and death? Was my condition causing delusions? In my final days was I descending into madness? It didn't feel that way. I was too aware of what had happened, enough to question its validity and meaning, if any. I remained sitting not knowing what to do. How could I explain that? I wasn't even going to try. I'd be thought of as deranged or high on too much morphine. Maybe I had put my tiptoe into a vast and never ending ocean. I'm not certain. I'm not expecting it to happen again. In my state, that had to be the last throw of the dice. It has been powerful enough to make me feel completely bewildered, overwhelmingly strong, yet humble. I wish I had more time. I'm left with an inexplicable feeling of gratitude for my life, even though I'm bloody disease ridden and rotting with the certainty of a slow an inevitable, creeping, painful death with all the degradation that this condition can bring. How can I explain that to anyone? How can I tell Hugh? It's not really something that's to do with what I'm trying to tell him. But I want someone to know who can have an inkling of what I'm trying to say. I notice the Ferrograph is still here so I decided I'm going to try and dictate this experience in my own words. I think Flora might understand. It may help others after I've gone. My life, the war and my disease are still with me but now I understand that just before the rain stops a bird can often be heard singing and from under the heaviest snow, appear snowdrops and new growth restarts. Life is continuous and not separate. These profound observations are brought to a halt as I feel the pain reappearing.

It's Saturday morning and everybody is still here. I find it comforting to have them around and I don't want them to leave. They warm me like the early sun, which seems exceptionally bright and alive to me this morning. It's burning off an early sea mist, which has rolled in across the Channel. Sunbeams, gleaming like torches, light up the grey sea reaching deep into the hollows of so many endless waves arching along their flanks of crystalline foam with spray scattering like a thousand separate stars as a weak wind lifts them and then lets them fall. I've never noticed things in this way before. My senses remain on high alert and I'm still feeling amazed from last night's experience. I was prompted to recall a quote I read somewhere by Vladimir Mayakovsky *'In the church of my heart the choir is on fire!'* This seems very apt to the way I feel. However, it takes only a sudden burst of pain to return me to my earthly reality and my grand vision is lost. These attacks are definitely increasing both in frequency and intensity. My medication and morphine mixture has also increased to match the attacks. I take my medication but I'm dithering as both my hands shake attempting to pick out my pills. These are all laid out in a daily sequence of times both day and night in my large blue pill case. Without this simple organisation I could never remember. I have to get Hugh to fill it when required as it's beyond me. It's then I recall I must hand my blue folder over to Hugh when he comes in. It's no secret. It contains my funeral arrangements. We'll talk about it later together with my Will and what that contains. Flora is first in to see me and as usual she's bright and breezy.

"You had a good night then, Dad? My, you have a glow about you I must say."

"Yes, I'm fine thanks. The pain has just got to me but it's coming under control, Listen Flora, something strange happened to me last night. I couldn't possibly explain it logically to anyone but it was breathtaking. I managed to put most of it all down on the recorder. Well that is what I could remember. It was like nothing I've ever experienced before. I've a feeling that you might have something to say about it. Would you like to listen to it now, please?

"Of course. Will I understand?"

"Just listen and you might know."

Out of anybody else I know she has an intuitive grasp of deeper things and has a spiritual side to her, and like me, intrigued by life and whether it has meaning.

She switched on and listened in silence. When it finished she looked up at me and said nothing. I could see her eyes questioning. After what seemed an age she spoke. "Oh my God! I don't know what to say. That's amazing. We've never known you have we Dad? What you've said is deep and profound. I'm shaken. Why've you never said anything before about this sort of thing? It's important stuff."

"If you haven't known me that's my fault. I wanted you to hear what happened because I know you are closer to this sort of thing than anyone else I know. You're right. It was amazing." In her breathless enthusiasm it was good to see she'd temporarily forgotten how ill I was.

69

"There's so much we don't know about you. You must tell us. You must" Her tone has a heavy insistency. "It's going to affect all our lives. Don't you see?"

"I'm trying to do that with what I'm telling Hugh. I hope you can all get something from it. If you can so much the better. We'll talk again later because I know it interests you. Now, what's for breakfast?

She smiled and hugged me. "What would you like?"

"Cereal, a boiled egg with Marmite soldiers, toasted crumpets with loads of butter and a large mug of sweet tea."

I certainly hadn't lost my appetite although my doctor had warned me that sooner or later that would happen and this Flora also knew. She asked me again if she could talk later about my tape, if I was up to it. I agreed. She's always had a spiritual side to her and I'm pleased she shows so much interest. I'm seeing now that each of them is going to be affected in different ways when all this is over but I am just hoping ultimately it will be to their good. This is in spite of the dark things they're sure to discover. This is the way I've planned it. It was at this point that Hugh arrived as Flora went to sort out my breakfast. I directed him to the drawer where he took out the blue folder headed up 'Funeral Arrangements.'

"Bloody hell Dad! You're doing your best to upset me, aren't you?"

"Of course not. It will keep you busy and you will have to make what arrangements are necessary but I think the instructions are comprehensive. Have a little read now if you want and ask me anything you want to. My requests and music are all listed. I've tried to keep it simple."

Hugh started to scan through and looked increasingly bemused. "Jesus Dad, where did all this come from?"

"It's just me. I'll tell you more later."

70

Flora arrived with the breakfast. In my heightened state it's the food of the gods. The tea is so tea like and the crumpets are so crumpet like. What more can I ask for as I wolf it down? My eating is manic and I suspect I'm refuelling my depleted reserves. Hugh and Flora are laughing.

"It must be the pills, Dad," said Hugh, "I think I'll take some!"

I manage a smile with egg yolk running down my chin and I guess they don't entirely understand the chemistry behind what is going on. Flora reaches over and wipes off the egg from my chin. At this point I'm aware of my acute and aching love of her. Why has it taken all these years for it to surface; perhaps it never needed to and had always been there. Once we had all eaten and that included Sophie and Mark they decided that they had to go and do some shopping. Hugh elected to stay behind with me. I'm getting worried about him as he seems to withdraw from socialising. As I've got worse he's become more withdrawn and that is not what I want. Maybe I'm asking too much of him or it's just a reflection of the circumstance he's in. After they've all went out, he opened up the blue folder and read through it slowly. I'm suddenly feeling overwhelmingly tired and close my eyes. I can hear vaguely in the distance Hugh speaking and then it's lost.

It's an hour or two later when I woke up and I feel awful. It's like a damp gummy hand has got hold of me. My chest is tight and my back is killing me. Every bone in my body seems to shriek as if on a rack. I'm being buried in a damp shroud of expired hormones and I'm gasping for breath. I know I'm not dreaming. I can barely sit up. After a struggle laced in cracking pain I managed it. I'm on my own, Hugh has disappeared somewhere. I try calling him but the words won't formulate. This is what I've feared and have been dreading. Dr. Adams warned me, I would lose my grip on bodily and sensory functions. Stabs of pain are running through my entire body. I got to the morphine and managed to open it but only with an intense and fumbling effort. I swigged on it liberally and after some minutes the pain subsided. In it's intensity it has brought tears to my eyes. My voice returns. I know I'm on a downhill run but I have to complete what I've being attempting to tell. Flora's words were so true. None of my children truly know me and I'm determined to reverse that process but I have to hang on with every fibre I have left. Eventually Hugh comes back in. "You okay there Dad?"

"I'm fine. Just a small difficulty or two." My voice has become fainter and it croaks "Look, I'm not up to talking about the funeral just yet so can we leave that be for a bit. I want to tell you about Stalag Luft 3 Safan. It's quite important."

He nodded, switched on the recorder, settling down with his notebook and pen.

"Stalag Luft 3 was a P O W camp designed specifically for captured air force officers. It was situated about 100 miles from Berlin close to Safan now called Zagan in Poland."

I remember this as it was only yesterday although I've never ever spoken of it before. It's opening up my memory floodgates.

"The Germans constructed it in such a way to make it virtually escape proof by tunnelling but two escapes did occur, which were turned into major films, *The Wooden Horse* and *The Great Escape*. Remember?"

"You were there, then, Dad?"

"Yes and this is part of the reason I'm telling you all this. I'll carry on while I am capable. Well, the camp became massive, covering about sixty acres. There were about 2500 RAF officers, 7500 American officers and almost another 1000 from Allied officers. To make life difficult the Germans raised the huts off the ground so that any tunnelling was easily detected. Also, the subsoil was of bright yellow sand so that it was immediately spotted if dumped on the grey topsoil. Tunnelling through sand was not a good idea because of the danger of collapse. The whole camp was wired up with seismographic microphones built to listen in on any escape activity."

"Wait there Dad." Hugh's eagerness was seeping out like water from an open lock gate. "Did you escape?"

"Not quite. I'll come to that later. In October 1943 the first escape took place. It was an ingenious idea. A gymnastic vaulting horse was built using wood from Red Cross boxes and any other source. Inside it was built big enough to hide a man and various tools made from tin cans and dirt containers. We took it each day with a man hidden inside to the same place where the tunnel entrance was hidden and carefully covered up after each session. It was undetectable. Three of our group got away and amazingly got back to England after a long trip through occupied Europe."

The door opened. It was Flora. "Dad, your promised Macmillan nurse has arrived to introduce herself to you. Her name is Kate."

"Oh! Show her in please. We'd better stop there, Hugh and carry on at another time." I was glad of the break because the effort was tiring me more than I would like. Kate was a tall and attractive Scots lady and I took to her immediately. She wore a tailored plum coloured trouser suit with matching low-heeled shoes. Her hair was fair, whilst cut close, remained long down her neck Her smile is warming and she shook me by the hand before being introduced to the others but not before I noticed she had spotted my growing bruising and numerous lumps on my arms and elsewhere. Sophie and Mark didn't want to intrude and decided to take a walk.

"I'm sorry," I said, "but I don't quite know what a Macmillan nurse does?"

"Let me tell you all, then we can talk about you and your family here. Is that okay?"

Her accent was softly Scottish and sweetly melodious. I told her that would be fine. In the background of my being, even whilst she was speaking, deep within my bones I sensed things were shifting, spreading threads of pain, which were subtly penetrating my arteries veins and blood like an advancing invincible army. I'm praying I don't have an attack whilst she is here. I so much want to hear what she has to say. As I listened to her the pain content faded slightly. Inwardly I smiled to myself and think if I was younger I could fall in love with her! There's something about Scots lasses. No chance of anything in my condition!

"I've been dealing with cancer patients now for many years and have seen most types of the disease. We're trained to spot what signs the disease is sending out and then we can begin to prepare the sufferer and the family to deal with what may happen. I've spoken with Dr. Adams and she tells me you're an exceptional patient and your level of acceptance is not often encountered. That's good. My role is to support relatives and family through every stage and we are often the only constant they can rely on as they try to cope with the impact on their daily lives. I can't take away the cancer and how awful it is to live with it but there are things I can do to help people cope. It's a journey for you and for your family and I'm here to listen to all your worries and concerns. I can help you and your family deal with emotional stress, hospital visits and any financial support and advice we can offer. I hear you're formulating your life's history to pass on down to your children. How's that going?"

"Yes. I'm trying but it's getting more difficult on a daily

basis. I'm not too sure how much more time I have to keep this up." I noticed she stared hard at me from head to toe and obviously she was summing up my expectancy but made no comment on how long I had remaining. She told me she would visit on a twice-weekly basis and after further conversation asked if Tuesday next would be ok? I told her I was going nowhere so she could come whenever she liked. There was something very definite about her I liked. She had a comforting and reassuring presence about her. I could do with plenty of that. We chatted for a while about the illness and the family and she decided to leave shortly after that. Flora, Bobby and Hugh followed her out. More conversations about me, why hide it? I know what's in store for me and I can totally accept it. I reckon if I'm lucky I've got about four to six weeks left. What I didn't know was that was exactly what Kate told them too.

* * *

I told Hugh that I didn't want to say anymore today, as I needed peace and quiet for some reflection of my own. The trouble with being ill you never get left alone and there are times when too many people becomes overwhelming. I've now got regular visits from District Nurses, night carers, Dr. Adams, Kate and now I'm being sent on a nightly basis Marie Curie nurses. I mustn't complain, they are looking after me brilliantly and ensuring my last days will be as pain free as possible. The pain's becoming relentless and I guess it's only a matter of time before a syringe driver will be fitted. It will then only be a short while before I can kiss my arse goodbye! Robert and Flora have arranged over the next few weeks to take time off from work to be with me and Dr Adams told me there was a bed in the local hospice available but I declined. I don't want visits from armies of strangers, vicars, starched sheets, the smell of death and antiseptic fumes from the countless rooms around me. I want to be here in my own place with my family and all my memories so when I die I shall know they will die with me. It's often been said that those who die in familiar places find it difficult to let go and return for months haunting the place and those who live there. I hope this is not the case. I don't wish to unsettle anyone.

When I woke up, Flora was sitting beside me holding my hand. As she spoke I can tell my hearing is beginning to go and ask her, in my raspy voice, if she can talk louder or into my ear. She's an intelligent woman but curiously I've known for some time now that she's spiritually unfulfilled. I first got an inkling of this when she was quite young and witnessed her in tears on top of a very large hill standing alone muttering to the sky, "I know, I know." I kept that incident in a corner of my mind. My days in the war don't appeal to her but she's more interested in Buddhism, what I did and how it impacted on my life. She doesn't know it, but all my regalia, certifications and books are left to her. Nothing would give me more joy than to see her walk on that never ending road, which goes onwards and never ceases. I can't tell her that. She will have to travel alone. She wants so much to know and with that level of curiosity I have little doubt she will pick her own path up the mountain. It's not for me to say. I smiled weakly, "Flora, when I've gone it is going to affect you all in different ways. There's nothing much I've achieved on this earth but I'm pleased to see you're interested in a spiritual route. You will in some way, I'm sure, be my successor in this respect. I'll talk to you at another time but as I've just woken up and I'm not quite ready for it.

"That's ok Dad. I understand." She squeezed my hand. My God, I thought, I've wasted so many years pissing about with things that ultimately don't truly matter. She's opening up for me a dimension I had closed the door on a while back. I'm finding it hard to keep tears from welling. She stared deeply at me, directly into the pools of sorrow coming from my eyes. She leant forward and held me tight.

"That experience you described on the tape has really shaken me, Dad. It seems like a signpost and I know I'll have to follow it and discover what it means, if anything. What's Hugh going to do with all this stuff you've been telling him?"

"He's turning it into a comprehensive document, and you will all get a copy."

"You being a Prisoner of War is astonishing. You never said."

"I've explained all this to Hugh who'll tell you why."

"My God, Dad. You make us feel inadequate and ignorant."

"Don't be. We're perfect even with our imperfections."

"Bobby can't get over it. He's shaken."

"He'll come to terms with it."

"Dad, I love you so much and I don't want you to go."

"Nothing in life is permanent, Flora. We all have to go at some time and mine is now approaching. I'm just dreading the time when I'm not able to communicate with you. I know what happens when it's coming towards the final moment with all those whispers and hand squeezes, so I have to press on before it's all lost."

Flora, I could tell, was considerably upset. In death there is always a sadness, deep and scarring, which can rip out the hearts of those who love you. I seem to be the least affected of them all. A total acceptance of my condition is in place; sadly for them they are witnessing my decline and unsightly demise. This makes me think that the hospice option would be kinder

77

for them as they wouldn't have to be part and parcel of observing the process of a messy and slow death.

The following morning Sophie, Mark, Flora and Robert came to say their goodbyes to me. I've never had so many hugs and kisses, perhaps I should be ill more often! When they'd left Hugh returned and asked, did I want to continue where we had left off? My voice continues to trouble me along with my hearing but I must continue. I got him in close so that he can hold the microphone near my mouth and I proceed to tell him in a croaky way what I was involved in as he writes what notes he needs.

"Three more tunnels were placed under construction, 'Tom' 'Dick' and 'Harry.' They were carefully hidden and concealed in both a washroom drain sump and beneath a hut stove."

"You were involved, Dad?"

"Oh yes. Most of us were. We all took shifts in the digging routine. The tunnels were ten foot deep to avoid being picked up by the microphones. They were also only two feet square. Every bit of wood we could find was used to shore up the sandy walls to prevent collapse. We got it from the hut roofs and bedding planks. It was amazing the camp remained upright the amount of wood we removed. We even made our own candles from fat skimmed off from our daily soup ration. An air pump was also made from bits and pieces so we could breathe more easily underground. Later the candles were abandoned as someone had worked out how we could hook into the camp's electrical lighting cables, On top of this we installed a small rail car system for moving sand more quickly. In all it was an amazing display of ingenuity under adverse conditions. The disposal of sand became more difficult so 'Dick' was used to dump it in. It also hid all our forged papers, maps and compasses. 'Tom' and 'Harry' would now be the escape tunnels."

"Hugh, let me pause a while, I'm finding this a bit tiring." My voice had descended into a whisper.

"I'll come back later this afternoon, Dad, if that's ok with you?"

I managed a nod, closed my eyes feeling the brush of life beginning painting me off the canvas.

Later that afternoon he returned and asked if I was okay to continue. I said I was but before I started I would like a large Glenmorangie. He smiled and got up and poured me a handsome measure. I wanted to say something to him about what he was doing.

"Hugh, how can I thank you enough for what you are doing for me? I know the others will appreciate it. I want you to know also how much I regret for leaving all this so long. But in some ways you would never have got this down if I told you years ago. Doing it this way, all what I've told you will, I know will be passed on."

"Dad, don't worry about that. It will be done. So can you continue where you left off?"

The scotch improved my voice. "At the same time we had a large intake of Americans arriving. Activity on the tunnels increased so we could enable as many Americans as possible to attempt escaping. With that amount of activity the Germans eventually smelt a rat and 'Tom' was discovered but not 'Harry.' Finally in March 1944 we completed 'Harry.' Sadly the tunnel fell short of the intended distance into the edge of the forest nearby but came up many yards short of where it was supposed. I wasn't among the seventy-six men who got out. A camp guard spotted the seventy-seventh and all hell broke loose. I was further back in the queue. Out of the seventy-six only three managed to make it back to the allies. Hitler was incensed and ordered a mass execution of all the escapees. Oddly, Goering intervened, as he was uneasy about the order. As a compromise fifty were taken and shot by the Gestapo. I can see now how fortunate I was. By Christ, we were bitter and I for my part had to spend weeks in solitary. All those wonderful warriors were slaughtered by Nazi madmen."

Here I stopped and began weeping out achingly loud. I could still see them after all these years. I can't bear to imagine their frightened faces as they were taken away for execution. Their faces will always be etched into my memory. They remain as clear as day. "I shall never forget them. I don't deserve to be alive!"

Hugh held onto me tightly. This display only aggravated my cough into a major spasm and next I was fighting for breath. My chest was on fire with pain and Hugh gave me a hefty dose of morphine mixture and quickly fitted me up to the oxygen cylinder. The attack gradually faded and a form of normality crept back into me.

"It's ok Dad. If that can't upset somebody what can?"

Composure returned and I continued. "Four of our band were sent to Sacshenhausen concentration camp and two to jolly old Colditz. I can never ever find it in my heart to forgive the Nazis. I have nothing but hatred and contempt for them. Interestingly the Camp Commandant, Van Lindenen was his name, was apparently appalled by the executions. Most of us there thought of him as a decent human being and he was no Nazi. He became a British P O W himself and gave the authorities much information leading to tracking down those murdering bastards. We could sense the war was coming to an end and all escape activity ceased. Then at the end of January we heard the Russians were not far away and subsequently we were rounded up by the German guards and marched for two days with very little sleep or food. Many of us were in a poor state. Some prisoners broke out to escape and the guards took very little notice. They knew it was all but over for them. I ended up in Stalag 7a at Moosberg. I was there until General Patton's 14th Armoured Division liberated us on January 29th. 1945. I shall never forget that day because it was also my birthday."

"That's some story Dad. No wonder you had a tough time adjusting when you got home."

"Yes, it was tough and I must have given you all a rough ride for a few years and I regret that so much and I'm so sorry for the way I treated you all."

"Don't be Dad. You must have taken a few years shaking off your trauma and I don't expect you were the only one who felt like that."

"Well, I did try to change but it had to proceed at its own pace and couldn't be pushed."

"That would have been some episode in any one's life."

"Well, now you know more than anybody what happened to me in Bomber Command and the RAF. There is little more I can tell you. I think I need some rest now for a while.

FOUR

Beauty in Death

Blasts of sunshine shot through the curtain gaps as he lay sleeping, almost approaching a coma. Outside rumbled angry spots of thunder. The grey stain of storm moved across the tossed sea as if hunting the sunlight, to devour it in vast swathes of darkening rain clouds and the flaky veils of sea mists. Deep down beneath the waters lay the wrecks of ships and their now ghostly crews once lured by the calls of material sirens. Scott was nearly home, being borne by the wings of angels he never knew existed but who now were beginning to whisper gently to him, calling him back home.

Later that morning I awoke and as semblances of cognition pumped into my senses I was aware of someone sitting there.

"Mum, what're you doing here?"

"It's not Mum, Scott. It's me, Kate."

My hand was being squeezed tightly. It was then my confusion cleared. "Oh! I'm sorry Kate. I'm a bit mixed up. I forgot you were coming." My voice quivered.

"That's okay, Scott. We all get jumbled up when we wake. I often stand there scratching my head when I get up. I can't make out sometimes what I'm supposed to be doing next. It often takes me an hour to sort things out. Well how's things?"

I didn't know how to answer that. Things were not good so I took the quickest route. " Not that good. I won't beat about the bush Kate. How long?"

"You lovely man. I don't often come across people like you. You seem fearless."

I interrupted her. "More sad than afraid. Tell me please."

She clung onto my hand and paused a moment, and smiled with an utmost warmth. "You've gone down hill fast since I last saw you. Two to three weeks at the most."

I paused. I felt the sudden rush of the endless universe pass through me and I knew I was being brushed by countless years of forgotten time. An enormous relaxation assaulted me and an ecstasy of bliss again released and rippled through my rotting body. Does this happen to everyone who's dying? How is it that from all this misery and degradation arises something beautiful like a lotus blooming, which it only does from dark and stinking mud? I looked at Kate. "I'm not unhappy you told me that. Funny thing … I feel real good. It gives me some time to sort things out before it's finished."

Both her hands were around mine and she leant forward and kissed me on the cheek. This strange happiness, I hadn't expected. Did it have something to do with the experience I had a short while back? I don't know but in a way it's irrelevant. I know now what I have to do with my family and then I shall be ready to let go. Kate talked to me about them that when the moment came its impact would change their lives forever. She leant close as she talked so I could I hear every word. She said she had seen this so many times. It was often wonderful how families could rally; get strength, and put purpose and meaning back into their lives. Someone's death often made life-altering changes to those closest to that person.

"I know this first hand Scott, because I lost both my

parents within a year of each other from this disease just over twelve years back. It gave me the resolve to become what I've become today. If it hadn't I would still have been sitting in some office processing away on meaningless information and contributing little to assist the suffering of people who really need help. It was their deaths that changed what I did."

I thought the loss of her parents wasn't too dissimilar from the loss of mine. My appreciation of her escalated. She had first hand experience of the cruelties of life and I knew she spoke from her heart and understood what she was talking about. I think she's a gift to me from the universe to comfort me in my dying days. Am I not fortunate?

She gently told me that my faculties were now in a state of decline and things I had to say and do should be done over the next week because after that I would in all probability be unable to communicate coherently. I nodded and whispered that I had already thought that would be the case. She told me that she was recommending a syringe driver should be attached the next day to alleviate my unremitting pain. Before she left she gently kissed my face again and told me I was remarkable and she would come over the weekend to talk to the twins and Robert.

That evening the Marie Curie nurse, Ella sat with me. Hugh has also taken to sleeping in the nearby recliner. It seems nobody wants to leave me alone. Hugh and Ella talked between themselves, as I now seem to be frequently drifting into another time and place. There is a different nurse each night but it's usually Ella and they're ready to handle any crisis or emergency. When Hugh gets tired of talking with Ella, it's often in the early hours of the morning he passes out in his chair and she covers him with a duvet and sits close by in the other room. She's waiting for anything that may occur with me that my family can't handle. My sleep is of the dying. It's noisy, unpleasant and abrasive to see and hear. I'm aware of the strain I'm causing everyone. Ella wakes me at six in the morning, which seems frightful but she has a home to go to. I'm washed, cleaned up and changed from top to bottom, which includes my man-sized nappies I've had to wear for some while now. The indignities of illness are unremitting and unforgiving.

PAIN! PAIN! PAIN! ... Not content with killing me it has to torture me and in ever increasing frequencies and ascending levels so that now it is almost constant. The hypercalcaemia has run riot causing back breaking, chest crushing, stomach smashing, pelvic pulverising, bone breaking agonies like a fiery salamander. There's not a part of me it will leave in peace. Yet I'm not quite ready for its assassination and its revelling delights from a pitiless sea of misery. It's coiling around me like an unguent python. The pain causes me to grimace, grind my teeth and groan out loud. I reach out for the morphine but only manage to drop it to the floor and know I can't pick it up. I'm left writhing. It's ten minutes before Hugh arrives and I'm on the verge of passing out. I covered from head to toe in a damp blanket of hot sweat. Kate and Dr Adams are also with him and they rush to administer a massive dose. I soon begin to relax but wisps of pain continue to lurk and telegraph throughout every part of my body. Kate tells me it's time to attach my syringe driver and I pray it will keep this monster at bay. I'm now realising how flesh becomes bone as suffering etches and digs out the flesh from cheeks for all to see, Smiles fade from once sensuous lips as they are replaced by tightening pain that stutters in arid Gestalts. I'm not wishing my family to enter into these dry deserts of misery but to learn something of benefit from all this. They are outside my jail together and can only look in at its bitter coldness and the waiting arms of a blissful death. From my cadaverous eye sockets I can melt snow as teardrops slowly trickle. The crucifying torture subsides as the syringe begins its pumping work. Normality courses through my stretched frame and I feel that now I'm able to speak, albeit in a hoarse croak.

"By Christ, that was the worst attack I've ever had."

Dr. Adams tells me that she could see that. The driver should keep the pain at bay but there would be no coming off it as I well knew.

"I know. I'm just grateful it's there and fitted."

We all spoke generally for a while until Kate said she would like to speak to me alone for a bit. Once we were on our own she said,

"That was bad. I could see that and the way you were reacting. That's how it will be from now onwards. The driver should keep the pain in check. The only thing is that now you'll lapse into frequent sleeps and deepening comas. You'll loose your vision and your hearing has, as you realise already diminished but that's always the last to go. Cognition is, I can see wavering. Your brain functions are also about to pack in. You may remain conscious but unable to respond to anything. Speech will go along with the ability to eat drink or swallow or respond to anybody although you may understand what is being said to you. Eventually that'll go also but whilst you are still breathing you'll know nothing. I don't mean to frighten you but if you were not the man I know you to be I wouldn't have told you. I except that you have already worked that out anyway.

I nodded. "That's okay Kate." I grunted at her. "I've made the adjustments I need to." I then told her of the release I felt when she first told me and subsequently the remarkable peace that came over me.

"That's incredible Scott. In all the years I've been doing this job I've only witnessed that once previously. You telling me that gives me strength and courage. It means that death is not to be feared and perhaps there is something warm and lovely beyond it. You see I'm learning from you!"

I smiled and told her in my raspy voice that I needed to speak to the family tomorrow and was there any chance she could be here, as they would need her? She agreed without hesitation. So we sat there quietly in silence, nothing needed to be said between us. We both understood and I felt a deep peace and love surround me.

I can feel life beginning to ebb away from me. Blessedly I'm relatively free from pain, thanks to the syringe driver, which also has adjustable settings to increase the dosage should it get unbearable. To me Multiple Myeloma is the Twentieth Century version of the Spanish Inquisition's torture chambers supplying a none ceasing assault on every limb, organ and functions of the body until inevitable collapse and certain death follows. Mercifully I'm not going to be burnt alive!

Today looks grey and murky yet still the sea gives emphasis to the openness of space and sky as it forever moves onwards, ever onward with its own unsophisticated beauty, transforming the mundane into a characteristic that is for ever extra special. In these last dying days of mine I wonder why I'd never seen this all before. I feel I'm smiling at the universe, which smiles back at me and is telling me it will forever protect me. How wonderful this is! I manage a deep sigh and remember that I've asked them all to come and see me, so that I can tell them how things are and my last instructions and intent. As Kate told me my faculties are beginning to fade. Every so often my mind goes off into a sort of pause where there is darkness, as if someone has switched the lights off. These moments are on the increase and I know that my brain is coming under attack. I'm not going to panic but I *must, must* get everything into some order. Physically I'm now looking a real mess like a spattered 'Ribena' bottle with purple bruising and bumps all over my body, signposting the attack I'm under. The pain is now under some form of control but because of the quantities of morphine going into me I keep lapsing into a semi-coma. I'm thankful I'm just able to retain cognition even at this advanced stage. Kate has been a real support for me and I've looked forward to her visits. I'm totally comfortable with her presence. She understands so much. I was deeply moved when she told me that she had seen many cases, but every so often, and only countable on the fingers of one hand had she been moved to tears by a patient. I, she said, was one in particular who stood out. She told me I was extra special. We both had a tearful moment or two. I was surprised at her sincere emotion and I loved her even more.

Later, the twins and Bobby together came to see me. They sat close by me and surely were noticing my increased deterioration in all departments. My voice has become a deep and hoarse whisper, virtually inarticulate and often not making a lot of sense. My hearing isn't too good and my eyesight is fading; yet I remain fully aware but in a greatly diminished state. Hugh switched on the Ferrograph. Goodness, this is some audio and written document he's preparing. If it's done right, my voice will ring out across generations like some old newsreel. With his intellect and skills I know he won't have a problem getting it together. I'm certain that not many people are recorded in their dying days, so in some ways this could be a bit of social history. I'm lapsing in and out of consciousness but I'm aware of my hands being squeezed and voices whispering into my ear but I can rally back and continue talking in an almost inaudible whisper.

"This is what I have arranged. My Last Will and Testament is with Stevenson, Le Carre and Slater in Plymouth. I've divided up various things I have, between you all and what I know you are interested in. I hope you don't squabble. My money and estate, which is over five hundred thousand pounds is to be divided equally between you. You should be able do what you want in life, easily." My voice trailed off. It is then I felt my eyes roll back in their sockets and I lost vision and drifted off into a form of unconsciousness. When I eventually surfaced they were still sitting around me. How long I had no idea. My sense of time was non-existent. In my waking moments I was drifting off to a time when Freda was still alive. In my grey coloured Austin A40 saloon, we drove off to a little known place at the time, Lulworth Cove and the magnificence of nearby Durdle Door. I remember how the place, the rock strata's and the intriguing Door enchanted the twins and Robert. The sheer beauty and its isolation made it special for all of us and I must tell Hugh that's where I want my ashes scattered so I can be part of the place and its magic. I think he already knows this. As I gradually came round I could hear them talking to me. I had one more task to do, which was to talk to them individually and alone.

Bobby sat with me, alone. He's always been a sensitive and shy individual. I'm able to speak, but only in a dreadful whisper.

"Don't be afraid, Bobby, and don't get upset for me. It's a natural and essential process that we die. The continuation of life relies on it. I'm unafraid now and in some ways I can't wait for the end. The stress it puts on all of you I can only apologise for. Forgive me won't you?"

"Dad, please don't be so stupid. We are where we are because of you. There is nothing to apologise for or to be forgiven."

I could see the tears in his eyes, which rolled gently and softly down his cheeks. He made no attempt to hide them but placed his arms around me.

"When I'm gone it will affect all your lives in some way and you'll be the stronger for it. Remember all the good things we did as a family and laugh at the daft things we all did. I shall never forget when you were about six years or more you had decided that Father Christmas didn't exist, it was all a hoax and when I crept into your room with your sack of presents I didn't know you had placed a trip wire across the bottom of the door and I fell over it. You sat up laughing your head off and pointing at me. "Got you, " you shouted. I didn't know whether to laugh or get angry. I laughed. A magic moment eh?"

"I'd forgotten all about that."

"Well don't, and make sure you tell Hugh of every thing you can remember."

"I promise."

"My wish is that you all get on well, settle down, get married and have children and add to this story for generations to come." A sudden gush of pain spread through my face, which by now has transformed into a large purple bruise. I winced heavily but it was under control. Bobby looked concerned.

"You alright there, Dad?"

"It's ok. It's ok."

I held onto him like a leech and told him what I should have told him years ago. I told him he was very special to me and how much I loved and cared for him and I didn't want to say goodbye. My words were upsetting him so I stopped and we held each other very close and in silence.

"I love you too, very much, Dad."

After a while I told him I needed to speak to Flora. He got up and kissed my face and walked quickly from my room. I felt the sadness in his departure and a piece of me went with him.

Flora came in looking as pretty as ever.

"You okay, Dad or would you rather wait for another time?"

"No. Time is something I don't have" My voice was barely audible. "Come close so you can hear me." I told her about my box and she might find some things that would be of help to her on her spiritual journey if she remained interested in that path.

"Most definitely, Dad, but none of us are enjoying this and we're all upset to say the least."

"Don't be. If you're concerned about the question of life and death, this will be a place for you to enter. You must have a great and penetrating doubt and get around yourself constantly asking, Who am I? What is life? What is truth? What is God? What is reality? All these questions I have left for you in numerous works in that box. Always remember if you get knocked down seven times you get up eight." A puzzled expression crossed her face I can sense her deep intrigue and that's how it should be. I told her of a true story I knew but hadn't now the strength to tell her but she would find it written down for her when she felt ready to read it.

"This sounds confusing, Dad"

"Just open your heart, not your brain."

"I don't know how."

"You're a woman, you know how without asking."

"Daddy, I don't want you to go. I love you so much. That side of your life's so fascinating. I want you here so much to help me."

"It's too late for that, Flo. It's a path you've to discover on your own. You won't regret it. I've done some things in my life, which I'm not proud about and I'm certain Hugh will track all this down."

She looked puzzled but a wave of tiredness and disorientation crossed through me. My eyes closed and I was momentarily aware of drifting off as the morphine infused my senses. Not only do I have unbearable body screwing pain beneath the blanket of drugs but my reasoning and intellectual functions are also being smothered. Without it however I wouldn't have these last few days. In the back of my mind I wondered what would happen if I could rip out the driver. At this point, I passed into a semi-coma. Some while later I surfaced as faint fingers of pain continued dimly to stalk through me like vultures looking for that extra meal. Flo was still sitting there and holding my hand. I know from her look of her distress how much she cared for me. I love her too in the same way. In this respect I'm privileged and blessed. My kids have turned out into loving, caring and concerned individuals. As a family we've had a deep love of each other. When they have their own children, those children will have the most excellent parents. What more could I ask for? I shook my head and looked her in the eyes and knew what she was feeling. Being part of their lives and they part of mine has created a unique bond, which nothing on earth can ever dislodge. I hope also that the other unpleasant things they will find out about me will not break that bond. I only wish I could be here to witness their lives, their successes, triumphs and even failures. That will not be. I already suspect what direction Flora is heading and that is giving me comfort. I ask her to talk to Hugh and Robert so they can pool their strengths and aspirations to get something worthwhile from this episode. She leant over and hugged me tightly and an immense sorrow erupted between us.

"All these things Dad and why now? I feel I've missed so much" She began to sob.

"Flo. I know I've made mistakes and it's the last chance I

have to place things in some sort of order." My voice has all but vanished. Now I can barely talk. I want no more emotion. "Promise me one thing Flo, I want you to read to me just as I'm going or just gone"

"Read? Read what, Dad?"

I pulled my ancient copy of the *Tibetan Book of the Dead* from beneath my pillow. The pages I'd marked were for her to read to me at the moment of my dying, my death and directly after.

"What's this? I've never heard of it."

"Don't worry about that. You might find it interesting and it's also now yours." She looked bemused. I told her not to worry or even think about it but take things at her own pace and just read to me where I marked and when the time came. I knew it was close now and I wanted her around me to do that if nothing else.

Later, after Flo had left, Hugh reappeared. He looked sombre and he's carrying his pen and notebook as usual. I know when all this is over he may have an outstanding vocal record and written testimony for their future families to add to. I bring him in close and tell him not to look so serious and there is nothing he should worry about. I'm beginning to lapse quite a bit. More and more blanks in my mind are appearing. Even with the protection of the driver I can still feel pain and sense the Myeloma marching ever onwards. At least when I'm dead the Myeloma will also die.

"Hugh you're my rock. Without you, Flo and Bobby would be none the wiser about my life. Promise me you'll do a good job eh?" At this point I broke into a horrendous coughing fit, causing me to gasp for air. There's nothing Hugh could do but place the oxygen mask over my face, which gradually gives me some relief until I'm able to breathe in my own time. I can taste blood in my mouth and feel it trickle down my chin, which he quickly wipes away.

"God this is fucking relentless and without pity. Dear God let me go! With a syringe of Phenobarbital and Dilatin and it could be over in moments!"

"Dear Dad," Hugh spoke quietly as he stroked my forehead and some calm returned to my system but I knew it was over. I'm letting go. What more can I say to him? He knows more about me than anyone else alive and somehow he has to make it live.

"Dad I'll get you a drink. Hang on."

As he went away I felt an enormous irreversible slippage in my mind and all that remained within me was a form of hearing that was rapidly declining. I heard him return but was unable to respond. I didn't attempt sitting. I was unable. I knew it was over.

"Here we are, Dad." He tried giving me the drink.

I could only faintly hear him but I couldn't see him. My brain has been paralysed, eaten away and I can only stare vacantly at nothing in particular, my vision gone.

"Dad! Dad!" He's shouting at me but I'm unable to respond. Hardly a muscle is moving. The drink he offered I couldn't reach or even see properly. I felt everything shut down as I drifted into a morphine heaven but noisy coma. I heard the alarm in his voice as he rushed out to call Flo and Bobby. It's now time and I know it's over. Kate and Dr. Adams arrived but I'm passing into the unknown. Flo is still holding the book and instinctively she knows what she has to do.

"He's going! Quickly! Quickly!" She grabbed the book and fumbled to the marked pages.

Scott could hear the sounds of the Merlin engines, the colours and the blasts of flak and guns of the German night fighters but knows now he cannot be harmed, he is now untouchable and knows he has to walk towards the light when it arrives.

He is almost gone and Flora knows this as she begins reading to him as he asked. She keeps her mouth close to his ear so if there is any consciousness he will hear her.

"Oh nobly born, Scott Anderson, the time hath now come for thee to seek the Path. Thy breathing is about to cease. Thy Guru hath set thee face to face before with Clear Light; and now thou art about to experience it in reality."

The drone of the Halifax's powerful Merlin engines continued their roar as he faded away, blasting at his ears as his slippage accelerated. Everybody he had ever known walked before him. He'd been here so many times before.

"At this moment know thou thyself, and abide in that state. I, too at this time am setting thee face to face."

A large sigh spluttered from him and he departed into the endless sleep. Flora was crying as they all were but she continued to read to him every passage he had marked. She wasn't going to cease. This was his dying wish and she knew it was important to him. The sons remained as Dr. Adams and Kate left. Flora continued to perform her ritual.

When she had read all the passages and there were no more she said, in-between sobs, "He was so dignified, right to the end and so brave I don't know where we're going to go from here. I'm devastated."

Hugh was quiet and a massive sadness was drawn into his face. "I've never seen anything like that, ever."

"Oh Holy shit," Robert was white. "That's unbelievable!"

The family weepily embraced each other and Kate and Dr. Adams returned. They had become part of the family.

* * *

They felt the deepest respect and proceeded to wash him and dress his body in clean underclothes and pyjamas. Hugh shut down his partially opened eyes and Flora got new pillows and a clean duvet and arranged him as if were quietly sleeping with his hands on top of the covers, resting together and gently removed his gold and silver rings. Bobby came back a while later carrying numerous bunches of flowers and they literally scattered them on and around their Dad. It looked like a scene from some old film. Hugh turned off the heating and opened the windows. There was a sense that they now knew something about each other and a father they hadn't had the faintest clue about. They had truly begun to meld together, aware of their common ancestry. Outside darkness was gathering in, stealing the light of an early spring evening. Above a new moon graced the sky and the planet Venus shone brightly. Flora carried in a box of scented candles and sticks of incense. These were lit and his room became full of the sweet scent of flowers, incense and the soft twinkling glow of dozens of candles. Scott looked pain free and a relaxation seemed to have entered his previously tortured frame. It was if he was gently asleep and it seemed hard to believe that he was dead. His struggle was over and he was now free from the assaults of birth, old age, disease and death. Hugh contacted the undertaker to come over later, once neighbours and others who knew Dad locally had the opportunity to pay their last respects. The house became full of people and was full with the pervading and gentle air of sweet smelling flowers and incense. A soft breeze blew through the open windows, yet all seemed so still. That moon, like a fingernail cutting, was for him, and the evening star glowed with an extra brightness welcoming him back into their sacred void as he was absorbed, ever upwards into the mysteries of the universe, free at last. A sadness saturated them. The end had come quicker than expected. He had always indicated towards his end that when he'd said and done what he had to he would let go. He did this. He gave up fighting and literally released himself. He wanted no more of it and willingly embraced death. It was a some hours later when two very sombre undertakers arrived dressed in black coats and wide striped trousers. They had with them a stretcher and a large body bag. The twins and Robert couldn't bear to watch and turned away. They tagged the bag with a large green tag with Scott's name and address and Hugh's phone number. Respectfully and very slowly they proceeded to carry Scott's body from the room.

"Goodbye Dad," a broken Robert stuttered.

Flora held onto a corner of the body bag. "Don't go, Daddy." Tears cascaded down her face and the undertakers paused a moment. This was a scene they had witnessed countless times. Hugh said nothing but comforted his sister who was now distraught. Gently they placed his body into the back of their darkened vehicle and drove quickly away to the undertaker's premises some miles away.

I felt the silence. It gripped the house, whispering from its foundations its own respect. It asked nothing of me or of Bobby or of Flora, its sole occupants. We'd buried our sadness into the cement and bricks of this lovely old house the second he died. We as a family were fused into this place. Mum and Dad had lived here. The memories of which would remain with us until the day we died too. We remained silent. Would speaking violate the air of sanctity that had descended on this place? Does this happen every time someone dies? We reached out for each other sitting in a small circle, and held hands. We wept, it was silent and soft until it was time to stop. I broke the spell, stood up, walked over to Dad's Glenmorangie and poured three large drinks.

"We all could do with one or two of these. Let's drink to Dad and wish him everlasting happiness wherever he may be."

We stood and drank the toast not certain what would follow next. Bobby asked when I thought the funeral might be? I replied about eight to ten days from now but would confirm that tomorrow if I could. I'd never managed to discuss the funeral arrangements with Scott as time had run out for him, so I was going to have to work it out as best I could with the others. My mind was whirling and I paused.

"I'm going out for a walk. I need some time on my own for a short while. I won't be long." Standing up, I walked from the room. Flo and Bobby said nothing but vacantly stared into their drinks. Time seemed to have stood still for them. Flora told me later, mysteriously that at the moment of his dying she felt as if universe had held its breath. She felt it was waiting for him. She was expecting the mysteries, of life and death, to be revealed. This didn't happen and the moment for her slipped away back into mundane reality. I always did have trouble with Flora's pronouncements on life and its meaning. This was no exception.

* * *

I dragged out the large wooden chest from behind the wardrobe. It was heavier than I'd thought. We gathered around it and saw that the key was taped to the side of the box with a strip of black duct tape. I peeled off the tape and removed the large ornate iron key and inserted it into the lock and gave it a hard twist. The lock made an audible click. We all glanced at each other not knowing what to expect. Slowly I pushed open the creaky lid. The deep chest was full to the brim and the top had several layers of red tissue paper covering whatever was underneath. I carefully pulled them to one side, folding each one individually and placing them gently onto the floor. What I saw caused gasps of astonishment from us all. What was there was, was no less than full Scottish dress of kilt, sporran, shirt, cravat, small dirk and socks and a ceremonial jacket. They were precisely and neatly arranged. An envelope lay on top of this which simple read 'To Hugh.' We were dumfounded, none more so then me. I carefully removed what I saw, placing the items out of harms way. I refrained from opening the envelope for beneath this were further layers of tissue paper but this time coloured purple. These were removed and carefully placed to one side. Again it revealed another set of identical items equally well laid out but the envelope was addressed 'To Bobby.' Nothing was said as surprise had gripped us all. Beneath this were more layers of black tissue paper, which I cautiously removed. Flo cried out "What!"

A tartan plaid had been placed on a magnificent white silk dress and again with an envelope marked 'To Flora.'. Astonished and with great care she took out the dress only to reveal a large sheet of paper, which simply had written on it, '*As you have now got this far, it's time for you all to read what I have written to each you. I love you all very much … Dad.*'

We agreed to move to separate chairs and not to say anything until we'd all read what he had written to us. I opened his letter, careful not to tear too hard and damage the contents. There was a mild shake in my fingers. I read the following,

'Hugh, my dearly beloved son, as you are now reading this I am no longer with you. I hope you like the Anderson tartan and will wear it at my funeral. This is important for it unites and brings together our past for all of you, a forgotten past, a link to where you all came from and which I neglected to tell you, for which I hope you will be able to forgive me. I know all of this may come as a shock to you, Bobby and Flora too. I have entrusted you to document every thing I have said and for you to present it in a logical and clear fashion. You will also find in the chest a history of the Anderson clan and an ancient family Bible going back two hundred years outlining our lineage. Amongst all this there are my research documents, notes, photographs and clues where to search further. You have a wonderful brain and I know you will produce something of lasting value, a testimony to our lineage and to your future one too. Don't be afraid of unpleasant truths you may find, either. Everything needs to be in the open. Take care of your brother and sister and of yourself. Maybe we will meet again. You know I love you so much. Goodbye, from Dad.

p. s. Can you scatter my ashes at Lulworth and from the cliff at Durdle Door. I wish to be part of that place.'

Behind the letter and attached was a picture previously unseen, of him in full flying kit standing beside a large Halifax bomber. With this was a woven badge of 78th. Squadron with its motto *Nemo Non Paratus.*

I bent my head low and controlled the urge to weep. In all my life I'd never felt so touched and loved. My sadness was intense. I vowed I'd do everything I could to fulfil my father's wish.

Bobby opened his letter, which began in a similar way, it said,

'Bobby, my dearly beloved son, when you begin reading this I will be departed from you. I think you always thought you were third in the queue as twins are a powerful combination to be dealing with. I assure you that was never so. If anything, you had a special place with your Mum and me. It was as if we wanted to protect you in your early days but you soon developed your own strength both physically and mentally and was a match if needs be for them both. Flora and Hugh love you dearly as I know you love them too. I'm anxious that things work out good for you from this my demise and get you to look at things in a brand new way. Don't waste time like I did and don't worry about money, cars and all that rubbish. Inside of you beats a heart of gold, which I sense is calling to you. Just stop and listen to what it says for it never lies to you. You will then know what to do. There is nothing to be afraid of. You will see I have attached pictures of you I've had all these years. As you will note they are of you at Durdle Door and Lulworth Cove so long ago when you were a young boy. Enclosed in the other small envelope you will find a flat fossil I found there. It's an ammonite, millions of years old. I think you will enjoy it. It could bring you good luck! Please have a family, as I know I would have loved them. Who knows, in your death one day we shall meet again and *be happy. With much love to you from Dad.'*

Bobby's reaction caused him to rush from the room. Flo and me could hear his sobs,

Flora was nervous to open hers. She had seen how the letters had impacted on us and she had no doubt that hers would not be any different. With care she gently opened up the envelope.

'My dearly beloved daughter, I think you will enjoy the plaid I've left to you and the white dress. They belonged to my mother, Caroline. I'd be honoured if you wore them at my funeral. Don't worry about the dress not being black because in Zen Buddhism white is the colour of mourning. As I am now gone from you, I can tell you, as the only girl in my family you had a special place in my heart. As you work your way through the rest of the box you will see I've left you various artefacts, books, documents and assorted cuttings, which I suspect will intrigue you. I have sensed your spiritual hunger and I suspect that your future will be linked along this route. The things I have left you, if anything, are a road map to help you along this path. There is a small envelope with this one I have left for you also. Inside you will find my mother's silver and gold bracelet and my tiny golden Buddha on a gold chain. It would please me to know you would wear them. I embrace and dearly, dearly love you. Be good and kind to all. Goodbye for now, Dad.

p.s. Our aspiration goes beyond the desire for well-being. Only personal experience can make you free.'

Flora like her brothers experienced an overwhelming rush

of emotion, She hadn't felt anything like this, as an unfathomable sadness engulfed every part of her. Her Dad, even in his death was opening doors for her, doors, which had been locked and bolted in the musty wrap of unknown time. She held out her arms to us and we embraced each other in a lonely silence. We made a mutual decision not to remove the next layer of tissue paper until the funeral was over. Anymore of what we might find we agreed could be too distressing and too much for us to take in right now. The lid was gently closed and Flora knelt down beside the chest and kissed it, stroking it softly at the same time.

* * *

It was the day of the funeral. Together with Sophie and Mark, masses of friends, neighbours, nurses, doctors, carers and those who knew and liked him gathered around as he was taken on his last journey. I had put all the arrangements together as Dad had requested. It had kept me busy with little time for reflection. By the standards of the time it was a strange funeral. All three of us wore exactly what he had requested. He had understood that his death would bring us together, creating a unique bond as we discovered the full impact of what he'd told us. Scott had requested flowers and the crematorium was full of the sweetness of hundreds of colourful blooms. The hearse very slowly drew close to the main doors and a solitary piper wearing the tartan of the Anderson clan played a mournful Scottish lament before finally leading the procession inside the crematorium. It had been stripped of its Christian symbols. In the centre of the main auditorium stood a magnificent copy of the head and torso of Maitreya Bodhisattva in flowing robes. He's the Buddha of the Future. The beauty of this work, its expression and gesture imparted a tranquillity to the proceedings. Bobby and I, Mark and others who had been close friends helped to bear the coffin in. It was his request that no strangers, priests or vicars should be present. A large palm like foliage was the only adornment on his coffin. Once the coffin was placed on the catafalque and the piper had finished I stood up at the lectern to speak as he had requested. I commenced with a quote from Meister Eckhart the Christian mystic.

"*The identity out of the One and into the One and with the One is the source and fountainhead and breaking forth of glowing love.*"

I told them of our deep love for him, the war years and the shock we had all felt on only recently discovering he had been a prisoner of war. As I was talking a recording was played that I had researched and found. It was of a Halifax bomber starting up its vast engines as it then proceeded down the runway to lift off with a thunderous roar. The mourners looked startled. When I'd finished the piper played another Scottish lament. When this had finished Flo and Bobby, hand in hand stood up to read their tribute. They each read sections between them. They explained that Dad as a navigator had a great interest in weather formations and meteorology. This is what they had written.

"So Dad, this is your weather forecast for the infinite future.

The deep depressions, the numbing greyness and the blasts of bleak winter that have dominated the weather front since last September are now lifted. Those distressingly low temperatures, freezing rain, snow, wearisome fog and the bone deep dampness that has enveloped and enfolded us all, is about to replaced by a ridge of permanent high pressure bringing with it prospects of halcyon days. As it advances, those dark clouds that have been lurking above, imprisoning us in their dreary despondency will all melt away. Those advancing ridges of high pressure will bring to you permanently good and superb weather.

You can anticipate, as it moves across, that there will be clear blue brilliant skies and a spotless sun; without a rain-cloud in sight. Temperatures will reach a constant 25/28 degrees. Coming up from the south you can also expect from the isobars an accompaniment of gentle summer breezes. These will cool you nicely as the warmer days unfold.

Every so often, … us here, … will late at night, or in the early hours … witness spectacular and deeply illuminating flashes of lightning. For those lucky enough to see, these will light up former dark areas for miles around and things unclear before, will no longer be so. Never before seen here, travelling high in the sky, to help you on your journey and carrying you on their wings will be flocks of migrating birds singing out to you their soulful cries as they voyage on their never ending way. They have flown across vast icy vistas from the grip of cruel and desolate landscapes. On the soaring thermal currents, they will travel with you to a new warm and pleasant land. For those travelling on this never ending journey, there will be a permanent assurance of kindly weather with endless warmth and sunshine, which will have no end. Through the seasons of life and death, you need never worry; for there can be nothing that can ever depress, harm or hurt you again. All the pain that comes from birth, old age, disease and death will, for eternity, pass away. The sunrise comes. The dew—drop slips into the shining sea. Bon—voyage beloved Dad."

After a pause for reflection the piper began playing once more as the Committal commenced and the curtains very slowly closed around his coffin. For us, the family, we had born this well, but now as the end came, cracks appeared. We said our final goodbyes silently and privately. The curtains closed briefly and when they slowly reopened he was gone. It was over.

The wake had finished and the guests had all gone. We three looked at each other in the now quiet house not knowing what to say to each other. Robert eventually broke the silence.

"Hugh, that was a great effort. You put so much into it."

"I promised Dad I would follow his instructions to the letter. Finding that Buddha figure caused me the most problems but he did tell me where I might find one, including that aircraft recording. He didn't want a long service, just something short and simple. That's what we gave him, didn't we?"

"We did our best." Flora said.

"It's going to seem strange without him."

They all agreed and I proposed to toast him on his journey with more ample measures of Glenmorangie, his favourite drink. It was then we agreed it was now time to examine his wooden chest once more. We helped drag it out again and when it sat in the middle of the room I once more slowly opened the lid. There was an uncanny sense of wisps of Scott emanating from the chest. Without saying anything we looked at each other. It was a strange sensation.

"Can you feel that?" said Flo.

I said I did but didn't want to mention it and Bobby said that he definitely felt the presence of something.

"Well, let's see what's here before we scare ourselves too much." I took a large gulp of scotch, let out a deep slow breath and removed the next layer of tissue. I let out a whistle of surprise. A note was pinned on top, 'Should you ever write a book all this might help.' Underneath this mounted in a frame was a solitary medal with a blue and white diagonal striped ribbon from which hung a magnificent silver cross. I gasped as I recognised it as a DFC a Distinguished Flying Cross. It was given in recognition of exceptional bravery during the war.

"Oh almighty shit, It's a DFC! That rotten man never mentioned a fucking word of this. I love and hate him even more now! This is incredible! I can't believe he would never say a word about it."

Flo and Bobby put their arms around me, as I was truly upset, angry, proud and happy all at the same time.

"He'd dictated all that stuff at me and never mentioned this. I can't believe he could have done that." After a short while my emotion abated. I picked up the frame and stared at the remarkable medal. My head shook in disbelief. I just whispered "Oh my. Oh fuck. Oh my!" Beneath it was another framed array of medals plus a gold oak leaf, certificates of commendation and his entries in The London Gazette and his DFC recommendation. This came complete with his personal log book, and all the Almanacs, star charts, navigational tables and various others. Remarkably, every book was bound in the same old brown paper he had covered them in all those years ago. In a separate envelope I found cap badges, navigator wings, accompanying these were ties, cravats and scarves. With these was a photograph of him in Squadron Leader's uniform. As a P O W he had been automatically promoted to the next rank above. This was something else he'd never mentioned.

"Did any of you know anything about this?" I looked

around at them but was met by a blank and stunned silence and shaking of heads. They had, like me, no idea. I carefully removed the items to find beneath several folders each marked for each century starting from the 17th century up to and including the last one marked 20th century. Slowly and carefully I opened them up. There in meticulous detail was outlined references, addresses, sources, trade journals, archival sources, old 18th and 19th century newspapers, birth and death certificates going back across the years. Coupled with these were suggestions for future references and the name of every child he could trace who had been born an Anderson in his family. Every so often there were question marks where research had been incomplete. This was going to take an age to wade through. Underneath the folder was a large black bag and it was heavy as I lifted it out. When I'd opened it up it revealed a huge well worn but extremely old Family Bible. This must be the one he'd mentioned previously. Inside the front cover was a host of Edwardian and early Victorian photographs of various generations staring back at me across time. As we stared at the photographs it was as if we were meeting for the first time. The next few pages, in immaculate copperplate writing was the family lineage from the 17th century as each successive generation had added and contributed to the family history. It concluded with Scott's final entries, themselves now incomplete. I sat back in my chair. "He was one big bag of tricks. How could he stay so secretive about all this? Yet in someway I now know what he was going on about so much. We didn't understand did we? God knows what you're going to find in your bits! They both agreed on this point. It was now Bobby's turn. He pulled away the next layer of tissue paper to reveal a label, which simply stated 'For Bobby. A new career?' At first he didn't realise what he was looking at. There were numerous camera lenses, colour filters and two extendable tripods. Beneath these were three cameras, two immaculate and valuable Leicas and an amazing Hasselblad. All top of the range stuff. With these were numerous manuals and dozens of rolls of film. A piece of cardboard covered a transparent folder, which contained about a dozen black and white photographs. They were of exhibition quality. Amongst them was one that got us gasping. In subdued lighting was in black and white a head and shoulders portrait of our Mum, as we'd never seen her before. She looked beautiful. So why hadn't we seen it before? Another was a stunning shot of a lightning strike on a tree, at night. A backdrop of dark brooding mountains added atmosphere by being silhouetted in the background. Where had he taken this? It was Bobby's turn to be amazed. "I never knew he did anything like this. Leicas, a Hasselblad, unbelievable! They're superb" he said as he passed them around. I whistled out loud. We'd no idea either. It was time for another drink. "I think we are going to need one or two of these."

Dad had indeed been unknown to us. It is a tragedy of modern day families that they barely take the time to connect, talk or communicate in a well-meaning way. Scott was guilty of this and he knew it. In his own fashion it seemed he had tried to put this to rights but not without causing some unintended shocks. He had indeed been unknown to us. Now with his death, he was attempting to reach out to us. Some may say it was too late as his full extent became more evident. Flora could barely bring herself to investigate her section. What she found was as she had suspected. On her note attached for her was a quotation 'If a man wishes to be sure of the road he treads on he must close his eyes and walk in the dark.' (St. John of the Cross. 'The Dark Night of the Soul'). Beneath was a large black heavily embroidered bag, which looked Japanese, with ornate patterns and fastened with a highly decorative button, which she carefully undid and reached inside and began to remove the contents. The first thing she saw was a photograph of him wearing an all black robe with what appeared to be an orange bag like attachment hanging from around his neck. She was later to discover this was called a '*rakusu*.' The next item was another small bag, which she opened up to reveal that self same '*rakusu*.' It came complete with a certificate of ordination and full details of when and where this occurred. It was also apparent, as she read through the material that Scott had a Buddhist name. It was Horin Sansho. What that meant she had no idea. There was also an old local newspaper cutting using the photograph of him, giving details she had first discovered. There was also an interview with him in which he explained why he was doing this. This was yet another factor in his life they really knew little about but by the way he had often spoken they were not greatly surprised. Next was a small bronze bowl with a soft padded stick attached. It was obviously a ceremonial gong or bowl of some sort. She struck it gently with the stick. It gave a sonorous almost mystical sound that filled the room as it softly vibrated before slowly fading away. It hadn't been struck for decades and it felt as if she had stirred a sleeping dragon deep inside her. Next there were various manuals and innumerable textbooks on various aspects of Buddhism. It appeared he'd been part of a Zen Buddhist group based in Cornwall. Maybe that's why he moved to Plymouth? There were also booklets on ceremony and ritual and Orders of Service. The last item she found was the black robe shown in the photograph. It had remained carefully folded from all those years ago and still with a gold brocaded attachment binding it together. It was immaculate. She looked at the others and nobody knew what to say. "Dad certainly lived a secretive life didn't he? He's been so thorough in the way he's left and presented us all with this."

I spoke, "When do you think he started to put all this together?"

"He probably intended it some time back but his illness must have spurred him on." Bobby surmised.

"My God I'm so going to miss him. He makes us look as if we have done nothing nor achieved anything." Flora began to weep before she was sobbing out loud as Hugh held her close, her head resting on his shoulder. She was unable to control it. Her Dad's illness, his death and everything that accompanied that, descended upon her leaving her with an unbearable sadness. It was some while before she was able to subside. Her outburst of grief caused us to go quiet. It filled the house and reached deeply into each of us.

He had reached out and touched them all in an unique and loving way. This was to be his finest achievement for what would soon be found would change their lives forever. They weren't to know this yet.

Outside a yellow sun gilded the ageing brickwork of the house giving to the structure a grandeur of light and shade and also lighting up a cobwebbed lawn and the virginal vegetable plot. A fading bonfire swept trails of dying white smoke into open windows of the house. The old burning leaves created a nostalgic air. It wasn't hard to understand the family's attachment to the house. Freda and Scott were gone, yet their presence remained. Flora, Bobby and myself strolled arm in arm across the old lawns and weedy structures surrounding the house. The entire place gave a deep. personal penetrating message of which kith and kin intuitively know. We knew this was our place. We had become part of it and had fallen deeply and irrevocably in love with the bones and spirit of the structure. The house was upright. Whilst imbued with the personal sorrows and happiness of its many past inhabitants, it remained straight and strong. We were locked into this place, its memories and its future. We'd become part of its foundations.

* * *

A grey sea lapped gently onto the stony shore of the cove. The countless pebbles and rocks shifted with a soft rattling sound as waves pushed them in numerous directions, Surrounding them in a rocky brilliance, towered unimaginable layers and levels of strata, millions of years in their making. They were silent witnesses to the turn of countless years, which has shaped and moulded their magnificence many times, before men walked upon the earth. Above the rolling waters, clouds parted and watery sunbeams shone in silver conduits lighting up the magnificence of Lulworth Cove. We had arrived early morning and were sat upon an old upturned fishing boat amongst damp rocks and pebbles surrounded by stranded seaweed. We contemplated the quietness and solitary splendour of what was around and above us. I flicked a few damp pebbles mindlessly to see how far they would go but my mind wasn't really in it. This day, his dying wish was about to be fulfilled. We had little idea how to do this but agreed to wait a short while later so we could compose ourselves suitably and later move on to Durdle Door to scatter the remaining ashes, which we would reserve for that part of the wish. Flora was more attuned to what was required and had come prepared. She had found amongst his items material suitable for the occasion, which she would read out loud.

"Shall we begin?" she said.

We agreed and tentatively began unfastening the urn to reveal a largish amount of grey ash, the earthly remains of our Dad. She asked us each to take a handful and then said solemnly,

"Let us not forget the importance of ritual, for it helps bind us together healing old wounds and hurts."

She then produced three sticks of incense, which she lit and planted firmly amongst the pebbles and rocks. The delicate smoke permeated across the cove.

"We offer this incense in which the sweet aroma of Dad's good deeds may ripen and spread throughout the universe for the sake of all living things. We his children, transfer to him all the merits of our own good deeds to assist and comfort him on his endless journey."

We then began to scatter half the ashes around the cove. The soft breeze helped scatter them but also blew some back onto us. Our clothes became grey with ash before we finished. The sun was now shining across the sea. Dad had now truly become part of this place, as he had wished. The atmosphere was sombre yet dignified and we were all touched with the gentle and emotional affection of the occasion. We said goodbye and farewell to him and set off on the short trip to the Door.

We stood looking down at splendour of this beautiful natural structure. The timeless arch, the long pebble beaches stretching both sides of it held a sense of antiquity, which was hard to deny. All was still and quiet in these early hours of the day. We all could remember coming here as children and how we had adored it so. It was unchanged. Still magnificent. We could understand why he wanted to be part of this area. We agreed that when our turn came to depart this life, we would want to join him and become part of it too. Flo again performed the same simple ceremony, which seemed so appropriate but adding at the end,

"*As rivers brimmed with water fill the ocean so charity practiced here benefits the departed. As water fallen upon a hilly place flows down to the valley so charity practiced here benefits the departed.*"

The three of us felt a deep and relaxing relief it was finally over. It was done and had been nagging away in our minds, as it was something of which we had no experience. Shortly after we took stock of the events that had brought us here; we walked across the valley and remembered how the setting of this location had always communicated to us from the first time we had come here. Nothing had changed; the old magic remained and was repeating itself once more.

FIVE

Bobby

It's been three months since Dad died. It feels like three years but I'm beginning to feel some normality re-entering my life. I sense those cameras calling me. His departure got to me much more than I realised and I know my life will change because of it. I feel ready for renewal but at times I can feel the clammy hand of depression brush across me. I'm not out of the woods as yet. Hugh has told us a good amount of what Dad had said to him. It's so unlike Hugh. He's communicating well with us. I feel he doesn't want to end up like Dad! He said he wanted to know about our lives, feelings, emotions and memories. I never found childhood the wonderfully happy event that some people do. My life was haunted by uncertainties and a degree of inferiority of my position in the family. Mum used to try reassuring me but Dad hardly ever said a bloody thing about anything. What he thought about things I never knew. He always seemed locked up in his head and preoccupied with God knows what. Perhaps his experiences in the war affected him more than I could ever know. His relationship with Mum was pretty much the same although she would put him through the hoops when she'd a mind to. Thinking about it, they seemed to be at a stage in their marriage when everything that could be said had been said. In retrospect, they were down an emotional cul de sac. Their game had resulted in stalemate. It was a situation that was convenient at times and could suit them both.

You know, when I'm on my own or lying awake in bed, even now I often hear her voice in my head. Her voice had certain patterns to it. When she was okay it was 'Bobby, Bobby, can you come here for a minute.' But when she was cross with me about something or other her tone would get short and terse and Bobby became 'Robert. Robert come here at once!' She could scare the shit out of me when she wanted to and wouldn't hesitate to wallop me when she thought it was needed. Her method of attack was a fierce slap behind the legs or a slipper across my arse.

The twins are two years older than me so as you can guess I perpetually saw myself as an outsider, a black sheep without a cause or at times the sacrificial goat. Things weren't all bad though. Most weekends Dad would like to go fishing and he would often take Hugh with him and me only occasionally. I could get an arsey attitude about that even though I didn't care for fishing. He never took Flora. It was a man and boy thing. He'd load up his car, a plum coloured Jowett Javelin, which was considered pretty racy in those days and off they would go. We were left behind and Mum would go to town to do the shopping, although we could see she was far from well. Flo and I got closer because of this and would often play in his old wood shed with water pistols. One of us would be inside and the other outside and we would fire at each other through the cracks in the woodwork. We always got soaking wet and couldn't stop laughing. Sometimes we'd take shots at spiders to see how far we could make them run or at worse drown them. I wouldn't do it now and I know Flora wouldn't either. Once we blasted at a poor old mouse who looked pretty pissed off with the proceedings but it did get away but not without a total bath. Looking back on that time now I can see there was an innocent sexual attraction between us although we didn't know what that was. We would often play around with each other and she would hold my cock, which gave me a funny but nice feeling and it went all hard. She used to like to see this and I would do the same thing to her 'thingy,' which she also seemed to like. It all smelt a bit strange if I remember but we both enjoyed how it made us feel. Later we got some other boys and girls into the shed and we would all show our bits and touch each other. It was never serious in that way and we would always be laughing about it. So we got to look forward to Dad's fishing trips with Hugh, and Mum's shopping expeditions in town. Hugh's trips with Dad were no longer a subject of jealousy but had become for us an opportunity for mutual fun and pleasure. The whole meaning of Mums and Dads, Nurses and Doctors had become an eye opener. Obviously this youthful experimentation couldn't continue as a little later when I for the first time unexpectedly ejaculated with what she was doing. Flora didn't quite know what it was but I think she had a good idea. I knew I was going to have to gradually call a halt to what we were doing and we did. Looking back on it, neither of us regretted it and I know we feel the same way today but it's never ever mentioned between us. I live with Flora in Paignton and that boundary is firmly in place and is never crossed. I think if it were I would be mortified and I want to keep it that way, as I'm sure she does.

Some years back, when I was little, Mum had been diagnosed as suffering with Parkinson's disease. Back then I didn't really know what that was. All I knew was that she had begun to shake a lot and was getting forgetful and her speech would often get slurred. She didn't smile too much either. I know now that was due to the facial muscles not being able to function normally. Her deterioration was rapid and towards the end her mind had virtually gone too. Dad became more attentive to her and I could see he really cared. That distance between them had lessened and he would often hold her close and stroke her head. I could hear him speaking softly to her but never enough for me to know what he was saying. I guess that was personal and private. It wasn't long after she lost practically every function and within a month she had died. He was depressed for some while after that, as we all were. Her loss got to us all but the twins suffered particularly badly. There has to be a special bond between twins with an unique flavour of its own that few would be able to understand.

Just like he did with his Dad, Hugh and I would sit out on the porch with Dad, as he explained how and what the star formations were and how to find them. I wonder if he ever realised he was repeating the very same behaviour of his father? We had another dog, Judy was her name and she came from one of Wren's original litters. She used to love it when we sat there and would settle close in between us and lean on Dad. When Wren had died Judy then took over. She liked us all but Dad in particular. He had this way of attracting animals. Perhaps it was his quietness and stillness he had when they were around, plus his firm and gentle manner. They seemed to know he was a friend and wouldn't harm them. Flo would often come out with mugs of sweet tea and if we were really lucky she would also bring out hot toast and crumpets. Oh they were magic moments!

Since Mum's death, Dad had moved emotionally closer to us. He'd always been as tight as a clam in that area but even with his move towards us I sensed there were still closed doors and locked rooms difficult for him to open. There was a sense of grief around him and I think we all had that but being younger we were able to get over it quicker.

When Dad went fishing I remember him saying to Hugh

that he did it to clear his head and to find time for peace and quiet. He seemed peaceful and quiet enough as he was. How much more did he need?

"There's nothing like sitting by the banks of the River Tamar or Plym." he would say, "It's often as clear as a bell. Nothing like watching the trout swim by and the numerous water animals and insects pass to and fro. That's so relaxing."

Sometimes he would uncork a little, get out the Jowett and take us all for a drive for an hour or two to the country. On the way back we would always stop off at a pub. We had to stay in the car and Dad would go in and come back with three bottles of ginger beer and packets of crisps with those little blue bags full of salt for us, before going back inside to finish his drink. These trips didn't happen too often but when they did we were delighted. The more I think back, the things I seem to remember.

I would sometimes read him poems from my old poetry book, especially those by Tennyson and Houseman both of whom he was particularly fond of. Looking back it seems strange that I did that but he used to say that it was relaxing having someone else read them out loud. This way, poems he said, would come alive for him. I think he thought I was creative. Now I think back he may have in his weird way been trying to bring something literary or artistic out of me, something different from the norm. When I started to read to him, Judy the dog would curl up between us in a brown ball and look up at us both as if she understood every word. Cocker Spaniels can be so loving. She was a beautiful animal. I can remember her so well, especially when I was helping Mum shucking green peas for a meal. Judy would sit beneath the table and make a rapid grab at any that missed the bowl and landed on the floor, her tail wagging like crazy.

In the course of later years I got to thinking of Dad as some kind of Second World War bunker, big, strong and virtually impenetrable. I remember this because I remember I had a girl friend who would often get me to stay with her overnight where she lived although it was owned by her aunt who also lived there. The aunt took to me considerably and we got around to discussing art, one of her favourite subjects. The Pre-Raphaelites, Turner the Impressionist movement and the genius of Picasso were amongst her favourite discussions. She was incredibly knowledgeable and even when I broke up with her niece she would still ask me over for tea and further discussions. I think she was lonely. She showed me her own collection of paintings, which I was amazed to see included works by the Scottish Impressionists, the Newlyn School and a fake Samuel Palmer by that now known rogue Keating. She was intrigued by my delight in the modern works of Edward Hopper and Jackson Pollack and got me to explain to her why I liked them. We became firm friends. Her name was Charlotte. Often I would drive my old black 350cc Velocette motorbike over to see her. We'd sit and chat for hours. She was a joy and a revelation. Her house overlooked the river with long lawns swooping down to the water's edge. We'd stroll around and sit looking across the river discussing literature and the arts in general. She told me later that she used to lecture in art and its history at Oxford University. That amazed me and I felt quite daunted. She got me over that with her easy going and friendly manner. In my visits there I realised she was giving to me an education, which brings me back to Dad. Big, strong and virtually impenetrable he'd never been able to talk to me, or open my eyes like this wonderful, warm woman. There were some contrasts there alright. Yet, remembering her and seeing

Dad in his dying days made me realise that the only miracle in life is that we are alive. Cures are rarely permanent and life struggles on until it ceases.

I never did take to fishing. I tried it a few times but found it boring staring at countless gallons of water flowing endlessly past all day. It sent me to sleep and Dad told me that was all part of it. "Fuck that" I thought. "I'd rather be reading about art, literature and poetry."

Dad was indeed a mystery to me and he never seemed to go that extra distance and reach out to the twins or me. It was as if he had other dark secrets. You never knew what he was thinking. I keep running through my mind the last few months he had alive and the prospect of his inevitable death, which seemed to wrought such a change in him. I guess that change had been going on a lot longer than we knew. This was apparent when we opened that chest. I was intrigued, like Flora and Hugh at his hints of dark secrets but so far Hugh has found nothing. That chest was carefully and meticulously arranged, poignantly presented with a simple humanity. It was not the hasty work of a dying man with only a few months left to live. In case you are wondering I'm also dictating all this for Hugh's benefit and for his records. Christ knows what he's going to do with it all. I hope it's the sort of thing he wants. Talking about these events has given me a recollection of how I had the hots for a pretty young ballet dancer a while back. We'd met at a party and I was lovesick for sometime. Flo remarked at the time that I was sort of a replica of Scott. Each new woman was a new country to be explored but would eventually abandon them when there wasn't anything new to find. So it was on to the next. This remark amused Hugh greatly but got me thinking I was misjudged and misunderstood. When I got round to thinking about it, obviously Flora had a dimension on Dad when she made that remark. What did she know that I didn't?

In those last days of his, we did manage to get Dad out a few more times in his chair but the main problem he would need his medication in strong doses and would frequently fall asleep. We're not here to urge him on. Everything has to be done at his own pace. Who were we to tell him otherwise? He would like to sit under trees gazing out at the sea and listening to the crash of waves on the rocks and shoreline. God knows what he was thinking but I suspect a lot of memories were pouring through him. I was surprised to see a small black rosary in his hands with ornate black tassels hanging from it and he was slowly moving the beads through his hands and at the same time his lips seemed to be muttering something. Flo had already noticed and she said it was probably a mantra of some kind or something similar. Clearly a spark still ran through him and his brain was functioning although his body wasn't. We'd decided to try a picnic although Dad was fast approaching the point where solids were getting difficult and mostly it was liquids only that he could take down. Trying to get them in his mouth could get awkward and messy. They would often seep down his chin and down his shirt. Flo would lean over and wipe them clean. Looking at what was happening to him I recall talking to the twins not long after he was initially informed.

"There's no hope for this as you know. His diagnosis is fatal and I've checked all I can and any prospect of stopping this is a non-existent. It was lost some time back when he first contracted Myeloma."

That came as no surprise to them both and Hugh simply nodded in agreement. Flora muttered something about not wanting to know that. We all had so many memories I'm not certain I can get mine all down. Unlucky Hugh being appointed archivist, researcher and general historian to our family, what had he done to deserve that? He could be in danger of being drowned under a sea of information. He's oscillating between us both picking up scraps of information, which we keep chucking at him willy-nilly. He's never without a notebook and pen. Neither of us has his sense of order. I'm almost envious of his skills and his organisational approach. I can sense he enjoys this aspect. It challenges his investigative and research skills. He can be so utterly focussed that for someone like me it's almost annoying.

Later that evening Dad had his nightly carers turn up followed much later by the Marie Curie nurse, Ella. She put Dad to bed with his beloved scotch, which he shouldn't be having, plus his usual medication and he very quickly descended into a deep sleep. We sat up and talked. Flora looked at us and said did we know that he said that without the morphine he would have given up some while back.

"I'm not surprised. So would I." Hugh replied saying that it was a cruel end to such an inspiring life and what had he done to deserve that? At this point Flora got up and said she would rustle up some food for us. I guess she wanted to avoid this conversation. She came back in fifteen minutes with a large bowl of noodles cooked in Soy sauce, garlic, chilli and ginger accompanied by large fat pink prawns and Chinese crackers. At midnight this sort of food has a magic uniquely its own. She said that Dad was very special wasn't he? We all nodded and six eyes momentarily were in danger of brimming over. For all his past mistakes, dalliances and reticence, another aspect of Scott had begun to emerge. Christ knows why he'd behaved like a poker player with the cards so close to his chest. In some low-key sort of way I saw him as a silent powerhouse, replete with strength, which reached down into unfathomable depths. He'd finally begun to surface towards the end. I said that few people like him could be found. Flora as usual, disagreed she reckoned there were more than we could imagine. She said that there was an element of God in all of us and that she was certain he operated through us in different ways. That's why we're all so different. There was a pause. She was always able to turn a conversation into another direction. She carried on in usual Flora fashion, cranking up and expanding the issues. telling us that all over the planet there were people who suffered similar misfortunes, if not worse. Suffering was an endemic condition of all living things. It was our core disease. We in the West live in affluence with every commodity on tap whilst rest of the world barely gets a thing apart from dictators or futures and commodity brokers fucking up the poor of the planet for their own personal gain. Neither Hugh or myself could disagree nor I'm sure Dad wouldn't have either. My memory is bobbing about like a jack in the box for I recall that this was one of her favourite debates. She would often get heavy and wanted everyone to feel guilty about certain issues. She's right in some ways but I'm not going to wear a hair shirt for what my ancestors started on the Stock Exchange or in Wall Street.

* * *

When Mum had gone Dad repeated what his Dad had done to him, unknowingly I suspect. He would send us off to our cousin's house, where Aunt Vera and Uncle Alf lived in a large rambling cottage named *The Lighthouse* in the small village of Lutton, close to Plymouth and on the very edge of Dartmoor. In retrospect I don't know why it was called that but perhaps it was a metaphor of some sort or someone had been addicted to

Virginia Woolf. Certainly it wasn't near the sea. I went there mainly at weekends but never longer than about four days. I liked both Aunt Vera and Uncle Alf. She was pretty and always laughing and smiling and it was hard to think she was Mum's sister. They were so different. He was big and gruff with large black bushy eyebrows and at the end of his muscular arms were a pair of enormous hairy hands. He had a sense of fun with us and we always got on well. Importantly they were kind and generous to us. Their daughter, our cousin called Trudi who was around about my age, I liked enormously, We'd laugh and joke a lot and start giggling and wrestling with each other. She was surprisingly strong and would get me locked in a scissors grip before kissing me a lot. Locked up like this she would give me a *Beano* to read and she would read a *Dandy* but that grip would remain. I actually liked it. Once, when we were alone she asked to see my cock, which I got out and showed her. She couldn't stop laughing, which made me laugh too and she then showed me her bits. We were so innocent then and similar to Dad with his girlfriend Emma when he was young, I grew to love her. She was a woman in miniature and she knew. When she helped Aunt Vera serve our dinner she would often but secretly try to give me an extra portion or two. Her elder brother Frank invariably spotted this. He would unmercifully rib her saying she loved me. Well, that made me blush and they would start punching each other at the table. Vera and Alf just ignored it all. That was an eye opener. I couldn't imagine Mum or Dad ever allowing that sort of behaviour at home. The love of a girl, eh? When it was time to leave for home she would give me big kisses on the mouth and I couldn't wait for the next visit. Dad hadn't a clue how I felt about her and I had no idea what his reaction would be nor did I really care. Vera would frequently come visiting and would often bring Trudi with her. I remember on one of her visits, without Trudi, coming down the stairs to find Dad laying on top of Vera across the sofa. I didn't know what they were doing but somehow it didn't seem right. I remember feeling uncomfortable but didn't know why. They quickly got up and she hurriedly left. Nobody spoke to me. So Dad in retrospect became an idol with feet of clay. Looking back on this, who of us hasn't made an error of some sort in our lives, which we would rather not talk about? In some ways, when I think about it, this reticent father of mine takes on an aspect of humanity. It brings him to life and I won't be judgemental about him in that way. Red blood did move through his veins after all.

Well, Flora and Hugh enjoyed those visits as well. They told me later that they suspected Dad of having a sexual appetite but couldn't bring themselves to mention it. Me revealing the Aunt Vera episode was a confirmation of those suspicions. Flora surprisingly smiled, "Dear Dad, so you weren't all wood."

Hugh said nothing but I saw he looked grim and uncomfortable. Perhaps he knew more than he was letting on? I guess he would have to decide whether he should include any of this in his chronicles. Hiding it, I thought, would be to present an incomplete picture and as Dad had said, he wanted a complete picture as possible, warts 'n' all of the family history. Nothing is more irritating when completing a jigsaw to find there are a few missing pieces. Today we have a different approach than they had in those austere years, which remained draped in the remnants of Victorian and Edwardian morality. I told them about Trudi and me and they just laughed and said that I was stupid if I thought they hadn't known. Trudi and I had become 'kissing cousins' and obviously at our tender age we had a thing about each other. If Alf and Vera knew they just ignored it. This was what I liked about them. For that time, they were in retrospect, advanced in their parenting. I remember hearing Alf saying that if you want to control a herd you must give them a big field to play in. How wise that seems even today! Looking back I think there is something timeless and perennial about that statement. There were times when Trudi would cuddle me close and I would feel something stirring in me. She used to giggle at me in my underpants and ask why I didn't take them off. Well, I was shy and didn't want it to get all hard and funny.

Flora interrupted, "Now isn't that sweet. Today it's just the opposite. Men are scared they won't get hard!"

I laughed and said how I got my own back by sniggering at her pointy little tits that were beginning to sprout. When I did this she would give me an almighty thump. Apart from Hugh, what we weren't realising is that we were talking as Dad had intended us to, in an open and frank way that he hadn't been capable of. He was reaching out to us still and would continue to do so for some considerable time yet until his mission was accomplished.

* * *

Trudi grew up fast and I couldn't keep pace with her. She was all woman and that caused all me uncertainties and my inferiorities came creeping back. Other boys were noticing her too and this would piss me off, as she seemed to enjoy their attention. I eventually became a cousin and not a 'kissing cousin.' So that is how we drifted apart from each other. I don't know if she ever thinks of me nor do I know where she is now or even if she is still alive. I often think of her for she was my first true love. I got down to feeling moody and depressed and took listening to sad music and generally being melancholic. My God I missed her.

Yet over time the pain lessened. Dad was deeply into his photography and would take pictures of me on my training runs with the athletic club I had recently joined but he rarely showed any of his shots to me. Now via Hugh, digging through that chest some of those photographs were now coming to light. Boy, did I look thin back then! I don't think Dad understood how hurtful he could be but I reckon now that is not what he really wanted. If he realised the niggling damage he was causing he would now regret it. He was so out of touch and so fucking remote it would cause a violent reaction in me. I remember laying in bed one evening swearing I would never, never ever want to be like him. It was about this time I joined the Communist Youth Party, partly from belief and partly to get back at him. When he eventually did find out he displayed some rare emotion by going through the roof! I guess he felt threatened. There wasn't a lot of point in him remonstrating with me as I certainly could punch above my weight in any argument he tried to present. I don't think he was used to that sort of thing. I got enjoyment seeing him flounder, unable to answer my points as he would often waffle and bluster with no reason or logic. The loss of Trudi had no small part to play, even in my later years for behaving the way I did. Dad could be so odd at times, as he seemed particularly fond of Trudi but seemed scared stiff of me having other girlfriends or of Flora having boyfriends. Why? I've never worked that out, perhaps it was all too much of a mirror for him. I had this Welsh girlfriend called Bronwyn who was three years older than me, which made me feel like a man because of that. I used to snog and grope her in our local graveyard. How romantic is that? But at least it was quiet and deserted. She was pushy and wasn't shy in asking me to do what she wanted. I learnt a lot from her! We'd stay out late, way past the time I was supposed to be home. I knew what to expect from

Dad when I was late. He could get verbally abusive and I'd be forbidden to go out for a few nights. One night I was really late getting home and got off my bike, let the air out of the front tyre, simulating a puncture and walked home and as usual he was leaning on the front gate waiting for me. Well, my little ruse worked that time but it wasn't something I could repeat. Why he was like that I shall never know. I know now that he'd been through and experienced a lot of hardship but he was so tyrannical and at times I could truly hate him.

All three of us are seeing more of each other than we ever used to. Dad's death has achieved that at least. Flora has invited Hugh over for a long weekend, which would get him away from the house in Plymouth. He was only too happy to accept. I'm really looking forward to him coming over especially as Flora does the cooking and she makes a pretty mean spaghetti bolognaise. She seems to be able to rustle up good food from practically nothing. I've enrolled in an intensive photography course and have been playing around with the cameras. How different the Leicas are to the Hasselblad as they all seem to be capable of different tasks, which the other can't always match. Well at least I'm learning things thanks to Dad. The only doubt I had is that I didn't want to become a duplicate of him, but taking pictures like he did would be no mean achievement.

When Hugh arrived we sat down for a few drinks, chatted a lot and eventually Flora went off to sort out the food and before long a delicious yummy aroma filtered through to our nostrils. However, Hugh seemed tense or was it just my imagination? He seemed withdrawn and I asked him if he was okay and was he finding the collation too much. He didn't answer immediately but said he'd rather eat first and then we could talk about things. We all enjoyed Flora's cooking and every plate was cleared. She should have been a cook. When we were all settled again I looked at Hugh who still wasn't looking his usual self.

"So what's wrong Hugh?"

"It's difficult. I Didn't want to say anything the other night." He paused and gazed down at the tabletop. "I've been going through the masses of stuff Dad left and have found a few more unopened envelopes, which of course I opened. In some ways I wish I hadn't."

I could see Hugh wavering and gave him a large scotch, which he bolted down. I have never seen him down one like that before.

"The first envelope was marked No.1. This is what it said." He pulled a letter from his inside jacket pocket.

"If this is you Hugh reading this as I hope it is, I want you to keep the most open of minds. You're about to discover a few things you may not like, nor will Bobby or Flora.

I know my shortcomings and I know where I went wrong in my life and have forever regretted those mistakes. I reckon my old aunt was right in her assessment of me. I haven't been too good as you are about to discover. Judge me, as you will. What ever that is it will be right.

Forever, your loving Dad.

Both Flora and I looked at each other and she asked, "What's this all about?"

I shook my head, as I hadn't a clue.

Hugh continued staring down at the tabletop looking pissed off. "I opened envelope marked No, 2. Give me another drink, will you please?" He pushed over his empty glass.

I filled it and he put his hand to his head and he didn't seem to know where to go from there. He asked for a minute or two, which for us was not a problem. He finished the drink off as quickly as the first and then asked for another. I've never seen him like this. His behaviour was wrapping us up in a sombre tone. Flora's Pavlova remained untouched as we sat there waiting to hear what more he had to say. All had gone silent and Hugh seemed to be struggling.

"What's wrong Hugh?"

He merely looked downwards saying he'd be would okay in a minute or two. Eventually, lifting his head, he looked at us both and asked if we remembered those weekends at Vera and Alf's and their children Trudi and Frank.

"We did have fun didn't we? Trudi and Bobby were special with each other." Flora gave me a knowing look, which caused me to smile. He then said those other envelopes were pointers of where to find more information. He had left very definite clues for me to find out what he intended me to find. It's almost like a detective novel.

"I dug around the drawers and cupboards of the house and as directed and eventually I found certain items, which I unravelled through various research sources, which is what I'm trained to do. Soon after that I found what I was looking for. I'll start with probably the most important item I found. It's a letter and I'm going to read it to you both now." He pulled another letter out from his inside pocket.

'My dearest...' Hugh omitted the name. 'I'm surprised and pleased at your news. Well it was a memorable evening we had wasn't it? I shall never regret it nor forget it. It was what we both wanted, wasn't it? Tell me how I can help you although I'm not often in the same place for long, as they post me around a bit but I shall do all I can. Once this is all over I'm

sure we can work something out between us and be
together again. I look forward to that time so much.
With much love...' Hugh left the name off again.

He looked at us both and I had a hugely uncomfortable feeling about what was to come. Flora went quite pale. Hugh continued by telling us he had married up the reply

'My darling, I shall miss you too and don't worry
about a thing, I shall be perfectly alright. As long
as Hitler doesn't strike us too hard we shall
survive. I shall keep you posted on how it's going
and can't wait for you to return and we can do it all
over again'

Hugh paused, "Any guesses, you two?"

I looked across at Flora who was struggling. We both knew but we couldn't say it.

"That was Dad writing to Aunt Vera and she to him. Her news in case you haven't worked it out was that she was pregnant with Dad's child. She gave birth to a daughter she named Trudi who Alf believed to be his. Trudi is our sister or half sister." Hugh bent his head down shaking it. "I never wanted to tell you that but how could I not. Forgive me please; it was probably best never said but I couldn't live with that secret like he did." We were stunned to silence. Hugh looked wretched and we reached out to him to let him know there was nothing to forgive. We all began to get watery eyed and I whispered, "Fucking hell!!. My lovely Trudi; you were really part of us and we never knew." The implications of what we had heard were far reaching. My relationship with her had been extra special and both Flora and Hugh knew that. I was shocked and devastated as I had almost entered into a sort of incestuous relationship without knowing it. It felt like an abyss had opened up in front of me. Flora from being pale had now gone completely white. She was rendered speechless. Hugh spoke again, "There's more."

"Oh What!" I almost shouted at him.

"Dear Aunt Vera had earlier already lost a baby. From Dad's and Vera's letters it was certainly his. There's no doubting it. Mum knew nothing about it. I've also discovered that Frank wasn't Alf's either but nor was he Dad's. I'm certain I know the name of who it was but he seemed to disappear. I found out where. It seems that loveable Aunt Vera was the town bike and Uncle Alf was so naïve he knew nothing. He thought all the events were related to him. Listen to this" Hugh unfolded a faded, creased looking yellowy and cream letter.

'Darling Vera, I'm so proud of you. We've had our ups and downs and you losing our baby all those years ago still upsets me so much and I feel it's my entire fault and I should be punished. But now we have between us two lovely children, Frank and Trudi, How lucky we are. I shall be home soon and who knows, we might try for another but only if you want to. I love you very much….Lots of love from your devoted husband, Alf.'

What he hadn't worked out was the time and dates when he was about or when he wasn't. If he had he would have cottoned on. I looked across at Flora and she was shaking her head. Hugh looked incredibly grim and said to me. "I'm sure there'll be more to discover Bobby, don't you? Once we've got over the shock of this I'll need to take stock before deciding what to do next."

"It seems he wanted you to discover this or why would he leave clues and letters of where to find this information."

"That'd crossed my mind too."

"I think he'd lived with it too long. Don't you remember him saying he wanted us to know everything both the good and the bad? If I recall, on more than one occasion before he died he hinted at a few things we weren't going to be too happy with. It seems this was the only way he could tell us. What do you two think?"

Flora looked up, still looking shaky. "I don't suppose that'll be the end of it. He must have intended for us to find out. I find it unbelievable. How're you going to get on with that family tree now I don't know? I wouldn't even want to personally. Poor, poor Mum. It was a blessing she didn't know. What he did was unforgivable."

"I agree with what you say Flora, but, Bobby, there's a little more yet."

"Oh no more please! What is it?"

"I got digging around and my research background has been very useful. If you'd both like to know, I've found out where Trudi is living and I have her phone number and address back at home."

"Bloody hell!" My heart began to race. And Flora held my hand tightly. "I don't know what to say." A sense of nervousness passed through me.

With that we discussed it at some length and I was in favour of not doing anything yet. This was something, which could be dealt with later, which both Hugh and Flora agreed with. They asked that when the dust had settled on this, would I be happy to make any approaches but only at my own pace and time. I nodded agreement.

"There's something else you might like to know. She's childless, divorced and lives alone. She works as a P.A. for a high flying oil executive with a well-known oil company."

Hugh is clever and totally thorough and I'm really impressed the way he's dug all this out. My initial reaction was that Trudi need never know but at the end of the day if we didn't tell her would be to rob her of a family she should be part of, or at least have a choice to decide one way or another. Undoubtedly her reaction would be the same as ours mixed up with anger and sadness. She was part of us and why shouldn't she be aware of the truth. In a strange way I felt closer to her than I did all those years ago. The twins felt the same too. We agreed to let time do its work before any approach was made to her. When I felt ready I would make contact and work it out from there. I asked about Frank. Was Hugh absolutely certain he wasn't Dad's son as well? He was certain. He had found references as to who the father might be and obviously it wasn't Alf. He explained.

"Checking back into Dad's diaries and log books he'd been posted to Yorkshire and for some time and hadn't been home at the time conception must have taken place. In an other letter to Dad she more or less admitted that she'd been 'indiscreet' with someone else. I dug around and there was a strong probability that the person was a lodger she had by the name of Stanley Weatherall, who I discovered was an essential worker at the nearby railway yards. He moved on once he heard the news and tracking back through the records it seems he died a few years back in a road accident. Where Frank lives I don't know but I'm thinking if I do find him it's not our business to tell him any of this. What do you think?"

I agreed totally and so did Flora. I said it could be very cruel and painful. Trudi's predicament, however was in a different category. The talking was helping dissipate our initial dismay and some colour had returned to Flora's cheeks. I think at this point we felt incredibly close to each other and for me more than any time in my life. Dad had at least achieved something out of this shabby pile of shit. We embraced for some time without a word being said. I thought of Hugh and how painful discovering all this in the way he had been led to must have been traumatic. What more was he likely to find? I turned away and poured them all large drinks. "What do we do now?"

"What we do now," said Flora "is that we carry on. The people I feel sorry for are Mum, Alf and Trudi."

I agreed that we should march on. "Dad certainly was a man of dark secrets. Who knows what he was thinking, asking Hugh to discover his murky past. He must have known how it would affect us. I have no doubt now that it was intentional. For him it was like going to a confessional and he's asking us for redemption and forgiveness. It's at best a gross and clumsy attempt to make us whole by completing the picture. It had no care or consideration in how it would affect us. Poor, you Flora. You must feel gutted having gone through that almost sacred ritual for him. It all seems so hollow and meaningless. An utter waste of time. What d'you think?"

"I feel conned and betrayed. Dad was a Jekyll and Hyde character and now as far as I'm concerned, a fallen idol. He wasn't good but mainly bad from what we've found out."

"Dad had loved us all in a remote sort of way but what on earth was going on between him and Mum?"

"Nothing much but by Christ he was crapping on his own doorstep having an affair with Vera all that time. They must have been clever in concealing it. What a cow! What a bastard!"

Flora rarely ever spoke in such a way but this has shaken her badly.

* * *

That night it was warm, so we sat out on the patio and listened to the sound of the sea not too far away. None of us felt much like talking. I gazed up at the stars and their constellations that he had so carefully explained to me all those years ago. I always enjoyed locating Polaris, the Pole star. It was relevant, particularly now. There was a constancy about it, it was immovable, always there, an object which never told you a lie. You could always trust it to guide you through the darkness and men knew it would never let them down. We were smarting, licking our wounds and wondering how and where this would all end. In an attempt to lift the atmosphere Flora and I invited Mark and Sophie over. Nothing seemed to matter anymore but I had earlier spotted Hugh talking into the recorder and I can only guess he's getting all this down on tape. So in a way he seems to be carrying on. I've decided to do the same. If nothing else he has shown me how treacherous people can be. Cynical this may be but true, as Dad had shown. How strange he left me the photographic equipment and the photographs. Like he also had, I too have a strong interest in photography and am almost tempted to branch out on a part time basis until I get good enough to give up the day job. This is just what he did. I at least have him to thank for that. He's also left us a considerable sum of money, which will shortly be coming our way. This will alter the course of our lives. I have to ask myself, am I being a hypocrite, appalled by his behaviour but willing to accept his money? He must have known all this and worked it out. He wasn't that stupid.

Later Sophie and Mark arrived bearing gifts, of Beaujolais and Rioja wines plus chocolates and French cheeses. How thoughtful they are. Mark adored Flora and I loved Sophie. She was paramount in my affections, beautiful, attractive witty and above all, intelligent. I was going to ask her to marry me and had planned it to be when she wasn't likely to expect it. So tonight was as good as any in spite of that shocking revelation Hugh had discovered. Sophie knew there was a high possibility of me asking but she had no idea when this would be. Even with all the events of the last twelve hours I'd decided to ask this very evening. I was feeling nervous about it and hadn't told a soul. It was to be a surprise for everybody. I'd brought a engagement ring a few days ago, which I kept buttoned up in my pocket. What on earth would they all think? I don't think they would be that surprised and she'd be unlikely to turn me down. I was also hoping it would lift the blues from us and get us into a more positive frame of mind.

I felt sorry for Hugh as he didn't seem to have anybody on the horizon although he had told me he was beginning to see Ella the Marie Curie nurse. I had noticed and so had Flora that they did seem to get on well as they used to sit up talking into the early hours. I hope it works out for him as she has a really attractive personality. I wouldn't be surprised if Mark asked Flora soon. They seem made for each other and go together like a mortice and tenon and it's a joy to see the closeness they have with each other. As I've said before, over the years I've always had a sense of exclusion from the family but looking back, a lot of it was my own fault for not wanting to join in with what was going on. They never really excluded me. With my own petty jealousies I excluded myself. Now I realise I have my own confidence, a confidence that comes with getting older and more mature, which leaves me unafraid of many circumstances in life. Even the recent events haven't dented that. If anything it has me made stronger and I hope it has done the same for the twins. I looked up at Sophie and I thought she looked stunning. She was wearing a soft pink short floral dress and had on a subtle pink lipstick, pink eyeliner plus mascara. Her big brown eyes glowed with a bright engaging warmth. I hugged her close and whispered into her ear that I loved her.

Holding me tightly she whispered, "I love you too."

Ripples of pleasure and sheer joy pass through me. Wonderful!

So there we sat in the warm night air and never mentioned the discoveries about Dad. That would have been a real downer as we were having a fun time. We ate all Flora's excellent off-the-cuff food and drank more than we should have done. Eventually I stood up, courage boosted by the mixtures of red wine.

"Everybody, I have an announcement to make." They looked up expectantly. I was surprised how firm and calm my voice was. My haven't I changed! I stared directly down at Sophie. I felt incredibly happy and expansive.

"My dearest Sophie, I've known you for some while now and as you know, I love you dearly, so much so, that underneath this starry sky and with these people present I have something to show you." A broad smile was cemented into my face. I reached into my pocket and pulled out the ring box opened it up so she could see it. "Sophie will you marry me?"

There was a slight pause and everybody remained quiet, transfixed. I saw her take a sharp intake of breath as she looked at the ring and then back up at me.

"I thought you would never ask. You stupid lovely sod! How on earth could I ever say no. Yes! Yes! Yes!"

She stood up, kissed me and hugged me and I could see the tears well up in her eyes. Everybody stood up and applauded, which made me feel like King of the World. My happiness was complete and I slipped the ring onto her finger.

For a while Dad seemed irrelevant to me. My course was going well and the photographic work was really beginning to pick up. I crave photojournalism but I'm going to have to be quicker off the mark and far better than I am now. Some of Dad's work was of such a high standard and would not seem out of place in that area. So for the time being I'm a weekend worker, christenings, weddings and even the odd funeral but I have greater ambitions. Dad's material and monetary legacy is changing my life, there's no doubt about that. Whether my wedding would change this I had no idea. We'd decided to marry nearer to Christmas or even in the New Year. Nothing was concrete. I told Sophie what Hugh had discovered about Dad. She was greatly surprised and taken aback. "You poor things. What a shock it must have been for you all."

"It certainly was but I can't get Trudi out of my mind and I know I've got to do something about it, but when?"

"Only when you're ready."

"Will I ever be ready?"

"I think you're close to that point now."

I agreed with her and knew it had to be done. That evening I called Hugh. He was still doing his researches but had found nothing else shocking. He'd found another envelope addressed to the three of us but he wasn't going to read it until we were all present to discuss it. He had Ella around so it wasn't a good idea to talk about anything. He gave me Trudi's address and phone number. I was startled to see that she was living yards from where I lived during my student days. How weird can that be? Both he and Flora had said they would come with me to see her if I thought it might help. I thought about that for a while but decided It would better if I went alone. It was days later and I was still staring down at the phone number feeling scared to try it. What was I going to say? Excuses flooded through my mind. I counted up to ten once more, took a deep breath and gingerly began to punch out the number.

* * *

The bus swung slowly around the long S bend. It was the same as it was all those years back; I knew the town well and never thought I'd be back for another visit. Where you lived is always something special whether you loved or hated it. I shifted uncomfortably in my seat with butterflies rising in my stomach and feeling really self-conscious of the bulky woman sitting next to me. She was wearing a large woollen tricoloured hat folded close over her eyes. She continually prodded out from her mouth a crooked and wet denture plate. I attempted looking out of the window as a distraction to recall some familiar landmarks. I wished I'd come by car. Not much had changed out there. There was the small hill that I remembered so well. Then the road dropped down over a bridge before the area became a town and the bus climbed upwards on the long hill between the houses. This part of town was where the wealthiest houses were found. Behind them I could see in the background the well-treed grounds of the college I went to. Its gold and black clock tower standing tall over the complex was pretty much the same as it was back then. Eventually the bus came to a halt.

"Bridge Park" called out the driver.

I knew exactly where he would stop and that hadn't altered either since I was last there. The woman next to me stood to get off the bus. I relaxed. This wasn't my stop but I was grateful for any delay. For obvious reasons they were more than welcome! The bus rattled on for a few more minutes until it slewed to another halt and the driver called out, "College Town."

I got up, put on my black Dannimac raincoat, pulled my overnight bag from the luggage rack and left the bus, nerves were eating away at me. The cream and maroon number 46 bus pulled away in a blast of black diesel fumes. I wished I was back on it. It was raining and the pavements glistened with a wet sheen. At a distance under the low grey of the early afternoon sky the wetness gave a polish to the square and the old bricks of the nearby Council Offices. I felt like laughing but thoughts of my mission squashed that feeling. Momentarily I remembered my student days and those indiscreet affairs and fumblings with different girls. But if you can't do that when you're young you won't get many other chances later in life. I headed in the direction of number seventeen Eastman Street. My heart speeded up at the prospect of what was about to unfold. I'd decided to spend a couple of days here, and before going to number seventeen I checked in at the College Hotel, which was probably the best in town. The lobby was elegant with oak panelling throughout. It was pleasantly warm with a luxurious wood fire burning brightly in the spacious Inglenook fireplace. Men in suits and ties and a few smartly dressed women sat in fat leather armchairs nearby. I ordered a room from the male receptionist who was wearing an ill fitting blue and gold uniform. He asked me to sign the register and turned the book around and pushed it towards me. I printed my name in the next vacant box and signed it and pushed the book back to him. He turned the register back round and looked down at my printed name, 'ROBERT ANDERSON' in large letters and I saw him do a double take before he stared up at me.

"Don't I know you sir?"

"I've no idea" I glanced quickly at his gold and black nametag. It read 'FRANK JAGGER.' A chill went through me. It couldn't be! It couldn't possibly be! He thought he knew me so it was a possibility but one I could do without.

"Never heard of you." I muttered unconvincingly, avoiding looking at him.

"I had a cousin with your name, sir, and you do look a lot like him if I remember."

"I think you're mistaken. Now could you give me my keys and show me where my room is please?" I affected a complete disinterest.

He gave me a long, long look and I knew he was certain that his recognition was correct. Jesus Christ! I was here to see Trudi and here was her brother like some hungry ghost living in the same place! I had a desire to run but that would be a real give away. I toughed it out and refused to look or talk further with him. I hadn't expected, nor was I prepared, for this. If they were both in the same town my revelations would be common knowledge between them in no time, which is what myself Flora and Hugh had agreed we didn't want. We hadn't thought it through sufficiently. Trudi was going to be hurt and he would be also, if it was indeed him but I had little doubt it wasn't him. He too had definite resemblance to the young Frank, Trudi's brother. A feeling of dread dropped over me. I checked into my room and barely noticed its spacious comfort. I looked at my watch and I had an hour or so before I met with Trudi. I took a stiff drink and called Hugh.

Flora picked up her phone and it was Hugh calling. He told her what Bobby told him and said unless it was unavoidable he should deny any knowledge of him and not answer any questions he might ask. Yet if Frank and Trudi lived in the same area it was going to be difficult for Bobby. If only in a small way Frank was still part of the family and was a cousin. Flora agreed without any hesitation. She also said that if and when he found out from Trudi and Bobby was still there it could get awkward. The poor man won't know what to think or believe. "What a load of shit Dad's dumped us in."

"It would have been better if we'd known nothing."

"I feel like going down there my self but Bobby wouldn't be happy. He feels he has to sort this out himself."

"I don't think we've heard the last of this. It's a right Pandora's box isn't it."

143

"I would say it'd be more like shit hitting the fan."

The twins discussed this at some length; that Trudi if she was agreeable should be part of the family. There was also the question of the estate and they were going to have to discuss how they could help her as she hadn't been included in Dad's last Will and Testament. They agreed that she had a rightful claim to some of that. The hours rolled on by and they each guessed that Bobby must have made contact.

I sat there for perhaps twenty minutes. Once I got up to go but mixed another drink instead. I crossed over to the window and looked out over the wet scene of the town. I gripped the window's woodwork, which surrounded the glass and saw my knuckles had gone white. I hadn't realised I was that tense. What I had planned was to get to her address, get it over with as quickly and politely as possible, then make my retreat but I knew it wasn't going to be that easy. I turned around and poured my third drink. At that moment my phone rang. "Who on earth can that be?" I picked it up. "Yes."

The phone oscillated in my grip, as Trudi's unmistakable voice spoke to me.

"How did you know I was staying here?"

"Let's say a little bird told me."

I didn't need to be a mind reader to know who that little bird might be.

She continued, " So will you be round soon?"

"I won't be long. I was about to leave in a few minutes."

She had no real idea why I was really coming to see her. She'd been amazed by my original call, nor had she any clue how she'd been found. I told her that Hugh and I were working on a family tree and she might be able to help us in a few areas. I'm such a coward aren't I?

I'd told her that I'd decided on the spur of the moment to try and find her. She asked me why I hadn't written as calling her was almost too much to take. I agreed that I should have, as my call was quite a shock. She added that it all sounded mysterious and intriguing. I asked her did she still want to see me?

"Not want to see you! We must have masses to talk about. You make sure you get here soon. I can't wait to see you. Stay for some dinner and take pot luck on my awful cooking." She paused, "How about it?"

"Well Trudi, I ..."

"Good," the phone said, "That's settled then."

"I'm not certain that's going to be a good idea."

"Nonsense! Of course it is. You get here soon, d'you understand?"

Her childhood bossiness hadn't changed from all those years ago and a deep sense of resignation trickled through me. This could get difficult. At least some more ice had been broken and she'd put me at ease. Once I put down the phone I poured my fourth drink and they weren't having the slightest affect on me. There was so much adrenalin pumping around me, alcohol hadn't any chance. I put on my raincoat, stepped out of the room and walked downstairs into the foyer. The clerk, Frank was still there. There was now no doubt Trudi had confirmed his suspicions. He looked embarrassed. I wasn't going to try and make him feel any better. That attitude would come in its own good time. I walked past him without acknowledgement, out through the revolving doors into the damp streets.

I hadn't seen her for so long now and had no idea what she would look like. I knew where she worked, where she lived and that she was divorced without any kids. It didn't sound promising. I walked slowly down the road feeling the cold rain on my face. I buttoned up my raincoat, turned up the collar, thrust my hands deep into the pockets and turned in the direction of where she was living. Running through my head were the things I would say and how I would say them. But game plans can and often do go wrong. Nothing was certain. A lot depended on what she was like. How I would get to the point of my visit I hadn't a clue. I passed a pub, an old haunt of mine, *The Hop Blossom* and was tempted to go in. It was one I had used many times as a student. I hesitated outside the door, breathing in the cold damp air, my misty breath disappearing ever upwards. I decided not to go in. I hadn't the time. Maybe on the way back would be a possibility. Eastman Street was just in front of me and her house was just a short distance along. My footsteps seemed to make a louder than usual sound as I walked along. Soon I was inside the spacious red-bricked porch of her Edwardian house. Pots of shrubs stood around the doorway. It looked stylish and it was smart. She had obviously done well. The wide lightly coloured oak door with its embedded art nouveau glass looked imposing and classy. A temptation to walk quickly away came over me. I fought it down. This had to be. Swallowing hard I clattered the heavy wrought polished brass knocker on to the metal plate. The door quickly opened and there she was. Neither of us said a word but just stared at each other for what seemed like an eternity. I hardly recognised her, she was a beauty. She had obviously taken some time and trouble over how she would look. Her dark hair was cut into a fashionable bob surrounding her fine cheekbones. She was wearing a tailored and beautifully cut pale blue velvet suit. Her figure looked as if she stepped out of a men's glamour magazine. She was immaculately made up and still had those flashing brown eyes I remembered so well. On her feet she wore a pair of dark red high heels. I was impressed. I must have looked shabby in my well-worn soaking wet raincoat dripping water onto the tiled porch.

"Trudi?"

"Yes Bobby, it's me. Are you going to stand there gawping all day. Get in here now and give me a big hug."

It was as though she'd never been away. I hugged her and she kissed my cheek. She smelt deliciously expensive and didn't pull back from my soaking wet raincoat. I didn't know what to expect but caution was the watchword. She took my raincoat and hung it up to dry out. I was ushered into the lounge. Like her it was chic. Two blue upholstered genuine Victorian Chesterfields sat alongside a blazing log fire. Expensive looking paintings in ornate gold frames were hung expertly and mingled with carefully chosen prints on deep red walls. Overall the ambience was warm and stunning. Flashes of inferiority came over me. She'd always had that affect on me. My heart raced.

"My," she said, "I would never have recognised you apart from that scar on your cheek. You're as handsome as ever!"

The scar ran diagonally from the corner of my eye halfway across my cheek. She stroked it gently, "I always liked that."

I felt uncomfortable. It was a scar I acquired when little, playing at sword fighting and had walked into a very sharp stick. "I wouldn't have recognised you either but as I look at you it all comes back to me especially your eyes. You were always going to become a woman and look at you now."

"Thank you sir! Let me get you a drink. Scotch ok?"

I nodded and she poured me a large Bells on the rocks with a small bottle of American soda to mix with it. She turned, stood straight and looked at me closely once more as she handed me my drink. "Just how we've changed! I can't wait to hear all about you and the family and what you've been up to all these years. I've got so many questions."

I started by asking what had happened to her since I had

last seen her. She'd always been able to talk a lot and that hadn't changed. For a while she forgot about her questions. I heard about her lovers, her jobs, including the one she had in Italy. She said she had often thought of me and wished we'd kept in touch. When Vera had died Alf had cracked up badly and was sent to a psychiatric hospital before he too eventually died of a major heart attack. After that she said she had gone a little wild with boys and lovers, falling in and out of love like a bouncing yoyo. She had carried on like this until she met her now ex husband.

"He had a property development company. He was an incredibly handsome man with shiny curly black hair and beautiful long black eye lashes over the most innocent blue eyes. He had a deep honey smooth voice. His name was Kurt van Larsen. He was of a Scandinavian and German mixture. Like lots of women I was bowled over. He was also a little wild and that included with women. He wasn't criminal in his business but he didn't mind bending the rules here and there if he thought he could make a profit out of it. I hated that, and with that, and his affair, it set us rowing with each other."

I was listening to this and trying to show interest but inside my mind was racing. I was wishing I hadn't come here.

"Look," she said, "I've been babbling on too much. Tell me all about you and the others and how you found out where I was."

She knew about Mum's death but not about Dad's and admitted she was sorry to hear that. "I liked your Dad, he was always kind and generous to me."

She was about to understand why. I told her about what the twins were doing and where they were heading in their lives. I explained where we all lived and why, together with our future aspirations. I spoke about relationships we'd had and she asked if I was married.

"No, but I hope to be by the New Year some time. Sophie is my fiancée."

"Now isn't that a pity," she quipped with an expression of mock sorrow. "You were always a favourite of mine and now I have no chance!"

I really wished she hadn't made that innuendo and I forced out an insincere smile. She wasn't to know and her ability for directness hadn't changed either. Outside I could hear the rain splattering on the windows.

"So that little bird of yours was Frank at the hotel then?

"Yes, of course. I hadn't told him I was expecting you nor did I know you would be staying at the hotel he works in. He just called me and said could I guess who he thought he'd seen? I put two and two together and told him. Did you not really know him as he recognised you?"

I said I wasn't sure and I wasn't going to open up with him until I confirmation from you that it was him.

"I'm sorry about that but as we live about a mile from each other how could we not communicate. I was going to tell him anyway but he got there first."

"Fair enough, but he did take me aback."

"He's really ok. He's married with a young son and seems to be very happy. I'm sure he would be very pleased to meet you properly. Anyway, what are you and Hugh doing about this family tree thing and how can I help?"

I knew my revelation was about to occur any moment. I felt a mild sense of panic. Pausing for a fraction I knew I would have to take this in stages. We'd been talking for almost two hours. I started by describing the circumstances surrounding Dad's death and how Hugh had been given the task of researching aspects of our relatives and ancestors. I told her how he recorded Dad almost up to his dying breath and that as long as it was passed on it would be heard for generations to come. I told her also that he was shot down in the war and had ended up as a P O W. I saw a frown cross her face.

"What's the matter?"

"Nothing really. It just seems a coincidence that when I was going through Mum's things I found a letter forwarded by the Red Cross. I could make out it came from a P O W camp in Poland somewhere but because the name had been snipped off at the end I had no idea who had sent it. It was very affectionate and could have been what we would call these days a love letter. What she was doing with that I had no idea, nor could I find from where it had come or who had sent it."

She was getting closer than I imagined she would. What I had told her must have rung a few bells in her head but she said nothing more, whatever she was thinking. Nor did I. Our light hearted tone and banter had just become serious. I then told her about Dad's box, what was in it and how it was all marked out for us individually together with the letters he written for each of us and what they had said. I was keeping back the important bits and told her about the funeral and the scattering of his ashes at Lulworth.

"That sounds beautiful."

"It was all rather moving, both Hugh and Flora did an excellent job. It wasn't until a month or so later that we all met up again. When we did Hugh looked pretty pissed off. I asked him what was wrong? He told us that he'd been going through various files and had made a startling discovery." At this point I felt myself faltering and could barely look at her. It was going to have to be said and I really didn't feel like being the messenger.

"It seemed Dad had left clues for Hugh to follow up, which he did. Dad originally, God knows why or how, was given the responsibility of going through your Mum's effects, which you and Frank now have. He took nothing apart from three important letters he'd hidden in various places in Freda's house. Hugh located these…."

"What are you trying to tell me Bobby?" she interrupted and sounded baffled. A frown creased her forehead.

"I have the letters with me now." I pulled them from my pocket. "Here's the first." It was Dad's letter to Vera. She read the letter intently. It was a while before she spoke An anguished tone had spread into her voice and I saw her lip quiver.

"My God! My God I know what you are trying to tell me."

"It's more than you realise, Trudi. There is no doubt you are our sister or half sister." I was close to tears as her pain was so evident. Her face contorted and a long soft wail came from her and she started stamping both her feet furiously on the floor as she drove her fists repeatedly into the arms of the sofa.

"No! No! No! It can't be true!"

"It's true Trudi." I reached out for her but she pushed me away.

"Why did you come here? Why?" She began sobbing uncontrollably.

I was going to have to be patient. This was a major shock. When she had calmed a little I carried on.

"When we all found out it was the same for us, as it is now for you. We were all deeply shaken and shocked just as you are now. We never wanted to harm or hurt you."

Her head was bent low and after what seemed an age her sobbing subsided. She was lost for words. I stayed silent. She broke the silence with a hoarse whisper.

"Don't you see? it would have been better if I'd never known."

She let me stroke her hand. "Trudi, the three of us took this decision. As I was the closest to you it was decided that I should break the news to you and it's been scaring the life out of me for weeks. You're part of us and we're part of you. To have denied you this would've been wrong of us. Whatever you think, Trudi, we're all part of each other in this. We'd like you to say yes and to be part of us and share our lives as we want to share yours. Only you can make that decision."

She said nothing but stared aimlessly at the floor. A thousand thoughts and questions must have been running through her mind. She shook her head slowly from side to side, I continued,

"I couldn't tell you by phone or letter that would have been even crueller and cowardly. I had to see you."

"I often thought of you," she whispered and her eyes were red raw and mascara ran down her cheeks. She looked shocked and very vulnerable. "I flirted with you tonight. What must you think?"

"I've had the same thoughts too. You weren't to know."

"There's a third letter, what's that for?"

"It's a letter from Alf to Vera. It's another matter, read it and I'll explain."

She read it. "What's wrong with that?"

"There's a lot wrong. Alf was always away a lot. From the dates in his diary there was no chance he could have been around at the time of Frank's conception. Hugh has constructed verifiable lists and dates of where Alf was. He suspected Scott but it couldn't have been him either because he was still up in Yorkshire and hadn't been home for at least three months, nor was he likely to be for some time to come. It was after this he found another letter Vera had written to our Dad. In it she openly admits of being indiscreet with someone else and had landed herself in a spot of bother. This concerns Frank. He wasn't Alf's nor could he have been Scott's because neither of them were around at the time. The chief suspect, according to Hugh, was the lodger she had taken in, a man called Stanley Weatherall. He seems to have left shortly after she had told Alf it was his. Hugh has been able to track him down but we will never know because he died some years back in a road accident."

"Oh fuck" she whispered, "I can't take all this in," and she reached out for my hand and held it tightly.

"Poor Frank. Poor Frank! What am I to do, Bobby? I'm so confused."

"That's for you to decide. We shall never tell him and he may need never know, But he may wonder if you tell him of your connection to Scott, that he too could be his son. You know it wasn't because of the date structures but he needn't know he wasn't Alf's either. That would stop any anxieties he might have. Personally I think it would be cruel and damaging to let him know otherwise. Our main concern is you. There's another thing. Your Mum had a miscarriage before you came along. That was Scott's also."

Her lip quivered. "This is all too much. Too much!" her fist was tight and she quietly pummelled the arm of the sofa. Her reply was disjointed and she had no idea what to do next. "You maybe right about Frank. How do I know?" She dabbed her eyes with a large blue handkerchief. "This is all too sudden and too much. I don't know what to do. I must think about it a while. I just don't know what to think. She looked up at me and her eyes held an imploring look.

"I don't truly know what you should do either, Trudi. All I know is that the twins and I want you as part of us. There are also some legal aspects we need to consider in your favour, if you would be happy for us to do so."

Again she said she didn't know and needed time to take all

this in. I agreed and asked, in view of the state this had left us, would she mind if I gave dinner a miss. She said that was okay as she was no longer in any state to cook anything anyway. She said she didn't want me to leave. I couldn't stay nor would I if I could have. I poured her a stiff drink, which she took with a trembling hand. Our eyes met and we were both full of sorrow. I loved her very much and always had but even more so now.

We held each other tight and she whispered "My brother," she paused, "My brother, I love you."

I looked at her directly and a tear rolled down my face. "Trudi, our lovely sister, you are welcome to come home."

I left her with my head spinning. Part of me wanted to run and another wanted to stay and help her. It was her life and it was better if she reached her own decisions. I felt an enormous sadness and a vast emptiness. All I wanted was us to be whole. I hoped and prayed she would accept us as her own. She had a strong mind and whatever she decided would be the right choice. I walked across the square, and decided to give the pub a miss and went into an Indian restaurant and ordered a Mushroom Jalfrezy with naan bread and side dishes. I ate mechanically without any enjoyment. My mind raced over the events of the last few hours. When I left the restaurant the rain had stopped but it was cold. I turned up my collar; thrust my hands deeply into the pockets of the raincoat twiddling the odd pieces of cotton and paper tissue, which remained there. I bent my head low and headed back to the hotel unable to fully assimilate what had happened. I was relieved to see that Frank wasn't on duty. I couldn't deal with him as well. I'd left Trudi with both of us feeling a strong affection for each other almost like those younger days. She had asked me to stay but I didn't feel that was safe or wise. Besides I needed time and space to clear my head and as I'm sure she did. When we said goodbye to each other we clung together like lost limpets and I felt a surge of love and pity for her. She'd lived in years of ignorance. It may have been better if she'd stayed that way. We'd promised to talk again soon and she'd let me know where she was. I'd walked away from her uneasy in the knowledge that I had altered her life and it could never be the same again. Had I really the right to have done so, but there weren't too many options on the table. Dad's legacy was beginning to behave like a falling row of dominoes. I got to my room feeling totally drained. I took a shower, shaved before falling into the bed emotionally sapped. Sleep consumed me in one mighty gulp.

For breakfast I had Kentish Kipper Savoury with anchovies and mushroom ketchup on wholemeal toast. After my second coffee I felt I was set to check out. If Frank were on duty I would deal with him. Once in my room I cleaned my teeth before packing the overnight bag. I put on my Dannimac and left the room. As I suspected I saw Frank was back behind the desk, and he'd seen me coming. He looked apprehensive. I had to put him out of his misery. I walked across to him and he nervously looked up at me.

"You were right, Frank, I am your cousin Bobby. I couldn't acknowledge that until I met up with Trudi, as now you well know. I met her last night." I held out my hand and he shook it with surprising strength and vigour. His broad smile made me feel ashamed I'd blanked him so rudely the other day.

"I knew it must be you and when I read your name and saw your face. I rang Trudi to tell her I thought I'd seen you. I was surprised to hear that you were on your way to see her to discuss the family tree or whatever."

"We did all that and I found out what I needed." This was

sort of a lie but I wasn't going to compromise Trudi. "Will you accept my apologies? I was a bit abrupt with you, wasn't I?

"Don't worry about it. No apologies are needed, Bobby. It's been a long time since we last spoke. I hope we can again soon."

It felt strange, almost endearing, after all these years, for him to call me by my name. I told him that Trudi had spoken lots about him. And I was certain that she would tell him all that had happened to us since we last had seen each other. He looked pleased and proud. I hoped she wouldn't undermine that with what she now knew about who his biological father might be. I silently reprimanded myself. Of course she wouldn't! Truth at times is painful and not always necessary. We embraced and I told him I was sure we'd meet again as his sister and I would be keeping in touch. I liked him. I felt bad as I left but if he knew the truth he would have felt far worse.

The 46 bus had the same driver as when I arrived. As it headed towards Paignton I knew my mission had been accomplished. It had been every bit as painful as I'd envisaged. I ran the events through my head realising that Trudi was a remarkable and successful woman. Like us all she wasn't immune to life's pain. I was relieved it was all over and now all I wanted to do was get back to Flora, have a stiff drink and tell her everything.

Flora was perfect, saying she didn't want to hear anything about the meeting until we met with Hugh. What self control! I'd have been blowing a gasket to know everything and every detail but she'd always had that cool element of self-control, which Hugh and I both envied. We drove over to *Pimlico* and met up with Hugh who poured some large drinks. The two of them went quiet, looking expectantly at me. I started with the unexpected encounter with Frank.

"I wouldn't have liked to be in your shoes. You're very brave, said Flora.

"My God!" said Hugh; he seemed stung, "Something must be wrong with my research."

"Forget it. You might be clever but you can't be expected to know everything. Frank lives and works there. You missed it. That's all."

He shut up. I told them how I had felt and how I got around to telling her and her stunned reaction and all the questions she'd asked. How could I express my emotion and the huge bond I felt with her? I wasn't able to convey that. Maybe they would feel that way too once they had met her. Beneath this, I said that I remained uncertain whether she would want to meet us again.

"Will she?" said Flora.

"I hope so, she didn't want me to leave."

"And what about Frank?"

I told them of my last meeting with him. For him to know of anything was not something we could get involved in. It was up to her to tell him or not. We wanted her with us and drank a toast in her honour. For some time we spoke of her and the things we had done and had said back then. It seemed like yesterday.

"Oh, by the way," Flora said, I forgot something. These arrived the other day."

She handed me two envelopes. I opened the first. It was from the local group of newspapers who said they were publishing a picture of mine I'd sent them of a kingfisher taking off with a fish in its beak. They also asked if I would be interested in doing freelance work for them on a regular basis. There was also a cheque for seventy-five pounds for the photograph. A large smile crossed my face followed by a strident whoop! My first ever sale! Hugh and Flora promptly toasted me. I wondered what the second could be about. The envelope looked expensive and the franking mark had some capital letters, initials I couldn't place, 'NPM?' Not too carefully I pulled the seal apart and pulled out a letter. My jaw dropped. It was from the *National Photographic Magazine*. A photograph I'd taken of an owl about to kill a mouse, which amidst all that had been going on I'd forgotten about, had won first prize in their national competition. They were going to publish it as their front cover in their next edition. Enclosed was another cheque but for rather more. One thousand pounds!

* * *

I hadn't heard from Trudi for over a week and was beginning to get anxious but it was for her to make contact. I resisted the temptation to call her, but It was not long after that she called. She said she was okay and had decided not to tell Frank what Hugh had found out. Apart from that she did tell him everything I'd told her. He too was amazed and had become quite emotional. She told a white lie, kindly to reassure him that Alf was his father and no one else and most definitely not Scott. She said she wasn't entirely sure that he completely believed her, but hoped that he wouldn't take it any further. There was a pause in the conversation,

"There have been enough emotions and too many casualties in this saga, hasn't there?"

I agreed and again there was a pause. I sensed she was moving to the central issue and felt an attack of butterflies in my stomach. What had she decided?

"Bobby, I've got over the initial shock now and have had time to think long and hard about this predicament."

Yet again she paused and I said nothing, not knowing how I was going to react to what she might say.

"I've had quite a few sleepless nights running this through my mind trying to decide what would be for the best. First one way than another. So I've made a decision and I hope all of you won't mind."

I began to have a sinking feeling at what her decision would be. She was going to reject our proposition.

"If all three of you want me to be part of the family and only if you all agree, the answer is yes please!"

I punched the air and let out a loud cry. "Will we have you! We can't wait! We want to meet you as soon as possible." I heard her laughing and crying all at the same time

"Me too. When can we meet?"

I told her I would talk to the twins and would get back to her as soon as I could. After we'd said goodbye I got back to Flora and Hugh. It was arranged for the following weekend. I called her back and it was agreed she was going to stay with us over the weekend. Hugh would come over lunchtime Saturday. I had to wonder if he'd found anything else from Dad's poisoned legacy?

I sat down quietly on my own and ran through the events surrounding Dad and the predicament in which he'd placed us. He'd a lot to answer for and he'd caused us all pain and heartache in various ways. Hugh, I'm sure, would find more skeletons and I felt so sorry for him having to be the harbinger of so many unpleasant things. He hadn't asked for it but he has a sense of professionalism, of which he is rightly proud. I know he'll take this to the bitter end if needs be. Dad hadn't been stupid. He must have known what fall out would occur from the storm he would create. He'd meant us to know. Was he trying to reunite us all? I suspect he was. He wanted us to realise that the isolationism, which surrounded him, was not what he wanted us to inherit. He had understood his own almost inescapable dilemma, of that I was certain. I began thinking he was emotionally damaged in some way to plot this unsafe course of action for us. What were we going to do? In one way we seemed powerless. He'd mapped out suggested paths for each of us, me with the photography, Hugh with the research and where that could lead him and with Flo he was definitely pointing her towards a spiritual path. His choices were correct for each of us but why had he done this? Couldn't we have found out for ourselves without this high drama? All I could see was disruption in our lives. His chart for Flora seemed appropriate and there seemed no danger of major change in her life. She was a seeker, always questioning the meaning of life and the nature of consciousness. That didn't seem to present her with doubts over her job. For Hugh and myself he'd thrown a level of uncertainty in our way. Hugh was questioning whether he should continue with his job in physics. I was hankering after a job as a photographer. Since he'd given me those cameras I'd never wanted anything so much. So far he'd never asked for us to forgive him. It was not a certainty that any of us could. I didn't hate him. I was beginning to pity him. He was achieving his ambition of making us change our lives to pursue something we normally only talked or dreamt about. Why hadn't he attempted this when he was alive? What a way do it! Unbeknown to me changes would be continuing for some time yet.

PART TWO

SIX

Flora

I've been amazed and shattered by the recent revelations and events surrounding Dad. It has jolted us all. He was a person we never truly knew, nor would he ever let us know him. Frankly I'm not even sure I want to anymore. What he did was disgusting. If nothing else he's caused us to look at our own lives and to try and work out what they mean and where we are each heading. I'm full of uncertainty and afraid. It seems to me life is treacherous, full of dangers and what you see is not necessarily so. I've no idea where I'm heading or why? My head has become a merry-go-round, creating conundrums about life. Since his death I've had countless nights of lost sleep. I've just been laying there, trying to make sense of this mess and I'm not a step closer. This was my Dad, for Christ's sake. What the fuck did he think he was doing screwing my Mum's sister? Not only that, he commits the grossest stupidity of getting her pregnant. Twice not once! Didn't they have French letters, Durex or Ona in those days? I know bloody well they did. And they weren't too different to what we have today. He must have been mad or the war unhinged him, given him a sense of recklessness. Did the thought of knowing that the next night he might not be alive have something to do with his attitude? Even if it had it wouldn't make it right. I've tried to work it out but can't find the answer. Not that's of much use now. I'd loved him but knowing what I do now, that feeling is decidedly in the balance. It turns out he was an arsehole. What sort of Buddhist was he? Obviously it hadn't done much for him. All this is going to take some time for me to come to terms with, if I ever can. The boys, I know feel the same way as me. They don't understand Dad's behaviour either. They've been superb and are both having difficult tasks to deal with. In this respect. I seem to have been let off the hook, or have I?

Dad always seemed to have a soft spot for me and looking back the same was with Trudi. Now I know why. He hardly ever seemed to get angry and the only time I saw him get really mad is when he discovered that Bobby had joined the Communist Party. With me he had always been gentle and caring and I can honestly say he never abused me in any way whatsoever. His legacy to me is intriguing but also a paradoxical reflection of his own life and behaviour. It's going to take some time to get my head around all this. With his spiritual aspirations how could he have done what he did? I can't help thinking that ultimately it was a callous betrayal of Mum and all of us. I've always suspected that he'd had a sexual appetite by the way he looked at certain women or when he got to read glamour magazines. Who knows what he got up to, spending long months away from home. For all I know he could have been a serial adulterer. The love I felt for him has taken a huge knock although I know he loved me deeply, unconditionally. I don't know whether I can recover from this and unless I can make some sense from it all I'm not certain whether I shall ever be able to forgive him. As a man he was interested in manly things, such as cars and fishing. Hugh and sometimes Bobby were often included in his trips while I was left alone with Mum who was ailing considerably at the time. He was kind to me but not in an exclusive sort of way. Well, it's got me thinking about my early and present life and I'm not sure where to begin. I guess at the beginning is a good place to start.

I can remember the day I was born.
I expect that will cause you expressions of ridicule, disbelief or whatever. But I know. I don't care what any one else thinks, for me it's true and that's all that matters. It's nothing to do with anyone else whether they believe it or not. It's my truth, not any one else's. I was born first and Hugh came out fifteen minutes later. So on that score I'm the eldest! Being born was painful and scary and the bright light of the world was startling. I'd been taken from my cosy warm place to a cold an airy space with no support or surrounding warmth. When you were born in those days the nurses would hold you upside down and slap your bottom to make sure you were alive and okay. It was painful and made me cry, which is what the nurses needed to know. I'm sure most of you won't believe me.

I was close to Mum but didn't really know Dad as he was away so much due to the war. I didn't understand war. Even at my young age it didn't seem right. Killings, mutilations and a host of other horrors appalled and horrified me. I would brood on these things under my bed covers at night and knew for certain it was wrong. I would also spend long hours sitting alone in churches thinking about this and what God might or might not be. There was something of a quiet peacefulness in churches. They helped me get my head together, rightly or wrongly.

When I was still tiny we had a new addition to the family, Bobby. As we grew older like all kids we fought and squabbled amongst ourselves and also with our playmates. When I think about that I suppose it was a form of war but which adults play more lethally. Dad was pretty much an absent figure. Initially we lived in Canterbury not far from the Cathedral. I recall this vividly although Hugh can't remember a thing. It wasn't until we moved to York that his memory cells came to life. Freda was a good and natural Mum who always put us first before anything or anybody else. She would have died for us if she had to. I can't begin to imagine what it must have been like for her living with all the hardships and uncertainties of war, never knowing if Dad was alive or dead. Yet we got through it all and we never knew until Hugh told us that he had been a P O W. Well, I think it's time to say a little about myself.

I vividly recall my first day at school with Hugh. How scary was that! It was so strange and menacing. There were lots of other children. Many looked frightened and were crying. There were others who seemed cocky and confident and teased those who seemed most upset. The classrooms seemed dark and were made mainly of wood with large wooden desks and built-in inkwells. The teacher had a big pictorial flip chart, which started off with the alphabet, A is for apple, and B is for ball and so on. We also had slates and chalks. I always had trouble writing the number two. These days it's known as a lack of spatial awareness. I made lots of friends, girls mainly and the boys would chase us about playing 'kiss chase' which horrified me. That meant if they caught you, you had to let them kiss you, Uggh! I'd one special friend called Tessa. I was a bit jealous of her, as she was so pretty with long blond plaits. The boys would chase her about all over the playing fields. I was left alone pretty much, being a bit of a plain Jane. I caught her out once kissing a boy behind the school annexe. I dissolved into laughter, which she wasn't too pleased about. As you get older you seem to lose touch with those you were friendly with in the past. That was the way it was with us and I've no idea if she is still alive or if she is where she used to live or what ever happened to her. It doesn't seem important.

Back at home not long after the war had finished Dad got a job with a photographic company but to do this he had a bike ride of over an hour there and back. Mum and Dad initially had little money so a car was out of the question until later. Mum got a job as a shop assistant in a local greengrocer's shop to help make ends meet. Every penny counted. There were times when they would row with each other mainly about money. Mum always came out the worse, as she wasn't able to match his argumentative skills. This didn't make him right. I thought he could be a bully. I would always support Mum. He didn't really get angry but was very cold, mathematical and steely when dealing with her. When she flared into a rage he would just burst into laughter, which made her even more angry. They weren't that happy together. Whether this was due to his wartime experiences I shall never really know. If it was, I suspect now that it might have had something to do with him looking elsewhere for what he wanted.

His spiritual side was strange and I knew so little of it. I've an amazing memory but can't connect with him and Buddhism. It was well hidden. When I listened to that experience he related on his tape recorder it sent me back to something that occurred to me when I was just eight years old. We'd all gone for a picnic at the base of a place known as Crooksbury Hill. It was quite high and difficult to get to the top. It meant scrambling up sandy gullies covered in prickly thorns and gorse bushes. I decided to try but the family didn't want to, they said it was too tiring. I set off alone. I really had to concentrate to get to the top. It was all very physical and I had to struggle to make it to there. My legs hurt and I was panting for breath. At the pinnacle was one of those Ordnance Survey plinths, which tell you in every direction where places are and how far away they are. I could barely see over the top of it, me being a bit on the small side. I'd put some effort in getting to the top and the views once there were stunning. I stood there transfixed as a warm breeze rippled through my hair. I stood still for some time. In some strange way in my silence and stillness I felt that I was being drawn into something but I didn't know what and I remember becoming aware of the quietness around me. For some reason I became very aware of my breathing. Something stirred inside of me, which caused me to remain standing stock-still. The enormity of the sky and the vastness of all that was around me transfixed me. How long this went on I can't say but it seemed like only minutes. I was too young to understand the passage of time. For a few moments in the time I stood there I had the incredible sensation that I was alone in the world, in the universe and amongst the stars. I was it, although I didn't know what that was. An vast sense of relaxation swept through me. That memory has always lived with me and in retrospect it wasn't dissimilar to what Dad had experienced and recorded before he died. As I remained standing, not moving, I had a feeling that all my pores were opening up and I felt the breeze cascade through and out of every single one of them. It felt beautiful. Everything around me and as far as I could see went into perfect slow motion, flying birds, tree branches and all living and moving things were bound in a perfect symmetry of motion. It was total perfection. My birth again flashed clearly in front of me. Momentarily, even at that young age I was aware of the deepest joy and happiness. Standing there and just for that moment my perceptions altered and I was no longer alive or dead. There was no me, nor had there been, ever. I didn't know what to say or how to express it. I was dumbfounded. Everything I looked at was glorious and radiantly beautiful and I kind of knew of my connection with an infinite past. I wasn't scared. All this at eight years old. How long I stood there transfixed I shall never know. I didn't want it to end and had no idea what was going on. When it did end I began to cry. I was aware of Dad eventually coming to find me. He looked at me oddly and asked if I was okay. I could barely hear him and tears ran down my face, which he gently wiped away with his large white handkerchief. I never told him nor did I tell anyone else, That memory has faded over time but left a lasting impression on me. There was something there he'd spotted. He said nothing either. After that I often saw him looking at me as if he knew something I didn't. Perhaps I knew more than he did.

That memory often surfaced causing me to feel a deep dissatisfaction with organised religions and my schooling. Somehow they seemed to be bound up together. What I experienced back then said more to me than anything coming out of the Bible and all that obscene bloodletting and spillage which seems to run through it from cover to cover. Education went hand in hand with it through its morning religious assemblies with those weird hymns, which I couldn't make neither head nor tail of nor can I today. There always seemed to be something missing for me. On top of this I had the anxiety of Mum's condition, which was going downhill fast. Then I knew nothing about Parkinson's disease. I recall one day she was trying to spread cold butter onto slices of bread but her hands were shaking so severely she had no coordination in any of her movements. She was all over the place and her hands wouldn't go where she wanted them. The butter was everywhere but the bread. It rapidly got worse in a very short period of time. She knew the affect this was having on us all. She was no fool and knew what the outcome would be. That must have been so distressing for her. Dad, to give him his due, was considerably attentive to her especially in the latter months of her life.

* * *

I enjoyed a good relationship with my brothers especially Robert. Looking back, most girls liked him as he was always fun to have around and had a permanent twinkle in his eye. I can honestly say that overall we were a happy family in spite of Mum and Dad's strained relationship. The only odd one was Dad who never really opened up about anything unless it was a car or a fishing trip. He wasn't hard on us, just so distant. One day I sat on the floor and was idling through his bookcase and found three red covered volumes of books on opera with lots of coloured pictures of posed statuesque naked Wagnerian Rhine maidens. That made me giggle. His father's signature, 'Percy Anderson' was on the inside cover. Then I found, tucked at the back of the bookcase and out of sight, a large brown volume entitled *The Facts of Life*. I'd never seen this before. You can guess what was in there! I can see why it was hidden from sight. That opened up my eyes. There were lots of photographs and diagrams, all very clinical and sexual. They could be called 'rude bits.' I was totally fascinated. I'd always suspected this sort of thing and this confirmed it. One Chapter was headed 'Masturbation.' The page was heavily underlined. Who'd done that I didn't know. It said it was the path to degeneracy and insanity. I didn't know what the word masturbation meant so I looked it up in the dictionary. It dawned on me. "Oh that. I do it most nights." I wondered whether I'd go mad too. I never heard of anyone who had gone mad and I knew most girls and boys who were friends with me did it also. Even in those younger years I was able to think those warnings were a load of rubbish. I never gave them a second thought after that. We did have lots of 'rude' fun in the woodshed, which was only natural and nothing to get concerned about. We're all still sane!

I ceased to be a virgin when I was sixteen. It wasn't that great an experience. It was all a bit messy and full of a fumbling rawness. His name was Sam and he was two years older than me. That happened in a nearby hay field where you could lay down and wouldn't get spotted. At the end of the day I thought the build-up more interesting than the clumsy gropes we went through. I did touch him but not inside his trousers. He had his hand inside my knickers and I found it rough and far from what I'd imagined. After it was over I felt sore. It also had hurt. I wasn't expecting that. I didn't ask if he'd done it before but he knew I hadn't. I never did it with him again as he seemed to lose interest in me after that. Well, as time rolled by I had several more experiences and they were certainly getting better. There was one boy called Peter who quite fancied me. I had the same feelings for him. We had sex as often as we could. Where he got his 'Johnnies' I never asked. We did it here, there, and everywhere. I thought he was *it* and saw myself married to him. I didn't tell him that, as this would have scared him off. It was not to be. He found a new love and said goodbye to me. I was devastated. After that I went off the rails a bit with men. I was up for anything on offer. Ultimately it was an empty pretence and I was all over the place. It wasn't until much later on when I met Mark that some real stability came back into my life. I fell in love with him.

This weekend Bobby and I are going over to *Pimlico* to speak with Hugh, as there are a few things to discuss between us.

More importantly Trudi is making her first visit to see us all. I think we all feel nervous and excited. I expect she too must feel the same. Bobby had the advantage over us of having met her previously. He went to great lengths to explain to us that she was a lovely and natural person who above all, was very warmly human. Bobby has changed so much and has become incredibly intuitive and full of perceptions. He's maturing. Also I'm pleased to see that he's been pursuing his wild life photographic portfolio. I've seen a few of his efforts and to say the least they are stunning. He's also been getting commissions from a few magazines and newspapers. Again the hand of Dad has altered a life. Hugh is as taciturn as ever. He looks like a man on a mission and I suspect all that he's sorting through has caused him a few problems and heartaches. I suspect he'll become a writer, either full or part time. Whatever we think of Dad, good or bad, he has unquestionably began changing our lives.

It's nearly lunchtime and Trudi is due to arrive shortly. I suspect she's feeling exactly the same as us. She hasn't seen us for so many years; the prospect must be daunting for her. Who wouldn't feel that way? The bombshell that dropped on her had to be an unusual and rare event, difficult to assimilate. My recollections of her are unclear and according to Bobby she has changed considerably and out of all recognition. Only her arrival and physical presence could complete the picture. The weather was warm and we sat on the patio sipping at very pleasant cocktails but our ears were strained to hear her drive up.

Hugh looked at me with a serious expression "Flo. I've found another envelope from Dad and it's addressed to you."

We all went silent as he handed me a large white envelope with Dad's bold writing in black ink marked, 'For Flora only,'

"I'm not going to open this today but only when I feel ready to do so and that could be a long way into the future. I will, of course, let you know what it says. We've more important things to see to. I expect it's more revelations. I think we can do without any more of those at present."

"I expect it's another pile of shit." said Bobby. "How can you not open it?"

"There's no hurry. It's not going to go away and right now is not the time and place."

"He's also left another, which I told you about and here it is. It's addressed to all three of us. As you can see his instructions are clear, '*Not to be opened until at least three years after my death.*' What am I supposed to with that? At the moment I'm not sure whether I want to open another bloody thing of his ever, ever! I feel so fucking angry. What was going on with him? But I'll do as I promised to show that at least between us three we have some decency and integrity."

I agreed. We would honour our pledges whether we liked it or not.

"Bloody open it," said Bobby.

Before any reply we heard the rasping growl of Trudi's Porsche crunching up the gravel drive. The envelope was forgotten. We all stood up and Bobby leapt up to open the front door.

She walked in. I saw a beautiful woman expensively dressed in a tailored light pastel pink Jaeger suit but looking nervous and afraid as she and Bobby embraced. To me she wasn't that unrecognisable. I could still recognise her face from all those years back. At that point I dissolved into tears. She did too. Hugh looked incredibly moved. We all stood with our arms around each other. Trudi and I wept, bound by the awful knowledge of our mutual past. Some minutes later we gained some control. Hugh looked at her reached out with his arms and hugged her tightly. "Welcome home, Trudi."

I couldn't speak. I just wanted to hold her as tightly as possible so as not to let her escape. She gripped me like a vice. Her fingers dug hard into my waist. I could tell she wanted reassurance. She didn't need to ask as we all wanted her with us, and to become part of us, which she'd been denied for so long. Bobby was the most relaxed of us all. He'd had a really difficult task as our messenger but unlike us he'd climbed the first obstacle. Without him it could have been more than awkward. What must she be feeling? Hugh led us all to the patio and fixed her a Whisky Manhattan. There was an awkward silence and I knew I had to break that.

"Trudi, all this must be quite a shock for you."

Her voice had become cultured and educated across the years. "What Bobby told me blew me apart and I didn't know what to believe and coming here today has really scared me. It's so unreal but here you all are, like me, older and we're not kids any more. I'm still trembling." She put her head down and held it with her hands before looking up again. "Part of me didn't want to come here and part did. I thought that if Bobby could go through with it so should I. I now know what he must have felt." She reached over to Bobby and squeezed his hand. "You all look so well and good I'd never have recognised you, but now I can see the things I remember about you haven't all gone."
We said the same about her.

So we sat there for hours, eating snacks, drinking and discussing our lives and our parents and what they were all about. Needless to say Scott and Vera didn't fare too well. Hugh in some ways is the most affected as he had discovered all this. Dad dictated

174

all that history to him and didn't even hint at this. How could he have done that? Hugh need never have said a thing but then he would have been behaving just as Dad did. We all found Trudi extraordinary fun. She got to teasing Bobby about his earlier escapades especially the ruder ones between them both. She told us things we never knew! She was so unabashed, so much so that he frequently blushed but he didn't seem to really mind. It was then we got a bit more serious and got back to Scott, Freda and Vera. Trudi was in a quandary as she had no idea about any of this and suggested that perhaps she should change her name. Hugh said that should be her choice, not ours and we would respect whatever she wanted. He started to discuss Dad's estate, how much it was worth and that we had all decided that we wanted her to be a beneficiary, the same as us.

"Stop right there," said Trudi, raising her hand at the same time. "I don't want a penny. I know it's so very kind of you all and I'm touched. I'm not hard up, as you can see. That money is yours by right and legally I'm not entitled to a cent, nor do I want any of it. You keep it, Enjoy that bastard's money. You've earned it. You've making me more than happy today and that's all I want from you all." A small tear trickled down her cheek and she shook her head. "Even if I was poor my answer would be the same. I've always wondered what had happened to you all and what you looked like. Through your efforts, which you needn't have gone to, I now have a family after all these years and I want to see you often, if you'll let me. Please understand though my answer about the money is a big fat NO!"

We all looked at each other and for a moment we were stuck for words. It seemed so unfair. Any doubts I had about her simply vanished and my admiration for her escalated. I think we all felt the same.

"Trudi, you must take a share, you could help your brother or a charity perhaps. Please reconsider won't you?"

"No. No. NO!"

I decided to give the matter a rest. Maybe another time. The boys said nothing but both leant across and cuddled her. She smiled and there were more tears from her. It was turning into an emotional afternoon. Why shouldn't it?

As the evening approached Hugh asked her was she still happy to spend the night here.

She paused a moment "Absolutely."

Bobby got up to get her bag from the Porsche. I told her I always had everything a woman needs stored in the house and said she was more than welcome to any of it adding the words, "Sisters are sisters and always share what they have."

A radiant smile crossed her face "Oooh! I do like the sound of that word, *sister*. Say it again, please, Flora."

I repeated what I'd said and we held each other's hands. She said there wasn't anything more she could wish for.

Hugh added, "We all feel the same and I'm glad because I've a surprise for you all after dinner."

I just hoped it wasn't another of Dad's blockbusters but by the way Hugh was smiling I knew it couldn't be.

The meal was very Italian with lots of red and white native wines to match. I think everyone was extremely relaxed if not a little pissed. But hey ho; occasions like this are as rare as hen's teeth and I think it was just what we needed. I made two desserts, which I was glad I did because they vanished at the speed of light. One was a Peach and Lemon Tart and the other a Lemon Mascerpone Cheesecake. Yummy indeed! After this we settled for an expensive Louis Bouron Cognac, reserved for very special occasions plus pots of coffee. I think much later into the evening we'd all become very mellow. Trudi is witty, cultivated and has a very engaging personality. Beneath it all is a woman who is as strong as iron when she needs to be, as we saw that over the issue of Dad's estate.

There was a bit of a lapse, so I asked, "Well c'mon Hugh, what's this surprise you said you had?"

"I thought you'd never ask! It's fireworks."

A collective *Whoo!* came simultaneously from all of us. With that Hugh got up and reappeared shortly with the most massive box of fireworks I've ever seen. They were spectacular and I made a note to share the cost with him and so did Bobby. The sky became alight with coloured flares, rockets, exploding clusters and all sorts of wiz-bangs I couldn't name. Eventually they came to a stop and we gave him a round of applause.

"I haven't quite finished yet," said Hugh.

He asked us all to stand back further. As a physicist and scientist I guess he knew what he was doing. He produced an enormous pair of fireworks, which seemed linked together. He lit the fuses and retreated. There was an enormous noise as this thing or things took off dazzlingly high into the sky cascading with a procession of various multi-coloured incandescent sparks, which then exploded with enormous bangs and whistling noises. Then with one final almighty bang, unfolded in the darkened sky in giant purple and white letters for a brief minute appeared the word *TRUDI* spelt out in coloured pyrotechnics visible across the night sky for all to see for miles around before gently fading away.

"Oh my God," I shouted.

Bobby grabbed Trudi and she was shaking her head in disbelief before running across to Hugh and clinging onto him.

"I'm overwhelmed. Utterly! I don't know what to say or how to thank you enough."

"No need. It was owing to you."

I can see Hugh has many sides to him and this has to be

the most beautiful thing he could've done for her. He really has a human side, which he keeps hidden, a bit like Dad, but when some thing like this happens I begin to realise what he's truly made of. How he got it all done and worked it out, is mind-boggling. Bobby hugged him close together with Trudi. Looking back on the day it was memorable and unforgettable.

We have become proper brother and sisters and now frequently visit each other. For Trudi it was a revelation and she told me it gave her sense of completeness. Nor did she forget Frank who must have felt left out of things. When we next went to visit her she had decided to ask him along as well and asked us if we had any objections. Of course we hadn't and it would be good for us to see him again. She really is kind and thoughtful. A date was fixed for a month ahead and he agreed to come over but on his wife's insistence, to come alone as it could be a very private and personal get together. I thought that said a lot for her.

Since that meeting at Hugh's I still had not opened Dad's envelope. Part of me wanted to and part of me wanted to rip it up and burn it. It was still on my dressing table where I originally threw it down. I knew I had to open it. Within me was a restlessness. I knew something was wrong in my head. Things were jumping around all over the place, probably due to the recent disclosures and events. I picked up the envelope and stared at the writing I knew so well. What was going to be in it? More horrors, more shocking disclosures? I put it back on the table, turned and walked away but stopped when only halfway across the room and walked back to it. I picked it up and savagely ripped it open feeling a strong surge of anger that he obligated me to do this. I pulled out several sheets of immaculately typed paper.

SEVEN

Slow Boat from China

When we got to Trudi's house Frank was already there. He smiled a nervous grin at us as he stood up. He was about six foot tall with dark long hair, which covered the top part of his ears and neck. There were small dimples around his mouth. He was dressed in stylish light coloured charcoal, complete with matching leather jacket, roll neck jumper, faded jeans and dark leather boots. He was good looking. Bobby went over to him and gave him a hug.

"Hi Frank, good to see you again."

"Hello Bobby, same here. I guess there could be some awkward moments here but let me see Hugh and Flora." He didn't lack confidence.

Trudi introduced us. Time does alter perceptions you carry about people. The brain fails to make adjustments for the process of time. He repeated what Trudi had said, that he wouldn't have recognised any of us although Bobby seemed to be the exception. We wouldn't have recognised him either. Again there were recollections of him that came to my mind. Trudi stood in the background as we all hugged and again I felt that surge of happiness run through me. Frank like us all was now an adult but also had his own family. He had no awkwardness and was direct and straightforward. If there was any awkwardness it was from us. As the afternoon went on, stories were exchanged of what we had all got up to when we were children and we talked a lot about events gone by, our memories of each other and what happened after we lost touch with each other. We all got on well and he laughingly said he'd always thought that Trudi and Bobby were in love with each other because they were always holding hands and she was always giving him bigger or extra helpings at the dinner table. I was surprised to see both of them blush and look at each other. They were smiling. We all burst into laughter and so did they. It was very relaxed but the conversation gradually got more serious. Inevitably it moved into the relationship between Scott and Vera. Frank had been fully informed by Trudi and admitted to being shocked by what she'd told him. There was a pause.

"Trudi assures me that your Dad wasn't mine but I've still got an uncomfortable feeling that's not the whole story." He looked directly at Trudi. " I'll ask you again Trudi, was Alf my true father or not?"

Poor Trudi, I could see she was in deep water. The room went deathly quiet and she'd lost her composure.

"Frank, I don't… I don't know of any other reason for you to think otherwise. Of course he was." She wasn't convincing.

"I've known you all my life, Trudi, and I've a feeling you're not telling all you know and …"

Hugh interrupted him "I did all the research and discovered all the evidence about Trudi but not about you. Isn't that enough for you?

I could see Hugh was trying to protect her.

"No it's not."

This was not turning out in the way we had expected and a feeling of dread came over me. Hugh like Trudi was being pushed into a corner. Frank was close and had spotted something about Trudi's demeanour that he knew only too well.

"You always were a rotten liar, Trudi."

She went white. Something was going to have to give. She'd been accused of being economical with the truth. She gave us an imploring look, which wasn't lost on Frank.

"Sort this out, you lot. Now." He stood up and walked over to her baby grand Salk piano at the end of the room, sat down, lifted the lid and began to play a beautiful rendition of Chopin's music, which I recognised as the Nocturne in E Flat Minor Op. 9, No. 2.

It seems Frank had many sides to him. He's impressive. I knew he was trying to send us a message with the music as its haunting refrain filled the room. I felt for him. Trudi turned away from him whispering low, "What am I to do?"

"There's only one honest thing to do, and you know what that is, Trudi." said Bobby.

Hugh nodded "There's been too many lies and deceits corrupting this family, you Trudi are part of this family. Do you want to behave like Scott? Unless you tell the truth now I'll have no more to do with it."

I knew Hugh meant what he'd said; he was never one to mince his words. I nodded my agreement as Chopin's music echoed around the room. Frank looked dignified and composed as he played but God knows what he was feeling. I could see Trudi had arrived at a decision. She was going to tell him. He finished playing, took a deep breath, shut the piano lid got up and walked back to us and sat down,

"Well?"

"I'm going to have to say what I never wanted to," said Trudi."

Frank's expression remained impassive.

"All I wanted was to protect you. I wish all this'd never happened. Forgive me."

She went on to tell him that Alf was almost certainly not

his Dad nor was Scott. She asked Hugh to give the details. Hugh spoke, looking sad. "Frank, forgive us all from trying to hide the truth from you. It wasn't done for anything else but to protect you and a concern for your feelings. Will you firstly forgive us?"

Hugh continually surprises me with how sensitive and human he really is.

Frank replied. "I understand and yes I do. Now tell me the truth."

Hugh spent half an hour without interruption. He started with Scott and Vera, the letters he'd discovered which related to Trudi. He also spoke of others about Vera's miscarriage, which was undoubtedly our Dad's. He discussed Vera's letters to Dad, which admitted to an 'indiscretion' and her subsequent pregnancy. She led Alf to believe it was his and his letter to her telling of his happiness in the forthcoming baby. He told Frank that none of the dates fitted Scott or Alf, they were away on war time missions and work for months on end and it just didn't fit. The culprit was in all probability the lodger who once he was found out did a swift exit. Frank remained as impassive as ever but when asked for more information Hugh told him the name but he'd died in a road accident and there was no way could he follow that route. For a moment there was silence and we were all looking at Frank.

"Oh shit! I loved Dad so much. He brought me up and whatever, he *was* my real Dad not that other arsehole. I loved him to bits."

Seeing this dignified and surprisingly cultural man cracking up was causing me an emotional problem. I wanted to reach out to him but he had to deal with this in his own way. His composure broke. His shoulders shook and he was crying. Jesus, we hadn't intended this but Frank had insisted and rightly so. Trudi held him close and I could see we were all very uncomfortable. In a way I wished this meeting had never happened but something told me it had to be this way. As Hugh had said it was time to end the family tradition of covering up and the deceit it bred. We got up and walked into the garden leaving them to be alone together.

After that the atmosphere went very flat. Nothing was said between us and I knew our hearts went out to Frank. He'd been very determined and brave. I liked him enormously. When we went back inside I moved next to him and put my arm around him. He very naturally leant his head on my shoulder but said nothing. I sensed the years unravel in him and the pain he must be feeling.

"Frank" I whispered in his ear, "We've all felt the same. We know how much it hurts." I stroked his forehead.

He lifted his head. His eyes were red raw. "Thanks Flo. I'm ok now I think. It's not me I feel sorry for it's Dad. He was cheated. What was my mother doing? And why?"

"It seems she had something that men liked and she must have known it but it got her into trouble."

"Some story I'll have to tell when I get home. To think I haven't seen you all these years and when I do this is what happens. It's unbelievable."

"When we found all this out, we were devastated too. We know how you feel, believe me."

He squeezed my hand hard and a faint smile crossed his face. We had a new friend.

There we all sat for a while and conversation slowly began to pick up although I felt in an emotional limbo. Trudi's cooking was far better than she had led us to believe. Sadly, our appetites had all but vanished and nobody was drinking much either. This was a situation that we hadn't wanted. In the kitchen Trudi pulled me to one side.

"My God, I'm mortified. I fucked it up!"

"No you didn't. Would you have wanted to live the rest of life with that lie? Would you? This was meant to be. All secrecy is now over. If nothing else we've learnt from all of this and that must be a bonus. Don't desert Frank; he seems to be an exceptional and lovely person. I for one would love to see him again and meet his family. It was hard for him if not harder than for us."

"You won't neglect me, will you?"

I thought my, oh my. In a few short months she wanted to keep us so badly. "Of course not. You're our sister and we love you very much."

"I love you too, Flo, and your brothers."

We hugged and I knew It was time to call it a day. I felt sorry for her and Frank whose world like ours was now irrevocably altered. His loyalty to his Dad was touching. I couldn't help thinking *"What the fuck is it about human beings who invariably cock things up from beginning to end. Life it seems is a series of errors one after another."* We eventually left Trudi and Frank together having agreed we'd all meet again soon.

* * *

I quickly scanned over the letter, there were several pages and it was immediately apparent it was not what I was expecting. There were no confessions. This was something totally different he'd written to me.

It started,

'*Dear Flora, this letter is not to discuss the various issues you all by now may have found out* about me and now more than likely loathe me. This is to tell you a true story, which helped formulate my later life. It may do the same for you. So just for now put to one side whatever you may be thinking and read this story.

It began just after the war had finished and concerns a good friend of mine back then called Bill Perrin. Bill was discharged from the forces based in India. During his time there he became fascinated with Eastern religion and decided that Buddhism would be his path, particularly Zen from Japan. We both had a similar interest but his question was more demanding than any thing I knew. He constantly asked himself 'Who am I?' or What am I." It bothered him constantly. Once he got back home he was unable to settle. He was wealthy in his own right but a very solitary and strange man. Once he landed in England he packed a tent and a few belongings and decided to walk across the entire south coastal paths of England to wherever it would lead him. He had no destination or goal in mind. Not long after he started he began having a recurring dream, which really bothered him. In that dream he saw himself, running along a beach and a Chinese man who was waving a clutch of papers at him was always chasing him but never caught him. The dream never seemed to go away. He had another problem, his mind was permanently preoccupied with that question, 'Who am I? What am I? Where am I? For him there were no logical solutions and it ate away at his mind and he would repeat these words over and over again constantly. In his self-absorption he thought he was going mad. He walked morning noon and night and this question and the dream continually stalked him. It was his koan; a Zen Buddhist practice of internal questioning designed to lead you to a profound spiritual awakening.

Flora, I've never forgotten how you looked that day, as a child standing on the top of Crooksbury Hill and watching you weep. Remember? Well I guessed something strange had happened to you and I think I was right wasn't I? This is why I am writing to you in such detail. There seems to be link running through all this, to which in some way you are connected.

One evening Bill was walking in the dark across a cliff top and still asking his haunting question when he stumbled on a hidden rock. As he did the moonlight suddenly appeared and what he'd fallen against shook him rigid. Standing in the moon's light stood a large stone Buddha. He was so shocked he promptly fainted. It was a while before came around when it was getting light. It was indeed a stone statue he'd collided with. It seems that he had 'inadvertently' crashed into a Japanese garden belonging to a large house nearby. The owner had spotted him and went to talk to him. After hearing of Bill's interests he told him he'd been a Colonel in the army and like Bill was deeply interested in Eastern philosophy and religions. He told Bill he could pitch his tent in the garden and stay for as long as he wished. He stayed for several months and I think the Colonel was sad to see him go. He'd enjoyed the long conversations about the East had over a glass of wine or two. Eventually it had to come to an end. Bill decided to move on. Something was calling him. His recurring dream and his perennial question wouldn't leave him. Bill was also a gifted potter capable of producing work of the utmost delicacy for which he won many awards. His walking took him down to Cornwall to the town of Mousehole near Land's End. He told me he was certain that was where he was meant to be. He survived well and opened up his own pottery and ceramic studio. He also married a local girl. But whatever he did, that dream, that question continued to haunt him. He had no peace.

One day, some years later there was a knock at the door and when he opened it he was more than surprised to see a Chinese man standing there who was holding a book. He asked Bill if he could help him. He wanted to know if there were any Buddhists in the area. Bill felt his blood run cold. He told him he was one. Bill was looking puzzled as was the Chinese man. He looked long and hard at Bill and proceeded without warning to tell him that he'd always had a recurring dream. In his hands he had some sacred Buddhist texts that he had to deliver to a person in the West. He said he could never catch him. He was always running. He lived in a place at the end of land. He said he'd searched everywhere on maps of the world but couldn't find that place. This was the closest he could find. It matched. He also said that when he got close to catching him he would dive away into a large mouse hole and vanish. Flora, work that out will you! Bill stood there and his jaw dropped and he burst into tears. The Chinese man first name was oddly, Charles. Both of them had been having the same dream for years separately across the ends of the earth. Astounding synchronicity! Their dreams were now complete. You may be asking what's the point of all that or what happened next? They held each close and both cried. It was all falling into place. From Charles, Bill learnt that a renowned Zen monk was coming to England and was going to run an intensive ten-day meditation in a remote Dartmoor farmhouse in a month's time. Bill jumped at the chance, he now might be able to come to terms with his constant question of 'who am I?" Bill remained a good friend of Charles for the rest of his life and Charles eventually dedicated a book to him. He also handed him some very important looking papers complete with impressive seals. He told Bill they were Chinese Buddhist texts meant for the west and were to go only to someone deemed worthy and who would treasure them and pass them on when he too felt it was time to so. For some reason he deemed Bill as that person. Bill remained astonished, this was a rare honour indeed. It was my good fortune for I remember going to that very same meditation retreat as Bill. One evening in a darkened room, lit only by a few candles he began telling us this entire story. The atmosphere was intense and you could have heard a pin drop. As it happened Bill reached for what he was seeking. He had the most intense spiritual experience the monk had ever witnessed. He had solved his question. Sengai, the monk, led him into a field where lambs were being born. One was born

dead and Sengai sat Bill in front of it and told him
not to move until he truly transcended the meaning
of life and death. He sat there alone for over
twenty-four hours meditating on this new problem. We
could see him out there and then we heard the most
enormous laugh and Bill was up on his feet and was
jumping for joy. He knew! Sengai wanted him as his
new heir and spiritual successor. Bill thought about
it, he was married and loved his wife and had other
responsibilities, so he declined. He didn't want a
monastic life or the responsibility of heading up an
order of monks. Instead he embarked on opening a
Buddhist hospice and formed an association to
promote the idea. It flourishes till this day.

Why am I telling you all this? I want to open
your eyes to what possibilities there are for you
out there. I know that you will understand that life
is a solvable mystery. I generally cocked up but you
are strong and I know you won't make the mistakes I
made. I want you to go where your heart leads you.
Ignore what you think about me, where this is
concerned it's irrelevant. I've always sensed your
sensitivity in matters like this. I just hope this
story can give you some inspiration to tread the
never-ending path.
I love you very much, Dad.

I slowly sat down and my hands trembled. My mind was
whirling. I felt utterly bewildered and confused. His letter has
blown me away. What am I to do now? I don't think I can take
any more of Dad's shocks or blockbusters. He was correct
though, it was true, I did understand Bill's dilemma. In a way

my childhood experience on the top of Crooksbury Hill wasn't so removed from his, albeit in a much minor way. Having just read that letter, Dad became even more of a paradox than ever before. I held my head in my hands just going over it time and time again. I was shaken and it was true. He'd spotted years ago all the things that concerned me about the mystery of life and the nature of consciousness. Life and death walked hand in hand. I know it and he knew it. He bloody knew about me, the devious bastard. How dare he touch me in this close way after what poor Hugh had to find out and tell us? How dare he! What more has he planned for us? Please God, no more.

Bobby was out so I called Hugh and told him what was in Dad's letter and the affect it had on me. He didn't say a word until I'd finished.

"Flora, I'm so sorry he did that to you. He seems to have done something to all of us. He'd no right but like it or not he's fucked us up in more ways than one."

Hugh is a person who rarely displays a lot of emotion but I could sense this had upset him. It was getting too personal for all of us. What we couldn't understand was why he'd left Trudi out of his considerations. I couldn't help thinking, *or had he*? Why was he playing this game? Perhaps his inability to communicate left him few alternatives and this was the only way he could handle it.

EIGHT

Trudi

You would find it hard to believe how startled I was to hear from Bobby. I remember thinking, who's that on the phone? When that dark brown voice said it was my long lost cousin Bobby I was flabbergasted. After all these years! I had to pause a moment to realise who it was. When we'd calmed down a bit he said he was researching the family history. I was intrigued. I was shortly to find out but not in the way I'd imagined. I'd always been very fond of Bobby even though we'd lost contact across the years. I'd often thought of him and had no idea where he was. I was totally curious how he'd found me and what it was he wanted to ask me about. When we put down the phones I was thrilled to have spoken to him and couldn't wait for his visit.

That call brought back to me a host of memories and whether Bobby could remember them all, I hardly knew. Looking back I think we were kind of rough and rude with each other. Even then I knew I could dominate him although he didn't seem to mind in the slightest. When Scott started sending him over here for long weekends. I thought I was in heaven. As a little girl I had no way of understanding what it was I felt but I guess I may have been in love with him. He certainly filled up my thoughts. My brother Frank got on well with him and my other cousins. We had enormous amounts of fun, although Frank would often torment me relentlessly about Bobby telling me I loved him. Bobby was a big sissy for loving a soppy girl.

I remember once, we were playing near the gravel pits, which were made up of large lakes of smelly water covered in reeds and ridden with hidden banks of weeds. We could both swim although Mum and Dad had told us we weren't to go there as it was too dangerous. Only a few months back one of our friends drowned here. He got tangled in the thick weed but whilst he could swim he couldn't get himself free. He began to panic and then became exhausted before he sunk beneath the water and died. We were mindful of that and splashed cautiously around the shore. We'd laugh for hours and hours and got wetter and wetter as we played splash fights. We'd skim stones across the water for hours to see who could get the most bounces. Bobby usually won. His record was nine skips. I remember once I saw something odd in the water. I went over and trod on it. It was squelchy and when I saw what it was I screamed. It was a dead black and white dog. It was bloated and decomposing. Around its neck was a knotty rope weighted down with heavy bricks. We ran home and I never wanted to go back there again. It was one of those memories that never leave you until the day you die. Yet those days did seem endless. They had their own special unrepeatable magic and I never wanted them to end.

Since Bobby had told me about his Dad and my Mum, it got me thinking. Looking back now I realise there were enough clues and signs that there was something going on between them. But as a kid I didn't make the connection. I was too young to understand. For instance, when Bobby's Dad was home he would often visit our house, especially when Alf wasn't there. I came home one day and the radio was on playing dance music.

I called out to Mum and she didn't answer. After a few minutes she came down the stairs with no slippers on and wearing her red and white striped dressing gown. Her hair looked messy and her face was red. I thought she must be feeling unwell and had gone to bed. She looked flustered. About five minutes later Scott came down. He was in his ordinary clothes and didn't look as he'd been to bed or was unwell. He smiled at me patted me on the head. He said he must be getting along and walked away. It didn't seem strange at the time but in retrospect it was obvious what'd been going on. Wasn't it? Bobby's Dad was always hanging around. Sometimes Freda would appear but as Mum's sister they didn't seem to get on too well. I can recall they had an enormous row about something that seemed to be connected to Scott, but what, I didn't understand. I recall Freda storming out and doors being slammed. Now I understand what that must have been about.

As I got older I thought, in my childish way I'd marry Bobby. I didn't really understand anything. I'm sure he would have been horrified if he knew. Sometimes when we were alone we'd play 'Mums and Dads.' We had pretend rows about money, food or whatever. Other times we'd get into bed together but not before we'd taken off all our clothes. In bed we had childish kisses and cuddled a lot and he'd touch me in rude places, which felt warm and nice. His willy would get stiff and I would stroke it, which he seemed to like. I don't think either of us had any idea what it was all about, nor did it happen very often. When I was about ten my breasts began to develop. I liked this as it meant I was becoming a grown up. Bobby would poke at them with his finger and make me laugh. Shortly after that I had my first period. That frightened the life out of me. I remembering standing in the bathroom with blood trickling down my leg and

193

not knowing what it was. I thought I was about to die. I ran screaming downstairs to Mum who looked startled. She cleaned me up and told me that what was happening is what women experience once every month until their middle age. She told me I'd started early. She then began to explain sex to me and how babies came about and because of this I had now to be very careful and not let any boy get me pregnant. She must have spoken to me for hours explaining this and that, not that I could take it all in. The end of my innocent childhood had begun. I felt curious and frightened about the adult world all at the same time. I was still a child but another small part of me was becoming woman. The significance of this brought into focus the fun games I used to have with Bobby in bed. I had a realisation what that was all about. I never allowed it to happen again. In some ways I now felt more grown up compared to him. He was still a boy and I knew so much more than he did. So in this way we moved apart, very gradually. I began to fancy other boys. My figure was becoming curvier and Bobby as an attraction was beginning to fade fast. I'd always liked him and I never really forgot him but there were so many more fish in the sea. I could tell boys liked the look of me and soon I was being asked out to the cinema or dances. Mum didn't mind. In this respect she was pretty good and always told me what I might expect; things like kissing and touching and not to get carried away. Her big thing was for me not to get pregnant, for if I did my life would be finished. She could be quite scary at times. After all, from what I now know she was an experienced campaigner at all this. I knew what she meant so I didn't get carried away, well not every time At least. I stayed a virgin although that on several occasions was in peril but I remained intact. There were several strong boy friends I had in tow and dear Bobby had become a memory. When we as a family moved

I never saw him again. Later I accepted a proposal for marriage. This was my first and only husband. I was so naïve I never realised he was two timing me right from the day we got married. Why do so many men do that? It was only after a couple of years that I discovered what he was at. I overheard him on the telephone.

"Jean, I love you and I'd leave tomorrow if I could. You know that."

That's what he said and I've never forgotten it. I confronted him and he owned up. Neither did I approve of the dodgy deals he got up to in business, which was causing severe friction between us. A short while later he left me and not long after that we were divorced. It would have happened sooner or later. I was childless and without a husband. He was a wealthy property developer and he wasn't ungenerous towards me. I got a substantial settlement. I decided on a move to where I now live. Not for one moment did I suspect the Andersons were nearby. I got a cracking job, which I still have and it's very well paid. Materially there's nothing I could want. I just feel a bit emotionally hollow at times, like something is missing from my life.

I'm going to ask you again now, can you imagine my astonishment when I picked up the phone and the voice said it was Bobby? I couldn't believe it. How had he found me? What did he want? Well, the day he was due over I was so anxious, so scared I couldn't keep out of the toilet! My butterflies were swarming especially when I heard that door knock. And there he was, older, more handsome and that same twinkle in his eye. He still had that kindly manner, which I'd always appreciated. You know the rest and I'm not going to repeat it all over again. When he left I sobbed my heart out. He, I now knew, was my half brother and I'd often wondered why I was so attracted to him. Perhaps that was why. I remember shouting out loud when he'd left. "Scott and Vera, what a pair of cheating bastards. I hate them!"

The three of them hadn't disowned me. They wanted me as part of the family. I hadn't got one and there was no way I was going to turn this down. I just wanted time to reflect on all the possibilities that could ensue. I had to think about them as well as myself and I didn't want complications or any of us to have any regrets. I love them all.

I love them all because they are so different to most people I've met. They have this relaxed and tolerant attitude to life and its problems. I know now how they must have felt when they found out about all this. Each of us has undoubtedly been affected in different ways. I can gather already from the little Bobby told me, it's changing their lives and I don't think it's going to stop there. I can't stop thinking about my parents nor of Freda and Scott. What a bloody mess they dumped us into. Did Mum love Scott? Did he love her or was it all pure lust? From what I've heard it was the latter. It seems Mum got around a bit too much and when I think back to all her dire warnings about me getting pregnant, that was rich, coming from her, wasn't it? Scott always made a particular fuss of me and he was my favourite uncle. If only I'd known! He was always kind to Frank and me and he seemed so wise. I really thought if I had a big problem I could turn to him. How wrong was I! It was him with the problem. He couldn't keep his dick under control nor his trousers on. Mum must have enjoyed it too and she couldn't keep her knickers on either when a man looked at her. I often wondered why so many men would knock on our door at times. She would tell me they were collecting the rent, coal or milk money and I believed it. Alf got on with everybody and he often said he liked Scott, as he found him helpful and informative about so many things. We all decided one year to go with Scott's family to a holiday camp near Christchurch. That summer was blissful and the weather was brilliant and we had the time of our life with both Dads throwing us into the sea, swimming pool and generally mucking about with lots of fancy dress parties. All us kids rode horses around plus enormous three wheeler bikes through the town. It all seemed such innocent fun without a whiff of sexy or adulterous goings on. Freda and Vera were still a bit reserved about all the jovialities of the camp and didn't join in too much. I now think that Freda wasn't too well and was jealous of Mum who was so different and outgoing from her. Did she suspect anything? I think that must have lurked at the back of her mind somewhere but she never let on. There was no evidence on that holiday that anything was going on. That for me, was how it'd always been.

My favourite, as you know, was always Bobby, and goodness hasn't he changed over the years. I always remember adoring him and used to look forward so much to his weekend visits. That's all in the past now but my memory maintains my fondness for him. His news totally devastated me but I know how difficult it was for him to tell me. It must have hurt him terribly. He has dignity and style and I'm one hundred per cent certain he and Sophie will be very happy. I hear now that their wedding will be in the New Year sometime and I can't wait. Just to think all those years ago I thought of marrying my newly discovered half brother! Bobby is so creative especially with those cameras that his Dad left him and he has a massive talent especially where wild life and nature are concerned. I'm sure he has a future in this direction. I've seen some of Scott's work and they are undeniably brilliant but he never pushed it. Bobby is on a par although he has a different approach. I've seen his work too and it is different but also excellent in its own right. He should pursue this course. Hugh finding me has made me so happy, so much so you wouldn't believe it.

Hugh I'm also fond of but in a different way. He has his own special qualities, which are quiet and undramatic. He's systematic and awfully well organised. If an aeroplane was in trouble he would be the sort of man I'd want as the pilot! He should have taken a career in politics. I think he would have done well with his research skills and detailed analysis of all the components of an argument. I sense also that his stability holds this family together. He rarely seems to make a fuss. If anything, Flora and Bobby think he's more like his Dad but Hugh's been brought up in a different generation and is far more open. He's obviously so very human and incredibly intelligent. When I heard he'd got a first class honours degree in physics I wasn't surprised. He'd told us that Scott also had a leaning in that direction. It's not surprising that Hugh's inherited something of that. When he's able I know he will continue his researches into the origins and development of the family. He said it was far away from being finished and he could see it taking another year at least as there was masses of paperwork to get through. However, he said, because of what had happened he says he has lost interest and his heart isn't in it. Understandable! We all admired his thoroughness and his unstinting acceptance of the promise he made to carry out his Dad's dying wishes. The next time we saw each other he called me over.

"Trudi won't you please reconsider our offer because . . ."

I cut him short. "Hugh, I thought I'd made it clear last time we talked about this. Do you have a difficulty in understanding the word NO?"

He sighed, "but it seems so unfair."

"No it's not. It's kind of you all but the answer remains the same as last time. Now that's the last time I want to hear about it. Understood?" I knew I was being steely but that's how it had to be.

He sighed, and shook his head and made a tutting sound before suggesting, "You might like to look at these." He handed me a pack of photographs. They were old black and white shots of both our families when we were all much younger. Some of them were of us as babies sitting in those old fashioned high backed carved wooden chairs that photographers used in those days to pose children. They made me laugh. The boy's dark hair was plastered down and the girl's blonde hair was fluffy, almost unreal with large ribbons and bows. There was a group of us. We had our best clothes on and looked surprisingly porky considering the food austerities of those years. Vera and Alf, Scott and Freda were also there as we all posed for those stiff and starchy photographs they went in for in those days. Our parents looked so young, barely out of their teens. I gasped.

"I've never seen these before. Where did you find them? Were they in that box? And what was he doing with them?"

"I don't know where he got them from and yes, they were in the chest inside the family Bible. There're lots of others and I'm trying to put them into some sort of order but like everything else it's going to take some time. There are pictures of some people who at the moment I don't know who they are. I'm wondering if you might know? I'll show them to you later."

I've got a feeling there'll be more surprises and discoveries to come.

Hugh told us that there was a time when he'd thought of joining the RAF like his father but instead opted for university. I told him that was probably the best decision he could have made.

He laughed. "Well, I don't know so much. I could have had had a flash uniform and be flying all around the world with women flocking after me!"

"Well, you haven't, so there. And just because you might have had a posh uniform doesn't mean us girls are going to chuck ourselves at you! Just you carry on with what you are doing." I leant over and poked him in the ribs with my fingers and he chuckled. He looks lovely when he smiles and drops that serious expression from his face. He's not an identical twin but there are strong similarities with Flora. Bobby doesn't look like any of them. He looks more like his mother and he certainly has the most easygoing personality of them all. Thinking of Hugh, I'm wondering whether he could turn this saga and what he has discovered into some sort of book? I've suggested as much and he just looks thoughtful but makes no comment.

Flora is a total sweetheart. In many ways she's an enigma. I wouldn't say she's the black sheep of the family but she's certainly different. She's total woman, devastatingly pretty with dark auburn hair, which cascades around her neck and shoulders. Her flashing green eyes are almost hypnotic. There's an unfathomable quality, which exudes from her even to this day. I can still remember as a kid she'd be talking or listening to you when she seemed to drift off into a daydream with a far away look in her eyes and appear to be disconnected to what ever conversation was in progress. I've noticed that she still does that today. It makes me wonder what's going on in her head. Even as a kid she used to come out with the strangest remarks. I recall once, she was looking up to the sky, which was dark and cloudy and it had begun raining. She asked quite seriously "Why does rain soak the good people as well as the bad. That can't be fair."

Who could answer that? She would often come out with odd observations that no one else would have thought of. I wouldn't say she was religious but there was something going on with her that pointed her in a different direction to most people. She seemed to think in a way that we never did. But she was very kind and would help me out when ever I needed it. I think she would give you her last penny if you asked for it. She didn't seem to care about money or material things. She had musical talent, especially on the piano and violin and had no difficulty in understanding how music worked. Frank liked her a lot, I could tell. That gave me my chance to get at him like he'd teased me about Bobby. Of course he denied it and would get cross. It was Flora who got Frank interested in music, especially the piano. Her music was important to her and later she branched out into drawing and painting. She would paint large fiery works. Very unusual, which wasn't surprising. Looking back, what she did was reminiscent of Blake. Some people thought she was weird but I remember Scott and the way he approached her. It was as if a sea of eggshells surrounded her and he didn't want to break them by treading on them too hard. He seemed to understand her and there was a definite and sensitive link between them both.

The unpleasantness of discovering who my real Dad was, was greatly softened by the way she treated me. I couldn't have wished for more gentle and careful consideration. She knew. Frank has also managed to struggle through this and I was so delighted he wouldn't deny Alf as his father. He earned a lot of respect from all of us and we were determined that he and his family should be part of us also.

NINE

Hugh

I was on my way up to the National Physical Laboratories based in Teddington. I was working on a complicated measurement project and it looked likely that I'd be there all week. The weather en route was deteriorating and flecks of snow began drifting down. I wasn't thinking of the project but of Flora, Bobby and Trudi. A thousand things were whirling through my brain and I tried slowing them down and concentrate on them one at a time but not with a lot of success. Christmas wasn't too far away but when I got to Teddington the roads and streets looked empty. Was it the weather? I found my hotel, *The Mulberry* and checked in. It wasn't great but it would do. It was six in the evening. Once in my room I unpacked my black leather Antler suitcase. I took care hanging up suits, trousers and shirts to let the creases fall out. I walked over to the mini bar, opened it, and selected a whisky, adding a good quantity of ice before pouring it into a heavy tumbler. Holding my glass my mind went blank. I stood staring out of the misty window at a dark and menacing sky. Soon I couldn't see it. Within minutes the wind had risen and the snow was falling hard. Flakes did a samba on the windowpane. It was turning into a blizzard out there. Quickly it became a major snowstorm. I turned away and mindlessly switched on the TV. I heard the snow was widespread over much of the country, reports that thousands of motorists and travellers were stranded and not going to make their destinations this night. I was glad to have made it to the hotel and knew if this weather continued I wasn't going to be able to get out to the Laboratories in the morning. I took stock of my room. The green flowery wallpaper looked faded and tired. It complimented the fat green upholstered armchair that looked as if had suffered over the years from the weight of too many bums. Mine became one of them. I was thankful the room was clean, dust free and warm. I sipped at my drink and began to think about Dad and the events of the last six months and how they had impacted on us all. I couldn't sit still for long and began pacing around the room. The recent events created thoughts and memories, making me restless. I opened the cream painted door and walked down a brown walled narrow and red-carpeted corridor. At the end of it was an exit. I pushed it hard and opened it. Great gusts of cold air and blowing snow wafted in. I didn't move or do anything. Snow was landing on me and melting immediately. I remained motionless. I clutched my glass, now almost empty, gazing vacantly out at the worsening weather. Everything about Dad's entire mess welled up inside. I wanted nothing more to do with it or him. The swirling chaos of the weather matched my mood perfectly. After a minute or so I shut the door, shivered and walked back up the corridor to my room.

Unlike the others I can't remember much about my early childhood years. My main memories were about fishing with Dad and getting him to talk, albeit reluctantly, about his wartime experiences. When I think about it he never really said much and tried to close the conversation down as soon as possible. Now I can see he left so much out. It was as if there is something missing in my life, which shaped and stretched out my feelings and emotions regarding others. I wasn't able to open up or experience degrees of emotion like Flora or Bobby could. The isolationism protected me from getting involved with people and in all probability, hurt. In some ways it made me feel superior. I despised displays of emotion. They were for the weak, the sentimental. It was all too mawkish. Was I too much like Dad? In my heart I didn't want to be. Over the years I'd ignored my heart and listened only to my head. I don't want to do that anymore.

My strongest memories revolved around my education, learning and university work towards my degree. Nothing else mattered. I had a few girlfriends but was never that much bothered with them. Flo and Bobby had new ones almost weekly. It was hard to keep track from one week to another who was currently in favour. I can honestly say I was never in love with the few I had. I don't think that would have bothered any of them either. Something good has come out of this for me. Seeing the impact on Trudi, Flora and Bobby has made me aware of my isolation. I was divorced from the pleasurable aspects of humanity. That's not going to continue. I guess I've been too serious a personality for most fun loving girls.

I went across to the mini bar and pulled out another scotch, poured it slowly into my glass and looked back out of the window. The snow looked blinding and everything outside had ground to a halt. Nothing was moving. It was totally quiet. Was I the only one in this hotel? There is a snug and cosy feeling when warm and dry and looking out into the bitter weather knowing you are safe and protected. It reminded me of when I was a kid laying in bed, buried under blankets and hearing the rain smack on the windows outside. Wonderful. I realised I was smiling.

I know I lack Bobby's creativity, which is now more evident than ever. Nor can I match any of Flora's artistic abilities at music or painting. Everybody said I was more like Dad. Physics and science protected me from getting involved in everyday interaction with others. I could get locked into a problem and all else would vanish. That is an aspect from which I now want to distant myself. Dad used to be my silent hero but not any more. His wooden chest is nowhere near sorted or emptied. I've catalogued everything I've found to date, births, marriages and death certificates plus information from various trade papers and directories of the time. I've scoured old newspapers in libraries and even found in *The Westminster Times* in the mid-eighteen-eighties, adverts the Andersons had been placing for domestic servants and cleaners for their home and business. This was something Dad had missed. How much else was there? Rather startlingly I had also discovered that Charles Anderson, Percy's father's father, had owned up to forty properties in north London in the Pentonville and Seven Sisters area. What had happened to them? Did Robert, Percy's father inherit them and sell them? There was no record of Percy getting any of them. So who did get them? Another mystery to investigate. Once I get going in this direction I'm fascinated and forget about the emotional nuances surrounding our family. It becomes an abstract assignment until some pertinent name or event reminds me that it all has to do with us. I mustn't let myself forget it's about people. It's not just a research exercise. I realise also I haven't told anybody about the discovery concerning the properties. I promise myself to do so.

Glancing up I can see that outside the snow is as relentless as ever. There was a call I had an urge to make. It had been in the back of my mind for some while. I had to stop putting it off. Picking up the phone I called Ella. She answered. Her voice was soft and sweet and I'd always enjoyed listening to her. As I hadn't spoken to her for a while she was surprised by my call. I could tell she was pleased I was calling. I felt uncertain about what to say. Why was I feeling so bloody nervous? I mentioned the weather and told her I was holed up in a hotel in Middlesex.

"It's snowing here too but not as bad as you seem to be getting. If it wasn't for that and it being so far away I'd come over and see you."

I felt a small jolt. "That would be more than welcome. I'd love to see you again."

"I'd like to see you again too. You hadn't called me for a while so I thought you didn't want to see me again."

At the back of my mind I realised that somewhere along the way with her I'd dropped into my isolationist protective role, my fear of relationships and being hurt. I didn't want this with Ella.

"Far from it. What with my work and all this family research I always seem to busy with something or other. I hadn't meant to ignore you and quite frankly Ella I'm feeling stressed with it all. So many things are running through my mind I needed a break from it with a real human being."

"What's one of those?"

"Somebody like you?"

There was a pause on the line. I didn't give her time to make a reply.

"When I get back on Friday would you like to come on over?"

"That would be lovely."

"Do you want to stop over?"

Another pause. "I hadn't expected that."

"Is that a yes or a no?"

"It's a yes."

We chatted a little more and when she had gone I felt a

surge of inward pleasure and noticed my sweaty palms had moistened the handset. I was amazed I'd asked her to stay over. Where had that come from? All I knew was that my fondness for Ella taken a leap forward.

Then I got to thinking that if it hadn't been for Dad and his illness, Ella was a woman I may have never had met. So many issues and unsolved connections continued to bombard me, infiltrating my creaking consciousness about Dad and his legacy. It also struck me as odd that the house name was the same as where the ancestral business links had been based. Perhaps that was a deliberate intention? It surely was no coincidence. There had to be a connection. Yet another mystery to look at. I gulped heavily on my scotch, letting it slowly warm my insides and give me some brief mental relief. Looking out at the blizzard I also thought about that envelope that after three years would be waiting to be opened. What was that all about? I decided it was time to go to the dining room for dinner.

PART THREE

TEN

Aftermath

Flora and I, together with Sophie, Trudi and Mark had been invited over to *Pimlico* for the Christmas holiday with Hugh. He told us that Ella would be there and so would Trudi, which pleased both of us. We couldn't resist a knowing nod and, '*I thought as much*' look at each other. We laughed. Poor Hugh, he does struggle where romance is concerned. We hoped it was going to work out for them both.

It was Christmas Eve and seven of us sat around Hugh's blazing log fire eating home made mince pies and sausage rolls courtesy of Ella and drinking mulled wine and rum punch. Inevitably the more relaxed we became the conversation got around to Mum and Dad and those wartime and post war Christmas's. It's odd, isn't it, that we can talk about them in this way as if nothing has happened? When Dad wasn't there it must have been difficult for Mum with all those shortages and no money to go around. Even Flora had trouble remembering much about them until Dad was permanently home. They did try to give us a good time and Christmas never really started until the night before Christmas Eve. Dad would bring home a big tree and we were kept busy making coloured paper-chains and Mum brought a large multi- coloured paper bell, cut in so many different patterns, which she would hang from the centre of the living room with all the chains and decorations radiating from it across the room. It was very exciting. Dad brought Mum a present and I suspect now he also must have brought Aunt Vera something as well, although there's no way of knowing. Mum would be in the kitchen preparing the turkey and all the other cooking associated with Christmas. She had made the pudding some weeks back and we had all taken turns in stirring it and making a wish. In their quaint and old-fashioned ways those times were memorable. We all had a turn in relating our memories and stories and how they compared to today's festivities. Ella fitted in well and was happy to relate her contribution of her Christmases in Stow-On-The-Wold where her parents ran a small hotel. I wasn't too surprised to see her and Hugh holding hands. Things have moved on here! I like Ella very much, she's such a caring person, intelligent and non pushy and I suspect very sensitive. I couldn't help thinking how the pair of them would get on. Undoubtedly she's the sort of woman that Hugh needs. She has a quiet fortitude that would suit him. He never made spontaneous decisions and I wondered what role his heart had in their romance? A lot I hope! He is in so many ways like Dad but I'm not going to tell him that, it could upset him.

As we continued I said, "Isn't it odd if it hadn't been for Dad's illness none of us would be sitting here together."

"I was thinking exactly that too," said Flora.

Hugh remarked, "He's still reaching out to us and won't leave us alone, will he?"

"Is there any good coming out of this mess?" Flora added.

"Yes, there is. I've got a real family now, who I love. I think that's something good, don't you?" said Trudi.

We couldn't disagree. I couldn't help thinking either, that if Hugh had dared he would have said something about him and

Ella as being something good too. That thought made me smile.

What would happen to us ultimately only time would tell. Could Dad have foreseen any of this? He may have to some extent, but not entirely. To me it seemed like a high-risk strategy. He never needed to have let Hugh discover this and if he hadn't none of us would have been any the wiser. But that was his intent. He must have known he risked our total condemnation. Oddly none of us as yet were prepared to go totally down this route. The jury was out on the matter. I thought it was time to change the subject as both Sophie and Mark were being left out of things. It was time for some good news. I grabbed Sophie's hand.

"Everybody, just to let you know we've fixed our marriage date. It's on the twenty first of January at Torbay, Paignton Registry Office, at two pm. You are all expected to be there!"

A round of applause echoed around the room and both Sophie and I were hugged and kissed by everybody. I felt happy and I know Sophie did too.

"Well done you two. Well done indeed" said Hugh.

I couldn't help wondering whether he might, in the near future, be making similar announcements about him and Ella. Maybe from Flora and Mark there could similar news. Nobody said anything about that.

* * *

We both wanted a very low-key wedding and that's what we got. We invited a few friends and work colleagues so in total there were no more than thirty at the ceremony. It felt strange to be getting married although Sophie was walking around all day looking like a Cheshire cat. She was happy. I've never seen her so happy. She wore a very fine light white dress with large pink polka dots and a small matching pink and black hat surrounded with a black ribbon and bow. I still felt hung over from the night before but for the groom that can be forgivable. It doesn't happen often does it? I'd thought of taking and setting up the cameras myself but that would have removed me from Sophie and the guests so I contacted a photographer colleague who agreed to take the pictures. I knew she'd do a good job. Not once did Dad get into my thinking and that was the same for all the others. It was a great day.

Earlier we'd bought a house nearby. We named it *Great Expectations*. We thought that was a bit novel! It also reflected our hopes and desires. It was a delightful Edwardian building with four bedrooms and wonder of wonders, a magnificent olive green Aga! Outside there was a huge wisteria tree and rose trees around the walls. Sheer heaven! We spent our honeymoon in the Normandy area of France. It was cold with frosty mornings but amazingly relaxing. Could that be the Calvados? I felt intensely happy with or without that drink and I knew Sophie did too. Not long after we got home I returned to my work and the photographic assignments became intensive. I was getting more work than I could have imagined, and was having trouble keeping up. Sophie was still working as a political researcher and we both loved our respective work. One evening she returned home later than usual.

"I've got something to tell you."

"What's that, honey?"

"I've been to the doctors and guess what?"

"What?"

"I'm two months pregnant."

For what seemed an eternity I froze and was struck dumb.

"Say something then!"

"What! Oh wow!" I jumped up, grabbed her, hugged her close and kissed her.

"You don't mind then?"

"Don't be so bloody stupid. It's the best news you could ever give me." I nearly fainted. I grabbed her and twirled her around the room. I couldn't believe it "I must tell the others." I was almost shouting and jumping up and down with sheer joy. The pair of us jigged and cavorted around the room laughing with huge grins and smiles. She told me the baby would be due some time in November. I was literally astonished by it all.

"There's more"

"What's that?"

"I don't want you to read too much into this but she's asked me to go and see her again in a few months time"

"Why, isn't that normal?"

"It is, but given Hugh and Flora are twins she wants to make certain whether or not I might be a possibility for twins. Honestly, Bobby there's little chance of that."

"Bloody hell!"

"If she suspects or can hear another heartbeat I'll have to go and have one of those new scans which can actually show on a screen what's going on inside!"

That bit of news got me thinking and to be honest, I wouldn't have known how to react even if it were true. I thought it better if she told Flora and I'd tell Hugh. Flora was beside herself with excitement and spent nearly an hour on the phone talking to Sophie. Women never seem to know when to stop talking! I told Hugh and also about the possibility of a scan. There was a slight pause, in his normal manner, before his congratulated us, then added,

"If Sophie did have twins then they'd be the third set of twins in the Anderson family."

"What!"

"I found out where Dad told me to go back in the nineteenth century about the first recorded account of twins in the Anderson family. There may be more but as yet I haven't found any. Then there was Flora and me and if you two, by any remote chance, had them then three sets in one family is pretty good going. Whatever, it's great news. You should both be very proud. Big kisses to Sophie from me."

Hugh began laughing; a not too common occurrence. Our news had touched him and I couldn't help smiling myself. I'm now looking forward to November although I know I've got to sit down and contemplate how the birth will affect our lives.

I'd now given up my auction house job to work on my photographic work full time. With the birth on the horizon I had to consider carefully whether I was doing the right thing but I loved it. I never knew where the next job was coming from or where it would take me. What was interesting was the amount of work I was getting from national and worldwide publications. I'd also got notification that on a split vote I was runner up in the National Wildlife Photographer of the Year award. I could hardly believe it. I had, using Dad's Hasselblad, taken a simple shot, a close up of a cow, just head and shoulders. I got down to the ground behind a fence to get the right angle and the shot gave the animal a remarkable sense of dignity. Apparently it was going to be used as a front cover of a wild life magazine. That picture was also syndicated globally, as evidence that even the simplest of shots are capable of a prize-winning performance. If it hadn't been for Dad's legacy none of this would have happened. Sometimes I was having trouble to keep up with the workload. It wasn't long after that *National Geographic Magazine* contacted me asking if I would call them as they had a proposition I might like to consider. I was totally surprised! Now if that was a work prospect it would be fantastic. An unbelievable opportunity. The photographers they used were amongst the best in the world.

That very week Sophie saw her doctor again who gave her a close examination. She told me her doctor looked very thoughtful afterwards and had said she wasn't too certain what she was hearing although Sophie's uterus was sitting higher than was normal. Because of that she had recommended her for one of those scans. I think by then we were both getting nervous. The whole thing was accomplished in days and the results were immediate. There was no doubt. Sophie was carrying twins. The impact of Sophie's news on us both was not what many people might have imagined. We weren't overwhelmed. We both took it very much in our stride. It was as if we had always known and it was no big surprise. If anything it was a matter of a quiet celebration followed by serious reflection and discussion. It's true to say we were unbelievably pleased. Of course we informed family and friends and reactions were positive from all. Hugh made us laugh by saying he didn't know whether to offer us congratulations or commiserations. Typical! Flora was beside herself with glee so much so anybody would have thought it was her having twins and not Sophie.

My meeting with the magazine was fixed for eleven thirty, two weeks away. I had to meet them at Brown's Hotel, Albemarle Street in London's West End. On the morning of the interview I was about twenty minutes early. That's an unwanted period of time, which caused me to mindlessly pace up and down the street dealing with an attack of butterflies, I attempted to pass time by extensive window-shopping but all the while feeling intensely nervous. The Hotel looked intimidating. I supposed that a magazine of this class didn't do things on the cheap. As the time crept closer I took a deep breath, walked up to the front of the hotel, pushed open the heavy swing doors and walked in.

The hotel had an expensive but warm and restful feel to it. I relaxed. It wasn't long before I was sitting in a comfortable and richly upholstered room clutching my portfolio in sweaty hands. The interview went well. Four people, The Senior Photo Editor, The Deputy Director of Photography, The Director of Photo Editing and the man who handled Assignment Projects, saw me. It transpired that they previously had a photographer lined up for a five-month contract for an assignment in South America. He was unable to fulfil that contract so that is where I came in. Would I be interested? They had, surprisingly, a portfolio of my work and knew what I was capable of. They looked over the work I had taken along and nodded approvingly. I was asked lots of technical questions about cameras and techniques, with which I had no problem. I guess they were impressed with my work, which they saw as highly original. The assignment would start in six weeks, which meant there would be a lot of planning. It also meant, if I got the job, I would be away from Sophie but I would be back home well before the birth. The interview came to an end and they asked me to wait outside. After ten minutes of minor anxiety I was called back in. I was offered the assignment together with a contract fee I wouldn't have believed possible.

On the way home on the train I experienced a feeling of incredulity. The time flew by. I was wrapped up in all that had happened and all the possibilities that this could bring. I barely noticed the rolling countryside flashing past the window. I was by comparison to many, a virtual novice. Dependant on Sophie's reaction I wasn't going to turn this down. The decision was going to have to be hers. If she didn't want me to go I wouldn't. It was as simple as that.

Back home I told her everything and I could see her mind racing.

"In some ways I wished he'd never left you those cameras. But I know you love the work and you'll back sometime in August won't you?

"Yes, if I go at all. You're my prime concern."

"You're not to turn it down. I know it seems strange but your Dad wanted something like this for you! It seems like he set it up. I'll be fine. I've got Flora up the road and Hugh and Trudi near by. They wouldn't let me suffer. I know that. I know you won't stop thinking of me and I won't stop thinking of you either. We both know that. Besides, if you didn't take it I wouldn't want you to die wondering what it might have been like if you had!" She hugged me close.

"Thank you, sweetheart, for making it easy for me, I won't forget that."

So with trepidation and some anxiety I accepted their offer and the contract terms. Arrangements were put in hand almost immediately and I got several briefings from various departments concerned with the project. The project was to photograph and record the lives of a snake eating tribe somewhere in the Amazon jungle, take pictures of the snakes and the tribe who also used the snake's poisonous venom for rituals and an aid in reaching states of ecstasy or altered states of consciousness. Some assignment! If this mission was successful I would have a rosy future with my camera. I could become an international photographer and after that there would be no going back to weddings and christenings and that sort of thing. When all my excitement calmed down I got to thinking again about Dad. Without him none of this would have ever happened, which raised the question, was I prepared to forgive him? I'm mixed up on this issue. I knew how I felt about Sophie and I could never hurt or betray her like Dad did with Mum. "I'm grateful to him," was about the best I could say. I told Flora, Hugh and Trudi and they understood totally.

The assignment was magical. I was working with seasoned professionals, which was daunting but I learned a lot and we all got on well. It was hot, intensely humid, and I never seemed to stop sweating. It was a dangerous mission but it was also a total success. I had some stunning shots, close ups of the snakes and a first in capturing shots of the tribe killing and eating the snakes and then using the venom for their sacred rituals. The tribesmen tried to get us to try it but somehow we had to refuse! One of our crew did try it and not long after looked seriously ill much to the amusement of the tribe. I got to trying some roasted snake as I didn't want to refuse and cause offence. It was a bit like chicken but it made me feel uneasy as you may imagine. What would Dad have thought if he could see the results of his machinations now? Taking those close up pictures of the snakes was scary as they were so unpredictable. Was it any more dangerous than Dad's bombing raids over Germany? I doubted it. Time passed by so quickly but when August arrived I was more than glad to be going back home to Sophie, Flo, Hugh and Trudi.

Sophie was fine and I felt really pleased to be back with her. I never realised how much I'd missed her, She was now quite large and it was a delight to stroke her bulge and to feel the occasional movement of the life inside. As amazing as my trip had been, nothing matched the way I felt about her and the prospect of twins. It was October before my pictures and the narrative about the tribe was published. Oh my, did I feel proud. *National Geographic* told me that I was being tipped as International Wild Life Photographer of the Year. Wow! I'm just a newcomer to this so I guess the only criteria is an ability to produce stunning photographs. This I had done. Their tip was accurate. I was a clear winner. After that my phone never ceased to ring with offers of work, interviews and offers of film and TV work. My life had changed.

The twins were born mid November. Poor Sophie had a tough time with thirteen hours of labour. Was it worth it? I say! For we now have identical twin girls who are an absolute joy for both of us. We're naming them, Hannah and Caroline. I can't help thinking what Mum and Dad would have thought. They were born within minutes of each other. They were chubby, rosy pink, happy bundles of sheer joy and had lots of dark hair. We both melted. I now had a real family of my own. Whatever else this is my greatest achievement. There has been nothing to match it, nor will there be. All this wouldn't have been possible without Sophie! Yet in moments of quiet I was aware of and couldn't shake off the ghost of Scott. He was always lurking close by. It was as if he was watching every move I made. But those cameras had given me a confidence I never knew existed. Since the award my life has drastically altered. Thanks Dad.

* * *

Like everyone who knew Bobby and Sophie, I had been surprised and delighted about the news of the twins. I too wondered what Mum and Dad would have thought if they had been here. Part of me is envious. It must be my maternal side showing. I never thought I had one. I called them both and offered my congratulations and best wishes and I couldn't resist telling Bobby how to look after Sophie. I'd asked her what she wanted, boys or girls. She said she didn't mind as long as they were human! I thought that was a wise reply. I liked it very much. I think she'll be an excellent mum. Bobby seems to be slightly terrified but to the rest of us it's amusing. It wasn't long after this I heard of his news from *National Geographic Magazine*. That seemed amazing and as long as Sophie didn't object it was an offer he couldn't refuse. He's come on by leaps and bounds since those cameras grabbed him. Again I paused to think of what Scott would have thought. I can only guess he would be pleased and proud to know what he'd engineered had been put to such good use. This was a major achievement and Bobby was fast becoming a big success story, in more ways than one.

A whole year has flown by and has given me chance to evaluate my own life and in what direction it's heading. That letter Dad left me has had a profound affect. He must have known it would or why would he have bothered to tell me. That bastard knew what he was doing and I was beginning to think that he knew more about us then we ever imagined. I can't stop thinking about it all. Dad's experience of the war must have altered the way he looked at things and I couldn't deny he had a certain philosophy, which he knew I would find attractive. Well, he was right. I do. Him being shot at, night after night and then having to endure the squalor of a P O W camp and a failed escape attempt and knowing people who were his friends being executed was no easy thing for me to dismiss. As you can see some of my initial fury has abated a wee bit. After all, I had a new sister and a successful brother. This has to be a large bonus emerging from all that crap. The sweet lotus grows only from the dark mud as I remember him telling me. Yep, he was right on that one. So it hasn't all been bad.

I've started reading the material Dad left me and as a result I've joined the Buddhist Society in Eccleston Square, in London and also attend meetings in Exeter. It's like I've always known what the tenets of Buddhism were without having to be told. The Four Noble Truths, The Doctrine of No-Soul, The Eightfold Path and the Middle Way all made perfect sense to me. Underpinning these was the Buddhist attitude of mind. What I was learning is that Truth has no label, no blind faith or belief but only seeing and understanding. There was no attachment, not even to truth itself. It felt as if a veil had been lifted away. These are early days for me and I sense that there is much more to come. I feel it in my bones and throughout my body. Those press clippings of him at his lay ordination were so surprising and the things he was wearing seemed to ring bells in my head but I couldn't put my finger on what it was. Yet I knew this was a route I would be taking.

Mark wasn't too happy about the direction I seemed to be heading. He said he felt he was losing me.

"Flora, what's happening to you? It seems as if a distance has opened up between us."

"Don't be silly, Mark. It's nothing of the sort."

"So what is it then?"

"It's just that I know this is what I have to do. I don't know why but it feels exactly right."

"It seems you've found a new lover."

His next question surprised me.

"Flo. Will you marry me?"

223

"There was a time I'd have said yes, and I would've done so without hesitation, but at this moment in time I'm not ready for it. I thought I was but not now. I'm sorry, Mark." I was upset with not accepting and felt mean.

"So it's not entirely a no, then."

"No, it's not entirely a no. It's just not the right time for me."

"When do you think that will be?"

"I can't tell you but I don't want to lose you either. But if you find all this too much you'd be better to give me up."

"I can't do that."

"I'm sorry Mark but later is the only answer I can give you." I gently squeezed his hand.

He looked up at me and I felt his pain. I'd no intention of hurting him but I knew what I had to do. He wasn't included in my plans right now. Those plans would take me away from him and whether he could wait that long I didn't know. I also understood I stood a good chance of losing him totally and if that happened, then that was what was meant to be.

Bill Perrin had left Dad a book about his experiences. He'd inscribed it inside 'To Scott who understands. Many thanks for all your help' That I thought was an intriguing inscription. What was it he understood? I had no way of knowing. I often thought of my Crooksbury Hill experience, which in retrospect I knew was spiritual. Scott had sensed this about me. Was this the 'understanding' to which Bill referred?

That reading from the Tibetan Book of the Dead I gave to Dad when he died also intrigued me greatly. Dr. Carl Jung had written a 'Psychological Commentary' on the text. It was in the synopsis that the book was a guide for the dead and the dying in the *intermediate* state of forty-nine days between the Tibetan belief of death and rebirth. When I examined it I found it was divided into sections dealing with the psychic experience of death. This fascinated me. I knew at this moment what Dad had asked for at the moment of his death. He was asking to be guided through the various realms known as *karmic* illusions, the states of consciousness, the diminishing lights and terrifying visions before rebirth occurs. This book took my breath away as it explained Jung's view of the *collective unconscious*. Life, it seems, is a disease because its outcome is always fatal. The ancient monks, he suggested, had glimpsed the dimensions between life and death and had twitched the veil from the greatest of life's secrets. I was astonished by what it claimed to reveal. I had no way of determining its truth. I only knew that I had to find out what life was all about, if anything at all.

I spoke to Hugh and Bobby about this and of the situation with Mark. Hugh as usual, paused in thought, and I could almost hear his brain whirring.

"Flora, you're an enigma. Dad knew that and so do I. It's very clear he had an agenda for us all. He was organised and methodical and I now think he knew exactly what he was up to and wanted to help us in some strange sort of way, perhaps a form of making amends. I also think he had a lot of regrets or why would he have gone to all these strange lengths?

I was surprised to hear Hugh's voice cracking slightly. It's been emotional for all of us and I know it hasn't finished by a long way yet. Both Bobby and Hugh understood my situation with Mark, which was supportive.

"You must follow your heart and not what you think is expected of you," Hugh said.

If anyone around here is a mystic I think it's Hugh, and Bobby is so creative I couldn't wish for better counsel from them both. Hugh is so surprising and sees more than we realise. He's like a clone of Dad when I looked back on all this. So what was I to do? Something was calling to me and I guess I would find out shortly.

What was a '*sesshin*'? It was an intensive Zen Buddhist meditation retreat. Dad had written about it in his letter to me. It seemed scary but offered me a chance to discover if there was anything to discover at all. I went for it. I found out where and when I could train in the UK. Later I found a place near Gloucester, which offered weekend retreats and a weeklong version. I went, and found it hard and it left me feeling disappointed and unfulfilled. There were none of those mind racking riddles or *koans* designed to loosen the intellectual hold on your mind, such as 'What is the sound of one hand clapping?' and a whole lot more. The majority of the system at this centre seemed to involve 'just sitting' which is hard but not what I was looking for. I wanted something more incisive, challenging. I stayed seven days but sensed my path lay elsewhere. The desire to find the 'truth' had woken in me and I was beginning to formulate a plan of what I should do. It was not going to be popular with Mark.

My relationship with Mark, because of the course I'm pursuing, has gradually diminished but we both know we still love each other. My aim is to discover this 'truth' if it exists at all. Mark is important to me but at the moment it seems that Dad has set me a task and I'm captivated, as he must have known I would have been. Mark knows this too but I'm hurting him as he'd presumed we'd get married. This is not now to be. I have to find what I am looking for. This question gnawed at me morning noon and night. If only I had stopped and thought what was happening to me. It was no different to that of Dad's friend Bill Perrin with his perpetual self-questioning. I couldn't see that at the time. I love Mark dearly and am torn in two over this predicament. We sit and talk for hours. I think he has an understanding about what is bothering me but that isn't an aspect of life we mutually share. If he wanted to keep me it would have been well for him to have heard my uncle Alf's words, '*If you want to control an animal it needs a large playing field to move around in.*' I told Mark my mind was made up I was about to embark on a mission of which I'd told no one about. Mark was the first to know I was going to Japan.

I called everybody over and we sat out on the patio wearing warm jumpers and coats, Trudi, Bobby and Sophie, Hugh, Ella and Mark were all there. Mark knew what I was about to say. I spoke about Dad's legacy to us all and how it was shaping our lives in different directions. What I was about to tell them in some ways was more radical than they would expect. I told them I was going to a monastery in Japan for as long as it took for me to attempt to discover what it was that was bothering me so much. I explained Dad's letter to me and how deeply it resonated inside me. With each of us he must have known he was reshaping our lives. Everybody looked aghast and Mark stared down at the flagstones.

"Please don't get upset. I may be away for only a couple of months or even a year, but I will contact you all frequently as I hope you will do with me."

"When you going?" asked Hugh.

"The middle of next month."

Trudi hugged me. "I'm going to miss you sister. You came into my life and now you're leaving it." A large tear ran down her face.

The group went quiet and I felt that I was betraying them in some way but I had to resist that feeling. I wanted them to be happy for me. Mark had already known but he was still disconsolate. I heard him say,

"Your fucking father. Christ what has he done to you all?"

Mark had got that right. Our lives were altering in a way that perhaps Dad hadn't entirely envisaged. He just gave us the maps we needed. Everybody was weepy and Mark told me he'd always love me.

"I love you too and if you still feel the same when I get back, who knows?" I replied.

He was taking it remarkably well and I knew I was loved, which caused me some heartache.

* * *

Tokyo: January 1977.

My Dear family and Dearest Mark.

Arrived here at two in the morning. Very bleary eyed and needed somewhere to crash out before I work out where I'm supposed to be heading. Tokyo never seems to sleep so I've found a small hotel that let me in. They are so polite and friendly and could teach us a thing or two. The next day I made enquiries about a friend of mine who lives in downtown Tokyo where she's been living for five years. I still have her number on a dog-eared and smudgy piece of paper. Joy of joys! She answered the phone and was she surprised to hear from me! She said she was leaving for the USA the following day for a week but would be delighted for me to look after her

228

apartment for the week. The Gods must have smiled on me! My timing couldn't have been better. Japanese houses or apartments are tiny compared to ours and have little furniture in them as they sit on mats and cushions around a very low table. They all seem to have those round wooden baths you must have seen on TV or films. They are so luxurious when you soak in them. We should invest in one for our own house.

Today I strolled around Tokyo. Boy, was it overcrowded and very cold. Much like home at this time of year? The men all seem to wear grey or navy blue suits or overcoats with matching skinny ties and they look so tired, weary and unhappy. Their faces seem to be expressionless or is that the version we have in the West for Eastern inscrutability? I think that if a Martian was to land here he would have taken off again pretty smartish. As I wandered further away from the hub, that greyness seemed to disappear and the streets became more colourful and were decorated with coloured streamers and lanterns and the people were smiling. Getting around can be problematic using a mixture of broken English and the odd Japanese word or two plus lots and lots of arm waving! Have you ever tried to speak Japanese? If you have then you will understand how hard that is.

Tomorrow I'm going to visit a few temples and that should be interesting. Will be in touch soon. Tell Mark I love him.
Love you all, Flora

I finished reading her letter and looked across at Sophie

and Bobby, Mark and Trudi. "Well she's got there and I hope she finds what she's looking for, and soon. Let's drink a toast to her. She's a remarkable and brave woman."

We raised our glasses and Mark looked very down. He was so in love with her and I wondered how long it would take him to come terms with this, if at all. I put my arm around him. "She'll be fine, you'll see. We know she loves you."

He could only nod his head several times but he couldn't look up at us. Poor Mark. He was suffering but the only cure would be time itself.

* * *

I've been let into the Spring Sesshin, a concentrated meditation retreat at Shokoku temple in a district of Kyoto. I'm really scared, as I've heard how harsh they can be. I'm a foreigner here and also a woman, which in some areas of this male run institution doesn't go down well. Apparently the temple is an important one and it certainly is impressive in size and grandeur. There seem to be carved dragons staring at you from every imaginable wall and corner including the ceilings! Dominating it all is a massive altar with a golden Buddha, overlooking the meditation hall. I know this is the style of Zen I've been looking for and it feels as though I'm at home. There is nowhere else for me. I made a silent vow that I would not leave Japan until I find what I'm looking for, no matter how long it takes. Dad had set me on this course and I am going to follow it through to the end. I was beginning to realise how much he understood but never ever said, even to me. The Roshi, or master, said that over the next seven days we would have to work very hard with up to nine hours of meditation throughout the day. There were also daily rituals and ceremonies, which added to the drama of it all. There is also a strict code of behaviour and formal etiquette for every occasion. Speaking is not allowed when the *sesshin* starts except when working jointly on some task and that had to be minimal. I'm the only westerner here but am treated with utmost respect. The Roshi gives his talks in Japanese but has kindly provided an interpreter for me so I missed nothing he was saying. After his first talk we are told to return to the *zendo* our meditation hall, for an hours meditation before going to bed.

I gathered from the trainees who spoke English that the Roshi considered me as a bit of a coup and hoped that I might want to stay there. I don't know about that but only the next seven days will show me. I'm missing my family terribly, especially dear Mark and I feel I've been too cruel to him and that hurts. I shall never forget that remark of his about what has Dad done to us all.

It's three in the morning, the darkness lit only by a few paltry candles. A cold draughty wind whistles through the opened doors. I'm shivering. A monitor is blowing on a large conch shell. It's the wake up call and the noise it makes is bloodcurdling. He's shouting at us that we have to get up. Another monitor walks behind him banging two large wooden blocks together. The sounds are frightening and electrifying. This is going to be awful! I'm petrified. Everybody is getting up and not a word is spoken. It seems so strange. Our bedding is rolled up and stored in separate cupboards at the rear of the zendo. Washing, teeth cleaning and using the toilets are over in a flash. We then ceremoniously march, bleary eyed into the meditation hall, which is illuminated with hundreds of candles. Our shadows seem eerily elongated flickering to and fro as we walk slowly along the polished floor around to our allotted meditation mats and cushions. A strong smell of incense drifts around us and the wooden blocks are struck sounding like thunderclaps as bells are rung. There's lots of bowing and I have to watch everybody else to follow suit. My first introduction to Zen! Not long into meditation my legs are killing me and the pain in my knees is agonising as I try the half lotus position of sitting. I'm unable to concentrate on anything with the pain and my head behaving like a full-scale jazz band with thoughts crashing around all over the place. What am I supposed to be doing? Why am I here? At five o'clock the morning chants begin, which is a welcome relief but with it all being in Japanese I can't understand a thing. There follows more bells and smells and wooden block clapping and prostrations, which if nothing else, relieves my aching legs and feet. This is agonising and it's only just started. How am I to get through another seven days of this sesshin? As soon as the chanting is finished we are each summoned individually before the Roshi. He quizzes me intently about my intent and my meditation. He speaks reasonable English, which surprises me. He spent several minutes with me, which was unusual. Sixty seconds was his average time with anyone! For my meditation practice he allocated me a koan, which seems to be a meaningless question but is a paradoxical story or riddle. It is not solvable by the intellect. It solution has to be intuitive. It's designed to bring about a spiritual awakening or test the depth of your understanding related to your part and meaning in the universe. This is what I dearly wanted. He gave me the riddle of 'nothingness' or Mu. This denied the basic premise of Buddhism, that all beings have the Buddha nature seemingly, but not so apparently. It made no logical sense. Everything was Mu, which means no or nothingness, the opposite of existence, which it was also not. How am I going to get my head around this? What would Dad have said?

That first day was agony and I was so grateful to get to bed at seven thirty that evening feeling totally exhausted but oddly satisfied. The next day it started all over again. I was beginning to centre and my jazz band head had become a duet, so something was happening. The pain was still there in my legs but it was just Mu. That seemed to lessen the agony. I kept at this for three days when on the fourth I found I was focussing more deeply than I'd been able to previously. Then something strange happened. I heard this enormous roar in my ears. I intuitively knew what it was. It was the roar of a Halifax bomber taking off. I was with Dad! I heard the flack exploding all around and saw the various colours of it. There he was in his flying kit looking straight at me as he prepared to bale out from the stricken plane. I gasped out loud and a great sob exploded from me. A monitor came over to me and signalled I should be quiet. I couldn't stop it and then in a body consuming rush my body became totally rigid with paralysis. I collapsed on to the floor, unable to move, and promptly passed out.

When I came to I was in my room on top of my bed. Every bone in my body ached and I felt the remaining wisps of a pervading all encompassing pain. A monitor and Roshi were staring down at me. Both looked sombre and serious, and Roshi just nodded at me.

My voice had returned and I croaked the question "Have I got enlightenment?"

"No," Roshi replied, "if you had you'd have no need to ask."

"What was that all about?" I told him what had happened and what I saw.

He gave me an intent stare. "It was an illusion but a sign of

233

what's going on inside of you. It shows some progress. Ignore it and walk on and away from it. It indicates you have a good level of concentration and is a good sign. Do not seek or try to repeat the experience. If you do your practice will become as a tomb. You will go nowhere."

I understood what he was saying and I promised I would do what he asked. He told me to rest for a few hours and when I felt like it I should return to the zendo. Later, when I had a moment I wrote a letter home.

* * *

I received Flora's letter and decided not to read it until Bobby, Sophie Mark and Trudi were present. So we arranged for a reading over the weekend. Ella was happy to come with me and I knew we'd become extremely close. A lot of that was due to us becoming lovers. I've been surprised at how happy she's made me. She's now a part of my life and I want it to remain that way. I haven't told the others but I guess they can figure that out for themselves without too much effort. Later that evening I realised that Dad's last envelope had still not been opened but there was still time to go before the dateline he had stipulated, We'd agreed we would wait as long as it took and for Flora to return before we opened it. I knew deep down that we were in for another surprise or shock but without Flora's presence we would wait for that. I opened up her letter to us.

Shokoku-ji Kyoto. March 25. 1977.

My Dear family and my beloved Mark.

The weather here is freezing with snow everywhere. Please be patient with me as I am at present only allowed one or two letters per month as it might distract from my practice. I have told our master provisionally that I might want to stay on after this sesshin for a while longer, which he was happy to agree to.

My God, I miss you all and all those home comforts and your food, which can really bother me at times. Here we get lots of pickles, rice, seaweed and Miso soup. Hey ho! This is my chosen path and I mustn't complain.

Getting up at 3.00am every morning can be exhausting but we do get to bed early. It's very cold and damp here but my meditations are improving. It's extremely arduous and I've never found anything so difficult as this but I'm determined to stay in Japan for as long as it takes. I keep thinking of you all and of Mum and Dad and their deaths. They can haunt my meditations in a disturbing way. In some weird fashion they seem to have come to life. I guess it's the subconscious kicking in.

Bobby and Sophie, how are the twins doing? I'd love to see pictures of them and all of you too. How's Hugh getting on with lovely Ella? I hope it works out for them. And Mark I don't forget you and I hope you won't forget me.
You are all always in my thoughts. Love and miss you all so much. Flora.

We all went silent for a while and I knew she was in all our thoughts. Dad has disrupted our lives as a family but not negatively so. In our own ways we are branching out into different areas and none more so than Flora. Bobby is due on an assignment to the Congo the next month and Trudi has received a promotion at her work and now has given control of a large department. I had my own ideas on what I might be doing and it would be removed from physics. I'd have to wait and see.

ELEVEN

Changes

The next morning all the participants at the sesshin were to do *Takhahatsu*, which is a ritualistic round of begging through the nearby streets. It was freezing out there and there was a lot of snow about. I put on as much clothing as I could but we had to wear straw sandals. Eek! We were given large straw hats shaped like giant bowls which covered our faces so we couldn't be seen. We kept ten paces apart and a ritualistic chant began as we walked, which sounded like *ho*. We accepted in our begging bowls everything that was given and what ever the food was we were obliged to eat it. My hands and feet were completely numb after an hour of non-stop walking the streets around Kyoto. A fish shop owner gave us warm *sake* and rice but the *sake* went straight to my head. Whoops! At the end of the day I felt it to be a most humbling experience, which we in the west don't appreciate or understand.

March can still be extremely cold here with snow continuing to hang about, and the only heating in the zendo is a small wood-burning stove at one end of the meditation hall. It might as well have not been there for you could see every one's breath exuding in great white drifting clouds. The cold is almost unbearable and I'm wearing as much as I can put on. I'm still concentrating on 'nothingness', which it doesn't mean, or mu. The sesshin is a few days from finishing and I'm not certain now if I want to stay here at this temple. It has got me started but I find the regime too harsh and fierce. I'd thought of taking a full ordination but something is stopping me. I spoke honestly to Roshi about it. He was gentle and nodded gravely.

"Always follow heart. Always heart. No head."

Now where had I heard that before? I knew he was right and I thanked him. I would stay here for a month or two after the sesshin was over and would move on to find Nakashima Roshi who lived about fifty miles from here. He was married and was a highly respected master who had a different way of conducting things, and from what I heard, was generally not so harsh.

The atmosphere is electric. It's the last day of the sesshin and nobody went to bed the night before as we sat up all night in meditation. How we would get through the next twenty-four hours was anyone's guess. I was totally immersed in the paradox and riddle of mu.

I'm nothing every thing is nothing. Nothing is everything! A strong current of something ripples through me. My eyes filled with tears as if I was standing on Crooksbury Hill all those years ago. I begin to violently tremble and I'm starting to shake, tears flood from my eyes. I'm sobbing out loud and lay down on my mat uncontrollably weeping. I was nothing, all my life was nothing, my dreams and aspirations, my personality are nothing yet in all this I am also every thing! My tears wouldn't stop. I know I'm close but not close enough. I have my interview with Roshi early morning. Again he stares at me intently.

"You are near. Immerse more, more, more till you know mu." He rang his bell and I was dismissed."

A thousand thoughts ran through my mind. What is the nature of consciousness? If all is consciousness, do rocks and stones have consciousness? If energy is consciousness, all form has and has not consciousness. When a rolling wave crashes on the shore what happens to it? Does it become part of the vast ocean again? That was where it started from anyway, so in one way it hasn't died. Is that the same for us?

I pushed on as Roshi had suggested. Everything was mu and I was too. The guy next to me began blubbing out loudly and softly alternatively. He gave a gasp and cried out "That's it. I know! I know! I was distracted listening to him and lost my grip on what I was doing. I was happy for him that he knew. So it can be done! I thought if he can find it so can I. But it didn't happen. I was an also ran. The sesshin came to an end and we all ended up in Roshi's quarters, the sesshin pressure off, eating cakes and drinking warm green tea. There was a lot of laughter and joy. Later *sake* was brought round and we all got a little merry. It was lovely.

Two days later I got a letter from home. What joy as several photographs fell out of them all and close ups of the twins as I opened the envelope.

Pimlico April 10th 1977.

Dearest Flora,

How's it going for you out there? It certainly sounds tough and painful and none of us would want to go through that. We check the weather reports each day in the newspapers and it certainly is far colder where you are than it is here. Aren't we lucky! We all have the deepest admiration for you. I hope, my darling twin sister that you won't be away from us too long. I love you very much........Hugh.

My lovely new sister I think of you every day and wish you were here so I could enjoy your kindly presence. Your departure really upset me but I

239

understand that is what you had to do although that sort of thing is a mystery to me. I'm doing pretty well at work and have risen to being in charge of a large team, which is daunting but the sort of challenge I need. I know you won't forget me, nor I you. Come home soon. I love you......Trudi.

Hi Flo! Hope you like the shots of the twins. I swear Hannah looks a bit like you! I hope you can endure what you are putting yourself through. It must be worth it. Nothing in life is easy and anything worth getting doesn't come easy. I know you have the strength and courage to do it and I know you will never give up. Promise me that won't you. Dad in some weird way sent you there and it was meant to be. I'm off to the African Congo shortly for a month or two on another assignment and I hope Sophie will be ok but she wouldn't have me turning work down as important as this. Sophie sends all her love and she misses you as we all do. Stick at it Flora and don't come back until you've got what you went to find. I love you so much.... Bobby.

I read and reread that letter over and over again. I felt myself reaching out to touch them. I noticed there was nothing from Mark. I cracked up and wept in the loneliness I felt without them. I had to carry on my quest. I found Bobby's encouragement moving and I knew he was right. I knew they loved me as I loved them.

* * *

I landed at Brazzaville in the Congo and within a few days set out with our team to the Queso district of the Sangha region. This was an important assignment for me and as I speak fluent French I was selected easily. We were to have a dual role, to study the Baka pygmies and to photograph the wildlife in the inhospitable swamplands of the former rain forest. This is full of gorillas and a host of other species that live side-by-side and are not bothered by mankind. This place is a Pandora's box of ecological wonders and has experienced climate swings for millions of years. Two thousand years ago the swamp was a giant rain forest, which now only exists in finger like strips stretching across the swamps. In the centre is a giant mysterious circular lake. Its origin is unknown and some scientists have thought that dinosaurs could have survived here, which to me seems unlikely. At night, when sitting around our small fire outside the tents it can seem unreal. There is the red glow from the fire watched over by a breathtaking night sky frothing with millions of stars. I've never seen anything like that in all my life. We chat quietly amongst ourselves and pipe tobacco floats tantalisingly across the night air. In the background are the chirping and twittering noises of countless nocturnal insects. Behind all this rests an awesome silence. I feel extremely privileged to be here. I can also feel guilty about leaving Sophie and the twins but then I think that Dad was away far longer from us during the war than I would ever be from my brood. That didn't necessarily make it right though. I also thought of Flora. Her departure was a gigantic step away from everybody and everything she had known and loved. How long before we would see her again God knows?

This land is magical. Its wild beauty is stunning. The Baka are in many ways isolated but many are still being used as slaves by others and the United Nations are investigating this point. I think Flora would have much to say about this if she were here. They are unsentimental about animals and kill them to survive. They never overkill or slaughter for sport, only to survive. They seem to have the greatest respect for nature and live harmoniously with and within it. I got some excellent shots of their rituals and customs. They have no written traditions. Everything about their history is told in song or through story telling since time immemorial and I hope that never changes. These shots are comparatively rare and I feel honoured to be allowed to have taken them. They treated us with respect and I suspect they are part of humanity's genetic ancestry that emerged from Africa millions of years ago. I'm hoping what our team is doing will contribute in some way to more knowledge and understanding of that possibility and of people worldwide. Flora would be impressed and I hope Hugh and Trudi will be too. What Dad would have thought of this? Amazement maybe? I've no way of telling. I don't forget, he in many ways is responsible for all this.

The gorillas were amazing and abundant beyond belief. They are such gentle and loving beasts foraging in the weeds of the wet grasslands. I feel honoured to be part of this assignment. They seem unafraid of our presence and we can get close to them and there's not one hint of aggression. They have a family structure where the dominant male, a silverback gorilla has a company of three or four females as his own. They are particularly gentle with their babies who ride around on their mothers' back . They seem to eat masses of grass, which they wash in water, shaking off all the dirt and roots before eating. They mix amicably with elephants and water buffaloes and not one species seems fazed by another. It seems harmonious in a way I wouldn't have believed possible. They are all vegetarians and the only fear they experience is when the odd carnivore cat or lion stalk them. I also spotted Sitatunga antelope in the forest where they shouldn't be. I got some rare pictures of them and of grey parrots both of which I know will surprise a few people back home. What they are doing here is a mystery.

It's been a fabulous trip but it took six weeks and by the end of it, as usual, I couldn't wait to get home. I'm really missing our twins, Sophie Hugh and Trudi too. In some ways I wish Flora hadn't gone away as she is so important to us and we are all missing her desperately. I often found myself thinking of her, alone out there, and putting herself through God knows what. As always, it was great to get home. Seeing Sophie again was sheer joy and I felt a lump in my throat as I grabbed hold of her. I never knew how much I could love someone. The girls seemed puzzled by my presence and I wondered whether they had any memory of me at all. I guess if they hadn't it was my fault not theirs. I called Hugh who wanted to know everything I'd been up to but I guess that would have to wait for another family get together. Shortly after getting back I submitted my work and commentaries back to National Geographic. It wasn't long after that they contacted me to say that they were extremely pleased with what I'd achieved. They said that my shots of the wild life and the Baka pygmies were exemplary, and some unique. Well I felt pleased and Sophie was proud of me. Would Dad have been? Yes, I thought, I'd stretched his legacy beyond what he could have imagined. I still didn't know what I felt about him and I'm still all mixed up in that area. I'm going to have to talk to the others about this.

* * *

Shokoku-ji Kyoto April 25th 1977

My beloved family,

How I miss you all so much and thank you for your lovely letter. It was a great comfort to me. Isn't Bobby doing well! Who would have believed what he has achieved in such a short time. I think we should all be very proud of him.

Just to let you know I'm leaving Shokoku-ji next month to go to another temple further down south. As and when I get the address I'll send it to you. The conditions here are harsh but the monks are so gentle and kind it takes out some of the sting. Still, I won't miss getting up at three in the morning every day and getting shouted at and whacked by the monitors! They are being over-harsh to be kind to us and spur us on to greater effort. In some ways it's been a shock to my system but I've gradually got accustomed to it.

How are you doing, Hugh, and Mark, together with Trudi? It's touching you all miss me, as I miss you too! I'm very tired at the moment and don't get much time for writing due to the work and meditation, so forgive me if this letter is too short. I promise to contact you again from my new address.

I send my love to you all ... Flora.

My master at Shokoku-ji called me to his quarters. I bowed respectfully in front of him. He sat on a cushion placed on his meditation mat. He looked as solid as a rock. There was a wise and kindly look reflected in his eyes and around the corners of his mouth. He had an ageless quality. His voice whilst terse was quiet and full of gentleness.

"Flora-san you have done much for beginner. I'm sorry you go."

Again I bowed deeply in front of him and thanked him for allowing me to be here and showing me so much. He knew of my decision to go to Nakashima Roshi's temple and seemed pleased for me. He told me that Nakashima had once been a disciple of his and gave me his personal letter of introduction for him. I was surprised and grateful. He told me that laymen also helped run the temple. Nakashima had two training centres, both close to each other. "You don't have to stay in monastery. If you wish you can rent room nearby and he won't mind as long as you turn up in time each morning! He right for you."

So I'm deserting the icy blasts of Shokoku-ji and am sorry to be leaving in some way. The monks lined up to say goodbye and presented me with a special cake they had made for me. Each one came up to me individually and said goodbye. Typical of their farewells was, "Flora-san we miss you much. You come back soon, real soon eh!"

This brought tears to my eyes. They are exceptional and gentle people and I love them all but I know that I have to move on.

I travelled to Nakashima's temple Kenkuro-ji and after attempting several times to tell various monks at the gate who it was I wanted to see I was eventually allowed to present my letter of introduction to him, which I did with a deep bow. His stature looked frail and he stood at about five feet, five inches tall. He was seated in a meditation posture. He wore his black robes and a brown coloured rakusu hung from his neck. His shaven but tanned head could not conceal the traces of greying hair or the large scar that ran from the centre of his head down to his lower right temple. His eyes looked black and had a curious flicker. Etched into his face was an inherent compassion and kindness. I was impressed. He paused for a while after reading the letter and then looked intently at me, his eyes glowered like a hungry hawk. He continued to scrutinise me closely whilst thoughtfully stroking his chin. I remained silent with my eyes respectfully lowered.

He nodded. "You are welcome"

He was as I thought, kind and gentle although I knew these masters could demonstrate a tough and harsh side if they thought they had to. The atmosphere here was so different to Shokoku-ji. It was a refreshing change and I'd arrived in time for a short three-day sesshin a few days away. A good beginning, I thought. A sixty-five year old nun leads the morning chants, and his mother who also acted as cook, helped him. Charming and unexpected. The temple was simple and had none of the grand décor and finery of Shokoku-ji. However, it had an amazing and extensive garden complex which in its beauty and construction took my breath away. The whole place exuded an atmosphere, a presence. It was something special. I felt at home.

There were only a dozen participants at the sesshin. It was a luxury getting up at four in the morning rather than three and not getting shouted at and banged about by the monitors in such a harsh manner as previously, or gawped at by temple visitors. It was warmer here and joy of joys there was a bath we could use every afternoon to alleviate the pain in our aching limbs. I don't know what my other Roshi had written in his letter but without any ado I was given the same problem of mu and its paradox of everything is and is not, nothingness. Well I didn't get far at this sesshin, it was too short to get my teeth into but it was a good introduction to how Nakashima ran things and how he conducted his interviews with us. He told me in an initial interview that I was welcome to stay here as long as I wished but I had to possess a deep faith knowing that my search would find an answer. It could be solved. I believed and had seen that others before me had solved the riddle, saw into their place in the universe and knew they had not been deceived. I told him I didn't doubt this and wanted to experience this myself no matter how long it took. I also said I didn't truly understand mu. It almost seems that there is nothing to understand. In a sense I don't know. I don't know what I'm supposed to understand or not understand.

"Good" he said, "You have right spirit and I admire your determination. You must strive morning, noon and night with mu and never let it go, whatever you are doing. You question understanding. If after much meditation and reflection, you honestly you truly say you don't understand, that would be compelling evidence since in truth you may find that there is nothing to understand. At a deep level it can be said that we understand nothing. All the scientific knowledge and philosophic wisdom that man possesses is but a pinprick in the vastness of the cosmos. All that is known is contained on the mere tip of the pin. Do any of us truly understand why trees grow, flowers bloom and the passage of the seasons. When we cease to think, it is then we reach the deepest levels."

I interrupted him. " I can understand that …"

He held up his hand and cut me short. "If you can truly admit and say that you don't understand, it is then that you understand very much indeed. Now go back and press on with your practice, with whatever you are doing, walking, working, sitting or sleeping" He rang his bell and I was dismissed.

I left Roshi's room with my head somersaulting with the significance of his words. They made some sense and in another way they didn't. I also wondered what Dad would have said about all this. Would he have had any insight or experience of what Roshi had said? I had no way of knowing unless Hugh finds more in his investigations about him in this respect.

* * *

I asked Ella to marry me. She didn't refuse! I was beside myself with glee and so was she. We held each other and together jumped up and down mad with a frenzy of sheer joy. If anyone had seen us they would have thought we were insane!

We drove over to Sophie and Bobby's place and I couldn't stop beaming like a searchlight. When we got there it was obvious to them both that something had happened between us. The air of expectancy was highlighted by the knowing looks they were giving each other. They guessed and boy, were they pleased. Bobby dashed across to his fridge and produced a bottle of Bollinger. He then said a strange thing. "Dad strikes again!"

I knew what he meant though and I had no doubts he was right. Unwittingly his illness had brought Ella and me together. There was no way he could have engineered that but no matter; we couldn't seem to escape from him even three years on. His hands continually reached out to us. It made me think about that unopened envelope but I knew we had to wait for Flora to get back before that happened. How long she would be was anyone's guess. We were prepared to wait. In the background I heard the cork pop.

"When's the big day then?" Sophie asked.

"I don't know yet." Ella answered. "We have to decide that when we've calmed down a bit."

Bobby was smirking. "The next question I daren't ask."

I thumped him playfully on his arm and spilt his

Champagne over his desert boots. He just chuckled. I'm glad he has a sense of humour and we were both laughing. I said we would like Flora to come to the wedding but whatever her situation was, that would affect her decision.

"We won't know unless we ask." "Bobby, if you can give me some more photos of the twins I'll write to her and tell all the news and see what she thinks."

Before I got round to writing to Flora I received a letter from her telling me of her new address and what she was planning for the future. She said she could possibly be there for another year. That was disappointing unless she would be able to break off what she was doing to come over for the wedding. I couldn't help thinking of Mark who was floundering about like a beached whale not knowing what he had to do. He never wrote to Flora and I suspect communication between them was at an all time low. His contact with us had also lessened since Flora went. That doesn't surprise me and I hope our friendship doesn't collapse entirely. He's a bright, intelligent man but like us all, prone to life's emotional twists and turns. So I wrote back to her immediately.

Pimlico May 27th 1977

Our dear Flora,

As you can see I've got your last letter and address so I hope this reaches you ok. Sophie and Bobby send you all their love and can't wait for you to come home and become a real aunty to Caroline and Hannah. I've enclosed more of Bobby's photos of them and some of us taken the other day

More good news! Ella and me have decided to get married either sometime this year or early next

*year, or maybe within a few weeks, which would get
rid of some of the suspense! Why wait! And of course
we want you there. I'll send you all the details when
we've set a date.*

*Mark is still very disconsolate so please write
to him separately. He's like a fish out of water and
we see little of him now. Whatever you do is your
decision but please put him out of his misery one-
way or the other.*

*Hope our news pleases you! Bobby's got masses of
work right now. I'm still into physics but not sure
for how much longer. Can't wait to see you again.
Hope it works out well for you at your new temple.
All our love, from Sophie, Trudi, Bobby and me.*

* * *

I got Hugh's brief letter and I was delighted at the photos of
them all, which brought a lump to my throat. I was so surprised
at Hugh's news about him and Ella and giggled with glee. I'm
sure they are going to be very happy together! I can't answer the
question about going to the wedding as I'm in no position to
know at the moment. Of course I would love to but a lot now
depends on my future here. It's possible I won't be able to go,
which would be a shame but there's not a lot I can do about it
especially as I've decided to take my ordination as a Buddhist
nun here. That will drastically alter everything again. This place
and Nakashima are perfect for me. I'm now extremely driven
and everything I do rivets into my koan of mu, morning, noon
and night. I take Hugh's point about Mark and it has been
amiss of me to leave him out of my considerations. What and
how I shall tell him I'm not certain. I'm a bit frightened of

damaging him further but I'm going to have to tell him. I picked up my pen and paper and stared down at it for a while, before beginning to write.

Kenkuro-ji June1st 1977

My Dear Mark.

I'm so conscious of neglecting you and I feel so bad about it, please forgive me won't you?

I owe you some explanations about what I intend and what my decisions are. Firstly, I've decided to become a Buddhist nun and of that I'm absolutely certain. It may only be for a short while but could be much longer. There are no guarantees. This is the only way I sense I can reach my goal. A nun as such is not for a lifetime. It's for as long as I want. I can walk away from it any time I choose. My ordination ceremony is four or five weeks away and after that, how long I stay here could be anything from six months to a year or two or more even. Now I know this is not the news you wanted to hear but for what it's worth, you are never far from my thoughts. If I have any misgivings it's that I'm missing a life with you. Secondly, let me go from your life and find a new woman, one that won't be so stubborn and single minded as me, one that can give you a decent life, one that I can't now give you. You richly deserve someone like that. I know I've hurt you and I'm so sorry. I'm not worthy of you. Forget me.

I'm writing to Hugh to tell him about my decision. I will always think of and love you. All my best wishes … Flora.

I was with Bobby and Sophie when Mark unexpectedly arrived at the door. I let him in and he barely acknowledged me. His face had a set and grim look. That morning I'd had a letter from Flora explaining her decision and that she'd written to Mark at the same time. I guess I know what he's arrived here for. He was tense and curt, almost rude. He said nothing but produced a letter and slapped it on the coffee table. I recognised Flora's distinctive bold writing.

"What do I do now?" he asked, " I suppose you've already heard?"

"Yes, we have," I said. "Mark, I'm so very sorry about this. It's gone further than any of us could have imagined. I don't know what to say."

"Read it." He roughly pushed the letter over to me.

I looked at the others and Bobby nodded at me. I picked it up and began to read. It was as I imagined. Under the circumstances and doing what she wanted, her letter couldn't have been anything else but this. Mark turned away and stared out of the living room window. When I'd finished he turned back again and looked at us all.

"I don't have much choice do I? She's married to a religion I want no part of and can't understand. I've lost her and I've no option now but to go on my own way. As I said once before, your father has much to answer for. If it hadn't been for him none of this would have happened. He's wrecked my hopes with the woman I loved and I shan't forget that."

I thought he was stretching the point far too far. Before I could reply he picked up the letter and without saying another word he ripped it to bits, throwing the pieces back on the table. He walked quickly out of the house slamming the front door as he left.

TWELVE

Two Weddings

It was the morning of my ordination. In preparation for this I stayed up all night in meditation, still focussing on mu. Deep inside I forever wondered and questioned its meaning. I've reached a stage in my practice where I'm totally locked into this riddle, so much so I'm abandoning any notions of nothingness and concentrating solely on mu. I've had some tantalising spiritual glimpses but they are not what I'm looking for. As my former Roshi had said "Don't linger or admire the view. Push ever onwards, never stopping and you will surely succeed." I kept to this as a sort of game plan. I knew I was ready for my ordination. In spite of minor reservations I knew this was meant for me. I felt no nerves, just a cast iron certainty that what I was doing was right. I also knew that Dad would have approved of what I was doing and maybe would have tried to be with me on this day. Thinking that, I had no bad thoughts of him.

The ceremony commenced mid-morning. It was made up of a long procession walking behind me, consisting of local guests and monks from other nearby and affiliated monasteries. In front were our own monks, the chief junior, guest master and chief cook. They were dressed in finery that I didn't know they possessed. The column of people was ablaze with black, orange, yellow red and purple robes. Nakashima Roshi solemnly led them in his full black and scarlet ceremonial robes. Whilst looking frail he was as upright as a scaffolding pole. And just as hard. I knew he was as strong as a tiger and his eyes, as ever, glowed with a distinct alertness. He was carrying in one hand a large object, which looked like a giant fly-whisk. I'm sure it wasn't! I now know it's known as a *hossu*. In his other hand he held a massive pole, which resembled a shepherd's crook but it was highly decorated with symbols and ornate gold embellishments. When we reached the shrine he turned and asked the audience to sit or kneel. I remained standing. There was much bowing, bells, drumbeats and incense. The monks began a slow deep and sonorous chant, which echoed around the hall. It could make the hairs stand up on the back of your neck. It seemed to go on forever. When it had finished the Chief Junior led me to the front where I knelt down in front of Roshi. He was now carrying a small bowl filled with perfumed water. He dipped in the *hossu* and liberally splashed water on my head. Producing a razor, he then passed it across my head right and left and the monks began another slow resonant but short chant. When it had finished he spoke, slowly and very clearly in Japanese, which I could now partially understand. The invocation was lengthy but I remembered certain passages very clearly.

"When we cut off our hair and the root of human ties, it is then that the truth manifests itself. When we change our clothes and live beyond the world we can attain freedom. In so cutting this hair we have nothing to cover our round heads and our square cut robes are symbols of enlightenment."

Tears flooded into my eyes but I wasn't going to let that distract me. Roshi proceeded to shave the right side of my head and when he had done so he passed the razor to the chief junior who then shaved the left side. Another monk collected my fallen tresses. I felt no regrets. A small round knot was left in the centre known as a *shura*. I was asked if I would permit it to be cut off. I replied "I do." And Roshi gently and carefully removed it. With much recitation I was encouraged to stand up and was dressed in a black robe known as a *koromo*. When this was done, I knelt again and was given my new name 'Sansho', which I had asked for in memory of Dad. After all, I felt he was instrumental in leading me here. 'Sansho' was written on a piece of paper. This and my new meditation mat were passed through the incense smoke and I had certain disciplines to recite. As I reached out for my mat and name a *kesa* or *rakusu* with five stripes was hung around my neck, which I then had to take off and place back on the shrine. With much ceremony and chanting before accessing a seven striped *kesa,* I bowed three times, took it off to the shrine and was then given a nine striped version, which I did not take off and was to wear at all times. Roshi had inscribed it in Japanese together with his bright red seal mark on the back. There followed more recitations and I was given my own begging bowl which was placed on the alter. I was then asked to recite my holy vows and the ten Buddhist precepts on how to conduct your life. This I did in Japanese. When I'd finished Roshi continued.

"Now the universe rejoices. The earth trembles and the petals of flowers fall. O Sansho Anderson, time, and your life will pass as swiftly as an arrow from a bow. Life and death are a grave event. Never rest, never pause in your practice. Always exercise charity and do not be proud or boastful when you come to enlightenment."

I felt like sobbing but I had to lead them all around the Great Hall three times to the accompaniment of the temple drum and the chanting of mantras. The atmosphere was totally uplifting. I felt I was capable of anything Roshi could ask of me. Once this was done I then led them out to the smaller hall. The ceremony was over and I knew I'd taken a huge step forward. Once in the hall, the monks to my surprise had prepared a special feast in my honour. Each one came up to me individually, made *gassho*, bowing deeply in front of me without a word being spoken. I felt deeply touched and remained standing and very solemn. However I soon got into the spirit of things when sake was served but unlike some I stuck at two little cups only! So it was completed. Next day I returned to my allocated tasks and daily monastic life. One thing I must say, my head is deliciously smooth but feels really cold! It's a marvellous feeling now being part of the monastery. I'm looking forward to the next sesshin in three weeks time. My black robes are now my life. I am now married and Roshi and the monks are my other family.

* * *

It was a beautiful spring morning, a fine day for a wedding. Magnolias, Camellias, a host of other flowers and various trees were bursting into bloom with the vigour of a new found life. I woke up to this and had a distinct attack of nerves. The bright sunlight hurt my eyes. It was the day of my marriage ceremony to Ella at Torbay Registry Office in Paignton. We'd brought the wedding forward due to Ella's property negotiations and she was due to move into *Pimlico* once we returned from our honeymoon. The mere mention of a wedding turned me into jelly. Still, what should I expect from the biggest decision of my life! The butterflies refused to go away and I wondered if Ella was feeling the same. My head remained throbbing from the night before and I was somewhat hung over! It'd had been a riotous evening with my friends and I don't quite know how I got home. If I can't get a little drunk on an occasion like this, when can I? I staggered out of bed and looked at myself in the full-length bedroom mirror. "Oh God," I said to myself. "What a bloody mess." I had suitcases under my eyes and I looked as white as a sheet. I groaned out loud and headed for the shower. The water revived me a shade but my head continued its incessant hammering. Fortunately the ceremony was several hours away but I thought getting back into bed wasn't an option, that wouldn't help. I had to keep moving! I got through the morning but my mouth still tasted like the inside of a gravedigger's glove in spite of mouthwash, drinking endless glasses of water and cups of coffee. There was no cure, only endless runs to the toilet. Gradually however, the hammering in my head ceased and colour began returning to my face. I felt slightly better and was able and ready to get cleaned and dressed up for our big day. I went to my old Harrods's oyster veneered walnut wardrobe, which came from my grandfather, Percy. I pulled out my never before worn white linen Pierre Cardin shirt, a light blue silk tie and my rather expensive dark grey double breasted Italian suit by Giorgini, plus my Italian black patent leather shoes by Brunori. I made sure I peeled off the price tag from the sole underneath so people couldn't play the game of spot the price tag when kneeling. It was then I remembered there would be no kneeling at the Registry Office. I couldn't suppress a grin.

The Registry Office was packed and many guests had to stand out in the entrance foyer. There were over one hundred people present made up from Ella's friends and family and also from mine. The place was a riot of assorted colours from the guests and so many varied flowers with their almost overpowering but beautiful scent. I noticed there were several of Ella's colleagues from her Marie Curie connection. They were all wearing their crisp sparkling uniforms and carried little matching posies of yellow flowers, which matched those in their hair. The twins looked wonderfully clean and smart but for how long? They are growing up so fast. Bobby and Sophie looked superb too. He was wearing a fetching light khaki safari suit with a red and white spotted handkerchief around his neck and the most enviable, very latest desert boots. All so unconventional and very much the photographer. Sophie wore a mauve close fitting suit with a large red carnation on her lapel, matching mauve coloured high heels and a navy frill front blouse. This she topped off with a tiny blue hat complete with a mini veil. Both Bobby and Sophie were to be our witnesses and they certainly looked the part for the occasion. Frank and his family arrived all looking immaculate. He was wearing a jet black light weight suit, which he contrasted with a bright white shirt and an immaculate crimson silk tie and shiny black slim fitting shoes. His wife, Charlotte wore a lime green suit and elegant matching high heels. Additionally she wore a very large black wide brimmed hat festooned with a colourful clutch of flowers. I attempted to speak to and shake hands with as many people as I could before moving to the front of the room and stood nervously waiting for Ella to arrive in the time honoured tradition of being five minutes late. My hands were sweating and I had a momentary thought that she had called it off! She arrived on cue and looked such a picture I gasped and almost wept. I felt so proud of her. She was wearing a cream coloured full-length cotton dress printed with sprigs of spring and summer flowers with matching high heels. On her head she wore a complimentary Juliet cap with a tiny white veil attached. We couldn't stop looking and smiling at each other.

The Registrar was a more elderly man with silver grey hair and kindly sparkling eyes, which took years off his age. He looked ideal for the job. We asked that if once he had gone through the legal requirements of his office and our wedding, we could read our own separate declarations to each other. We had five each, making ten in total. He paused a moment and stroked his chin, smiled, "Well, I don't see why not. It's not going to harm anyone, is it?"

So he performed the legal part of our ceremony and we made our solemn pledges, exchanged our rings as tokens of our love for each other. We then kissed and our audience clapped loudly amidst some cheering. The Registrar held up his arms signalling the guests to be quiet for a few moments. He told them we had a few things we wanted to say to each other and for them to hear what we were saying. So I started as we turned and faced our guests. Slowly and clearly I began to speak. My nerves had vanished.

"My darling Ella, we met in sad and strange circumstances but looking back on it, it was meant to be. I was always attracted to you but never in my wildest dreams did I even suspect it would lead to this. We've made our vows and now I want to make these further pledges to you. One, I shall never betray or desert you come what may. Two, I will help and assist you in every possible way and never expect you to be the traditional wife beholden to her husband. Three, I promise to kiss you at least twice a day for the rest of my life. Four, everyday I shall tell you that I love you and finally five, should we occasionally fall out I shall still keep to what I have promised to you today. Whatever happens I will always be prepared to say sorry or admit when I was wrong."

I leant forward and kissed her gently on her mouth.

Ella stood back and looked me squarely in the eyes and spoke loudly and openly.

"Hugh Anderson, my beloved Hugh, I've heard what you

had to say and indeed our meetings were under the saddest of circumstances but I always felt that there was something between us both. I too never imagined it would come to this. I'm so glad it has."

Her eyes never left mine for an instant and she continued.

"Hugh, I too have promises to you that I also intend to keep. One, whatever you wish to do in life you will always know I shall support you whether or not in my heart I like it or not. Two, from our conversations I suspect it won't be too long before your life takes a new direction. I want to be there for you and to help and assist you where I can. Three, I too will always want to kiss and make up should we fall out at times. Four, everyday, as long as I'm able I shall tell you how much I love you. Five, come what may in sickness or ill health, God forbid, you know my prime concern will always be you. You are my number one priority. I love you so much."

She leant forward and kissed me. We held each other tightly and hugged. For a moment you could have heard a pin drop. Then a beautiful eruption of noise came from the hall as clapping and cheering got wrapped up in an appreciative cacophony of sound. I don't think there was a dry eye in the place and that included us both as we turned to them. We held hands tightly together and we waved to them all. Even the Registrar seemed moved as he moved up behind and whispered, "That was beautiful. Well done, well done!" He shook my hand and gave Ella a peck on the cheek and added with lovely smile, "Now that's something I very rarely do."

We moved out of the hall across to Oldway Mansion where we had arranged the reception. The building is most suited for weddings with its assorted rooms and large hall. It's a romantic construction boasting an elegant colonnade, an Italian garden and French architecture. Well, of course, at the reception there was the usual raucous speeches directed at me by all and sundry with some embarrassing anecdotes I would rather have forgotten. But that's what the groom has to expect isn't it? Yet I was inwardly aware of other emotions bubbling below the surface. When my turn came to say a few words I said that there was one person missing from our family who we dearly wished could have been here. "That's my twin sister Flora, who as many of you know is still in Japan and couldn't be here today although we've had a message from her. So can we please stand and drink a toast to her and wish her every success and good health and we are counting the days until we see her again." I also felt Dad's presence very strongly in my psyche but kept that to myself. He is still here with us all and never goes away. Perhaps one day we can draw a line under his chapter but that never seems to happen. I pushed his memory aside and told them all that in ten days time we were off on our honeymoon on a hot air balloon safari over Kenya for three weeks. Boy, was Bobby envious! He told me later he'd always wanted to do that and wished he could come along as the photo opportunities were endless. No chance! His next assignment, he told me, looked like being in India dealing with how sacred cows and elephants are treated. I'm certain he'll do a first class job. Sophie seems well adjusted to his new life style. If she thinks otherwise she's not saying. I guess she has little choice. She has had to turn her job into a part time one but I don't think she minds at all. When everybody finally left in the evening we were exhausted. As I told Ella, today was the best day of my life. Ever.

The following morning as I was drinking a cup of coffee I heard the letterbox rattle. A letter from Japan had dropped onto my doormat. Of course it was from Flora. As usual I wasn't going to open it until all the others and myself were all together. We

261

arranged this for Sunday lunchtime, which has now become much of a routine for us and gave a chance for us all to be together and catch up on all the latest chat and gossip. On Sunday, at midday we sat around the large wooden patio table with glasses and a couple of chilled bottles of Sauvignon Blanc. I pulled the letter from my inside pocket and handed it to Trudi to open and read it to us. There were several photos inside.

Kenkuro-ji July 20th 1977

Hello you lot! How you doing over there? What's that good old British weather doing? It's not too bad here much like home I guess. So Hugh, by the time you get this you may have been married a few days perhaps. I can only guess it will be a shock to your system. Ho! Ho! Honestly I really would have wanted to be with you but I was there in my mind and couldn't wish for a lovelier Sister-in-Law. I send you both all my sincere and best wishes. I'm sure it all went well and to plan, knowing you Hugh! I had my ordination ceremony some days back. Enclosed are photos {not up to Robert's standards} showing me receiving my robes, head shaving and presentation to the other monks. Hope you like them. My, don't I look serious! And don't laugh at my shiny dome!

I want to see pics of the wedding … urgently. D'you hear! I can't see myself getting away from here for some time to come yet but as soon as I know I shall of course let you know. Am progressing with my training and that's all I can tell you about at the moment. My path is remorseless and never ending.

Please, please send me Cadbury's chocolate. I dream of it constantly!
All my love… Flora.

It's true to say we hardly would have recognised Flora with her shiny new head and she's lost so much weight too. Her Pre-Raphaelite auburn wavy hair, her crowning glory, has gone and I can't say nor can the others that we like the shaven head at all. She's almost unrecognisable. There were other photographs of the temple and surrounding grounds. It does look a stunning place.

Bobby spoke. "There's an assignment here I reckon. Just look at that temple and all that gold decoration and a western woman being ordained as a nun in an all male monastery in far off Japan. Who's the old guy there with the giant fly swat and the sheep dog trials crook in his hands?"

His remark caused us to giggle. He said what we thought but dared not say! Bobby carried on with a smile. "I get it, he must be Mr. Big, her boss, her master or Roshi as she refers to him. I must say, joking apart. he looks impressively scary."

Trudi said, "Boy, she looks well into it doesn't she?"

"We all know Flora. She never did things by halves, always head on. You have to admire her though. She's got real guts to go out there alone, knowing nobody or nothing. Now look at her." I said.

"Yes, but she lost Mark in the process."

There was a momentary silence. "That's true but she's married to her vocation instead. I hope it's enough for her."

"What's that hanging from her neck?" Bobby pointed to her photograph. "I guess it's something to do with the ceremony. She looks pretty dignified in that robe, don't you think?"

We all agreed. Bobby carried on. "I'm going to have a word

263

with NG and the BBC to see if there is any mileage in this for them. It looks a good story to me. Could be good publicity for the temple and if it happened it would be a chance to see her again, presuming she doesn't get back here first, that is."

We passed her photos around. It struck me how at home she seemed in a totally different culture, and so serene standing there posing with her master and the other monks. I felt an overwhelming surge of pride and love for her.

"D'you think we'll see her again?" asked Sophie.

"Don't say that!" I said. "Of course we will even if we have to go to Japan to see her."

"I reckon we should give it another year and then we'll consider what we should do. If we have to go there I think that's what we should do. What do you think?"

"Sounds reasonable."

"We've still got that bloody letter to deal with yet." Bobby reminded us..

"We'll not doing anything with that until she gets here. That's for certain."

"Agreed."

"I just hope it's not another of Dad's can of worms."

"Don't bet on it."

"Jesus, his legacy has caused more soul searching and heart ache amongst us all. Yet there have been strange and unexpected developments for some of us, so it hasn't all been bad has it?"

"Maybe, but that's the trouble with war heroes, they seem to dwell in their own little retrospective world. Dad did, didn't he?"

"Yes that's true."

"Well, I guess that was part of his problem, he wouldn't talk to anybody about anything of importance. You only have to look at us lot and what's happened to us all to see the proof of that!"

"Let's forget him now. I propose we drink a toast to dear Flo." I stood up and lifted my glass with them all and drank to her happiness for always and success on her quest.

Bobby said he would prepare an album of our wedding and would send it to her as soon as he could. Almost as an afterthought, he turned and asked me, "How you doing with all that compilation and research? We never seem to hear much about it."

I smiled. "It's coming along. There's quite a bit to do yet but I can see the end in sight. I think you may all be surprised.

THIRTEEN

Dying

Two years have now passed since my ordination and letters still continue to be exchanged between us all and I did get the wedding album. Oh my! Wasn't that just grand. I often look at it to think of back home and how so different it looks to things out here. I'm always wondering what they are all up to, Bobby and Sophie, the twins Hannah and Caroline, Hugh, Ella and of course Trudi. I've written to Mark a few times but he's never replied so I guess he's given up on me. That's not surprising is it?

I've now become Chief Junior, which is an important post in the monastery and carries a lot of responsibility, which I have to fit in with all the daily rituals, meditations, sesshins and any other tasks they care to throw at me. I have much to run and take responsibility for. When I've got a spare moment or two, which is rare, I sit back and run through all the events that led me here. Dad looms large in the frame and I can't seem to throw him off. It wouldn't be untrue to say that I'm not too sure whether I want to do that or not. I did regret missing Hugh's marriage to Ella but I also had my own ceremony to attend at about the same time. This made a trip back to England impossible. Part of me wanted to go and part of me didn't. It would have been a major distraction.

What of my family? I see from Hugh's letter that Sophie will be giving birth to her third child in the next six weeks. Phew! It would be dishonest of me to say I didn't feel envious.

I do! Brother Bobby in the meantime continues to globe trot for National Geographic from one continent to another on seemingly endless exotic assignments. Lucky him! And now he's also doing work for the BBC. There was a chance he would make it here for an assignment but it was dropped for budgetary reasons. Shame! He's become highly regarded in professional photographic circles according to Hugh's letter. I don't doubt it for a second. It's strange to think how good Dad was with his camera and along comes his son who far exceeds anything he did. I bet he would be proud.

As for Hugh, he appears to still be in limbo land. He plays his cards pretty close to his chest. In this way he is so like Dad and never lets on what he has in mind. But overall he's nothing like him. I definitely sense from what he's been stating in his letters that there will be a change in his life. What this will be and when I've no idea. Like everything about Hugh, it takes time. Ella carries on her work with the terminally ill as a Marie Curie nurse. My God, I admire her so much. She makes what I'm doing look worthless and incredibly selfish. Hey, I can't dwell on this. We all have our own paths to pursue. Mine is so different to most but I have to live with that and all the flack and criticism that I sometimes encounter.

I often think of Trudi and how I found her such a delight. It was such a shock to her to find out the way she did about who her father really was. She's a very brave lady and we all took to her at once and I think she felt the same about us. It was like the connection had never been broken. A definite blood link exists between us all and I see no separation with her from us. She became my sister and then a short while later I went away and left her. That is a definite regret on my part. It hurts to dwell on it and I know I must not. I have to push onwards with no refuelling stops. I was pleased to see from Hugh's letter that she's now become a director of the company she works for. My, isn't she one talented and hard working woman? She deserves every inch of success. I love her dearly. I just can't wait until I see them all once again.

What of me? I've still not found out what I'm searching for although I'm focussed intently on my koan practice. Maybe it will hit me in the near future. I know it's obtainable and I know I *will* crack this paradoxical riddle. I've seen others do it and how it's changed their lives. That encourages me to even greater efforts. I made a vow and I intend to stay with that.

It wasn't long after my return letter to them all that I received another letter from Hugh. It was unusual to receive such a swift reply and I immediately thought that something must be amiss.

Pimlico, August 14th 1979.

Dearest Flora, I'm sorry to have to write this but darling Sophie lost her baby. There were complications and the baby was stillborn. It was a boy. We're all completely devastated. Poor Sophie, she's been so brave and making such an effort to carry on, business as usual. We know this is not the case. She is really in some emotional pain. It's plain to see. Bobby is totally broken up and I've never seen him sob so. They were going to name him Bruce Robert Anderson but now they are going to have to bury him with that name and never see him grow up. It's so bloody sad. We all hurt badly.

It would be good, Flora, if you could write to them soon. It would help them, I'm certain. Sorry to give you such sad news.

Hope you are well.

All my love Hugh.

I wrote back at once.

Dear Sophie and Bobby,

Hugh has just written to me telling me of your very sad news. I'm so, so very upset for you both to hear that. It's really made me cry. Words seem so inadequate. I feel such sorrow but it must be nothing to what you are going through. Don't give up trying in the future when you feel are ready. That may take some time and only time can perform its slow healing process. Promise me please, you won't stop trying. I really do want to be an aunty in the true sense of the word. The more the better. Oh dear, I'm getting tearful, which isn't helpful. I'm going to include your names in our morning's recitations asking for you to find peace. If it's any comfort to you both, you will know that I and a dozen monks or so will be chanting for you and Bruce Robert Anderson every morning here in Japan, to move you all to some peace and understanding. I shall leave your three names there until this trauma is reduced and over. I'm sure you will let me know but I can only imagine it will be sometime yet.

I feel so bloody useless, please forgive me because I love you both so very much and never stop thinking of you.

All my love … Flora.

When I'd finished writing I leant back and sighed deeply, feeling a profound sorrow. I thought of the Buddhist premise that ultimately life is suffering. Life is pain. Separation from that and those we love causes pain. This I now understood with a concrete certainty. Without warning I felt a blanket of total misery suddenly enfold me, tearing at every part of my mind and body, its rapid intensity escalated so much so that I collapsed on the floor and began weeping loudly and profoundly as my body was taken over with a total racking pain. Years of pain and agony burst over me. Total pain! Every limb was reduced to an incompetent painful paralysis. I began to gasp for breath. I was unable to move an inch. I must have stayed this way for some small while, gasping to catch my breath, unable to move, thinking that I was going to die. It was then Gaido, our chief monitor, came to my room and found me. Putting his arms around me he said anxiously,

"Sansho-san. Please no more cry."

He hauled me up into a sitting position. I barely heard him. My entire mind and body were experiencing degrees of pain I'd never felt in all my life. My body felt so hot it could have been on fire and perspiration gushed from every pore of my body, soaking my underclothes and penetrating my robes. My head was covered and running with rivers of hot sweat. I could barely breath. The pain of everyone in distress that there had ever been was in me. There was no end to it from beginningless time to the endless future. My mouth opened and shut but no sound was able to escape from it. Gaido attempted to calm me. After what seemed an age there was a vocal release, a loud and plaintiff wail screamed and shot from me. It echoed and bounced around my tiny room. He rushed to the water bucket and came quickly back with cold wet cloths, applying them rapidly to my head and neck, attempting to cool me down.

"Missy Flora, Sansho-san, please, please take deep slow breath. This pain go soon. Please do, please, deep slow breath now."

I could hear him vaguely in the recesses of my psyche and robotically did as he asked. Deep slow breath in. Deep slow breath out. I kept this up for some while and he stayed with me, continually giving me support and encouragement. He really is so very kind. He laid me on my futon, covering me with a warm blanket. Gradually I felt normality return and had barely begun to wonder what had caused this sad and dramatic reaction, when a deep sleep swallowed me instantly.

The next day I'd recovered but when I walked, it was a similar feeling to having night cramps in the legs and every step felt sore and stiff. I still didn't understand why my body had been attacked so, and wondered if I should see a doctor. Soon the late summer sesshin would commence, and I was not going to miss that! I hope my body is up to it. This is an important date in the monastery and a great emphasis was placed on it as it was supposed to coincide with the time that the Buddha found enlightenment. There are many contradictions to when that actually was. For me it doesn't entirely matter. The doing is what is important. I tried not to think of what had caused that attack the night before. The issue of pain and suffering, I remember Dad talking to me of so many years ago. I didn't truly understand but now I know how right he was. It was then the unopened envelope flashed into my mind. The three years deadline had long passed. I couldn't help thinking it would stay unopened for some time to come. Why should that came into my mind? I don't know. In reality I was more concerned for Sophie and Bobby.

I've been cleaning out the meditation hall before I go to the kitchen to give cook some much-needed help. After last night's experience I feel strangely serene. I'm not going to analyse what it was about or why it happened. It just did and I can only stay being continuously immersed where possible in my practice of asking what is mu? I've also got an odd premonition that this sesshin will be important for me. It's been some years now since my first ever sesshin. I know that in many ways I've changed along with my approach to practice. I know that Roshi values me highly although I haven't had an enlightenment experience to show for years of unremitting effort. Let's hope this next sesshin will prove to be different!

The last twenty-four hours told me how much I love this place. Since I've been here I've been on *Takhahatsu,* the monks begging round more weeks than not for over two years in all sorts of weather. It can be a mixture of pouring rain that drenches you through to the skin, freezing ice and snow, which would turn my feet and hands so numb I could barely hold my wooden begging bowl or walk properly due to the intense cold. The sun can also be unbearable in the summer months as I become drenched with rivulets of heavy sweat running down my back, chest, arms and legs. It could have been raining! When it got that hot all I longed for was to take off my immense straw hat to get some air to my body and feel the warmth of the sun on decently ventilated skin! I'm not really moaning, because I love the people here just as I did at Shokoku. They are remarkably dedicated and gentle and bear no resentment to me a westerner. I join in their laughter, their tears, their fears, hopes their gossips and petty intrigues and feel no separation from them, or they from me. Gaido's help and concern showed me that. They are my extended family. This I truly know.

The issue of Sophie's news gave me an unexpected jolt, bringing home to me the pain that life can cause. The experience and the apparent truth of it hammered itself into my receptive consciousness. It won't go away. Later that afternoon I spoke to

Roshi about what happened to me the previous day and what I was feeling about life and suffering. He said nothing for a short while when I'd finished telling him. He looked at me very sharply and intently and as was his habit, he thoughtfully stroked his chin.

"What you experience is true. You have truly felt it. It hangs heavy in Sansho-san's heart. Sesshin tomorrow our most important. Take experience with you but with open heart and do not try to recall. You have to press on with mu. Always ask, what is mu? You can do. Remember, a quickly obtained awakening never as deep as one that takes so many years as you have strived. You have taken time. You have learnt much. I see this. You don't." With that he rang his bell and I was dismissed.

The formal ceremony began that evening, heralding the commencement of the sesshin the following morning. I could sense a tension in the air as the proceedings went on. Although I was now an old hand at sesshin I was never immune from that tense air of expectancy. We assembled in the meditation hall, which was dimly lit by spluttering candles. The head monk assembled the participants, about twenty-five in all, and allocated sitting places for each. As Chief Junior I already had mine at the head of the hall close to the altar facing the other meditators. I instructed newcomers on the various disciplines of the monastery. This entailed how to enter and exit the zendo or meditation hall. Enter in on the left and bow, exit on the right, turn and bow. I showed them how to prepare their bowls for meals and how to behave when the food was coming round and how to tie up their bowls when they had been washed and cleaned. There were to be no leftovers. All had to be eaten! Additionally they were shown how to use their utensils silently during meals. I also showed them how to get on and off their cushions quietly. The air around us was now becoming cloudy with 'Mainichi Koh' incense, which was burning in bundles from the various shrines that stood up front of the hall. The sights, sounds and smells added to the anticipation and the rising atmosphere amongst the participants. When I was satisfied all the preliminaries had been attended to and they understood that they were now all under a strict no talking rule, I led them, single file, into the main hall, which by contrast was a blaze of lights and the air throbbed with the hypnotic beat of the giant monastery drum. The sitters all wore formal meditation attire and lined up in two rows across the hall facing each other. When the bell was struck we made gassho and bowed to each other as a sign of our mutual respect and recognition of our shared aspirations and understandings. An air of expectant excitement filled the hall as the rear door swung open and Roshi slowly walked in attired in full ceremonial dress. He filled the hall with an awesome presence as, firm and upright, he moved slowly forward, striking the base of his staff loudly on the floor on every other step. Even now, from me, he could command the utmost respect. His principal aides in attendance were also similarly clad in ceremonial robes. We all knelt and bowed with our heads touching our meditation mats. Roshi began in a slow and steely voice by explaining the monastery rules and those of the sesshin. No talking allowed. Only a single-minded devotion to our practice was the order of the day whatever that discipline he would allocate to us later. He told us neither to divert our eyes nor to look around at others or the surroundings as this was distracting and disrupts concentration for others and ourselves. He then talked about mealtimes and our approach to eating.

"Do not eat too much. You should eat only two thirds of

your capacity and food will be vegetarian. No fish or meat whatsoever. Eating too much can make you sleepy and interfere with your concentration. If you are worried about this, refuse what is offered. It is better for your concentration. You will not die! Eat quietly and do not crunch your pickles, as this can be irritating to others." He then exhorted us all to extend our finest efforts and endeavour as if this was our last chance on this earth to reach understanding for we could die in the morning! I then ceremoniously served Roshi his green tea and small cake and when he had finished we were allowed to eat and drink ours. This simple act symbolised the journey of hearts and minds together and confidence in the master and his devotion to us in attempting to open our mind's eye. He then interviewed each of them separately but I was not required to attend as I already knew what I was to do. Shortly after this the nine o'clock bell was struck and we retired to our beds. Six hours later the journey of a lifetime would begin.

Some were so nervous and excited they barely slept through the night. At three-thirty a.m. the temple horn was blown seven times to wake us up. Gaido was chief monitor and tore amongst us, his black robe billowing all over the place. He shouted loudly. "Wake up! Get up! Do you want to the find the truth or not? If not you best stay where you are in your soft little beds! The fight is now on. C'mon on get up and get ready for the fight of your life!" The slower movers out of bed he booted with his foot. He was like a Sergeant Major in the army and really scary to those who didn't know him. After teeth cleaning, washing and toilet, all in total silence, we rushed to our places in the zendo as incense wafted across us, adding mystery to the dimly lit proceedings. The gong was struck, booming mysteriously round the walls telling us the sesshin had commenced.

For me I knew this was a do or die opportunity. I'd never felt so ready for this in all the time I'd been in Japan. As the clock ticked on I felt like I'd swallowed a solid rock as I bore down on Mu! Mu! Mu! I attacked it with every thing I had. I was locked into it like never before but it wouldn't crack or open up for me. In what seemed no time at all and frustratingly so, the bell was struck and we had five minutes quick walking meditation, which also relieved the pressure on legs and feet. I refused to be separated from mu. I was utterly locked into it, so much so, it was mu walking not me. The bell was struck again and we made our way back to our cushions. Again a forty-minute period went by and we were yanked off our seats by the monitors and ran to line up for the first interview of the day with Roshi, who would test us on where we were at with our practice. We knelt in a formal row outside his door. Meetings with him in this way were often nerve racking and frightening and to confirm this we could hear him shouting at some hapless meditator who was going in the wrong direction. Some went in and he would dismiss them before they even had time to kneel. It was my turn and I knew I had nothing to say. His eyes on fire, he bellowed at me. "Next time bring answer. Nothing stupid!"

I made my prostrations and left hurriedly. We then had the morning rituals, which I always enjoy and they have an anchoring affect for me. I know some don't like ritual but for me they were inspiring with numerous prostrations and the deep slow chants of the community. Thankfully this was always followed by breakfast and like all meals was done ceremoniously. Great for maintaining concentration. During the day my concentration began to deepen as I locked horns with my practice and continued to question, 'What is mu?' Without realising it I was beginning to puff and pant heavily and my hands were clenching hard. Gaido whispered softly in my ear. "Quietly Flora Sansho-san. Others here."

I gave him a gassho but bored deeper and deeper into mu than I had ever done before. WHAT IS MU?" It was at this point, and quite suddenly everything disappeared in a flood of white light. Filling my ears yet again with the deafening noise of an RAF bomber and I knew it was flying over Germany. I was intensely cold, as the plane began dropping its deadly payload killing God knows whom down below. This was again similar to one of my earlier experiences a while back, I saw and heard flak and fighters filling the night sky. Noise. Noise and blood and the wounded screaming everywhere! It all came back! Life is pain! Life is suffering! Then I saw Dad standing in front of me in his officers uniform. Tears were running down his face. I reached for him in my mind but couldn't touch him. In his arms, he was holding a small baby boy. I knew at once it was Sophie's. The face of the baby then became Trudi's face! Pain! Too much pain and now tears were flowing down my face too. I *knew* I couldn't stay here in this mental prison. I had to move on! Move on and continue only to digest mu. Don't dwell on this vision. It's false. Carry on. Always carry on. Do not stop to admire the view or dwell in sorrow. Abruptly the vision vanished as quickly as it had come. Mu had cut it down. Then as quickly as it had vanished I found I'd ascended into the black quietness of space. For a moment I could see the entire universe stretching endlessly before me. Galaxies, giant stars, awesome planets of varied colours and sizes spun into a breathtaking and seductive panorama. What magnificence! Was this being what God was like? FORGET IT FLORA! Just mu and only mu! Nothing else! I dismissed, or mu dismissed this illusion. I bored ever inwards asking what is mu? Part of me began crying out for forgiveness for all the harm and wrongs I'd ever done. But there wasn't anybody who could forgive me. At this point I got an almighty whack across the shoulders from the monitor. "Don't think! Just mu!" he roared at me. I hardly felt the whack and his shout I barely heard. It did the trick, though, and I got back into my question and out of my head. He spoke more quietly into my ear.

"Become a baby again. Just mu, nothing else but mu. From pit of stomach not throat or head!"

I was building into a white-hot ball of heat and I could sense electricity around me. Then the bell rang for the interview. I tore to the front of the queue, breathless and with an internal fire burning within me. At my interview with Roshi he listened to what had happened to me but said very little. All he said was that one more giant leap was required. Press on harder! That was all he said and I was quickly dismissed.

Three days have now passed at the sesshin and I've never felt so positive about how I'm progressing. It all seems so tantalisingly close. I'm on fire or rather mu is on fire. I'm not certain which. Even the menace of the monitors and their whacks across the shoulders with their flat sticks doesn't faze me like it used to. They are now a positive and welcome encouragement. The whacks and roars they fire at us are ultimately kindly acts to goad us to find the truth we are looking for. So I pushed on harder, deeper and deeper. A phrase from Dogen, an early patriarch of Zen flashed into my mind. "*I came to realise clearly that Mind is no other than mountains and rivers and the great wide earth, the sun and the moon and the stars.*" I had read this many times in the past but this time it was unusually vivid, so much so it shook me. I sensed something was happening. All I could do was press on with mu. Ignore the emotions and feelings. Quite suddenly I felt a soft giggle bubble up inside me as at this point the bell struck for our interview with Roshi. Without realising it I again sprinted to the line up and was first in the row of participants to see Roshi. When I heard his bell ring summoning me in I quickly rose up and sprinted into his room without thinking, still with the remnants of that giggle. He looked intently at me and simply said, "Show me mu."

Without thinking I grabbed his bell and rang it hard three times before tapping hard on his statuette of Buddha, whilst laughing out loud. Without waiting for his dismissal I promptly turned and walked from the room. If I'd stayed longer I would have seem him smile.

At the next interview it was a similar performance. I had pushed open the door of mu the merest fraction but it still wouldn't swing open for me. The excruciating pain in my legs didn't prevent me from charging rudely into his room at the next interview. Again he asked me to show him mu. I was breathing hard and bubbling with a rising elation within. I reached for his wooden blocks, picked them up and struck them hard together. The resultant 'clack' of sound seemed to spread across the universe. I felt amazingly free and unrestrained.

"Sansho-san," he said quietly. "Do not leave yet. You now face the final hurdle, the hardest part. You must be fearless, let go and jump into the void. You now much more free. Return to your seat. Bore harder deeper into mu. You almost there. Attack that iron ball with all your strength and might. Do not be separated from it. Do zazen all night if you think sleep separate you from mu. You will not tire. With you sleep not necessary." He rang his bell. I prostrated myself before him before leaving his room. I was determined to stay up all night and not let go of mu. When night fell and the nine o'clock bedtime bell struck I picked up my cushion and headed outside to a small hillside nearby where I found a flat spot beneath a tree. It was a brilliant night sky and I think every conceivable star was shining down on us here in the monastery. I resisted the temptation to admire it all and instead focussed intently on my practice, pushing and burrowing further and further into mu. It was relentless. Early in the morning I heard the temple clock strike and as it did a large pinecone dropped from the tree under which I was sitting. It struck me hard and unexpectedly on my shaven head. The sound of the clock and the pinecone caused a moment of sudden realisation. The pinecone, the chimes and I are formless together and made from the same organic matter we are all made. Why not! It seemed so obvious! We were the same. This wasn't an intellectual understanding. It was much different. This small event gave me vast encouragement and without feeling tired I strived and pushed on until I heard the rising bell and the mystical note of the temple horn summoning all to rise, wash and do what toiletry was necessary before marching silently into the dimly lit zendo once more.

I felt alive, very, very much alive without an obstacle or tiredness in sight. All was mu and I was mu. I sat and embraced mu like an ardent lover. It was in my very being, my mind, my breath and all around me. Of that I had very little doubt. Roshi summoned me in at the first interview of the day. He said nothing as I sat in the required formal posture in front of him. He surveyed me at length and I wasn't afraid of him.

He spoke. "I saw you last night under the hillside tree. Tell me what you understood. I proceeded to tell him very slowly and carefully what had happened. When I had finished his questions were unexpected. Some I could answer, others I hesitated with and could only make a faltering response.

"How old is mu? Who is mu? Show me mu. How tall is mu? What colour does mu have. Show me mu when having a bath. When eating breakfast. Where is mu in pain and suffering?"

When he had finished he looked directly at me. "Maybe some masters would sanction this tip of the tongue experience as the real thing. What would you have me do?"

Without any hesitation I told him that I didn't want him to sanction my feeble effort as an enlightenment. I guess this is what the sly old tiger had in mind anyway! I told him I had many insights over the last two years. This was the most significant but I was going to soldier on for deeper understanding. I wasn't prepared to accept approval for this effort. I was going to travel onwards to full realisation.

"I admire your spirit and courage, Sansho-san. Push on to the top of the mountain. You are still half in cloud."

When I returned to the zendo for the next painful session of aching legs and knees I felt strangely light as though I was becoming transparent. I attacked mu in an assault I'd never ever mustered before in all my years in Japan. I was desperate. I was going to nail this or die in the attempt. This was how badly I wanted it. For the next ten hours I hammered on mu's iron door until I felt it beginning to budge a little. Every thing I did through the day and night was only mu. 'I' wasn't involved. I'd ceased to exist. The monitor Gaido did not let up on me. It was as if he knew. I felt as if I'd died to myself. 'I' no longer existed. 'I' had passed way. I could feel myself laughing and half crying but it wasn't me it was mu. I was perilously close.

The bell struck and it reverberated throughout my whole being. I was the bell! I floated, or so it seemed over to the interview room and once more was rudely first in. I made my formal prostration to Roshi. Like a hunting tiger he stared with an intensity, looking right through me. I waited and eventually he spoke, initially paraphrasing Dogen's famous words, the same words that had come into my mind a while ago.

"*People who obtain enlightenment come to realise clearly*

that mind is no other than mountains and rivers and the great wide earth, the sun and the moon and the stars. All is mind. A piece of string is eternal and boundless. The pure white ox is as your mind, pure, vivid.."

My body began to shake. Heaven and earth disappeared, disintegrated into a million fragments. Utmost and complete joy struck me. An earthquake hit me. I felt as if I'd been shot! Everything around me vanished in a brilliant gold and silver rush of illumination. It was an ecstasy of unparalleled delight. For what seemed an age I alone WAS. I was at the centre of the universe I was there. How long this went on for I can't say but I *knew.* My vision reoriented and Roshi's face reappeared into focus. He was smiling broadly and our eyes met and we both broke out into laughter. "I *know!* I *know!* I really do *know.*" I was laughing and crying all at the same time and my fist thumping the mat on the floor. "There's absolutely nothing. There's nothing to realise! I'm everything and everything is nothing. Its been in front of me all these years and I couldn't see it." My body continued to shake and tremble from head to toe. Crooksbury Hill hadn't lied to me after all. I'd been too young to know. It was there all the time. It never left me. I'm so, so grateful. I couldn't say another word, my throat ached with joy and words wouldn't come out. All I could do was lay my head in Roshi's arms with tears streaming down my face as he gently stroked my head and back. "Well, well Sansho-san, this is a rare achievement indeed. I have watched you these years now and never doubted you could do this. What you have reached, I can tell, is called the 'Attainment of the Emptiness of Mind.' Very rare. You will be much honoured." Eventually I stood up, thanked Roshi for his amazing patience with someone so stupid as me, made my prostrations and left his room still half blubbering and laughing all at the same time.

Later that evening as the sesshin was moving to a close I sat in zazen unable to control tears and emotions of all kinds including the giggles and feeling profoundly privileged for being given the opportunity to come to realisation. I was trying hard not to make a noise to disturb others. Gaido, who had whacked me so enthusiastically crept quietly up to me and whispered gently into my ear. "Congratulations Missy Flora Sansho-san. It's wonderful isn't it!"

Very unconventionally I seized his hands in mine and squeezed them hard, whispering, "Gaido, thank you, thank you so very, very much. Thank you for pushing me so hard. Without you I wouldn't have made it."

He smiled, said no more and bowed very deeply and respectfully in front of me and I made a similar response.

At the evening interview and discussion, l felt unbelievably free and was still experiencing a state of shock with emotions alternating between laughter and tears. Roshi again told me that I had reached a rare and unusual level of achievement. He proceeded to tell me that there were many degrees of self-realisation and the depth was without foreseeable end. My practice, he said was now to change and he gave me instructions on how I should now proceed. From this point. I subsequently worked on over three hundred koans over the next eighteen months and 'passed' through them all. I knew all this was for me and was meant to be. Whilst concentrating on my practice I continued with my allotted tasks and still look forward to Hugh's letters and news of home. That letter of Dad's has still not been opened. They are waiting for me. Sophie seems to have got over her tragedy but I suspect the memory will always be with her. I felt it was now the right time for me to now try and go to see them and knew I was going to have to ask for permission. Shortly into the New Year later

Roshi summoned me to his room. He looked unusually solemn.

"Sit down Sansho-san."

I duly sat down wondering what it was he could want. He reached behind him and revealed a small bundle of documents, richly embossed with grand looking red seals with gold and black tassels.

"These, Sansho-san, are for you. Before I tell you about them I will say your record is one I have not come across before. I despaired of ever finding any one who has achieved what you have achieved." He paused. His words were always terse and to the point. "I wish to appoint you as my spiritual successor, the inheritor of Buddha's Truth and his Truth manifested through me. Will you accept please" He bowed with a deep gassho in front of me."

I sat, totally dumbfounded. I didn't know how to respond, all I could do was to let tears roll down my cheeks. He wept too. He turned his head away from me to privately wipe away his tears with the sleeve of his kimono. With that moving gesture, I knew I loved that man and would be unable to refuse his request in spite of the awesome responsibility it entailed. I simply prostrated myself in front of him and simply choked out the words "Yes I do."

There was a silence as I remained in the prostration position not wanting to move.

Eventually, he spoke. " Sit up please. I can now die contented. There are many things to say, but I shall talk to you after the ceremony."

I hadn't realised that a ceremony would be involved but he told me he would instruct me on what to do and what to say.

So it was a week later the monastery community was summoned and lined in rows around the main hall. The ceremony was thankfully short. Roshi again in full attire carried the sealed documents he had previously shown me. Quite suddenly and unexpectedly I had a fleeting memory of Dad's story about Bill Perrin being chased by the Chinese man holding sealed documents with dangling tassels. The story had come full circle. Roshi placed on my head his very own Abbot's hat, which he held in place with his hand as we walked down the middle of the hall. This caused me some mild embarrassment. I could sense the puzzlement and awe that the assembly felt as we moved slowly up the hall accompanied by the beating of the drum, the ceremonial gong and Gaido blowing hard on the temple horn. When we reached Roshi's chair, he flicked his *hossu* across it several times and told me to sit in it. This I did still wearing his hat. He then stood in front of me, took three steps back made gassho to me and did three full prostrations in front of me. I was extremely solemn but couldn't prevent a small tear trickling down my cheek. He then stood, turned around and addressed the assembly. He explained to them what had happened since I passed through Mu and my achievements since that point, which were unique and he had never come across before. He then announced that I was appointed his true spiritual successor and Abbot in-waiting at the temple. He handed me the seals, which gave me my cue but I had to remain seated. In a slow clear loud voice I thanked everyone, in Japanese, especially Roshi and Gaido for pushing and guiding this ignorant western woman to something I would never have believed possible. I would carry on as before attending to my daily chores and work and wanted no special treatment or there would be trouble! Everyone laughed and there was a spontaneous round of applause, almost unheard of for such a reserved and conservative people. There then followed formal speeches and pledges of allegiance with plenty of bells, gongs, chanting and incense. One by one the assembly walked in turn towards me and each made three prostrations in front of me. It seemed to go on forever but that was an illusion of time. I then thanked them all and exhorted them to greater efforts. If I could do it, then surely anyone could make a similar or greater achievement. I would carry on here until I was needed elsewhere or whatever Roshi wanted me to do. With that I stood and Roshi banged his staff three times on the floor and we slowly filed out in silence to a small celebratory feast. The monks came up to me and offered their non-formal congratulations. Beneath all this I was thinking of my family and I was suddenly missing them terribly. Writing and exchanging photographs was fine but it couldn't replace real physical contact. I hadn't seen them for years. I felt I must see them soon. I was aching to see them in a way I'd never felt previously. If something didn't happen soon I would request permission to visit them. Later that day Roshi called me in and with amazing coincidence told me he would be sending me back to the UK for six months, then on to the USA to establish a branch of the monastery there. Underlying this he told me that Zen was floundering in modern day Japan and the West was the place it should now develop, as there was much interest in it and a demand for Japanese Masters to visit. I would be leaving within three months or even in weeks as soon as arrangements were finalised.

* * *

I've just received Flora's last letter addressed to me but written to us all.

Kenkuro-ji. January 1981

Hello Hugh, Sophie, Flora and Trudi.

How you all doing there in sweet old England? What I would do for a pint of Courage Best Bitter and a night down the pub with all of you instead of the occasional cup of sake rice wine! There's so much I want to know about you all and so much I have to tell you as well. How's things, Bobby? Where are you off to next? Hope you're not making Sophie a photographer's widow! Hannah and Caroline must be very grown up now. I really can't believe I've hardly seen them since they were tots. They must be over five now. That can make me ashamed and very sad for not being a proper aunty. Will you forgive me? What about you, Hugh? You still doing research? I really did think you would be off doing something else by now. Who knows? You may have placed your foot one stride forward in a marathon and not even known you've done it. Hope Ella's fine too. Is she still working as a Marie Curie nurse? And what about you dear Trudi? What I would do to see you again and have one of our all night gossips. They were such fun, weren't they?

Well, here's some good news you should be pleased to receive. I know I am. It looks like I shall at last, be allowed home for a while. I'm being sent back to establish a branch of Rinzai Zen in the UK and then on to the USA. It will take up to six months or more to establish. That's a bit scary, but I've been here some years, as you all know and it's time for a small change.

I have to also tell you I found what I was looking for. But I never felt able to tell you all. It was intensely personal and I wasn't sure you would understand. I guess I got a bit too precious about it but that, I think, has passed and I feel I'm able to mention it but with a wee bit of caution. Do you know what? It was in front of my eyes all the time and I never ever could see it. There is nothing I can say about it but just to say how profoundly grateful I am to everybody, especially to you for your unstinting support all these years for something that must have been difficult for you to understand. What would I have done without you? Thank you so much for keeping contact with me during, on occasions, difficult times. I especially feel this way towards my Master, Nakashima, who led me, a stubborn ignorant woman to a place I could never have imagined. I still haven't got over it. Anyway, enough of this I guess you may be wondering when you will see me. Surprise, surprise, It could be any time in the next three months or even weeks. As soon as I know and plans are finalised I will let you know.

I think you should also know, I've been appointed Roshi's spiritual successor. It doesn't get much bigger than that over here! Apparently he says I've achieved a rare degree of insight that very few are able to obtain. This is a very extraordinary honour indeed and I only hope I'm up to it.

I'll let you know when I'm expected back and when I do perhaps we can open that darned letter eh! My word! My family! I'm so excited at the thought that I shall be seeing you again soon. By the way, I don't know about you all and I haven't mentioned it before but I've given a lot of thought towards Dad. I have forgiven him, totally. I feel I owe him an enormous

*debt of gratitude and realised that I'd never really
stopped loving him. Without his sly manoeuvring I
would have never achieved what I have. I know this
is what I was looking for but never knew it. He was
human and capable of error like us all.*

*Goodbye for now. You're never out of my thoughts
and I love you all so very much. Much love, from
Flora.*

We were thrilled that, after all this time, we are about to meet our sister again, my twin sister, my missing half whose absence makes part of my life seem empty. Without her I've sensed a vacuum in my life. I guess that's the power and bond between twins. After all this time I've sensed a subtle change in her letters. She is calmer, philosophical and in some ways a sense of sadness impinges on what she writes. She really is a big hearted and courageous woman who we are lucky to have as one of us. I turned to them all to explain; "I don't think we should expect her to be the same Flora who left us over four years ago. Do you? She's a Buddhist nun now, complete with a shaven head. She's obviously been through stuff we probably couldn't begin to imagine."

Bobby spoke. "This is really, really good news, and like you I'm sure, I can't wait to see her again. I don't know what a 'spiritual successor' means or entails but for Flora to mention it in the way she did it's obviously very important in her world and we should respect that, shouldn't we? I expect she's changed a lot and I'm not expecting the Flora who arrives here to be the same as the one that left years ago. Anyway we've changed too. For a start we're married and that makes for its own changes, doesn't it?"

"Whatever she's become and looks like, she'll always be

Flora, my half sister to me but I prefer full sister. She's extra special to me, and was so kind and caring when I needed it most. I'm taking her down to the pub for that pint of Courage, shaven head or not!"

We all had a good giggle over Trudi's comments and agreed that was what we should do.

"When you think about it," said Sophie, "I can't believe she hasn't seen the twins for so long now. Was it really that long ago? They're now getting on for six years old and they often ask about her, their mysterious aunt who's a nun living in Japan."

"Interesting what she feels about Dad. That's something I'll decide on when we open that bloody envelope that's been hanging around in my dressing table drawer for over six years. What do you lot think?"

"Me too," added Trudi.

"Agreed. I'm in no hurry to see what's in it. Knowing him something dreadful!" Bobby said.

About a week later I started to write back to Flora but received another letter from her saying that plans had moved on quicker than she had imagined. She would be here in three weeks, not three months! She was flying on a Japanese Airlines flight but would be stopping off at Bombay en route for a few days to catch up with some old friends of hers who were living in an ashram close by, who she dearly would love to see. She was so excited and it showed in her letter, which bubbled with anticipation and happiness. She'd be arriving at Heathrow on the tenth of March and would telephone once she had arrived. Obviously we felt the same joy and instantly started making preparations. I would write back and ask for the flight number and time of arrival and arrange to pick her up at the airport. I wasn't having her making her way down here alone from

London. Ella would make the welcome home cake, Trudi would make all the side dishes, and Bobby was 'official' photographer. Sophie was to prepare the main course. We knew she didn't eat meat or fish although she had to eat what was given on her begging rounds meat, fish or not. We weren't going to impose that on her so Sophie in usual meticulous fashion set about designing a suitable and delicious vegetarian meal but with no pickled radishes or seaweed that we knew she had always eaten there! They both were careful not to make the menu too rich and also decided between them to make light desserts that wouldn't be too much for her. We could only try and see. I put myself in charge of decorations and décor. Not difficult, a few balloons and paper chains here, a few there plus a huge 'Welcome Home Flora' banner across *Pimlico's* porch. I'm just not the cooking type. Anything for a quiet life! I couldn't help wondering if she could still cook the best spaghetti bolognaise in the world like she used to. I was going to put her to the test.

The last letter I received from Flora gave all the flight and arrival times so I was well prepared. A fortnight later she flew into Bombay to visit her old friends.

* * *

Several days before she was due, I arranged the large banner across the porch, which simply read *Flora. Welcome home at last!* The letters were bright blue on a background of soft yellow, so that they really stood out. I brought great stacks of balloons and a handy blow up pump to inflate them with and stacks of multi coloured chains and paper decorations. The ladies set about preparing their chosen meals ready for cooking. There were some days to go but I decided to start hanging up the decorations and leave the balloons to the day before as they have a way of deflating after a few days. We began to get excited and even a little nervous. Isn't that ridiculous! When I was up a ladder stretching out to pin some ghastly coloured floral thing onto the wall I heard the phone ring. I jumped down, walked over to the phone and picked it up. A voice at the other end said "Is that Mr. Hugh Anderson?"

"Yes it is"

"Mr Hugh Anderson living in a house called *Pimlico* in Plymouth?"

I felt puzzled. "Yes. Who's calling?" It had to be a bloody newspaper that'd got wind of Flora's arrival back here.

"Mr Anderson, my name is Peter Wilson calling on behalf of the British Embassy based in Bombay."

A start went through me. What is this about? "Yes?" I didn't know what else to say.

His voice was exceedingly grave. "You have a sister, Flora Anderson, a Buddhist nun?"

"Yes. What's going on?" What he said next I was unable to believe.

"Mr Anderson, I'm awfully sorry but it's my very sad duty to inform you that your sister died two days ago in Bombay."

I felt my blood curdle and panic ripped through me. "What! What are you saying?"

"Mr Anderson, I'm so sorry to have to tell you this but it was an accident and …"

"I don't believe it! It can't be true!"

"Sadly Sir, I'm afraid it is true."

"How?"

"She was taking a bath at her hotel and a live electrical appliance fell into the bath. She died instantly."

I couldn't speak. I just groaned out loud in acute agony and slumped like a sack of wet washing into the sofa.

"Mr Anderson, I can only imagine how you must be feeling

about this sudden and unexpected news and this is not the moment to go into details. I shall ring you about this time, in two days time to discuss further details. In the meantime I'll leave you my number should you need to speak with me. Written notification has also been sent directly to you containing full details and circumstances."

I fumbled for a pen hardly able to write down what he was telling me.

"Once again Sir, my sincere condolences." The phone went dead.

I couldn't take this in. Flora dead! It wasn't possible. She was due here in a few days time. It wasn't true. Yet I knew it was. I couldn't cry. I was numb from head to toe and a total paralysis gripped me. I didn't know what to do, what to say. My heart rate accelerated and breathing got difficult. Nothing. I must have sat there for half an hour with a myriad thoughts cascading through my head. My twin sister was gone. Something had been cut from me, torn out of me. Surely this must be some sort of cruel joke? I knew it couldn't be. It was beyond belief. Utterly beyond belief. The pain was kicking in fast and I knew I had to act to tell the others. This was going to be hell on earth but it had to be done. I was going to have to ignore my own feelings, push them into the background and get on with telling Bobby and Sophie, Trudi and all those outside the family who knew Flora.

You can imagine the reaction I received. My first call was to Ella. I didn't know what to say or how to say it. I could barely raise a stutter.

"Hugh, what's wrong. What are you trying to say?"

I blurted it out in a rush. There was a long pause.

"Oh my God! It can't be true. It can't!"

Ella was distraught. "I'm coming home right now Hugh. Tell me it's not true."

"It's true. The Embassy have written to me and are calling me back in two days. I'm pole axed. I don't know what to do. I have to ring the others." I put the phone down without saying another word. God how was I going to tell Bobby? I called him, mercifully he answered the phone. I was more worried about his reaction than me having to tell him. I told him in a disjointed and emotionally inarticulate way what had happened. There was a silence down the phone that lasted an age.

He spoke quietly but clearly "Hugh, would you repeat that again please."

I repeated what I'd said.

"Oh fuck! Oh almighty fuck! "

I could hear him beginning to sob. I stayed on the line. I wasn't going to go until he wanted to put down the phone. I was having great difficulty in handling this. Bobby eventually regained composure and I knew his tears were under control. He found it unbelievable and wasn't able to take it in. He saw it as a nightmare that only happens in films and books. This time it was knocking on his front door.

"What do we do now?"

I told him that I had still to contact Trudi. We would all need to meet either tonight or tomorrow before the Embassy rang to discuss what arrangements we had in mind.

"Make it tonight please. We'll come over to you."

I agreed. My next call would be to Trudi.

Trudi wasn't in when I called a few minutes later. I left a message telling her it was urgent. It was a few hours later she responded. In between time Ella returned. We had a very emotional time and she understood the loss of a twin was a sadly unique event and did her best to console me. I was finding it incredibly difficult to absorb. For us all, a dark and bottomless abyss had opened up in front of our eyes. Shortly after, Trudi called. Ella answered and told her I was here. Afraid for her, I took a deep breath and stutteringly began to relate what had happened. Her reaction was what I expected and to hear her cry out in obvious pain and grief caused me to become upset again and I had to get Ella to take over until I stopped.

Trudi's reaction was no different to ours, full of agony, tears and disbelief. "My poor darling sister. This is unbelievable. My lovely Flora. I wanted to see her so, so much. I can't believe it! It can't be true! Tell me it's not true! This is so cruel." Her sobs were breaking up what she was trying to say. "All those plans we were making. What are we to do?" She could barely talk. I realised she'd had a special bond with Flora and now in one way, that was shattered. In another, they would always be united, more so. She agreed to come over early evening.

We sat together in an atmosphere of aching sadness lapsing into long silences. We went through every possible permutation of what might have happened and what might have been had she got here. The big question was, what did we want to happen to her body.

"Should we cremate or bury her?" Wondered Bobby wiping a fat tear from his eye.

"What do Buddhists do in these matters?" asked Trudi

"I don't know."

"I don't think it matters to them."

"Don't you think we'd better find out?"

"Dad was cremated and he was a sort of Buddhist wasn't he?"

I spoke, "I think I know what she would have wanted."

"What?"

"She did mention that Kenkuro-ji had a cemetery for deceased monks and others were cremated on open funeral pyres. I think we should ask the Embassy to return her body there, to the temple and her master Nakashima for burial, and I think we should all attend. What d'you all think? That is what she would have wanted. She loved the place and came to regard it as her home and the people there as her brothers and sisters. I've no doubt that would have been her wish."

There was a silence as they all looked at each other, then back across at me.

Trudi spoke "Part of me would have wanted her here but I understand what you are saying Hugh and I'm prepared to agree to that."

We felt the same, but her desire would be paramount. None of us disagreed. It was agreed that when Peter Wilson called from the Embassy that is what we'd ask for and would be prepared to pay any extra cost involved.

"I don't know if her master knows about this horrific event but he's soon going to. I'll try calling him. He speaks reasonable English, so Flora said. I'll wait to the Embassy calls and we will try to work it out from there. If not we'll just turn up anyway."

The Embassy rang as promised. I told Wilson of our decision, and as a Buddhist nun that was what she would have wanted. Wilson agreed and said they would put the arrangements in place so that her body would arrive at Kenkuro-ji in about four days time. He also said they had fluent Japanese speakers who would talk to the temple and make the necessary plans required and inform Nakashima of our imminent arrival.

The following day Wilson called again and said that every thing was in place. Flora's remains and ourselves were expected. He said nothing of their reaction. He also told us that he had made arrangements for our collection and delivery.

It was a grey and murky morning that we took off on a Japanese Airline flight heading for Osaka-Kansai International Airport where we would be met by Embassy staff and driven to the temple. It was much nearer the temple than Tokyo airport, which would have been almost three hundred miles from our destination. Sophie had arranged for the twins to be looked after by her Mum. Ella had some seriously terminal patients who were relying on her to be there so she was unable to come with us. She said she would be thinking of us all and was so sorry she was unable to attend. Sad, but her patients were paramount and needed her. We understood. So there were four of us on this most unhappy journey. We didn't speak much and locked ourselves away in our private thoughts and memories.

The plane touched down at Kansai Airport approximately twelve hours later. Local time was eight hours ahead of what we were used to. Once we had cleared airport formalities we were met by two dark suited, courteously efficient embassy officials. They directed us to a large shiny black Jaguar car. They told us that Flora's body had arrived the day before and was now at the temple. The journey there would take us about two hours and was outside the main city. There had been no need to book hotels as the temple had prepared guest rooms for us, which we appreciated. We drove through towns and the countryside of old and modern Japan but barely noticed it. Our minds remained elsewhere. This whole trip had an air of unreality about it. I don't think any of us were capable of taking it in. It was all too sudden. Too quick. Shock weighed heavy upon us all, heightened more so the closer we got to her temple. The Embassy staff pointed out places of interest en-route, probably trying to loosen up the atmosphere but we found it hard to respond. Eventually they stopped talking and we continued in silence. Not long after one of them spoke. "We are now in sight of Kenkuro-ji."

We stared from our windows at a large squared walled area about ten foot high, which was dominated by a large wooden Japanese style red and black lacquered arch, the entrance to within. The car came to a halt outside and with some foreboding we got out. This was her domain. We stood where she must have stood and it felt painful for us all. There was an air of unreality about it. Standing a little way inside the entrance was a figure that I knew to be a monk, wearing black robes and with a shaven head. The Embassy men walked over to him while we stood where we were. The monk bowed to them and they returned the gesture. A brief conversation ensued. When it had finished they walked back to us and explained everything was in hand and the necessary arrangements had all been made. They would return the day after the funeral and deliver us back to the airport to catch our flight back to London. They explained we should follow the monk who was to guide us through the temple gardens. He apparently spoke passable English. We each thanked them for their kindness and we would be waiting for them when they returned. A soft wind was rustling the leaves of trees and bushes just like Flora had mentioned in one her letters. There was a sense that she was here with us. The monk approached us and bowed low. None of us really knew how to respond, so awkwardly we followed but self consciously the example of the Embassy men.

"My name's Gaido. You are most welcome, Andersons, on this sad day. I was good friend of Missy Flora Sansho-san."

Trudi gasped and a sob stuck in her throat. This was bringing Flora and what she did here to life. Sophie gripped Bobby's hand hard. Gaido bent his head but I saw the sorrow etched into his face. I remember Flo mentioning Gaido occasionally and it now seemed so strange that here he was, and we were meeting him in such dire circumstances. He was no longer a name written in ink on paper but real flesh and blood. I wondered what his thoughts might be.

"Follow please." He turned and began walking slowly ahead of us.

We followed ten paces behind and none of us knew what to expect. Bobby seemed most at ease and contented himself by taking shots with his camera. The gardens were breathtaking, like nothing we had ever seen before in England or elsewhere. A stone and pebble path meandered through the grounds, like the body of a giant dragon and towards an important looking temple building up front. Was this the path she had mentioned so many times, from which she had swept leaves? It seemed so strange, unsettling, and almost profane that we were entering her world, a world that we only knew from her letters and the odd photograph. Gaido led us past a large lily pond surrounded with immaculate banks of grass and azaleas. The pond looked as if it was connected to another garden. It wasn't. It was an ornate dry landscaped garden, which led directly to the building. All was not what it seemed. The dry landscape had been made with raked sand to resemble water and the trees and bushes planted resembled imitation floating islands in a sea of sand leading up to the building. Masses of surrounding bushes and shrubs had, with topiary, been made to resemble rocks, mountains, sea birds and ships! It was stunning. I felt we were treading in Flora's footsteps. Her deep attraction to this place, none of us had a difficulty in imagining. Her domain was coming to life. At the end was a stone bridge made of two natural large flat stones supported in the centre by a solitary rock on which they rested. This led to a large open pergola, surrounded by numerous sweet smelling flowers. Bobby became aware of the sanctity surrounding this place and I was pleased he stopped taking pictures. He did say it didn't seem respectful to do so. It was then we saw a solitary figure standing motionless and clad in a black and gold kimono style robe. Gaido indicated us to stop. 'Roshi is here.'

We knew this was Flora's master. It was Nakashima. This was like a movie coming to life. Gaido walked towards him, stopped, bowed in front of him and then moved behind him. Roshi advanced towards us with incredible stature and dignity. His presence was overwhelming. His face carried depths of knowledge and wisdom. His age seemed impossible to tell. This was the man who Flora had the utmost love and respect for. I could instantly understand why. She had written of him so many times and at last in these dreadful circumstances here he was. It seemed unreal. I felt dreadful, and tears were close to the surface and I heard Trudi suppress a cry as Sophie held onto her. Bobby was gulping heavily. He stopped short of us bowing very low. He said nothing.

We made a poor attempt at returning the bow. I spoke nervously and falteringly, not knowing how to address him or what the protocol should be. I knew he spoke English.

"Forgive us sir, we do not know your customs and don't know how we should behave and …"

He cut me short by holding up his hand and shaking his head. "It is not important, I understand. Sansho-san's family most welcome. This for all very, very sad. Sansho-san my successor. There has been no one like her. We find it hard to believe. I am sad for you too. It hard for us all."

He paused and turned his head low and sharply away from us. I could see his eyes were full of tears. I felt sad for him and could understand Flora's connection with him. We looked at each other and were moved. He soon composed himself. He had incredible dignity. "We talk later. Follow me. I will show you rooms and Sansho-san's also. Later temple and what she did."

We each had small room, which were immaculately clean and in simple Japanese style, with a futon, low table, mats cushions, a wall mounted scroll and indoor plants. We were told our meals would be brought to us. The beautiful simplicity of it was miles away from our complicated social structures and the need to have masses of possessions.

We were left alone to sort ourselves out. I felt like downing a large scotch to calm my frayed nerves but I guess that was out of the question. Later Nakashima and Gaido returned and gave us a tour of the temple. We were ushered into the meditation hall, the zendo, but had to remove our shoes before entering. It was steeped in atmosphere, which was almost mystical, heightened by the Japanese statues, lingering incense smell, religious artefacts and above all the large golden Buddha on the central platform.

Nakashima stopped at the head of the hall and pointed to a mat on which sat a large round black cushion. "This Sansho-san's. It will stay here until new successor found."

This was almost too much for us and I heard Trudi gasp and spontaneously she then slowly knelt, held and then kissed the cushion placing her cheek close onto it. We all looked away including Roshi. It hurt. We then headed across the outside compound to the accommodation area. He stopped at one entrance. "This her room," and slid open the flimsy Japanese door. Again we removed our shoes. Nakashima remained silent as we looked around inside. He and Gaido remained outside.

Again it was an interior of utmost simplicity. Tatami mats covered the floor. The room was constructed in a Shoin-style architecture with a bay projecting into the garden. There was a decorative alcove in which hung a Japanese scroll and a built in wooden writing desk, again giving a view into the garden. Then came a surprise. Alongside the desk stood three framed photographs, almost intrusive in this austere unintentional stylishness. There we all were, the family, including the twins, one of Bobby's photographs, Flora in her monastic regalia and most breathtakingly of all, a picture of Mum and Dad. It must have been taken on one of our holidays to Lulworth. Her forgiveness, it seemed was total. Before we could truly react, Nakashima had entered and spoke.

"Her room is as she left it. She was expected to return. Shall leave room as it is, until ready to change or new person fit to be here."

With that remark the true extent of his regard for our sister was becoming clearer. What web of circumstance brought these two together across half way across the world? They were of alien cultures but melded and understood each other without difficulty. It was as if they had been as one. We were then escorted to his own rooms with Gaido where he sat us down and green tea and small Japanese cakes were arranged to be brought to us. He began to discuss the funeral procedures and what would happen and did we have any requests that we might want included. We had none. He said the funeral ceremony would be modified, as a traditional affair might prove too much for us, not being used to the culture for such occasions. He mentioned that his own monks could also find this difficult. I thanked him and said we were here to say goodbye to our sister. She in some ways was now as much their sister as she was ours and he should do what he felt was acceptable to all. He looked deeply at me and bowed his head. He was human and couldn't fail to understand. After our talk we got up to leave.

"Wait." He whispered to Gaido. They both stood and did

a full prostration in front of us. Before we had time to gather our astonished reactions they were standing again.

"You are of her. This we not forget. You honour us by being here. Even bigger honour you let Flora be buried here with us. I not find another like her. This we never forget and we honour you too as part of her."

Gaido produced a small bundle and handed it to him. He turned, bowed and handed it to us. "This for you. Her kesa and robe."

We didn't know how to react. He took the initiative, moved over and embraced us. There were six wet faces in that room. When we left our minds and emotions in a whirl. The impact of simplicity struck us all. I realised that was the first time he had simply called her Flora.

Later that evening our conversation turned to Dad.

"What would he have said if he knew this would have been the outcome of his legacy?"

Trudi spoke, "He could have never worked this out. I think he would be proud in some ways but ashamed and grief stricken in others. What's happened here is almost beyond belief. The respect and honour they are giving her is astonishing and deeply moving. It's an incredible chain of events, a wooden box, a family history, a collection of things he thought would be helpful to us and worst of all those hidden clues, which you Hugh have had to deal with, leads us to this temple in Japan."

Bobby glanced round at us all. "It's still not over. Once Flora's funeral is done we have to return home and decide what to do next." They had no doubt I was referring to the unopened letter.

It's the day of her funeral and we are all very quiet, solemn, uncertain of what to expect or how we should perform. After a breakfast of what Flora had frequently mentioned, rice, pickles, miso and green tea we changed into our black funeral wear, suits, complete with black shoes, and black ties. Sophie and Trudi, to fit in with decorum wore long black dresses, matching shoes, white blouses and black matching jackets. They had, to avoid clashing with Japanese and monastic sensibilities, previously asked if they could wear their large veiled black hats, as is the custom in the west. Permission was given without any debate or forethought.

Roshi had understood that we would find the proceedings incomprehensible and alien. He was as good as his word and had shortened the two-day ceremony down to one and made drastic alterations so as not to cause us concern or consternation. Gaido was released from his formal role and was to be our escort and interpreter. At around noon he called for us, looking very grave and focussed. He told us what to expect and what would happen. As an honour, we were to lead Flora's sarcophagus in and take the procession down through the ranks of monks lined up on each side of the hall. We did this and Trudi held onto my arm with her head bent low. Sophie and Bobby were behind us. Trudy and Sophie's black veiled hats did not look out of place. They added their own tribute. When we reached the top of the hall Gaido indicated five chairs that had been placed there for us. He sat in between us. The ceremony was incredibly ritualistic with lots of low bows, beating drums, gongs, bells, cymbals, chanting, prostrations and umpteen offertories. We could have easily been divorced from the proceedings had it not been for Gaido's running commentary. A picture of Flora was brought in, which made me gasp and startled the others too. It was presented to Roshi who then placed it on the altar, lighting a bunch of incense sticks before it and bowing low three times. The reverence and dignity these monks and Nakashima-Roshi conveyed to her funeral touched us all greatly. We couldn't fail but to understand more of her life at this beautiful place. Trudi wept throughout, her shoulders occasionally shaking and she leant her head heavily on my shoulder and held my hand tightly. Bobby had his arm around Sophie who was obviously shaken by how Flora was being honoured. He looked grey, visibly moved and upset. I was saying goodbye to my twin sister in a foreign land thousands of miles across the other side of the globe, probably never to see her burial place again. I was alone with the thought that together we'd shared the same womb; locked in as one, until the day we were born. We were parted then and now death had completed that separation, physically parting us for all time. It's a separation of bodies but not of minds. Our minds or spirit, will for as long as I'm alive, be as one. I drew comfort from this. I'm like Bobby, heartbroken, a great chunk of me is lost and gone with her. We'd never understood until now just what she had achieved here. Gaido saw my distress and placed his arm comfortingly around my shoulder. He gently guided us through the ceremony, which he continually stressed had been shortened for our benefit. When the proceedings within the hall were over he told us we were to lead the procession behind the gold, purple and white decorated sarcophagus carried by monks with Nakashima-Roshi following close behind. It was, he told us, the funeral ceremony of an Abbot! That was breathtaking. Then there would follow various monks in order of seniority. A giant bell was struck as we moved off and it would strike for one hundred and eight times, a number Gaido told us was of high significance in Buddhism. He further translated what the Chief Disciplinarian was saying in his loud slow clear voice. It was that "Houn Horin Sansho has entered Nirvana the True Source of all Peace. As this day fades from us so her life has also. Her name is utterly virtuous and pray through her for advancement on the road to enlightenment." There was much more said, which was for the monks benefit. Various offerings were then made of food and sugared water, and there was a considerable amount of bells and gongs and short swift chants. We moved closer to the open sarcophagus and stared down at her coffin knowing she was only feet away from us. The monks and Nakashima stood back and we stood tearfully and each touched the coffin and said our individual farewells to her. We turned, our heads bent low, tears in our eyes and all the monks including Nakashima-Roshi made a gassho and bowed low towards us. We responded in kind and were led away by Gaido. I understood there was more ceremony for them to go through but we had done what we wanted to and it was time to retire to our rooms and reflect on the day's events.

We were due to be collected by the Embassy car about lunchtime. We didn't speak much. We were all locked into the memory of Flora and what she had achieved. I was amazed and overwhelmed by the monks. Their kindness, respect and generosity was unparalleled. How wrong had I been with my stereotypes about the Japanese. These prejudices had now evaporated. It was only now, in this sorrowful episode, had we come to understand the startling impact she must have made on this community. We'd made the right decision in allowing her to be at rest here. She would have wanted that. Whatever happened in the future we would not forget her.

Later that morning just before our car was due to arrive Nakashima-Roshi and Gaido came to say farewell. There were the customary bows between us and we were getting a bit more used to that after such a short time. It has much to be said for it as a social greeting.

He spoke. " We are sad to let you go, brothers and sisters of Flora."

I knew he spoke sincerely. We too felt affection for this amazing man.

"We are sorry to leave you too."

"Anytime you come here, most welcome and honoured. I thank you again for your kindness to me and the monks here."

"You too are most welcome at our house in England, anytime." I produced my address card and handed it to him and he passed it to Gaido.

"Gaido will come soon. I know. He will be welcome with you?"

"We can't wait to see him again." I turned to him and thanked him profusely for his care and attendance in helping to get us through a difficult day yesterday. I then offered him a western handshake. He beamed with delight and Roshi smiled. "He will come to you soon. Will let you know. I have something else for you. He produced a small packet. "These were her food bowls and the last one is bowl she take on Takhahatsu to collect food. Very dear to us but you must have."

This man was full of kind surprises. I turned to Sophie, Trudi and Bobby and handed them his gift. "Your gift is generous and we are moved by it. We will have a shrine for her back at home and will send you photographs when it is finished. Meanwhile, please accept this gift from us for you both. They belonged to Houn Horin Sansho our sister." I handed them Flora's small black velvet box. Inside was her golden Buddha necklace she had left behind, given to her by Dad, plus her two bracelets, one of silver, the other of gold. He opened it slowly.

To my surprise he turned his head away from us and Gaido kept his head low. Both were obviously touched and considerably moved. They gratefully accepted them. With these exchanges I felt we were inextricably linked. Then a monk hurriedly arrived to tell us the car had come. Both Nakashima and Gaido came with us to the front gate. I don't know who felt the saddest, us or them. We embraced, something they were not used to. They stepped back and bowed low once more. We knew this wasn't the last we would hear from them. A link had been forged between us in England and them in far away Japan, thanks to Flora. It was also an indirect result of Dad's influence and perception of where Flora's future might have lain, although he would never have worked this one out. So we left in the same Jaguar car we arrived in. Both Nakashima and Gaido stood there until we passed out of sight.

FOURTEEN

Revelations

It's now October and almost six months have now passed since Flora's funeral. The leaves are falling. They seem to me to be emphasising the passing of life from one state to another. At the moment they have a poignancy I've never really noticed before. I guess it's to do with what's happened to us over the last year. An empty void has enveloped us in the absence of both Flora and her unfaltering and steady stream of letters and news from Japan. Life around here is not the same without her. The letterbox will clatter in the mornings and I still maintain the silly hope that there will be a letter from her. There never is, of course. We each have a deep yearning for her, which we know can never be fulfilled. As her twin I've had my own unique demons to deal with although I'm careful not to reveal that to the others. I've started to bash the scotch a bit, especially on my own late at night. It helped initially, soothing the pain but the end result is often not the one I'm looking for. Ella is getting concerned for me but her presence keeps me under some control. Too much scotch only magnifies my sadness and is no real help at all. The truth is that Flora's death has altered the way I view the world, what's happening in it, my own role, my job and ultimately what I want from life. All these things have been called into question. Others have told me previously that my life was due for a change. Maybe Flora's death will act as a catalyst for that change. Her passing, like Dad's, has in one way bound us together but the jollity has left us. Whilst closer, we're not seeing each other so much as we used to and there's a feeling of a dark shadow hanging over us that wasn't there before.

When Flora wrote of 'enlightenment' I didn't understand what that meant. I still don't. I've been reading about it in an effort to understand what it was driving her along and to a lesser extent Dad. I keep thinking if it could get to him, a hard-bitten wartime bomber crewmember with a DFC it had to be powerful stuff. Having seen Kenkuro-ji, Nakashima-Roshi, Gaido, the monks, their monastic way of life and simple dedication, I suspect I have a few clues but am far from total comprehension. Dad certainly has caused a domino effect on our lives.

Between us all we erected a small shrine for Flora at *Pimlico*. It isn't elaborate. It's made up of a photograph taken in Japan of her in her robes, which stands next to a Buddha icon. A permanent vase of fresh flowers is in place plus a candle that is constantly alight. We also placed alongside an incense holder and carefully arranged around were her meal time bowls and the begging bowl. All this stood on a heavy gold and purple brocaded silk. On the wall behind was centrally mounted a Japanese scroll. We attempted to recreate her shrine in her room at Kenkuro-ji. On the wall alongside were hung two frames. On the left was framed her regalia and robes with another photograph of her and her various certificates relating to her ordination. On the right was a framed photograph of Dad and mounted with his citations, medals, oak leaves, cap badges and navigator wings. When it was complete Bobby came over with his family and took several pictures of what was done and several of us all together, including Ella and Trudi, which I would send to Kenkuro-ji. I intend also to explain to Roshi the role Dad had in causing her to come to Japan and his own lay ordination. Before I could do this I received a letter from Gaido who said he was due here in the New Year to attempt to follow up on what Flora had intended to do. Could he stay? We are more than delighted to put him up and help out with anything he needs. The connection will be kept alive. Isn't it strange, I thought that through all this we have this link and deep bond with people and a culture of which we know so little. I can't help thinking it has a profundity. I don't want it to wither away and be forgotten.

Dad's letter remains unopened and the thought niggles away at me. I have spoken to the others several times of late and we are all in agreement that the last thing we want is another of Dad's bombshells or nasty little secrets descending on us. I frequently hold it and am tempted to open it but never do. The fact that it exists is bothering me a lot lately. Something I have to live with and it's become a weight around my neck. The only way to get relief is to open it and bring this episode to a close. It may not be anything but if that is the case, why those instructions that it was not to be opened until at least three years after his death. It's certainly well past that. Bobby suggested we do it at Christmas but Trudi thought there would be a possibility that whatever was in it could put a damper on the festivities. It could upset our thinking about of Flora at that special time. Ella came up with the best solution. She said we were all going to be together on November 5th for a fireworks party, so why not do it then? It was a simple solution to which we all agreed.

Guy Fawkes night was, as usual, damp, wet, rainy and complete with a biting wind, which drove us indoors quicker than normal. Eating baked potatoes in the wind and rain was not enjoyable. Literally a damp squid! It didn't help that Ella couldn't be there as she was called away, yet again, on an assignment to sit through the night with a family whose Mum wasn't expected to last the week. Poor Ella. As a Marie Curie nurse her nights are never her own! Once indoors I made mulled wine and hot drinks, served with the now well seasoned baked potatoes and large dollops of best butter and a tangy Godminster Vintage Cheddar Cheese. We chatted away for some time and sipped at our drinks but at the back of our minds was that envelope. At some point later on there was a break in the uneasy conversation.

"Are you going to open it?" asked Bobby, "or do I have to do it for you?"

There was a good part of me that didn't want to open it, more so than to open it. I gave a deep sigh, got up and said, "Well, here goes." I went over to the cupboard, and opened the drawer and pulled out the envelope, which was looking a bit tired and faded after all these years. Turning, I went back to the group and stood in front of them staring down at the fading blue ink written in Dad's clear and bold handwriting. I couldn't think of anything to say, instead I looked up and tossed the envelope into Bobby's lap. "You open and read it. I've had enough of finding out about Dad's little tricks and games. Now it's your turn. You give it a go will you."

"Okay."

Bobby took out his small red Swiss army pocket-knife, opened a blade and slit through the top of the envelope. The noise of opening paper filled the room with a rustling and crackling heightened all our expectations. He began pulling out a large folded, cream coloured sheet of paper that we all could see was covered in Dad's writing.

"Shall I read it aloud?"

The others looked at me and I nodded agreement. "You do that so we can all hear."

He glanced slowly up and down the letter before proceeding to read loudly and in a slow clear voice. In the background outside there continued a succession of bright flashes and loud bangs from numerous fireworks in the vicinity. I don't think they were noticed.

Pimlico. October, 1974.

My Dear family, Flora, Hugh and Robert,

(I immediately noted the date. He was well aware even then of what he was doing. He'd written this well in advance. I also noted there was no mention of Trudi.)

What can I say to you all? Two or three years may have passed since my death, which won't be too long after this letter and maybe by the time you read this your lives will have moved on to something better. I sincerely hope so. In writing this I have thought long and hard whether it was right to do so. As you can see I decided it was. I know I haven't a lot of time left so I'm trying to make up for the worst of my misdemeanours. I hope firstly that the money has enabled you to do what you want in life.

Hugh I left a task, which I suspect he has, on the way, not enjoyed doing. I'm certain his revelations about me to you were not enjoyed either. However, knowing Hugh, he will pursue this to the bitter end and see the job finished. I thank you, Hugh for that and am so sorry to lumber you with the task of finding out so much unsavoury stuff.

You will by now have some understanding of what my life has been about and I've been so anxious that you know, not just about me but all the other Andersons way back in the past. I wouldn't be

surprised if you didn't want to hear another word
about them, and I wouldn't blame you.

Bobby paused reading for a moment and looked around at us all. We were locked in to what Dad had written way back then.

"His voice, I can still hear it, as if it were only yesterday. It's like he's never gone away. He's rightly guessed we'd find out about Vera and Trudi so why the fuck hasn't he mentioned that episode. He couldn't have been that cowardly, surely?"

Nobody spoke but the silence said it all. Trudi looked uncomfortable. He carried on. The letter answered the question.

I expect you consider I've betrayed every decent
standard this family would acknowledge. I NEEDED you
to find out and I'm so sorry I lacked the guts to
tell you. I'm not asking for your blessings or
forgiveness, just a small iota of understanding that
I was human and riddled with faults like some old
rock face. I only ever wanted what was best suited
to you and that may explain why I left you each
separate items the way I did. Of course I will have
no way of knowing if the guidelines and maps for your
lives and my legacy I left you will have made your
lives any better. You may, of course, have decided
to have nothing more to do with me. I can understand
that.

Now before reading any further, put this letter
down. I now want you Hugh to go and pull out my large
wooden chest in which I kept all my researches.

Bobby paused and folded down the letter. "Now what's this all about?"

"God knows. I cleared that chest out a while back. It's empty unless there's something I missed. I've got all his documents and diaries and ancestor's diaries. I missed nothing. I bloody hope this is not going to be another of his nasty surprises surfacing to give us all a hard time."

"What do we do now?"

"I'll pull out the chest and when I have, carry on reading."

I dragged the chest in and across to the centre of the room. It sat there, the focus of our attention like some corrupted talisman. It felt much lighter than when I first started dragging it out for my investigations. I paused, took a deep breath. "There we are. Now you can carry on."

Bobby picked up the letter and carried on reading.

Looking at the chest head on you will see around the entire edges there are placed decorative wooden bosses. If you look on your left hand side, facing you. you should see four wooden bosses running down the length of the edging. Run your hand down the length of this until you reach the third boss. Stop there. Stand back from it a fraction and then thump it hard with the butt of your palm.

I looked at Bobby and he at me. We looked around at each other, mystified.

"Oh no, it's going to be another of his surprises." I groaned.

Sophie said, "This is all very creepy, like some old detective novel or horror film."

"I feel uncomfortable about this. What's going to happen?" said Trudi.

"There's only one way to find out. Give it a whack, Bobby."

"Let's see if he says anything else before we do that."

Bobby scanned the letter. " No, there isn't very much more. If you can bear to wait, this is what he says.

If you've got this far then you now know all.

I'll end this letter now and all I can do is profoundly apologise to everyone for all the trouble I know I have caused you.

I wish you all well. All my love to you. Dad.

"That doesn't add anything more to what we know. Time now to find out what he was going on about. Do it Bobby!"

He took a deep breath, leant back and struck the boss with some force. "Ouch! That hurt" Nothing happened. He stood back shaking his hand.

"Again! Do it again! Its been dormant for years. Whatever it is may be jammed up."

He struck out again and this time the boss made an inward then an outward movement, which was followed by an audible click. A largish but concealed drawer slowly and silently emerged along half the length of the bottom edging of the chest. We gasped and you could have heard a pin drop. Wonderingly we looked around at each other unable to say a word and jaws hung open as we gazed down into the drawer not knowing what to expect. Inside, clearly visible was a largish brown envelope and on top of this, covered in a large transparent tissue was a photograph. Bobby reached in and pulled the contents out. He could see what it was and silently handed them to me. He looked thunderstruck. I took a sharp intake of breath.

"My God!" I stared down at the photograph and a cold shiver ran down my spine. I was staring across the years and a lump came to my throat.

"What is it?" asked Sophie.

I didn't really hear her but stayed quiet for what seemed an age before turning to Trudi. " I think this is for you, Trudi."

She took it from me and stared at it for ten seconds or more. She gave an inward and audible gasp before bursting into tears and dropping the photograph on to the table. In between the tears all she kept repeating was the words "I remember. I remember."

I picked up the black and white photograph, which the years had not faded. It looked as if it could have been taken yesterday. I passed it to the others. Dad was staring out at us. He was wearing a Squadron Leader's RAF uniform complete with all his insignia and medals including his DFC that we'd never before seen him wear. He looked extremely dignified and proud. There was a faint smile on his face. More surprisingly his arm was around a small girl, wearing a black dress and shiny black shoes. There was a ribbon tied in her hair. She had an impish grin on her face. Unmistakably it was Trudi. She was as we remembered her all those years back when we would play with her at her house. Bobby moved round and placed his arm around her and she leant her head into his shoulder muttering quietly the words "Why now? Why now?"

Beneath my breath I was cursing him. He'd gone and done it again when we could have best done without it. I turned the photograph over. There was an inscription on the back which must have been written at a later date. It said *To my beloved daughter Trudi. Know that I loved you very much. I'm so sorry. All my love from Dad."*

The photograph took us all aback. It'd never been seen before and I wondered how and where he'd managed to keep it concealed for so long. The words 'All my love from Dad,' were difficult to immediately digest, especially for Trudi.

I poured a large scotch. " I need this. Anyone else?" Not one of them refused. I poured out largish ones all round and the room went quiet except for audible sips as the photograph was passed around.

"Where do we go from here?" said Bobby.

"This is where we go next." I brandished the large brown

lumpy envelope, which in bold blue ink in Dad's unmistakable hand was written Trudi's name. She was still weeping slightly. There was something so sad, in seeing this successful woman reduced to a state bordering on devastation. She muttered, "He didn't entirely forget, then."

I knelt down in front of her and offered her the envelope. "Trudi, this is addressed to you."

Her hands were shaking tremulously as she took hold of the bulky envelope. How long it had been in that chest there was no way of knowing. An air of heightened expectancy descended. Trudi paused and looked around.

"I'm frightened. I don't know what to do."

Sophie sat next to her and gave her a long hug. "You're with us darling. There's no need to worry. We're all here for you. You can't be harmed. You'll be fine."

I felt so much pity for her. What Dad had caused her to be put through could instigate a breakdown. Even *he* couldn't be so harsh and unthinking. The dried tears shone on her face under the room lights as she shakingly and slowly peeled open the envelope before reaching inside. She pulled out another smaller lumpier envelope to which was attached a folded note. Before reading this she felt inside once more before visually checking she hadn't missed any thing. She attempted a light-hearted response. "This beats Christmas doesn't it?"

We all smiled. "It's a bit like one of those TV game shows." quipped Bobby.

Trudi unfolded the note and silently read it through. Some composure had returned to her. "I'll read it to you."

Dearest Trudi,

I denied you much and I hope that what's in the envelope will reveal the extent of my guilt and shame

I felt about my previous denial of you. I hope this
will go some way in making restitution. Please don't
reject me.
Love from Dad.

She looked around at us all and began opening the envelope not knowing what to expect. When it was fully opened she reached in and pulled out a transparent plastic folder leaving the remainder inside. Its very visible contents caused us to gasp and her mouth gaped with a look of total astonishment. She emptied the contents on to the table. Out fell, held together with an extremely large black plastic clip were five separate bundles. The bundles were fifty-pound notes.

"This can't be true. It can't" Her voice had sunk to an incredulous whisper. "I can't take this. I can't."

"Oh yes you will. Not a chance of you refusing Dad's bequest to you. "You can and you will."

Although like the others I was stunned I was adamant she wasn't going to turn this down.

She shook her head from side to side. "This is ridiculous."

"He's given us what he thought was right. Now it's your turn. You refuse this at your peril. Just think what you could do with this, even help Frank and his family if you wanted." Bobby leant towards her and I could see how serious he was. He was on the verge of anger.

Falteringly she asked, "How much is there?

"Wait a moment." It was obvious each clip contained the same number of notes. I counted the first and made a total of two hundred notes. That made a total of ten thousand per clip. I told her, "In all fifty thousand pounds."

Her face went white. "This is all too much. I can't take it in."

"You're going to have to. There's more to come I think. Pull out what's left, Trudi. Don't be afraid."

She pulled out another plastic folder, which looked as if they contained legal documents. She gently dislodged them. For a moment she couldn't comprehend what she was looking at. Attached to the front was a sheet of headed notepaper bearing the name Stevenson, Le Carre and Slater. Centrally placed, in bold capital letters and underlined was her maiden name, 'Miss Trudi Jagger.' She didn't know the company or firm but I pointed to the heading and told her they were Dad's solicitors. As she turned over the separate sheets it was apparent what she was looking at but she wasn't realising. It was the deeds to a property she had known well, and hadn't we all?

"I don't believe this. What is it?" Her voice cracked.

We were finding it hard to believe also. She handed me the file.

"You read it Hugh, please. It's all too much for me," and she buried her head low into her hands as Sophie held tightly onto her.

"Give me a short while, Trudi. I just need to read this through quickly to understand what's going on."

She nodded agitatedly. I read it through reasonably quickly, enough to understand the situation. I took me about five minutes. Not a word was spoken. The only sound was Trudi's sniffles. I already knew the answer to my question to her before I even asked it. "What was the name of the house where you lived in Lutton when we used to come down for long weekends?"

She paused a moment. "It was *The Lighthouse*. Why you asking?"

I hesitated a moment or two, and then smiled at her, "Congratulations Trudi. You're the proud new owner of *The Lighthouse*. In fact, from what I've just read you've been so for some years now, even before Dad discovered he was terminally ill."

She held her head in both hands and her jaw hung open. "What! Tell me this isn't true!" Her eyes flooded and she didn't know where or who to look at or what to do. She was transfixed. It was all getting too much!

We began to smile and Bobby and Sophie let out a loud whoop, jumping up and down together and he shouted out, "About bloody time! At last he's done something right in his life for us. Well-done Trudi. Come here." He moved towards her and gave her a huge embrace and kissed her cheek. She was still in a state of shock. Her head lolled back as he held her and her arms hung loosely down by her sides. She was incapable of a reaction. She'd gone totally limp, and I thought she was about to pass out, but she held on. This was a fireworks night that had rocketed off in a way we never would have dreamt of. In a space of thirty minutes she had accumulated fifty thousand pounds and a reasonable sized property. Not just any old property but one full of memories, one where she'd spent most of her early years.

"How? Why? Please will somebody tell me? My head's on fire." She wiped the tears from her eyes with the back of her hand.

"It seems from what I've read here that Dad had been the owner of *The Lighthouse* for quite a few years back. He must have had some idea he was going to leave this to you. None of us here had a clue. It was it seems another one of his secrets. He used his solicitors to let the property out on three monthly contracts, which they still do to this day. When he received the news of his fatal condition he transferred in proxy the ownership of the property to you, Trudi. It would remain this way for a minimum of twelve years when they would then contact us or if of course you hadn't contacted them on receipt of these deeds to establish your ownership and to inform them how you wished to proceed in the future." I stopped and looked at her. "He didn't forget you. What d'you think now, Trudi?"

She gave a huge sigh and a small smile flitted across her damp face. "I'm lost for words. This is utterly unbelievable! It seems so unfair to you all."

"Don't worry about that. We've all done well by Dad and we've no complaints. have we Bobby?"

"None whatsoever. I'm delighted and happy for you Trudi. You deserved it. What I can't make out was why he put us through all this. Why not immediately or leave instructions like he left us all in this chest of his. Overall it doesn't make sense."

"I always thought he couldn't be all bad but I was beginning to doubt that and now he's left me all this. I think I know why he did it this way. He couldn't face the shame of having to face us all if this ever got out. Time needed to pass and our anger to diminish. Although none of us knew his secrets I think he felt he couldn't die knowing he left us in ignorance. Beneath it all I suspect he was a man in considerable torment, he had to reveal it all. From his behaviour I would say he loved us intensely. The shame was he could never really show it. He always seemed nervous around me but was always so kind to me. I remember that photograph being taken. He came round to the house when Dad wasn't in, only Mum. He was dressed in his uniform and Mum washed me and dressed me up in my best clothes and I was taken off to the photographers. I've never seen that picture before this day but when I saw it, it was like yesterday all over again."

She was interrupted by the sound of a popping cork. Hugh was holding a magnum of *Dom Perignon* complete with a set of glasses.

"Well, out of all our sadness comes something we can

322

really be happy about. The devious old spider certainly wove a web around us all. Lets drink to him."

Trudi spoke. "Let's not forget that Flora was the first to forgive him. He never forgot me did he? Guess what? I forgive him too."

"Me too," said Bobby and I agreed.

"Firstly, shall we drink to dear Flora who's been so central to all our lives?"

We raised our glasses and drank to her and her memory.

Trudi was now smiling, "I know my sister would have approved all this so here's my toast. To Scott the loveable secretive devious bastard!"

FIFTEEN

Renewals

A lmost another six months have slipped on by since Trudi's inheritance. Time seems to wing its way so fast that we hardly ever notice it. I'm delighted and so is Ella now that she is expecting our first child in four months time. We can't wait. I would never have believed that I could be so thrilled. I've completed my promise to Dad and my researches into the Anderson family its history and how uniquely it has impacted on each of us. It's complete, all three hundred and fifty pages of it. It's quite a record to hand down and I've printed up several copies and made copies of every thing Dad told me and what Bobby, Flora and Trudi contributed, including myself. Additionally I've included every record, newspapers, church records, birth and death certificates, diaries, trade journals, directories and anything else I uncovered. I managed to get back to 1586 although that is slightly speculative. I hit a blank there and there seemed to be nothing more I could trace. The most interesting part is the recent history, all of what Dad told me and how he led me on to discover to those unpleasant truths. I've included all those, and the circumstances involved, also our own personal reactions and observations to what happened and how it impacted on each of us. So there is now a complete record up to this moment of writing. It just needs adding to by each member of the family and their successive generations as time goes on. I feel pleased at what I've done, although there were times I nearly threw it all on the bonfire. I hope each one of them keeps their copy and will update it from time to time. Our expected baby will certainly be an addition on my copy.

Flora, quite rightly, continues to fill my thoughts and hardly a day can pass where I don't think of her in some way. Her death, and its appalling suddenness was a profound shock to us all. When no one's around I still find myself talking quietly to her especially in front of her shrine. She can be a source of comfort to me. I don't mention this to anyone else. I almost expect her, even now to turn up on my doorstep, as she often did, her arms full of fresh farm eggs and vegetables. "Bloody hell, Hugh boy, thought you could find room for these!" Sadly this'll never happen. I live and feel an enormous sense of loss. That will never leave me. Now knowing what she had achieved and the esteem in which she was held, it all seems so unfair. She could have gone onto greater things. I don't suppose she would see it that way though, probably put it down to *karma* and just accept it. She was an amazing person with an extraordinary but quiet and determined dynamism. In her world, after her death, she is now regarded in awe and considered almost saint like. Hard to beat, eh? Gaido stayed here for a while and told me, before he left for America that Nakashima had erected a permanent shrine in her memory. It was situated at the entrance to the temple, where it could not fail to be seen. He went there every day to pay her respect. She'd affected him profoundly. Her path was a direct result of Dad's intuition regarding what he correctly guessed she would be deeply interested in. She'll not be forgotten.

Bobby, since he got his hands on those camera, has completed a total transformation. Who would have believed it? A frequent prize-winner, now working with NG magazine, various TV channels and film companies, he's become pretty hot stuff and much in demand. He now travels all around the globe on dream assignments most would die for! He's had his ups and downs especially when Sophie lost her baby. She might not enjoy his frequent absenteeism from her but she always encourages him and never complains. He let me know recently that they are now trying for another baby. I really hope that happens for that would truly add some icing to their cake. Next month he's off to the Arctic to film a seal cull. Rather him than me! He loves his kids dearly and always brings them and Sophie goodies from wherever he's been. I'm deeply proud to have him as my brother.

Trudi got over the trauma of her shock inheritance. She tried to give us a gift from the money but of course, like she had done before to us, we refused. She eventually told us she had helped Frank and his family out with a generous cash injection. She really is a most kindly and thoughtful person. She continues to let out *The Lighthouse* until she eventually decides what she will do with it. I wouldn't be surprised if she sells up and moves into the place. Like us, she always loved it there and it does hold many fond memories. She's changed her job, which surprised me. She's become the Managing Director for a firm in the burgeoning communications industry. You don't get many woman getting into that rarefied stratosphere. She must be a real whiz kid! None of this goes to her head and she remains Trudi, as we have always known her with all her strengths and frailties. We're lucky we've got her and I know Flora would be pleased about that.

Behind us all has lurked the shadow of Dad and I'm hoping we've got away from that as our individuals lives have shaped out the way they have. We all at one point despised him but I can see that he always travelled hopefully. He was obviously depressed not just with the illness but from what had gone on in his past. I now feel that he was under a lot of pressure from his own conscience. As a result of that in his own weirdly dramatic fashion he had tried to give our lives meaning. He wasn't that concerned with what we thought of him but did want our love in spite of the wrongs he had committed. He regretted his relationship with Vera. I know this from what he had written in a small note tucked in behind a picture of Mum I'd found. He wrote of his disgust with himself for what he described as biological errors! Some terminology that! I haven't told Trudi or Bobby that but I will do some time in the future. To live with his secrets must have placed a deeply corrosive burden on him, Sure, he liked women, most men do, but he made a mistake of chasing too hard and too close to home resulting into all sorts of difficulties. Full marks to him for his wartime exploits and even more marks for acknowledging his mistakes and attempting to rectify them even in the strange manner he did.

It has taken me some time to get everything together and that doesn't just include the family records. For some while people have been telling me I was due for a change in the circumstances of my life ... new directions and that sort of thing. That never seems to happen and has been a long time waiting. The family affair, Ella and our forthcoming child is something of a change in circumstance, don't you think? Dad did change the outlooks of both Bobby and Flora. All he did was give them the tools to do the job. He didn't do the job for them, they did it all themselves. I've often thought, has he changed my life in any way? You can judge for yourself. If anything, I realise that people, circumstances and things are not always what they seem if you care to look underneath the surface. This process has taught me that. There was a time when looking at the entire Anderson family and clan I felt I wanted nothing more to do with them. Then I'd find another interesting tit bit and I get back into them again. I discovered that Dad wasn't the only philanderer in the family. There were at least three other illegitimate children. The fathers were my great granddad Robert and great, great-granddad Charles. Robert's child was a girl named Alice, her mother, called Victoria, owned a hat shop in Pimlico called *Fenwicks*. What happened to her is a mystery. She vanished somewhere and no trace of her is available. Great, great granddad fathered two boys by the same woman. Her name was Philomena Longmate and she was a married woman living in Hackney. The boys were called James and the latter was called Albert. What happened to them is again a mystery, there seems to be no further trace of them. Looking at this information puts Dad's episode into perspective. A family trait or an inherent male weakness? I won't make a judgement. If anything I think because of all this I've become more tolerant of others. I now try to look beneath the surface of issues, my role in society and the job I was doing. I say 'was' because I quit a while back to take up teaching. I now teach physics and science to sixth formers who are hoping to reach university. I love it. It's so rewarding and I often ask myself why I didn't take it up earlier? In a strange way, doing all that work on the family history and knowing what he went through, must have in an imperceptible way instigated changes in me without me even realising. There has, however, on top of all these things been another major shift in my life.

I always envied Bobby's creativity, his now well-honed

photographic skills and Flora's penetrating and intuitive mind plus her musicianship and artistic abilities. I was always the solid reliable old plodder whose forté was science and physics with a much-unsung path through life, or so I thought. Recently, something remarkable and unexpected happened. I had shown my completed and finished research in its made up state to a colleague of mine. It comprises a good deal of narrative, charts, foldouts and chronological tables, not only for the family back then but the important news and events of the times. I tied in corresponding photographs not just of the family but photographs of those events and happenings where possible, together with relevant social comment of the time and age both contemporarily and retrospectively. Those events must have impacted on their lives back then as today's events impact on ours, shaping the structure of our lives. Backing this up were copies of every newspaper reference, trade journal entries, copy of diary pages, letters and any other material I was able to find. It was presented in both colour and black and white and I'd bound it in board, the pattern of which, was in the Anderson clan tartan. I consider it as a piece of research quite different to anything else I was used to and have not come across anything similar. My colleague was fascinated and told me he couldn't put it down. Later he told me he had a good friend who owned a publishing group and would I mind if I showed it to him. I agreed and thought nothing more of it. Not long after, there was a thud on my doormat and my research had been returned. The letterhead was in a bold red and blue, complete with a fancy logo which read *Jupiter Publications Ltd*. It was from their Publishing Manager, Polly McGraw, thanking me for letting her read it. It more importantly asked if I would contact them as soon as possible with a view to discuss publication of my work. I wasn't expecting that and when I told Ella she almost gave birth on the spot!

"I knew! I knew, Hugh Anderson, you had it in you."

We embraced. "I'm amazed, I really am." I went quiet.

"What's wrong? Aren't you pleased?"

"Of course I am. Of course but I can't get Dad out of the picture. He's struck again hasn't he?"

After negotiations and a certain amount of readjustments, consultations with an editorial team and discussions on the relevant artwork my work was published as a book. It was called *A Secret Family*. Within a few months it had, surprisingly, become an unlikely best seller, the sort of coup publishers dream of. It was ranked with unlikely successes such as Edith Holden's *The Country Diary of an Edwardian Lady*. As a result of this various literary supplements, radio and TV stations were interviewing me. Reprints of the book quickly followed by yet more and I was earning some reasonable cash from this. My delighted publisher asked if I had any thoughts about a possible follow up, a sequel or any other related ideas. Rashly I said I'd been thinking of that too. She asked me to let her have my proposals with a synopsis and an ideas regarding the first few chapters.

"O God," I thought, "What have I let myself in for?" To be honest I had no real idea at all. However I liked the idea of my work being so successful and I knew this could be where my future truly lay. But could I write? Would I now able to walk creatively with Flora and Bobby! I thought about it for a while and a plan began to formulate. I covered my desk in further research notes, books and flow charts, which I always used in my work as a physicist and plotted a possible narrative and story outline together with a host of possibilities and myriad of endings. After a few weeks I had the bones of what I would write, ready for my publisher's evaluation. I switched on the

Amstrad PCW word processor not before sorting my notes into some form of order and then began to write.

'I looked up at the Halifax parked low on the tarmac. My Black Beauty. It emitted an aura of menace, disturbing in its mat black paintwork, a weapon designed for the purpose of waging war. It was a far cry from the rickety Blenhiems and Hampdens I'd been recently trained in. She was to be mine, Flying Officer James Macmillan, pilot, now posted to 78 Squadron of the Royal Air Force, 1940.

A scary prospect. I'd heard of so many aircrew shot down, killed or never to be seen again and I know I'm a highly likely candidate to join them.

My thoughts revolved around the mechanics of war as I changed from my uniform into some casual clothes. I needed to be alone to get things in perspective. I picked up my fishing rod and set off through the woods but not before I stopped at the 'Anchor' for a pint of ale. When eventually I reached the river, the banks and water were deserted. I cast my line and sat down and watched the gentle river flow on by as the lazy float bobbed on the surface surrounded in the reflections of an afternoon sun. The sounds of war had not reached me. It was a glorious English summer's day. I sat back leaning against an old willow tree. Memories of my childhood began to surface ...'